LADY KILLER

Ki turned to stare at Longarm, thundergasted as he said, "Jessie's gun rig is missing. So is the Stetson with the throwing star she wears. She hasn't gone back East. She's gone hunting!"

"Hunting sneaky," Longarm replied, "if she lit out dressed sedate with her gun and star carried sly. Unless and until that drug wears off, there's just no telling what she might do. Cocaine don't affect your coordination, just your head. So she can still go after folk like a well-oiled killing machine, and we don't even know who she might be after!"

TABOR EVANS

LONGARM

AND THE LONE STAR RUSTLERS

J

JOVE BOOKS, NEW YORK

LONGARM AND THE LONE STAR RUSTLERS

A Jove Book/published by arrangement with
the author

PRINTING HISTORY
Jove edition/August 1990

ISBN: 0-515-10381-0

Jove Books are published by The Berkley Publishing Group,
200 Madison Avenue, New York, New York 10016.
The name "Jove" and the "J" logo
are trademarks belonging to Jove Publications, Inc.

PRINTED IN THE UNITED STATES OF AMERICA

10 9 8 7 6 5 4 3 2 1

Chapter 1

When the starless sky commenced to glow hellfire red to the east the Panhandle Kid reined his stolen mount to a walk in the stirrup-high chaparral. He wasn't being considerate to the jaded thoroughbred he'd helped himself to at gunpoint, for the Panhandle Kid prided himself on being mean to men, women and livestock. He'd killed his first cat at the age of seven. Bare-handed. But dawn was no time to be raising dust with at least a sheriff's posse and likely the Texas Rangers trying to cut your trail in such open country.

The Panhandle Kid's wolfish grin grew wider as the eastern sky grew ever more scarlet, for he knew he wouldn't have to worry about rising dust or hoofprints in his wake if he was reading that eerie sky right. He'd never heard what New England fisherfolk said about red skies at night being a sailor's delight while a red sky in the morning was time to take warning. But he did know a red Texas dawn usually meant thunderous cloudbursts from the Gulf of Mex-

1

ico were coming any time now. A horned lark flushed out of the scrub ahead of him, and the Panhandle Kid drew and threw down on it without thinking, but held his fire as the fool bird skimmed low above the chaparral, searching for another place to shelter from the coming storm. Shooting songbirds on the wing was usually a pleasant way to pass the time on the owlhoot trail, but a good old boy had to conserve his ammunition when he only had so much in a world filled with lawmen out to do him dirty. He knew he had to stick to serious thinking till he could make Fort Stockton and the good old Santa Fe railroad. There was that one Harvey Gal, serving meals by the depot like she thought she was some sort of high-toned society lady and, if he had time, he'd teach her not to turn down the one and original Panhandle Kid when he asked polite. Anyone could see she was just begging for it. Gals only wore them engagement rings as a come-on, lest old boys think they might not be popular. He'd use the coming cloudbursts to cover the distance while most other riders would be sheltering sissy, and then—

"Drop them reins and grab some sky!" called a stern voice from somewhere in the scrub ahead. But the Panhandle Kid had a better notion, or at least he thought he did. He drew and rolled from the saddle at the same time, meaning to play the same lizard-belly game among the bushes. But on the way down he heard a Winchester clear its throat, and when he hit the dust he could only lay there, breathing fire and staring numbly up at all those bitty morning stars pinwheeling against the red sky.

Then somebody had unbuckled his gun belt and rolled him off it like he was supposed to be Cleopatra rolled in a fool rug. The Panhandle Kid howled in sincere agony, protesting against such cruel and unusual punishment. The huge dark figure looming above him, outlined against the now ominously crimson sky, told him, not unkindly, that the worst was over and his best bet, now, was to just lie still and wait for the inevitable, adding, "I got you close to the heart and you're likely bleeding pretty good, internal. But look on the bright side. It's fixing to rain fire and salt any minute and you don't have to worry about getting struck by lightning, like me.''

The Panhandle Kid tried to prop himself up on one elbow, felt even worse, and just lay there, gazing up glassy eyed to demand, ''Who are you? How'd you know I wasn't streaking for the border the way I wanted one and all to suspect?''

The tall stranger who'd just shot him replied, in a conversational tone, ''I'm the man you've been out to meet since the day you left home with the contents of the poor box and the parson's horse, old son. In this particular instance I happen to be U.S. Deputy Marshal Custis Long. But if it hadn't been me it would surely have been some other lawman. For as the Good Book says, the wages of sin are death, and you've been one sinful son of a bitch since you chose of your own free will to follow the owlhoot trail.''

The Panhandle Kid smiled weakly and muttered, ''I've heard of you by rep. You'd be the one they call Longarm, and I take some small comfort in knowing I was outfoxed by a lawman known to be so sneaky. How did you know I was headed this way, Longarm?''

The tall, tanned federal deputy shrugged and said, ''They told me *you* was sneaky. I was on my way to pick you up for transport as a federal want when I got word you'd busted out of the county jail I was heading for. Lucky for me and unlucky for you, I was at Fort Stockton, changing from the Santa Fe to an army mount, when word came over the wire about your daring breakout. As you no doubt hoped, both the county and state figured you'd be well on you way to the border by now, Mexico being closer than any place you ain't wanted. And though the Rio Grande runs less than thirty miles south of Sanderson, the riding down that way is a mite rough, so when they told me you'd had time to choose, and chose the mayor's fine thoroughbred for your

3

getaway, it occurred to me you might be headed somewhere else, like the rail line I'd just got off. That particular line runs to points north, like the Texas panhandle you was said to haunt in your misspent youth, so, seeing I was heading this way to begin with . . . I'm sort of hungry, now. I got some blueberry muffins in my saddlebags that I bought off the Harvey Gals at the depot as I was riding out to meet you. Don't go away. I'll be right back."

The Panhandle Kid tried to rise again. But he couldn't. He was still cussing about that when Longarm returned with a big fist filled with muffins instead of that Winchester. He hunkered down on his haunches by the fallen desperado, saying, "They've gone a mite dry on the outside, but they're still soft and yummy when you bite in deep. I'd make us some coffee to go with 'em, only it figures to rain any second. So there's no sense trying to start a fire. Here, try one. They're almost fresh from the oven."

The Panhandle Kid groaned, "Are you loco en la cabeza, Longarm? You've shot me mortal and now you're trying to feed me cookies?"

"Muffins," Longarm corrected, adding, "I know you're done for. But you ain't gut-shot and I got more than I can eat myself. Open your mouth and I'll shove one in for you if you're too weak to feed yourself."

The Panhandle Kid started to protest. Then he somehow found himself with a mouthful of blueberry muffin. So he chewed and swallowed before he allowed, grudgingly, "They are good, ain't they? Might you have bought 'em off a sultry dishwater blonde who sports a flashy rhinestone ring?"

Longarm swallowed, thought, and decided, "I wasn't flirting with the waitress behind the counter in the Harvey House, but I do recall the engagement ring you just mentioned. I hope you don't mean to stick me with a last message for your true love. No offense, but none of the gals slinging hash up yonder struck me as your type."

The Panhandle Kid didn't answer. He was just staring up

at the red dawn with blue saliva and wet crumbs sliding
down his gaunt cheek from his gaping mouth. Longarm felt
the downed outlaw's throat, nodded soberly, and muttered,
"I sort of wish I'd killed you more direct. I just hate it
when you boys check out in the middle of an interesting
conversation."

Fort Stockton was a heap closer than the county seat at
Sanderson, so that was where Longarm headed with the two
horses and the remains of the late Panhandle Kid. Even so,
it wasn't easy, for that summer storm rolled in from the
Gulf just as he got the body lashed facedown across the
saddle of the purloined thoroughbred, and naturally both
brutes commenced to shudder and spook as hail came down
and the Thunder Bird flapped gusts of wind and shit lightning bolts among the crimson and purple clouds rolling low
above the shiny wet chaparral.

Riding through a Texas gully-washer presented many
problems to ponder, since flash flooding could get you in
the draws while the lightning lashed down to lick the rises.
Longarm knew the only thing that could scare Comanche
was lightning on the Texas plains. It was easy to see why,
as he drove the two spooked mounts on through the unsea-
sonable weather, trying to avoid both higher and lower
ground while mesquite all around burst into flame only to
be doused by the pelting rain and mothball-sized hail. He
hadn't taken time to pick up a slicker in Fort Stockton since
it hardly ever even clouded over in West Texas at this time
of the year, so he was soaked to the skin in his tobacco-
brown tweed suit and nearly deafened by the hail drumming
the soggy brim of his pancaked Stetson. It was on rare
occasions such as this he forgave his boss, Marshal Billy
Vail of the Denver District Court, for making him dress up
so sissy on official business. For had he been wearing the
more sensible summer costume he'd have had on otherwise,
he'd have to worry about catching an ague as well. Some
of those wind gusts had an almost arctic nip to their wet

teeth, and wool was the only known textile that stayed halfway warm when it was soaking wet. Folk back East read a lot about cowhands dying of gunshot and getting gored. Having worked as a cowhand in his time, Longarm knew twice as many more got killed by chills and fever. Working out of doors in the uncertain climate west of the Big Muddy could play hell with a man's innards, and many a man who could lick his weight in man or beast had gone under from what had started as a summer cold.

So when the storm blew over as unexpected as it had started Longarm knew better than to rejoice. They were still out in the middle of nowhere as the Texas sun of summer came out to turn the soggy results of the storm into a steam bath.

He reined in, dismounted, and tethered both mounts to handy mesquite branches. Then he unsaddled them, dumping the one saddle, corpse and all, upside down on the soggy soil to catch the drying rays of the once more ferocious sun. He wiped both mounts as dry as he could with damp saddle blankets while they commenced to brouse mesquite pods in blissful ignorance of basic western hygiene. Then he peeled off everything he'd had on but his boots, pants and gun belt, and draped them over chaparral branches to bake dry, or as dry as cloth would bake in a steam bath at any rate. He found a standing pool of rainwater, filled his hat from it, and watered both mounts. Then he used some to wash down the last of those muffins and some Maryland rye he'd brought along for such medicinal purposes. Then he paced back and forth, smoking a somewhat soggy cheroot, as he let the world dry out some more. It took no more than an hour or so. The thirsty soil and rapidly drying winds soon had things back to normal, which in West Texas in high summer meant hot and dry as hell. Then he got dressed again, loaded the saddles and the Panhandle Kid back aboard, and rode on to Fort Stockton, hoping he'd saved them all from a summer cold, which could kill a horse quicker than it could a man, since a man could breathe through his mouth once his nose got stopped up total, while no horse could.

They got there around high noon, more in danger of heat stroke than anything else, now, so the streets of the bitty town grown up around the army post were deserted as well as dusty as ever.

First things coming first, Longarm rode directly to the town livery. As he dismounted and proceeded to dismount the dead man across the other saddle, a stable boy came out to ask how come he seemed to be depositing a dead man on their doorstep. Longarm explained, "These two critters have been through hell. I want you to water and oat 'em both. Then they'd best be run into your corral out back. The army bay might not chill in a shady stall but this thoroughbred requires some thoughtful treatment indeed. The poor brute's a show horse used as a racehorse by this rascal at our feet. He belongs to the mayor of Sanderson, who'll be sore as hell at both of us if you let him die or even go lame. So don't let him."

The stable boy took the reins of both mounts as he nodded at the thoroughbred and said, "He's sure got handsome lines. Is it true what they say about this breed being sort of dumb?"

Longarm replied with a nod, "It is. This dead gent stole him with just that in mind. No cow pony with a posse rider on it could hope to overtake a thoroughbred in a cross-country night ride. Cow ponies have too much sense to let a man ride 'em to death. Fortunately for the mayor and this horse, I cut the rascal off before he could manage that, I hope. I got to talk to your local law about this cadaver, now. So make sure you take good care of these poor critters and I'll make it up to you before I leave town, hear?"

The stable boy nodded and led the spent mounts inside. But as Longarm turned away from the doorway he saw he didn't have to look up the town law. His riding into town with a dead man had occasioned considerable interest in a town that didn't even have an opera house. So a heap of

7

gents seemed to be strolling his way now. One of them was sporting a brass star on his vest. He didn't look pleased to see Longarm standing there with a dead man sprawled in the dust at his feet, so before anyone could do or say anything ugly, Longarm called out, "I'm the law, too. Federal. I'd be U.S. Deputy Custis Long and this used to be Harold W. Thayer, better known as the Panhandle Kid. We met at dawn just south of town, with results you can see for yourselves."

The town constable nodded and replied, "We've heard of both of you, Longarm. I answer to Wellington Lee, no relation to that Virginia boy who surrendered to the damn Yankees, and I sure wish I'd been there, considering how fast they say both of you are, or was, on the draw. To what do we owe the pleasure of the Kid's company, Longarm? Last I heard tell, he was streaking for Old Mexico with half of Terrell County right behind him. They put out an all-points on him. Even alerted the Mex rurales on him."

Longarm nodded and said, "I feel sure he figured they might. That's why he was headed the other way. I brung him here for the simple reason that I had to bring him some damn where and this was most convenient. I was on my way to pick him up when he lit out from the Terrell County jail. I ain't about to drag him all the way back to Denver in his present condition, and I reckon my boss will settle for a death certificate from your coroner. And I'd like to have his picture taken as well. My boss can be a picky rascal when he sends me after a want and I come home empty-handed."

The town law stared dubiously down at the cadaver. Thanks to the heat it was already starting to bloat a mite. He decided, "The doc can fix you up with a death certificate, seeing the gent is plainly dead. Flynn's photographic gallery by the depot would likely be able to fix you up with a sepia-tone suitable for framing. But, ah, who's supposed to pay for all this consideration, Longarm? It ain't as if anyone here in Pecos County had Wanted papers on the rascal, you know.''

Longarm smiled thinly and said, ''Count your blessings. He was on his way here when I cut him off. Naturally I mean to pay for any chores I ask another man to do for me. I'll even spring for his burial if you boys will only keep it simple. I'll go along with you as far as a box and a hole in the ground. If you want to sprinkle his coffin with bunches of roses, you're on your own.''

The town law chuckled and said, ''Roses are out of season and he ain't worth a nosegay of tar-weed flowers to anyone in this here town. Leave it to me and the boys. Where might you figure to be when we've tidied up and it's time to present you with the tab?''

Longarm frowned thoughtfully and said, ''I hadn't studied on that, yet. I got an army mount inside I have to take back to the fort before I leave for Denver. I ain't sure I'm done with it entire, yet. The Kid was saying something sort of interesting just as he lost interest in talking, and I'd hate to go all the way home only to find I'd left some loose strings dangling. What time this evening might a train come through, bound for the panhandle and points north?''

Constable Lee said, ''The next such train ought to be here around four this afternoon. There ain't no night train such as you desire. But you ought to be able to make the afternoon train if we all get cracking. What say we agree to meet at the depot, oh, say three-thirty?''

Longarm hesitated. It was tempting. He knew they could have him fixed up with proof he'd gotten his man in the time they had to work with. The stable boy would doubtless run that army bay back to the remount officer at the nearby fort for two bits. Longarm knew that should he fail to board that afternoon train he'd be stuck here overnight, and a small Texas town in high summer was no place to be stuck without good reason.

He pursed his lips in consideration, shrugged, and said, ''If I mean to catch that afternoon train, I'll see you at the

9

depot like you suggested. If I ain't there, it means I'll look you up later, after I figure out why I had to stay a spell."

"Was you figuring on staying?" asked the town law. "And if so, how come? I thought you just said you'd finished your errand in these parts."

"I hope I have. I got to take it up with a lady the Kid said he was fond of. She may not know anything, but I won't know that before I ask her. So that's what I'd best do next, see?"

Chapter 2

The Harvey Restaurant chain was set up mostly along the right-of-way of the Santa Fe and its affiliates. Old man Harvey knew what he was doing. The Union Pacific and Burlington lines had started to attach dining cars to their cross-country varnish, but the newer Santa Fe still ran sort of primitive, so passengers were expected to eat during jerkwater stops. It didn't take all that long to refill the boilers of a locomotive, so that meant eating short order indeed, and before Harvey had come up with his grand notion many a passenger had been forced to run back to his or her train before coffee served late could be saucered and blown. The plain and simple but nicely kept up Harvey stops were crewed by short-order cooks who could deal blue plate specials as fast as many a tinhorn gambler, and Lord only knew where Harvey got his neatly uniformed waitress gals, for they kept getting married up almost as fast as the company could train them and ship them west.

They were trained good and picked for beauty as well as the quick minds and strong backs that went with the job. Longarm had yet to meet a Harvey Gal he hadn't admired. For even though they almost always said no, they always said it with a sunny smile and never even cussed when a customer ran for his train without leaving a tip. They were usually too busy serving someone else at the time.

But as he strode into the Harvey House at the depot this time, he saw everyone seemed to be in back, clashing pots and pans together amid gales of female laughter. He sat down at the empty counter, and when nothing happened he lit a cheroot.

He'd only smoked it down a third of the way when the pretty gal who'd sold him those blueberry muffins came out from the back, wiping her hands on her apron and laughing about something. She stopped, stunned, when she saw him sitting there. Her flaxen hair was pinned up neat as ever but this time she had on a seersucker smock instead of her brown uniform. She smiled at him uncertainly and said, "We weren't expecting to serve anyone before the two-thirty westbound pulls in, sir. As you see, I don't have my uniform on and—"

"I see you are a blonde lady wearing a mighty handsome engagement ring," Longarm cut in. "You may not remember me. I passed through sudden the last time. But I'm the law, and we seem to have things more interesting than blueberry muffins to talk about, Miss, ah . . . ?"

"Phelan, Terry Phelan," she replied, with a worried frown. Then she brightened and said, "Oh, I remember you, sir. I did sell you a dozen fresh-baked muffins yesterday evening, right?"

Longarm nodded and said, "They were swell. I got to share 'em with an old boy I met up with out in the chaparral. He sort of mentioned you in passing. Might the name Harold Thayer mean anything to you, Miss Terry?"

She looked sincerely puzzled. He tried, "Some called him the Panhandle Kid."

She dimpled at him and said, "Good heavens, that sounds like a hobo nickname. I'm supposed to know this person? We do give handouts to the poor things at the back door from time to time. Departing passengers leave so much on their plates and it seems a shame to let it go to waste. But the cooks have the final say on such matters. We girls never deal with riffraff."

"Well," Longarm said, "the Panhandle Kid was worse than most bums in this bummish world, ma'am. But from the way he mentioned you I got the notion he knew you as a customer, at least."

Longarm started to describe the nondescript young outlaw. Then he decided, "I can see a lady in your position serves a heap of grub to all sorts of gents. It's my hope I'll have a photograph to show you later. It sounds more delicate than asking you to leave your chores and accompany me to the local undertaker. How late might I still find you here, Miss Terry?"

She didn't answer. She was staring at him in dismay. When he repeated the question she licked her lips and said, "I get off at six, as soon as we clean up after the last afternoon train, but what was that you said about . . . an undertaker?"

"Oh, your admirer is dead, ma'am. It was him or me. I'm taking you at your word you didn't know him by either of the names I just mentioned. But, you see, he was an adventurous youth prone to use all sorts of names as he was passing through. So I'd be obliged, later, if you'd just gaze on his features, on paper, I mean, and tell me for sure whether they mean anything to you or not."

He shifted his weight to rise. But the Harvey Gal leaned over the counter almost close enough to kiss him as she pleaded, "Please don't get me in trouble, sir! It would mean my job if the company even suspected I knew someone wanted by the law!"

He assured her, "The Kid ain't wanted, now. I know the company rules. I've met Harvey Gals before. You have my

13

word I won't drag your name into any mire it don't belong in. I just have to make certain the rascal meant nothing to you. It's my considered opinion he was just jawing about a pretty lady he'd admired as he was passing through. I can't say I blame him, but you look like a respectable gal to me and I'm sure we can clear the matter up without pestering Mr. Harvey about it.''

She pleaded, "Why can't you just drop it, then? I mean, if he was just some randy fool I might have served flapjacks to one time, Mr., ah . . . ?''

"Long. Custis Long." Longarm went on, saying, "It ain't that simple. There was nothing on the Kid's yellow sheets or criminal record to connect him with this town or anyone in it. That means nobody here knew him as an outlaw. It also means, since he was on his way here when I cut him off, that he knows Fort Stockton better than Fort Stockton knew him. Some of the loot from his last stickup is still missing and he was recognized and nailed by the law just one county south, if you follow my drift.''

She looked as if she was clouding up to cry all over him as she protested, "You can't really think I'm some sort of bandit's doxie, holding his ill-gotten gains for him like some sort of sporting Jenny!''

Longarm resisted the impulse to hum a few bars of "Whisky in the Jar" as he told her, "I figured your name had to be Irish. I don't think Thayer is, but I could be wrong. I met an Irishman named Cohen one time. As for the sporting Jenny of the old ballad, you don't look like her, to me. But if you *did* know the Kid, by some other name as sweet, and if he *did* have some gal here in town you might know as well—''

"Please leave me alone!" she cut in, sending a nervous glance over her shoulder at the kitchen door. "I don't know hardly anyone here in Fort Stockton. It would mean my job if I even recognized any bad girls on sight! All the bad girls stay out near the army post, anyway, and I'm supposed to be in bed by ten at my respectable rooming house and—''

"I'll be back when that afternoon train comes through," he cut in. Then he added with a reassuring smile, "That way I'll just seem like another customer, showing you pictures of my wife and kids or something. You only have to say yes or no and that'll be the end of it. Unless you say yes, I mean."

She gulped and asked, "What if I say yes? What if it turns out to be someone who's eaten here regular enough for me to remember?"

He rose from the stool, saying, "Let's eat the apple a bite at a time, Miss Terry. Odds are he was just jawing. He did mention that handsome ring you're wearing, so he likely knew you'd been spoken for and . . ."

Then she was running back to the kitchen with her apron to her beet-red face. Longarm stared after her, shrugged, and muttered, "Women. Sometimes it ain't even safe to talk to them polite. If the fool gal don't want gents noticing she's been spoken for, why in thunder is she sporting that big old ring?"

He went back outside. It hadn't gotten one lick cooler and he'd meant to have at least some apple pie in there, if only they'd been serving. He crossed to the shady side of the street and spied a Western Union sign ahead. But he saw no reason to spend a nickel a word before he had something serious to wire the home office. He'd inform Billy Vail he'd gotten his man and was headed home once he knew for sure when that might be. In the meantime he was still hungry. He found a hole-in-the-wall beanery presided over by a fat Mex and a heap of flies. He didn't think he'd better risk that fly-specked lemon merengue pie they'd just sliced open. So he ordered chili con carne and black coffee, both too hot to land on. The chili wasn't bad and the coffee was so good he ordered a second cup. He was working on it when Constable Lee came in to join him. The older lawman sat down at his side, saying, "They told me you'd just ducked in here. You must be hungry as hell. We got the Kid planted in a potter's field on the unfashionable side of the tracks. The sky pilot from First Methodist said some words over him, even though we said he didn't have to. You know how sky pilots are.''

Longarm swallowed and said, ''It might have done the poor soul some good. The Methodist minister, I mean. There's just no way anything anyone can say up here is going to do the Kid a lick of good down yonder. What about the photograph I asked for?''

The town law hauled a small sepia-tone print from an inside pocket and handed it over, saying, ''Flynn took this as we propped the box up to the light for him. You owe Flynn a buck and a quarter, now. Don't he look as if he's just asleep?''

Longarm studied the grim portrait before he put it away in his own coat pocket, muttering, ''Assuming one sleeps with his eyes half open. I'll take care of the photographer before I have to leave. Want to show the picture around some, first?''

Lee shrugged and said, ''Nobody in these parts knew the rascal in life. Lots of folk came to the burial, though, hot as it is outside right now. Some gal bawled and said he looked too young to die. But when I asked, she didn't know him. Some gals just like to cry at funerals.''

Longarm felt tempted again. He knew he could still catch that early train and Terry had asked him not to pester her about the dead rascal. Billy Vail had sent him to bring the Kid in or, failing that, do just what he'd done to the bastard. He had no orders to dig up the dead past of a dead and buried outlaw, and he knew that if he had to stay over the money would come out of his own pocket. Billy Vail could be a bastard about expenses incurred in the field unless they got results. So what results would Billy buy, once that Harvey gal looked at the sepia-tone to either deny she'd ever seen the gent or, at most, that she might have served him a blue plate special one time?

As if to show great minds ran in the same channels, Constable Lee said, ''If you're looking for confederates of the Kid here I'd say you was baying up the wrong tree. That posse that chased him the wrong way last night picked up some suspected cow thieves near the border. They was driving Texas beef by moonlight when the boys bumped noses with 'em just this side of the border. They got 'em locked up in the Sanderson jail. Not the cows. The cow thieves. The owner wants the cows back. Why don't you ride down to Sanderson if you want to question owlhoots about the Panhandle Kid?''

Longarm grimaced and said, "Not hardly. The Kid was a stickup artist, not a cow thief, and if the herd was branded Texas and recovered in Texas I have no jurisdiction.''

Longarm swallowed the last of his coffee and added, "I'm glad. For stock stealing keeps your Texas Rangers busy enough. Texas caught the rascals and Texas gets to deal with 'em.''

Then, interested despite himself, he asked, "How do they know the riders they tripped over were herding stolen cows? Lots of outfits drive at night in high summer. It's one hell of a lot easier on the beef as well.''

Lee shook his head and insisted, "I just told you. The rightful owner wants 'em back. The men caught driving 'em in such mysterious ways naturally said they was pure as driven snow and only herding said cows to a buyer in New Mexico. But they didn't have no bill of sale, and when the county wired the Circle-Star—''

"We're talking about Circle-Star beef?" Longarm cut in with interest indeed as he recalled that brand of old.

Constable Lee nodded and said, "Yep. Them cows was the branded property of Miss Jessie Starbuck, and she seems mad as hell about 'em winding up so far from home. Them old boys must have been new in Texas if they thought they could get away with stealing Starbuck cows. The Comanche learned a generation ago not to mess with that big outfit. You wouldn't know it to look at her, but pretty little Jessie Starbuck inherited the outfit from her daddy when he got

17

killed by crooks from other parts, and they say by the time she got done with 'em—"

"I know the story," Longarm cut in with a pained expression. Lowering his voice he added, sort of wistfully, "I know Jessie Starbuck personal. And you're right. Anyone running off so much as a piss ant wearing her brand was just begging for trouble."

Constable Lee brightened and said, "There you go, then. Why don't you mosey on down to Sanderson, get in on the investigation, and grab yourself some credit. Miss Jessie ain't just pretty, she's said to pay handsome rewards on recovered stock."

That sounded even more tempting than catching the early train back to Denver. More than one pretty lady would be waiting for him in Denver, Longarm knew, but none of them could match Jessie Starbuck when it came to rewarding a man, and as far as he knew, she still liked him.

But he knew he didn't want to get mixed up with her again, much as he wanted to. For there was more to his odd relationship with Jessie than the fact that they were in love with one another, or as much in love as fate allowed such a star-crossed couple to be.

Longarm made less riding for the Justice Department than Jessie Starbuck spent on tips and play-pretties and, if he had been the sort of man who'd let a woman pay his way, he'd had many a good offer long before he'd met Jessie while investigating the murder of her father and saving her from the same syndicate of big-time crooks. Had he made enough to keep a lady like Jessie in the manner she'd grown up accustomed to, he still might have hesitated. For despite his often free and easy ways Longarm couldn't resist the lure of fighting for justice in an unjust world, and he'd been to far too many lawmen's funerals to risk any pretty lady's premature widowhood.

Even if he had considered himself bulletproof, Jessie Starbuck had her own risky row to how. For though the Good Lord knew she didn't need the money even a full marshal like Billy Vail drew, she fought for justice her own way. As an unlicensed and undeputized crime fighter in skirts, Jessie Starbuck was prone to use her considerable wealth and influence as well as a mighty fast draw to deal with evil as she saw evil, and as she saw fit. So, as Longarm had half-jokingly warned her during many a sweet pillow conversation, even if they ever did get hitched he'd likely wind up having to arrest her.

His beanery counter reverie was shattered by Constable Lee breaking into it with some dumb remark about cows. Longarm came back to reality with a dull thump and said, "I just said the pilfering of Texas cows is none of my business, even if I do just happen to know Miss Jessie Starbuck. If there's one thing we're agreed on, it's the fact that she can take care of her cows as well as her sweet self. The Terrell County law just proved that by recognizing her famous brand by moonlight. I'd just be in the way if I stuck my federal nose into the Texas beef industry."

Lee shrugged and said, "You could be right. What do you reckon will happen to them cow thieves now that they've been caught so famous? I'd purely hate to have to face up to Jessie Starbuck like a shit-eating dog with her beef in my possession, wouldn't you?"

Longarm shrugged and said, "Depends on who they might be and how Miss Jessie feels about 'em. She's got dozens of Ranger captains and at least one U.S. marshal she calls Uncle because they used to bounce her on their knees when she was little and her dad was the biggest rancher in Texas. It won't take her long to get copies of their yellow sheets. If they got serious records I'd say they were in a heap of trouble. She has a couple of Texas judges she calls Uncle as well. On the other hand, she's a generous hearted gal and they might get off, total, if she decides they were just cowhands down on their luck. You've heard the tale of her dad and Quanah Parker, haven't you?"

"Nope. All I know about Quanah Parker is that he used to be the half-breed chief of the Comanche. Led the tribe at Adobe Walls that time. Hear he's gone straight and living white these days."

Longarm nodded and said, "Jessie Starbuck calls him Uncle Quanah. We're speaking of when he was still wild. Being you're a Texican, you doubtless know the Comanche killed more whites than any other nation in their day. Jessie's father did a lot to calm them down. The event of which I speak took place during a blue norther on the Staked Plains. The Indians had been raising too much ned to pay proper attention to hunting that year. So the cold snap hit 'em hard and hungry. Parker and his band were holed up in a cottonwood draw, half of 'em down with the ague and all of 'em half starved to death. The army and Rangers were both tracking 'em. They were, in sum, up shit creek without no paddle."

Lee nodded and said, "I recall the bugs they caught off us did kill more Comanche in the end than the army and Rangers put together. But where does Old Alex Starbuck fit into all this?"

"He saved their red asses. They'd been raiding him pretty regular, even took hair from some of his vaqueros. So Quanah Parker must not have known whether to shit or go blind when Starbuck rode into his camp with thirty head of beef and a modest proposition."

Lee stared thundergasted to demand, "A Texas rancher feeding his own beef to *Comanche*? Whatever could he have been so drunk on?"

Longarm chuckled and said, "He told Quanah it was Christian charity. The chief was a Christian, on his mother's side at least. Naturally Quanah wanted to know what the catch was. He knew he had to agree to most anything if he aimed to save his people. Starbuck told him there wasn't any catch. He had beef to spare and he'd heard some neighbors were hungry. He knew, of course, that Quanah would have found some excuse to wriggle out of any promises extorted under such conditions, so he never asked for any.

He just left the beef with the Comanche, rode home, forted up and waited to see what came next.''

Lee asked what came next. So Longarm told him, ''Nothing, as far as the Circle Star herds were concerned. The Comanche went on fighting everyone else a few more summers. Meanwhile they left the Starbucks alone. Jessie told me one time how she'd been introduced by her father to Quanah in the flesh and feather when she was still in pigtails. He used to stop by for cake and coffee now and again, between raids. You see, he was in their debt the way an Indian understands being in debt. They feel it's all right to break a promise they never wanted to make in the first damned place. But Quanah Parker hadn't been asked for any promises and he knew it was wrong to stomp a good neighbor. So he never. He likely got a kick out of giving a bitty white gal ponies and bear-claw necklaces. I know Jessie said it gave her some enjoyment. They respected her more, later, when they found out she'd fight mean as hell if she had to. There were other bands who weren't as friendly as old Quanah's. So by the time she was in her teens she'd swapped some shots and taken back some beef run off when her dad was away and she'd been left in charge.''

Constable Lee whistled in admiration and said, ''I'd heard Miss Jessie was sort of tough for such a pretty lady. What's all that stuff about her chasing after owlhoots with a big silver star pinned to her hat?''

''That's not supposed to be a badge she wears in her hatband on such occasions. She was partly raised by Oriental house servants. I forget the Japanese name of them throwing stars, but that's what she's got stuck in her hat as a sort of ace in the hole. Should push come to shove, when she's low on ammunition she can sort of throw that starry creation like a bitty buzz saw. That's what some say, anyway. She's been more sedate since the last of her daddy's killers wound up as dead as the Panhandle Kid.''

That hadn't been an outright lie. Jessie had calmed down a mite since her first almost suicidal rage in the wake of her father's murder. Of late she'd taken to going after crooks with almost ominous efficiency. The buzzards moving in to wrest control of Starbuck Enterprises from what seemed a demure young Texas debutante had taught her there were more crooks than she'd ever dreamed there might be in the land of opportunity. There was more to the family business than the herds her dad had started out with. Starbuck Enterprises traded in everything from beef to tea and silk from the Orient and she had everything from cotton choppers to steamship skippers on her payroll, cuss her sweet expensive hide.

To change the subject, Longarm said, "I got my own small problems, here in Fort Stockton. I don't see how I'll be able to leave this evening, seeing you're so lacking in proper railroad service. How would you go about finding a place to board overnight if you were in my boots?"

Constable Lee frowned thoughtfully before he decided, "I'm sort of glad I ain't in your boots. We don't rate a proper hotel, but you might try the Widow Watt's boardinghouse. I'll be proud to point her place out to you. Don't know if she'll go for your staying just one night, though. I understand she charges by the week. Five dollars, room and board."

Longarm said it was worth a try, since he just hated to spend a whole night in a saloon or pool hall. Lee led him outside and up the street a piece to point out a mustard frame house with spinach shutters and trim. Lee said, "I don't know the gal any better than you do and you can see it's on the sunny side of the street, with the same hot enough to fry eggs if you don't mind 'em dusty."

So they shook on it and parted friendly. Longarm saw what Lee meant as he stepped out into the afternoon sun and felt as if that egg was frying atop his fool hat.

It didn't get any cooler until he'd knocked on the big green door a spell and the Widow Watt, if that was her in that thin house dress and sort of wilted red hair, opened up to favor him with an icy stare, saying, "Whatever you might be selling, I've already got it, or else I don't want it."

Longarm smiled down at her to explain his true reasons for darkening her doorway. It didn't hurt to smile at her, for she was sort of pretty in a cross and heat-wilted way. She let him in out of the hot sun, but said, "I don't know, Deputy Long. I don't have anyone boarding upstairs right now, this being the slow season, and if I did, I'd still charge 'em five dollars a week. How can you expect me to divide five by seven? I only went as far as the fourth grade."

Longarm suggested, "How does a dollar a night, with no board, strike you, ma'am? That's what most first-rate hotels charge, and I've found a couple of places in town to eat."

She looked less annoyed as she asked, uncertainly, "Don't you feel that's a mite steep? I don't run anything like a fancy hotel here. I just hire out some spare rooms and serve down-home vittles at five a week and . . . Let me see, now, one dollar a night times seven comes to . . . two dollars extra? How does seventy cents sound? Ain't that about right?"

"No, ma'am," he said, "you'd be cheating yourself. If you want to be picky, seven times seventy cents comes to four dollars and ninety cents."

She looked as if she was going to cry as she protested, "I told you I only got as far as the fourth grade, durn it!"

He soothed, "You were only a dime off. Most folk can't do half as well without pencil and paper. I'll be whipped with snakes if I can work it out for a week exact to the penny, and anyone can see I'm treating a poor widow woman inconvenient. Why don't we just settle on one pure dollar and not strain our brains in this heat?"

Before she could figure it was seventy-two cents she was groping for, Longarm pressed a silver dollar on her. So she took it, saying, "Well, if you think it's fair I'll just show you where you can bunk. It's upstairs."

He followed her, sort of admiring the view. As if she'd read his mind she told him, halfway up the flight, "I'm

23

sorry about my appearance this afternoon. I wasn't expecting gentlemen callers and in truth it's so durned hot I still feel like I'm wearing my late husband's old army coat.''

He told her she looked just fine. He suspected she'd slipped into the thin cotton dress to answer the door. For as a born and raised Victorian, Longarm knew Victorian manners were mostly for show, and a lot of ladies who'd never dream of appearing in public without corset and stays in high summer tended to lounge about or even do their household chores as bare assed as Eve. He tried not to wonder what this one would look like stripped to the buff. He was only going to be in town one night, and that thin cotton didn't leave all that much to the imagination in any case. As she led him into a plainly furnished but clean and bright dormer room she informed him the sanitary facilities were just down the hall and that her pals called her Martha.

He said she could call him Custis, in that case, and moved in shucking his tweed coat and vest. He hadn't known how hot it really got in West Texas until he felt the dry air hit his damp shirt. As he hung his coat and vest on a handy wall hook Martha Watt stared soberly at the .44-40 riding cross-draw on his left hip. She murmured, "My land, I'm glad you told me you was the law. That gun sure looks big, now that one can see it more plain. My late husband brung a big horse pistol just like that home from the war. He rid for Texas as a cavalry lieutenant. That was long before we married up, of course. I was just a young child during the War Between the States, of course. You didn't serve in the war, did you, Custis?''

He had, but he said, "I was pretty young at the time as well.'' Old war stories were old bore stories, and if her husband had told her he'd packed a Colt double-action for the blue or gray he'd likely been full of shit. Many a man who now said he'd done wonders and ate cucumbers in the Union Cav had really been in the quartermaster corps, and it was even easier to fib about a Confederate record since few if any records of the lost cause were on file anywhere, fifteen years after the south had surrendered. Longarm preferred to disremember the war he'd run off to as a fool teenager. Too many bitter memories still tended to start trouble in saloons of a Saturday night and the few times he'd tried to tell folk who hadn't been there what it had really been like, they'd refused to believe him. A real vet could always tell a bullshit artist from the real thing. For it was only the bullshit artists who told war stories with a sensible plot.

Having found a safe place to leave his coat and vest, Longarm informed his heat-wilted landlady he had errands to attend to. As they went back downstairs, he said, "I'll likely have supper at the Harvey House at the depot. If it ever cools off, I mean to ask a few questions wherever I can meet up with those who might have some answers. I can't say when I'll be coming home to go to bed upstairs. It could be sort of late. Do you reckon you could let me carry a spare key, Miss Martha?"

"I don't have one," she said. "I generally lock up around nine. By that time nothing in town is open but the saloon and, ah, houses of ill repute. I don't allow no boarders under my roof who frequent saloons and worse."

He thought and said, "I don't blame you, ma'am. But I hope you understand I'm a lawman searching for lost treasure and I just can't say where the trail may lead. You have my word I won't come home drunk. But nine in the evening could be cutting it sort of fine. Maybe if I was to borrow your key just a minute and run it over to a locksmith . . . ?"

She shook her head and said, "There ain't no locksmith here in Fort Stockton. If there was I'd have more keys, of course. You just go ahead and pound the door when you get back. I'm a light sleeper to begin with, and if it ain't too late I'll likely still be up and about in any case. In high summer we don't like to waste the cool shades of evening on sleeping. It's about the only time we can get anything done without getting all perspired."

He said he'd try to get back early and left. He'd thought

it was hot and stuffy inside. The late afternoon sun gave him yet another hot lick and he was tempted to run back inside.

But he settled for a saloon on the shady side of the street instead. By now he suspected poor Martha was wandering her halls naked as a jay, again.

As he leaned against the bar, sipping a needled beer that tasted warm enough to pass for frothy tea, he wondered why he kept wondering about an all right but not outstanding redhead's state of attire. He hadn't been on the road long enough to get all that hard up. Like most healthy men his age, save for downright sissies, Longarm liked women just fine, and seldom refused to kiss one, lest she take him for a sissy. But he didn't consider himself a skirt chaser. He seldom mixed business with pleasure and, damn it, he'd be back in Denver by the time he could launch a proper campaign with any fool gal down this way.

As he sipped his warm beer to kill time he found himself thinking about gals back in Denver he didn't have to wage a campaign to get at. There was pretty little Morgana Floyd, who was ever grateful for the time he'd rescued her from a runaway streetcar, and there was that China doll at the Golden Dragon who said she'd just die if anyone ever found out she liked a white man's eggroll half that much, and of course there was always his old pal up on Sherman Avenue and . . .

"What are you *doing* to your fool self?" he muttered into his beer suds. The barkeep down at the far end looked up from his newspaper to ask if he wanted to order another. Longarm shook his head and replied, "Just talking to myself." So the barkeep said he'd noticed how hot it was and got back to his reading as Longarm kept his thoughts to himself some more.

He knew what was eating him. It was Jessie, or maybe it was the excuse he had to look her up again. He told himself it was highly unlikely she'd come personally to Sanderson after those fool cows. Whether the cow thieves

26

stood trial there or not, the rich and powerful Jessie had better things to do than attend a small-town trial. She'd told him one time, not meaning to brag, how she'd had tea at the White House with President Hayes and old Lemonade Lucy, who never served anything stronger than tea, First Lady or not. Nobody important enough to visit the White House when she was back East was likely to be in any part of Texas this time of the year. If he went all the way down to Sanderson just to look at ragged-ass cow thieves Billy Vail would call him a fool, with simple justice. The gal he was trying not to think about wouldn't be there and, even if she was, then what?

Thinking about Jessie was a lot like probing at an aching tooth with your tongue, even though you knew you were only going to hurt your fool self some more. He knew her. He'd had her. That was all there was to it and all there could ever be. A man who liked women and could usually take 'em or leave 'em had to face the simple fact that now and again he'd get hurt. Getting in too deep went with getting in women at all. He'd fallen for gals before that just couldn't be, and he'd managed to survive. It wasn't as if Jessie Starbuck was the only one he'd ever been tempted by. There'd been Roping Sally, the only gal he'd ever met who could rope and ride better than he could himself. She'd been grand in bed as well and Lord only knew what might have happened had not poor Sally been killed by those land grabbers.

He started to order another drink. He told himself not to. Mooning over might-have-beens over a needled beer was no way for a man to behave. He wondered what old Kim Stover might be up to these days. Like Jessie, Kim had nearly led him into the dark temptations of unholy matrimony. She owned a mighty fine herd in her own right and . . . But like Jessie, she'd been too rich for him. They'd gotten back together a few times as well, and every time they had they'd both sworn it would never happen again. For it hurt like fire to part with such a special lover and, if

27

a man had a lick of sense, he'd stick to gals he could part with less painfully when the time came to part, as it always did. For a lawman who specialized in hunting down far-flung fugitives from justice had no more right to marry up than a damned old tumbleweed did, and there were some few gals you couldn't settle up with any other way.

Jessie Starbuck was one such gal, damn his weak nature. He knew, deep in his bones, that unless he stayed the hell away from her they'd likely both wind up in a heap of misery. For what use was a man too proud to take money from a woman to a woman who left his day's wages on the table as a tip? He thought about that time she'd ordered fancy French wine without thinking, and the fight they'd had once she realized their fancy meal at that fancy joint was going to cost him a week's wages, and offered to pay, herself! She'd told him he was being silly when he'd said he was a lawman, not a pimp. But that made him think about the sweet swell way they'd made up, afterwards, and just thinking about her soft sweet flesh, and the way she knew how to move it, made him hurt so bad he had to stomp outside again and cuss back at the ferocious old sun.

But even as he cussed it, he saw it was getting lower. He hauled out his pocket watch, saw he'd killed more time than he'd imagined, and headed for the depot.

The train they were setting up to serve wasn't due for a few more minutes, but Terry Phelan was all gussied up to serve it with a smile in her fresh blouse and trim brown skirts. She stopped smiling when she saw Longarm enter. He moved over to her counter and sat down anyway, saying, "Howdy. I sure could use some pie and coffee. Apple or cherry, if you've got it. Some flies I met earlier have put me off lemon merengue for the time being."

She served him quicker than some men could draw and fire a six-gun, her training overcoming her obvious reluctance to talk to him. He failed to see why. The other four Harvey Gals out front were too far down the counter to listen in, and wasn't the fool blonde supposed to serve all comers?

She moved out of easy earshot before he could bring up the photograph he'd taken from his coat to stick in a shirt pocket. She'd likely noticed the edge of the sepia-tone peeking out at her along with his cheroots. He shrugged and dug in, for now. The pie was mince. He decided not to raise a fuss. He'd told her anything but lemon merengue and it wasn't a bad mince pie. The coffee was even better. The Harvey chain had coffee down to a science. They knew passengers off a jerkwater didn't have time to let coffee cool. Yet they managed to keep it just warm enough in those fancy tanks against the back wall.

By the time he'd demolished the pie they could all hear the whistle of the incoming train. Longarm tried to catch Terry's eye. A fat cheerful Harvey Gal came over to take his order instead. Longarm asked her for a second cup of coffee. He wondered how the two gals had worked that out so confidential.

He muttered, "Women!" and nursed the second cup as he tried to figure a way to be nice about it. He didn't see why Terry was acting so shy about just glancing at an infernal photograph. But if she thought she could get rid of him by pretending he wasn't there she had another think coming. If push came to shove he could simply flash his badge, line the whole crew up, and make 'em *all* look at the infernal picture of the dead outlaw.

He knew he wouldn't, of course. He wondered if that was what Terry was counting on. The real mystery was why she was counting on anything. Even if she'd been the secret lover of the Panhandle Kid and had his loot hidden away for safekeeping, she was acting dumb as hell. For she had to know that all she had to do was say no and he'd be stuck. There was no way he was going to get a search warrant on no grounds at all in the time he had to work with. He wondered if he ought to explain that to her. He decided he'd better not. A lot of crooks were dumb about the law, and if she was a crook there was no sense educating her.

The train rumbled to a stop outside. It had barely come to a full stop when the stampede commenced. The passengers must have known there'd be no Harvey House where they'd stop to jerk water at their regular suppertime. The others crowding in around him looked as if they'd just been drug many a dusty mile in high summer. A young mother with a bawling baby sat down next to Longarm, trying to bottle the baby and feed herself at the same time. Longarm said, gravely, "I'd be proud to wrangle that infant for you while you coffee 'n cake yourself, ma'am."

She shot him a look of suspicion and utter gratitude at the same time. Gratitude won out. So the next thing Longarm knew he was holding the fool brat in his lap and trying to get some warm and likely sour milk down it as it whimpered and sprayed his shirtfront. Its mother was too hungry to notice. She wanted more than coffee and cake. She was stuffing her face with chili in the short time she knew she had to work with. Longarm called for service in an authoritative tone. The fat Harvey Gal came down their way, blinked in astonishment at the sight of such a tough-looking man nursing a bawling baby, and asked what she might do for either. Longarm handed her the half-filled baby bottle, saying, "This smells sour. Could you rinse it out and fill it with fresh moo juice before that train pulls out?"

She dimpled at him sweetly, said she sure could, and proceeded to do so before the young mother could grasp the situation and protest to Longarm, "Oh, no, I couldn't."

But he said, "You just did, ma'am. Milk don't keep in such hot weather, and if this child wanted to drink cheese he or she would have said so."

She said, "It's a boy." Then, in a more worried tone, she murmured, "Ah, how much do you suppose they charge for milk in such a fancy place?"

He followed her drift. He'd noticed how threadbare her travel duster was. But he didn't want to insult a proud young

30

woman, so he said, "I'm sure it comes free, with the coffee, ma'am."

The fat gal returned with the fresh milk. They didn't mess about in a Harvey House. As she handed it back to Longarm she started to say something. Then she caught the look in his eyes and turned away to serve another passenger. She was a smart old gal. Longarm liked her, even if she was awfully fat. The engine bell outside was clanging now. That only meant not to order a second helping. But the young mother must not have been as used to traveling by train as the others. She grabbed her kid back from Longarm with an expression of sincere thanks and ran for her coach seat, baby, bottle and all.

The others went on eating. The next time the fat gal came down to his end of the counter Longarm asked how much he owed her for that bottle of milk. She dimpled at him again to reply, "Nothing. I guess I can be as sweet as you can when I see a gal stuck with a hungry baby and run-over shoes."

He smiled back at her in a way that made her sort of blush as he said, "I hadn't noticed her shoes. But I can still smell how sour that bottle was. Seeing we're both so sweet, could I ask you a sort of delicate question?"

She fluttered her lashes to reply, "I'm not that kind of a girl, just my luck."

He chuckled and confided, "I came here to talk to Terry, platonic, about personal business. I couldn't help noticing her getting you to change places with her so she don't have to come to this end of the counter. I was wondering if you knew how come."

The fat gal shrugged and said, "She said you were sort of fresh. I said I didn't mind, as long as we had this counter between us. If you are trying to get fresh with her, forget it. She's engaged to a fancier dresser big enough to take you on, cowboy."

Longarm scowled and said, "I'm neither a cowboy nor trying to be fresh with her and she knows it. Would you be

31

kind enough to inform her I've been trying to be nice but that my nicer parts are commencing to feel strained."

The fat gal asked if he was trying to talk dirty in some sort of secret code. He growled, "I'm not talking about nicer parts the way you seem to have took my meaning. Terry knows who I am and what I want. You just tell her to get herself up this way sudden, lest I commence to treat her dirty indeed."

The fat gal gulped and moved away from him. The crowd was rapidly thinning out as the bell outside began to toll in earnest. Terry still waited until everyone but Longarm had left before she came down to his end of the counter with a resigned, perhaps somewhat frightened, expression in her eyes. She asked, in a defiant tone, what on earth he'd just said to Flo. He said, "Nothing that could get you fired. She told me it's a matter of public record that you've been courting with some fancy Dan who likely wears a tie in the daytime. I want you to look at a face less couth and tell me what you can about it."

As he got out the photograph she bit her lower lip and asked if he couldn't come back later, when they weren't so busy. He shook his head and lay the sepia-tone faceup on the counter between them, saying, "Don't push it if you don't want me wondering why. Look at the damned picture, girl!"

She obviously didn't want to. But she did. Then her eyes got wide as saucers and she had to grab the counter to keep from falling. She threw back her head to murmur, "Oh, Mother of God! Thank you! Thank you!"

As anyone else might have, Longarm found her reaction mighty peculiar. He said so, adding, "All right. Where have you seen this gent before?"

She grinned ear to ear at him, saying, "Nowhere. He's nobody I've ever known well enough to remember."

Longarm asked if she was sure. She picked the photograph up and calmly regarded the features of the late Panhandle Kid. She shook her head firmly and said, "He could have stopped by one time as a face in the crowd. What's the matter with him? He looks sort of odd, now that I study this more.''

"The picture was taken under unusual conditions. I'll take your word you didn't know him as well as he might have thought he knew you. Some men talk about women sort of silly. Would you mind telling me how come you went to so much trouble not to gaze at a total stranger's picture to begin with?''

She'd recovered her composure. She shrugged and said, "You told me you were the law. I was afraid I might get mixed up in something ugly. Is this man dead? He sure looks dead.''

Longarm took the picture back with a nod but he didn't put it away. He called the other Harvey Gals over and asked them to admire the sepia-tone as well. Fat Flo said, "Oh, him? Sure. I waited on him myself a week or so back. The only way I remember is that he was asking about Terry, here. He asked if that ring she's still wearing was for real or show. I told him she was spoken for and he said we'd see about that. I didn't like the way he said it. Do you think we have to worry about him coming back?''

Longarm shook his head and said, "Not hardly. He used to be a wanted outlaw. Now he's just a local legend, if that. But I see I may have saved you ladies some trouble with the rascal, and now that it's all ancient history we can all forget about it, only, dang it, I wish I'd caught that train.''

Flo smiled rougishly to opine, "That young gal with the baby was sort of pretty and you sure made friends with her sudden.''

Longarm just smiled at Terry and said, "You see, it didn't hurt half as much as pulling a tooth might have. Had you only told me sooner, I wouldn't be stuck here tonight.''

Terry asked him with sudden concern how she'd managed to do that to him. He said, "No matter. What's done is done and I found me a place to stay." Then he paid his

33

tab, left a tip for fat Flo, and left to see what else there was to be seen in such a dinky town.

There wasn't much. Once you'd seen one West Texas sundown you'd about seen them all unless the western sky was clouded up enough to notice.

Constable Lee caught up with him again at that same saloon. Lee said, "We just heard more about that case down to Sanderson. Miss Jessie Starbuck's pressing charges to the limit. Seems them cow thieves shot one of her riders who disputed their claim to her beef. They'll swing for it if her rider dies. Even if he pulls through they'll be making little rocks outa big ones until they're old and gray."

Longarm stared soberly down at his suds, saying, "I told you she was firm but fair. I told you it was none of my business while I was at it. What can you tell me about a Harvey Gal called Terry Phelan, wearing ash-blonde hair and a big diamond ring?"

"I know the gal you mean. They do serve fine coffee. But that's about all I can tell you about the lady in question. Them Harvey Gals is from out of state and keep to themselves as a rule. Why do you ask?"

Longarm pursed his lips and said, "I'm not sure. I couldn't help noticing she acted sort of devious when the truth was in her favor. You're a lawman. Can't you sort of feel it in your guts when a witness is feeding you cracked corn for oats?"

Lee chuckled and said, "Sure. Witnesses lie more than rugs. What's she supposed to be witnessing for you, Longarm?"

The younger but no doubt more experienced federal lawman said, "Nothing, now, and the hell of it is, the other gals who work with her back her up. The Panhandle Kid mentioned Miss Phelan and that handsome ring as he lay dying. I followed up on that by showing her the picture Flynn took for me. I'd best get around to paying the photographer while it's still on my mind."

"They'll have closed for the night by now," Lee said.

"It's just after six and it'll soon be too dark to take pictures in any case. What was that about the lady's diamond ring?"

Longarm glanced at the wall clock as he said, absently, "It was real. And a real diamond that size costs more than you and me make between us in a year. Another waitress told me the gent who gave it to her is rich. He'd have to be. Yet he lets his true love sling hash for way less than I make. How do you read that?"

Lee shrugged and said, "I don't know the gent. What if he's already married up? You know how some traveling salesmen are, and she's sure a pretty gal."

Longarm shook his head and said, "No traveling salesman could afford to bestow a rock like that on a stopover play-pretty. I agree Terry Phelan is a beauty. I can see many a rich man willing and able to take her away from all this hash slinging. So that leaves either unwilling or unable. I reckon I'd best delve a mite deeper into small-town gossip. The gal said she gets off work about now."

He left some change on the bar and strode out into the orange light and purple shadows of the gloaming. Sundown came sooner this far south, but he could see he still had an hour or so of tricky light to work with. He moved toward the tracks on the dark side of the street. He circled wide of the depot and found a Santa Fe tool shed to lean against, deeply shaded on his side with the sky glow lighting up the back door of the Harvey House just fine. There were lamps burning inside. From time to time he saw movement. But a million years later she still hadn't come out and he was wondering if he'd been inspired a mite too late. It was well after her quitting time. What if she'd already headed home? He had no idea where her rooming house was, save the fact she'd said it was close by.

Then, just as he was certain he was on a fool's errand, both Terry and Flo came out the back door, dressed in their own summer frocks. Longarm stayed put. The art of trailing called for not pressing the quarry too close. The two gals walked a few yards together. Then Terry stopped and her fat friend seemed to be trying to persuade her to come on along. He could tell they were arguing about something. Then the sensible fat gal shrugged and flounced away up the main street. If Flo was headed for that rooming house, Terry wasn't. She spun to head along the tracks through the gathering dusk. Had she not been wearing that light-colored frock Longarm would have had to follow closer on her heels to keep her in sight. But he knew that if he just kept her at the limit of visibility she could turn and look back for all he cared. He was dressed darker, except for his work shirt, and it was still a darker shade of blue than her dress.

As he tailed her he tried to figure where in thunder she could be headed. They were two city blocks from the depot when she whipped around a corner and he broke into a trot to keep from losing her. He thought he had when he eased around that corner into a dark cinder-paved side street. Then he spotted her up on the porch of a one-story frame house and slid into a doorway so he could watch her without being seen. He'd no sooner done so before the door opened and that was that. She ducked inside the dark house. Unless someone planned on doing something naughty with the lamps lit and the shades up, playing Peeping Tom was just asking for a bucket of slops or worse in his face. Folk inside a dark house could see out better than anyone could see in.

He waited where he was, dying for a smoke. A million years later, or more like forty-five minutes later, she came out again, smoothing down her dress. He muttered, "Yep, that's timing it about right for a quickie, considering how pretty that blonde is, you sneaky rascal."

He didn't follow Terry as she headed back to the center of town. He waited until she was long gone. Then he moved directly across the street, well down from the still dark little house, and eased on up, wondering just what he was supposed to do once he got there.

For on the face of it, there was no federal law covering a small-town romance on the sly. He'd look dumb as hell and have a tough time explaining if he simply barged in, gun drawn, to throw down on a man whose only crime was getting engaged to Harvey Gals. On the other hand, he'd look even dumber, and deader, if the cuss inside had more on his conscience than stringing a gal along with flashy jewelry. There had to be a better way. But he couldn't think of any, and he had to do something. For he was the law and something mighty mysterious was going on in these parts.

He got to the last house but one and leaned against it to study some more. The windows of the mysterious love nest were naturally wide open and the two of them had doubtless sweat like pigs while doing what he felt sure they'd been doing this early in the summer evening. He heard somebody moving around inside. Mighty busy for a man who'd just torn off a piece on such a hot occasion in the external sense. Longarm listened, trying to figure out what he was listening to. Then he heard a brassy snap, followed by a dull thud, and knew. The cuss was packing his traveling bags, in a hurry, as if he might be planning on leaving town soon.

Longarm eased back and turned to stride back the way he'd come, grinning wolfishly. There were still a lot of ways it worked as well. It was still possible Terry had known her flashy Dan would be leaving town a spell and so she'd just dropped by after work to see him off friendly. Or she might have dropped by to warn him a lawman was sniffing about, asking lots of questions, and thank God it hadn't been him in that photograph. Either way, if the rascal was packing in such a hurry he meant to board the first train he could. That one stopping at four in the afternoon had been the only one bound northeast. But a man in a hurry to leave town might not care just where a train might be bound, as long as it was leaving soon. The boys at the saloon would know when and if there was a westbound coming through after dark.

There was, in a way, albeit they told him at the saloon he was talking about a freight train if he was talking about a westbound stopping for water at all. They said it was due

37

in about an hour. Longarm said that sounded close enough and ordered a beer. But this time he told the barkeep not to spike it. There were times to get liquored up with the boys. Only this might not be one of 'em.

Chapter 3

Dandy Dunbarton, a handsome road agent wanted by almost as many women as lawmen, knew better than to wait for his train at the depot, now that he'd been warned a federal deputy was in town and asking questions. He'd put his oldest and darkest suit on over the Remington .45 he carried in a swivel holster and waited until just before that westbound freight was due before he made his way to the rail yards with his fancier duds packed in a handsome pigskin suitcase. The water tower was just up from the depot, of course, and he scouted that for lurking danger before making his way across the tracks to take up his stand. You couldn't hop a freight just anywhere. An empty gondola car close as possible to the engine and far as possible from the brakemen riding in the caboose was usually the best bet. Brakemen seldom expected to catch a hobo in a roofless gondola, so they paid most attention to the empty reefers, and if a brakeman still wanted to pester Dandy in a forward gondola, well, that was why his gun carried five in the wheel.

The depot across the way was dark at this hour, bless its sun-silvered shingles. For the ticket agent had gone home after that late afternoon passenger varnish pulled out, and the Harvey House had no sensible reason to stay open after dark, either.

Yet there must have been more moonlight shining down on the yards than he'd expected, for when a feminine voice called out the name he'd been using in Fort Stockton, and Dandy just froze, Terry Phelan still managed to spot him. She was easier to see as she crossed over in her light summer frock. Dandy just had to return her kiss. But as they came up for air he told her, "Had I wanted you here I'd have brung you along, little darling. Go on back to your rooming house before they suspect you of keeping company with a lowlife like me."

Terry protested, "You're not a lowlife, William. I told you I understood how you'd gotten in trouble with the law over that moonshine your business partner was making without your knowledge or consent. I want to go with you. Why can't I go with you? If it'll be safe for you on that big California ranch your family owns, why wouldn't it be just as safe for the both of us?"

Dandy chuckled dryly and said, "I told you I'd send for you as soon as I could, didn't I? How would it look if I showed up on the family doorstep with a gal I'd been riding freight trains with, unwed? My maiden aunts would likely suffer mortal strokes. You just go on back and keep your pretty little trap shut until I send for you, hear? I doubt that nosy federal deputy will pester you again. But if he does, well, I've been studying on that since you told me he might be on my tail."

"I'll never tell him anything about you, darling," she assured him. "I was so scared when he said he had a picture of a man he wanted me to look at, knowing how mean they can be about moonshining, but—"

"Never mind that dead outlaw," he cut in. "I've been

thinking it might be a good notion to feed him a red herring if he comes sniffing about again. None of the other Harvey gals but that fat one have ever met me, and she wasn't supposed to. But women gossip and he's sure to find out you've been keeping company with someone around here. If he asks about us again, I want you to tell him, innocent eyed, that you have indeed been sparking with a gent called Jim Dunbarton and—''

"You said your name was William Brown, dear," she cut in.

"I lied. I told you true I was in a little trouble with the law, didn't I? My real name's Dunbarton. That's what he'll have down on any warrant he's chasing me with. Should he show you a picture of me, tell him right out that it's me, lest one of the other gals make a liar outa you. Then tell him I left town yesterday, bound for Amarillo on some business I didn't tell you much about. That'll inspire him to wire ahead to the Rangers and go looking for me where I ain't, see?"

She nodded soberly and said, "Gee, you're smart. But Flo knows I went to see you tonight. She tried to talk me out of it. She keeps saying you're no good and that you're sure to get me in trouble."

Dandy Dunbarton laughed, without real humor, and said, "She must have some brains under all that lard, after all. All right. Confess you did say adios to me tonight in that house I hired. Let him search it if he likes. He won't find anyone there before the rent runs out at the end of the month. Tell him I told you I was bound for Amarillo, like I said. By the time he gets back to you some other trains should have pulled out. Maybe it's just as well he searches high and low for me here in Fort Stockton before he sends out an all-points. If you can keep him flustered half the day I'll be a good eight or ten hours west by the time he even gets about to guessing. I'd best get off this side of the Colorado and . . . Damn, I'll need more money than I'm packing if I

41

have to hole up a spell in some Arizona jerkwater where I don't have no pals.''

''Won't you be able to sell that diamond I gave back for a lot of money, dear?''

He answered, coldly, ''Where, and how? That rock is hotter than I am. I dare not try to sell it this side of a big city where some jewelers understand such matters.''

Terry's jaw dropped and she demanded, ''Hot? Do you mean to tell me the engagement ring you gave me had something wrong with it, dear?''

He favored her with a disgusted look and growled, ''Grow up, for God's sake. Did you really think I'd give any gal such an expensive rock if I'd bought it with my own money? Look, honey, I'm an outlaw on the run, okay? We've had our fun and it's been grand. But now get out of here and leave me alone. I've got me a train to catch and it'll be here any minute!''

The Harvey girl stared at him in dawning dismay as she said, ''Oh, Flo was right! You were just trifling with my heart all the time and now I guess you feel I was pretty dumb, even for such a country girl!''

He shrugged and said, ''Look on the bright side. You know you loved it.''

She gasped and informed him in a wounded voice, ''That was just mean and spiteful, William, or whoever you are! I've a good mind to march right back to town and tell that nice Deputy Long all about you!''

Dunbarton sneered down at her to say, ''Go ahead. Make sure I'm caught. For when and if I am I mean to tell them just how innocent you are. How would the folk having breakfast at the Harvey House like it if they knew the waitress serving them liked me to lick her love nest clean as any platter?''

She gasped and sobbed, ''Oh, you wouldn't! You couldn't! Why are you being so cruel to me? I just don't understand!''

He told her, flatly, ''Sure I could. If that lawman catches

42

me I'll have to. He's sure to ask lots of questions about my stay here in Fort Stockton. As to understanding, hell, if you understood men half as well as fat Flo you wouldn't be such an easy lay. It's over, you pretty little dimwit. No use stringing you along to cover for me now that I know Flo can place me here in town tonight. I just need to get out of it, sudden, and then you can tell the law anything you like. Who knows? He may lick the plate as well."

That did it. Terry spun around and staggered back across the tracks, tripping over more than one rail with her eyes blinded by her tears.

Longarm waited until she was out of sight before he stepped out of the shadows of the water tower to say, "Evening, Dunbarton. You sure have a way with words. If that didn't set her straight I don't know what might have."

Dandy Dunbarton felt a bucket of ice water pouring over him, going the wrong way from his calves to the nape of his neck as he tried to come up with something, anything, to do or say next.

Longarm was facing him from less than thirty feet away, but, like Dunbarton, his hands were still empty. Dunbarton saw the lawman favored cross-draw. He knew he only had to get to the grips of his own six-gun and the swivel holster would do the rest unless the cuss was too fast to qualify as human. That was something to study on. He swallowed hard and said, "You have the advantage on me, amigo. You seem to know my name and I don't know your name and rep."

Longarm had been disappointed by brave talkers before. So he replied, "My name ain't as important as the fact that your own is on many a Wanted flier, Dunbarton. You're under arrest and I'd sure like to use anything you say or do against you. So what's your pleasure, you son of a bitch?"

Dunbarton swallowed again and said, "I'm still pondering my next best move. Would you mind telling me, for openers, where the hell you was staked out all this time? I

43

was under the distinct impression I'd scouted yonder water tower.''

"I figured you might. So I climbed up the ladder a ways to let you poke about at ground level and feel secure. I was just about to come down and get you when I spotted Miss Terry coming. Not knowing how deep she was involved with you, I thought it best to just hear her out. I'm pleased to see how innocent she really was. Now, about that gun you seem so undecided about . . .''

Dunbarton knew it was ever best to make one's move while the other man was in the middle of a sentence. So he made it. But Longarm had been hoping he might and he'd had gents slap leather in the middle of a sentence before. So the stillness of the night was sundered by two gunshots and illuminated by the muzzle blasts as well while Dandy Dunbarton spun like a top with two rounds in his chest to wind up on his side on the railroad ballast, almost as surprised as hurt.

As Longarm strode over to him, Dunbarton raised his head from the dust to gasp in wonder, "How . . . how did you do that?"

Longarm finally got around to drawing his six-gun as he explained, casually, "Derringer. I'd heard about that swivel holster. You shouldn't have been such a creature of habit. I was sort of hoping you'd feel you had the edge on my cross-draw rig. So I was covering you with a palmed derringer all the time. I know it don't sound fair, but you was hardly fair to that poor little gal, and this is real life, not one of Ned Buntline's dumb wild West yarns.''

He kicked the downed outlaw to roll him off his own still holstered gun. As Longarm hunkered down to disarm him Dunbarton protested, "That hurt, damn you! Are you trying to kill me?''

Longarm straightened back up with a pistol in each hand, saying, "I already killed you. You just ain't figured that out yet.''

Dandy Dunbarton heaved a great sigh, vomited a pint of

44

blood, and didn't answer. Longarm nodded and muttered, "See what I mean?"

But he wasn't lonely long. For in any community of less than a thousand or so souls, counting the nearby army camp, gunfire before bedtime tends to attract quite a crowd. Some of 'em were even packing lanterns. Terry Phelan and her fat friend, Flo, were among the first to arrive on the scene. When she saw her recent lover stretched out so bloody and dead she started to scream and then she fainted instead. Flo caught her on the way down. Longarm holstered his .44-40, stuck Dunbarton's six-gun in his gun belt, and helped Flo drag the unconscious Harvey gal clear of the still growing crowd. Flo gasped, "I have to get her back to our rooming house before she says something dumb!"

But Longarm took out the sepia-tone of the Panhandle Kid and handed it to Flo, saying softly, "I wrote an address on the back of this, thinking I might need it later. I can't carry her for you. Get her there the best way you know how and I'll join you there as soon as I can."

Flo naturally asked where and why. He said, "Their little love nest. It's deserted total right now. She'll no doubt know where the bed might be. We got to recover her some before she has to face the clucking of curious women in that rooming house, see?"

Flo did. She said, "Goddamn if you ain't one sweet soul! You knew about them, right?"

He just told her to get cracking and went back to join the crowd. Constable Lee had shown up by now. He asked Longarm, "Did you do this?"

So Longarm said, "I can not tell a lie. His name was James Edward Dunbarton, better known as Dandy and wanted for murder, rape and burglary. It wasn't a good idea to wake up when he was burglarizing your bedroom. The funny part was that he was never wanted federal. I never suspected he was in town. But he must have found out I was. So he made a run for it with the results here before you."

Then he drew Lee clear of the others to confide, "As a paid peace officer I was authorized to nail any wanted man I might meet up with. But I'd say you had more jurisdiction over the final results of his resisting arrest. Texas is one of the many states he was wanted in, and there's considerable reward money posted on the cuss, if you feel up to the paperwork."

Lee brightened and said, "I do indeed and this is mighty neighborly of you, Longarm!"

The unselfish federal lawman shrugged modestly and explained, "May as well keep the money in the family. My boss frowns on us putting in for state bounty money, and I just hate paperwork. I can settle up with your coroner and photographer Flynn before I leave for Denver in the morning. Right now I'd like to sort of fade away before I get asked all sorts of fool questions. I got enough of a rep to live down, and I suspect that mean bastard never would have given me the chance to gun him if he'd known just who he was talking to."

Dim light was showing from the open windows of the house when Longarm arrived, sauntering casual. Nobody seemed to notice when he mounted the steps and knocked softly on the door. The fat and flushed Flo let him in, grinning roguishly as she confided, "The door was locked. I had to climb in through a porch window. You'd have surely fallen down laughing had you been here to see me with my skirts hitched up like so."

Longarm smiled down at her to reply, "It's a good thing you're so athletic. How's Terry doing?"

Flo led him back to one of the two bedrooms as she told him, "Out like a light, poor thing. By the time I'd hauled her in here and got her atop a bed she was carrying on sort of crazy. So I found some whiskey in the kitchen and made her drink as much as I could get down her."

As the two of them entered the dimly lit bedroom Flo

sighed and added, "I might have given her a mite too much."

Longarm moved over to feel the limp wrist of the blonde laid out for a wake atop the covers. He told Flo, "Well, she's still alive." Then he took out the engagement ring he'd taken from her dead lover's vest to put it back on Terry's finger. Flo wanted to know about that, too, of course. So he said, "As you must have figured by now, that polecat never meant to make an honest woman of her. But she thought he was sincere and by now the whole town must have seen her flashing that fancy ring at 'em. It's likely to be close as it is. You may not have been the only one who ever saw them together. Come sunrise he'll be famous as well as dead. Her best bet will be to tough it through and just tell anyone who asks that, sure, she'd served flapjacks and such to the sneaky rascal, but naturally her one true love was and still is a traveling man who comes through now and again. You're going to have to help her carry it off, Flo. You're going to have to tell her what I just said. I doubt she needs a moral lecture from the man who shot the rascal."

Flo stared soberly up at him to say, "You're wrong. I got some of it out of her as I was knocking her unconscious. You never gunned a rascal, Custis. You rid the world of a total bastard!"

"I'm glad you see it that way, too. Now all we have to do is sober her up, make sure she's calmed down, and sneak her back to the rooming house."

He bent forward to gently pry open one of Terry's eyelids. He whistled and muttered, "She's going to have to sleep at least some of it off. Trying to get her back on her feet this side of midnight just figures to make her puke all over us and she still won't be able to enter that rooming house halfway sedate."

Flo sighed and said, "I had to do something, the way she was carrying on. We might get away with getting her to the rooming house so late, just this once, as long as they

47

see I'm with her. The landlady will no doubt sniff. I'll just have to say we was setting on a porch with some gentlemen friends and lost track of how late it was getting. But it ain't like it was only one of us, unchaperoned.''

Longarm chuckled and followed her back out, saying, "I noticed you thought fast on your feet when I handed you that baby bottle one time."

She led him to a parlor sofa and as they both flopped down she said, in a sad little voice, "A gal has to learn to use her brain when it's the only charms the Good Lord ever granted her. I hope the landlady don't laugh when I tell her I was out all this time with some gent. I know what I look like. But it still hurts when folk laugh."

Longarm skimmed his hat aside and leaned back expansively as he assured her, "Nobody decent would ever laugh at you, Flo. I think you're a swell gal and it ain't your fault you're sort of pleasantly plump."

She made a wry face and said, "Don't I know it! I've tried to lose weight ever since I was a kid and all the other kids teased me and called me a butterball. I know you don't believe me, but I don't eat half as much as the other gals at work and I never touch sweets at all!"

He soothed, "That's likely why you have such a fine complexion. I know some folk put on more weight than others without really trying. I eat twice as much as my poor boss, Billy Vail, and he still looks like a sort of mean, smooth-shaven Santa Claus. He's way fatter than you, by the way, and yet his old woman still acts mighty fond of him."

Flo shook her head and insisted, "It's not the same when a man gets fat. Nobody I'd want is ever going to fall in love with me. I've had boyfriends now and again. Some men seem to think fat gals are easy. They may be right. But it hurts like fire, even when you want it, to have a man making love to you just because he can't get anybody pretty. I wish just once . . .''

Then she blushed like a rosy peach and turned her face

48

away to murmur, "Land sakes, whatever must you think of me?"

He put a gentle hand on her shoulder to assure her, "I told you what I thought of you, Flo. I said you were a really nice little gal."

She laughed, bitterly, and insisted, "I never wanted to be a nice gal. It was inflicted on me by a cruel fate. I know you know I'm good-hearted. I can't help that, either. But fess up true, wouldn't you just laugh like hell if I was to ask you if you found me pretty enough to . . . you know?"

Longarm managed not to laugh, albeit he did feel awkward and sort of panic-stricken as he swallowed hard and tried, "You're just teasing me and you know it. For, sure, I'd just love to treat you naughty as anything, if things were a mite different. You're a woman and I'm a man and you know how men are, Flo."

She turned to face him, eyes glowing with an almost unholy light as she said, "I don't know near as much as I'd like to find out about men. Did you really and truly mean that? Would you really want to make love to me, like I was slim and pretty, if I asked you to?"

He hadn't even thought about it and didn't think he'd better. For while she wasn't exactly repulsive—her face was sort of nice, in fact—he didn't want to hurt her and, grasping that straw, he said so, explaining, "You'd wind up sorry and I like you too much to let that happen, Flo."

She sighed and said, "Well, at least you didn't laugh right out at me. Thanks for the gentle turn-down, Custis."

He frowned at her and insisted, "You don't know what you're saying, girl. Are you sure you weren't at that whiskey as well? I'm a tumbleweed stranger, just passing through this one night I'll be in town. You don't want to go getting passionate with any man you'll likely never see again."

She muttered, "Speak for yourself. I guess I know what I want or don't want. Maybe it's the very fact that we're only ships passing in the night that makes you look so yummy to me right now. It's sure a lot more vexing to spend a night or maybe even two with a good-looking man, only to have him start ducking around corners on you, just as you were daring to hope that, this time . . . Oh, never mind. I said I got your meaning. What else do you think we ought to do while we wait for Terry to wake up? Might you have a deck of cards on you, young Lochinvar?''

Longarm muttered, ''Aw, hell,'' and hauled her in for a kiss. He meant it just to show he didn't find her all that ugly. Then she started kissing back in a way that felt pretty indeed. She took his free wrist in hand and directed his hand down to her lap, spreading her massive thighs as she did so, lest he lose his way to where she seemed to want to be grabbed.

So he grabbed. Most men would have by this time, and once he'd edged her skirts up to fondle her right he discovered she was more than ready. Her pleasure spot was already wet and turgid. As he began to soothe it with gentle strokes of his fingers she moaned, ''Oh, Lord, don't make me waste a climax like this, Custis! Let's go in the other room and do it right!''

He wanted to, but he still felt obliged to ask, ''Are you sure? I doubt we have more than an hour or so and that has to be the end of us, for keeps.''

She pleaded, ''I know! I know! So why are we wasting one more second on this goddamned sofa!''

That sounded reasonable. He knew she'd never forgive him no matter what he did, now. So he scooped her up to carry her into that other bedroom. This seemed to surprise her. For she stared up at him in adoring wonder to tell him he was ever so strong.

The bed in the spare room of the hired house only had a bare mattress on its springs. Flo refused to strip bare, despite her aggressive passion, before he'd kicked the door shut to plunge them into total darkness. By the time they were both going at it stark in the dark, Longarm was a mite sorry there wasn't at least a speck of light on the subject. For with all her duds off Flo felt downright lovely in his bare arms. Her

50

breasts were firm as well as massive, and there was a lot to be said for a gal having that much meat under her upthrust pelvis as he entered her to discover she was built surprisingly small where it really mattered. It felt like he had a virgin with two pillows under her behind and he was glad she'd told him she was no such thing. He'd have never bought her being green at the game of love in any case, once she commenced to move in time with his thrusts. Flo had a heap of muscle under all that lard and a lesser rider might have been thrown from her love saddle by the bucking performance she put on.

He knew she wasn't just trying to please him when she moaned that she was coming, almost at once. He knew he sure wanted to, now, but between the sudden surprise and his lingering moral doubts about all this, he found it sort of hard to catch up with her, and so as he pounded her in search of his own pleasure he brought her to climax again and again and she seemed to want the whole world to know it, judging from all the dirty words she kept yelling.

He came in her at last and there was a lot to be said for taking some time doing that, as well. He kissed her fondly and asked if she'd please shut up before they started selling tickets out front. She sobbed, "Oh, thank you! Thank you! I feel so happy I could just die. But now, of course, you can't wait to get out of here, right?"

She had, in fact, hit the nail on the head. But he felt he owed it to her to just kiss her some more and soothe, "Does it feel like I want to take it out, honey?"

She contracted on his shaft, moaning, "Oh, Jesus, thanks for calling me honey, even after you've had me. But you can't mean to do it again, can you? I thought men had to go to sleep right after they'd come in a gal."

He didn't answer as he let it soak in her, wondering if he really did want to try again. For she wasn't at all bad, but it was sort of a tiring chore unless a gal was really pretty. He knew, now, the kind of men she'd been with before. He decided he had to do better. For a cuss who'd

51

shoot fish in a barrel and just roll over and go to sleep was pushing an easy lay to cruel and unusual punishment, even though she did seem used to it.

Then the door popped open to spill lamplight across their entwined naked bodies, and as they both gasped in embarrassment Terry Phelan stood there, bleary eyed, to manage, "Oh, dear, I don't know what to say, Flo. I heard you calling out and . . . What have you been doing with that naked man?"

Flo laughed weakly and said, "It's a good thing we're all Irish. You know what we've been doing and would you please wait out in the parlor for a minute, damn it?"

Terry said, "I feel sick. I'm so ashamed. Not about you two. About me, and that terrible man, in this very place!"

Longarm told Flo, "I'd say the party's about over, honey. The sooner we get her home the better."

Flo agreed, albeit cussing some, and begged them not to look at her as she began to get dressed. Longarm would have preferred Terry somewhere else than staring at his semi-erection as he hauled his own duds on. But they were all in this together, now, and with any luck, nobody else would ever know.

It was just after midnight by the time Longarm made it back to the Widow Watt's place after stopping at the saloon to steady his nerves after getting the two Harvey gals discreetly home. There was a lamp lit somewhere deep in the innards of the house and old Martha had told him she sat up late, but it was late above and beyond the call of duty, now, and he cussed himself for having had those last few drinks. He'd figured he'd needed them, not so much as a reward for a job well done as in hopes of getting to bed, at last, unwound. They hadn't unwound him enough to mention. That quickie with old Flo had used up some of the inner flutters a gunfight tended to generate. But Terry busting in on them like that had left him even more keyed up with a semi-erection to boot.

He eased on up the porch, recalling how Flo had gotten

into that other house despite its locked front door. Given the choice between getting shot as a burglar or waking up a redhead who'd just about managed to fall asleep in a late cooling Texas night, he decided he'd best at least try the door latch before he did anything wilder.

But as he reached for the knob the door swung inward and said redhead hauled him in, gasping, "Oh, Custis, where on earth have you been all this time? I've been so worried since they told me you'd been in a shoot-out near the depot!"

She must have been, and drinking lonesome while she waited, judging by the bourbon on her breath as she kissed him smack on his surprised lips. As he kissed her back, ever courteous to his elders, he noticed she'd been waiting up for him in a silky kimono. He wondered if she was aware it hung open down the front of her. She likely was. For as she sort of ground her red-fuzzed but otherwise naked mound of venus against the front of his tweed pants she murmured, "Ooh, might all this be meant for little old me?"

He hadn't, in fact, been thinking of her half this disrespectful. For in the first place he'd only considered her his landlady for the night, and in the second place the poor old gal had to be almost forty. But as he cupped a silky buttock in each palm to hold her closer and kiss her more French he was glad he hadn't managed to get really reeling at the saloon. Being a woman, Martha naturally felt obligated to ask, "Oh, Custis, what are you *doing* to me? I feel so fluttery!" and they both felt him answering his own way through his pants. That was a mighty dumb place to keep a hard-on. So he picked her up and headed for the stairs. He knew that if he asked her for directions to the nearest bed it could break the spell. So he headed up the stairs with her in his arms for the bedroom he knew about. She sort of sobbed that he was so masterful and asked him how he'd gotten so strong. He told her it was clean living and she laughed and said they'd just see about that.

In point of fact Martha felt light as a feather after packing fat Flo less than half as far. He packed the much slimmer redhead into the room she'd hired him and placed her gently on the bed as she moaned, "Hurry, hurry, and do you have any matches?"

He allowed he did, in a curious tone, as he sat down beside her to tug off his boots. Hoping she didn't mean to set fire to anything important, he handed her a waterproof match from his shirt pocket and she lit the bedside oil lamp as he was peeling off his shirt. She lay back with a satisfied little sigh, saying, "That's better. Oh, my, you do have a lovely body, Custis!"

That made two of them, he saw, as he kicked off his pants and rolled aboard her without bothering with his socks. He'd noticed in the past that gals found making love in the dark less romantic when they had a build they were proud of. Old Martha had every right to feel proud of hers. Ben Franklin, bless him, had once made note of the fact that as trees die from the top down, so did a gal's face age first and, hell, Martha's face was still pretty enough, and her body seemed that of a teenager fixing to grow up curvy as hell. He propped himself up on locked elbows to admire all of her as well as the sight of his love-slicked erection going in and out of that handsome red thicket between her slender, wide-spread thighs. She lay there with her own eyes closed and a dreamy little smile on her lips in the kindly lamplight. Her Texas-weathered face had a mite more, well, character, in bright sunlight. In this more flattering light she didn't look a day older than he did and, what the hell, if she did have a few years on him there was a lot to be said for experience. For despite her angelic expression she commenced to move her hips as no fool teenager built like that was likely to. So he was getting the best of both worlds and it sure felt grand, despite the fact that between fat Flo and those last few drinks at the saloon he was getting there slower than usual.

She didn't mind at all. She started moving faster. Then she locked her legs around him and opened her eyes to stare up at him adoringly to hiss, "Faster, darling! I'm almost there and if you stop now I'll just die and . . . Jeezusss, yessss!"

She went limp as a poleaxed steer for a spell. Then she felt it still moving in her and moaned, "What's the matter? Don't you like me?" So he went limp himself and kissed her hard as he faked one for her. It seemed fair enough. Gals did it all the time when they wanted to catch their breath. She ran her nails up and down his spine, crooning, "There, there, Mamma knows how to kiss it all better, baby." So while he'd intended to just act inspired for more, the old-fashioned way, when he finally did get to come in Martha it wasn't exactly where the Good Book said a man was supposed to if he aimed to go to Heaven.

She blew a mighty fine tune on the love flute as well. He felt it all the way down to his toes. But her generous treatment of his old organ grinder inspired him to roll her over on her back some more to do it to her again, less sinful, albeit some sky pilots might not have approved of the positions they wound up in during his protracted fourth grab for the full pleasure of her company.

As they shared one of his cheroots, afterward, she told him he was quite a man and asked if he thought she was a dirty old woman. He said, "Of course not. I was just as hard up, as you may have noticed. Folk who don't get it regular always tend to go a mite wild when the rare opportunity arises."

She told him he was so understanding as well as a swell riser. Then she added, "I may as well confess I got all hot and bothered the first time I saw you hang up your coat. I could tell by the way your shoulders filled your damp shirt that you were really strong as well as handsome. I married young, and liked it the first night. But my late husband was a smaller man, in every way, and I reckon we took to sort of naughty tricks to keep us both well satisfied."

Longarm grimaced at the low-slanted ceiling. He just hated it when women brought up other men they'd screwed, and he didn't see why so many of 'em seemed to want to. They got sore as hell when a man mentioned another gal he'd been playing slap-and-tickle with. The cuss who'd dubbed 'em the fair sex hadn't likely been with all that many women. Most of 'em were unfair as hell about such matters.

As he stared up through a thoughtful smoke ring it occurred to him, as it had before, that maybe that was what made some few ladies in his life more special. It wasn't as if certain gals were prettier or screwed better that made a man miss 'em so. He hardly ever even kissed a gal who wasn't *sort* of pretty, and nine out of ten gals screwed great, with the tenth a sort of interesting novelty. It was the feeling of *honest* love-making that made a man fall hard for a gal, even when he didn't have a hard-on. That old Irish song about the Rose of Tralee had surely been written by a man who'd been lucky in his choice of women and had the sense to know it. For Mary, the Rose of Tralee, had been the sort of woman most men never found. Like the song said, it hadn't been that she was fair as the first rose of summer, or even that she'd been smiling and listening to his brags as they'd strayed by them pure crystal fountains. He found himself softly singing, "Oh, no, 'twas the *truth*, in her eyes ever beaming, that made me love Mary, the Rose of Tralee."

Martha snuggled closer but naturally asked him what on earth had gotten into him. He said, "Nothing. Lying here like this just reminded me of an old dumb song. Lord knows how come."

But he knew exactly why. Had an old pal like Kim Stover, poor Roping Sally or, damn it, Jessie Starbuck just asked him the same question, he'd have felt perfectly free to answer, without any fear of being misunderstood. There was more to feeling good with a gal in one's arms than the fact that nothing else felt better. Longarm liked most women, this way. He was good at getting 'em this way because he'd learned to sort of play 'em like a trout, and it sure felt grand once he reeled 'em in. But a man had to know how to handle women, lest they wind up sore at him for no sensible reason. He never knew how far it was safe to relax and just act natural, unless he was with someone like good old Lonestar. Her eyes were ever truthful, even acting down and dirty, and he always knew just how wild she wanted to get, because he could trust her to tell him exactly how she felt. He recalled that time she'd started to feel her period coming on, and just told him so instead of making up coy excuses, and how that weekend had been swell, anyway, as they just enjoyed each other's company and settled for kissing each other goodnight after they'd sat up reading in bed a spell. He smiled wryly and snubbed out the cheroot as he considered Jessie could be in that condition if she *did* come to Sanderson about them cows. But it didn't work. He knew most of the month she was raring to go.

★

Chapter 4

Longarm didn't recall falling asleep, but he knew he must have when he woke up in broad daylight to find old Martha fooling with him again. He yawned and said, "Now that's mighty considerate of you, little darling. But I'd best go down the hall for just a minute, if you'll pardon my talking so indelicate to a naked lady."

She laughed, lewdly, and said, "Make it snappy, then. I just love it in the morning, don't you?"

He laughed, sat up, and told her he just loved it any old time. Then he asked her what time it might be, and when she said it was around nine he said, "Thunderation! The day's almost half shot and I got chores to tend to before I have to catch that train!"

She sighed wistfully, let him go with a last fond jerk, and said, "I'd have let you sleep longer if I wasn't so passionate. I know you have to leave, damn it. But you can always catch the four o'clock eastbound if you miss the one coming through at noon. You surely don't have all that many things to do here in town, right?''

He swung his bare feet to the rug, saying, "Wrong. I have to pick up some papers, pay some bills, and get an army mount out to the post before I catch train-one. So I'd best get cracking."

She told him to hurry back as he left the room, naked as a jay, to find the dinky bathroom at the end of the hall and get rid of all that needled beer. As long as he was back there he enjoyed a refreshing whore-bath at the sink with scented soap and a heap of cold water. But when he sauntered back into the bedroom he saw he might well have spared himself the effort. For the redhead, in every way, was kneeling across the rumpled bedding, presenting her peachy upthrust rump to the open doorway. He chuckled fondly and sauntered over, rising to the occasion as he approached all that sweet temptation. So when he took hold of a hipbone with each hand he just had to step right in. For she was mighty slippery as well as wide open to welcome it. She giggled and said, "I told you you had the time."

He started thrusting in and out, with his socks planted firmly apart to balance his center of gravity while he assured her that sometimes chores just didn't seem as important as they did at other times. She hadn't been kidding when she'd told Longarm she loved it in the morning, and her energetic responses increased his own fervor. And then, of course, she made him screw her right, and so by the time he got to the town lockup it was pushing ten.

Constable Lee had the death certificates and photographer's bill waiting on his desk. Longarm said, "I have to see about running a pony back to the remount service. Could I leave the money here with you, pard?"

Lee said, "Sure. Anyone can see you had a rough night. Was it thinking about these death certificates that kept you from a good night's sleep?"

Longarm smiled thinly and said, "Not hardly. I'd often

suspected I might have gunned some men in the war who might not have had it coming. I've never gunned anyone, since, who didn't deserve to die. So I seldom lose much sleep over a shoot-out. It only makes me broody when I consider *losing*."

Lee chuckled and said, "I know the feeling. I was pleased as punch the day I shot my first damn Yankee. Then I mosied over to get a better look at the dead cuss, and I've always wished I hadn't been so nosy. He couldn't have been more than sixteen and his dead eyes was staring up at me like a little kid who'd been punished and couldn't see why."

Longarm didn't want to listen to old war stories any more than he wanted to listen to old love stories about dead husbands and other lovers. So he was barely listening, at first, as the older lawman continued, "Dealing with outlaws ain't half as confusing. You take that bunch they caught down to Sanderson, now. They're fixing to hang high for what they done and nobody will care what they look like, as long as they look dead. That Starbuck rider they shot just died. So it's murder in the first."

Longarm didn't want to hear about Jessie Starbuck right now, either. But then Lee said, "One of them cow thieves is just a kid named Willy Shepherd, age fifteen. But you know what the wages of sin are, and if he was old enough to gun a grown man—"

"Hold on," Longarm cut in with a puzzled frown, "I know a young cowhand called Willy Shepherd. The name stuck in my head because it struck me as an amusing handle for a cowhand and because I was there when he asked Miss Jessica Starbuck to give him a chance as a rider. She thought him a mite young and asked my opinion. I told her to let the kid rope a corral post for us and, when we saw he roped just fine, she signed him on. I mean, as a Circle Star rider. I fail to see how they could suspect young Willy of stealing Starbuck beef, seeing he's *supposed* to be keeping company with the same."

Constable Lee shrugged and opined, "He must have decided to go into business for himself. It ain't all that unusual for a cowhand to steal from his own outfit. Miss Jessie surely would have said so if the kid and his pals had had her permit to drive 'em this far west, by moonlight.''

Lee hauled out a smoke for himself and lit up before he added in the same laconic tone, ''They wouldn't be holding Shepherd and his Chinaman leader in the Sanderson jail if the lawful owner of them cows had not wired, personal, to press charges.''

Longarm almost let his own cheroot fall from his astounded lips before he recovered to insist, ''Back up. You say a paid-up Starbuck rider was driving Starbuck beef with a trail boss of Oriental appearance?''

Lee nodded and said, ''Yep. Chinaman or part Chinaman called Kee-wee or some such heathen notion. I've misplaced the wire they sent, asking if he was on our Wanted list. He wasn't, so it didn't seem important. I got enough regular owlhoot riders to worry about without Chinamen who've already been caught.''

Longarm said, flatly, ''There's something wrong going on down to Sanderson. There ain't that many Orientals by any handle in the beef industry, on either side of the law. I had Willy Shepherd down as a dumb and decent young cuss, and Jessie Starbuck's own segundo is a hitherto honest gent of part-Japanese persuasion who answers to the name of Ki!''

Lee nodded and said, ''That was it. I noticed it sounded sort of like my name, albeit I'm pure white on both sides. You reckon Miss Jessie's foreman went bad on her? I'd surely never trust no Oriental breed to guard *my* property.''

Longarm shook his head firmly and insisted, ''If there's one thing I know about old Ki, for he's sort of mysterious, I'd be willing to bet my life he'd give his life for Jessie Starbuck. I've seen him almost do so, more than once. He helped her dad raise her and she's risked her own life for him in the past. So how in thunder could she have ever pressed charges against him for stealing stock on her? Even

61

I know Ki has authority to buy and sell stock or anything else in her name!''

Lee shrugged and said, ''Don't look at me. I don't know neither of 'em. Maybe they had some sort of falling out. What if she had to fire him for lusting after her fair white body, the way they say such Oriental gents lust, and what if he just decided to take some of her cows with him as he was leaving? That works, don't it?''

Longarm grimaced and said, ''Now you're really talking dumb. Ki would stab himself with one of them Japanese hurricane knives before he'd do a thing to make Miss Jessie sore at him. He's devoted to her as a redbone hound, and vice versa. I got to get on over to the Western Union. They must have wired something stupid to Miss Jessie. She'd never have pressed charges had she known it was her *own riders* they'd caught driving her beef!''

He got there soon enough. Longarm wore low-heeled army boots with possible running in mind. He assured the startled telegraph clerk he wasn't cussing Western Union. Then he filled out a yellow telegram blank for Jessie and another for the law down in Sanderson. He spent more money assuring Terrell County he could vouch for Ki, young Shepherd and likely their comrades as a U.S. deputy marshal. The Western Union clerk charged him a heap of his own nickels and assured him both wires would arrive within less than an hour, day rates. When Longarm asked how long it might take to receive any answers, the clerk shrugged and told him it depended on how soon anyone wanted to wire back any answers. So Longarm went out to do some shopping, just in case he found his fool self stuck with a sixty-mile ride. There was a rail line through both towns, but nothing but sixty miles of dry chaparral between.

His personal McClellan saddle, Winchester and bedroll would still be in the tack room at the livery, Lord willing and they hadn't suffered any recent burglaries. He'd have heard by now, in a town this size, if anyone had stolen that army bay he'd left there. He was glad now old Martha had kept him in bed so late. Things would have been more complicated if he'd returned that army mount first, as he'd planned.

He went to the nearest general store and cheered the old gal behind the counter by asking for a sack of oats and a pair of ten-gallon water bags. Once he'd seen to the comforts of his mount he bought extra matches and .44-40 shells to fit both his saddle carbine and side arm. Then he bought some canned beans and tomato preserves and of course a couple of dozen cheroots. While he was at it he bought extra clean socks and underwear. He told her she'd best throw in a new hickory shirt, seeing he'd no doubt wind up in Sanderson sweat stunk, and that reminded him to ask for a bar of naptha soap. The soap in his saddlebag at the livery could be too mild if this hot spell didn't let up. Soap had to be powerful to cut through grease with the little water a man had to spare on a long dry ride.

He toted his bundle to a liquor store across the way and stocked up on a pint of medicinal Maryland rye while he still had the chance. Then he toted everything to the livery and had them water, oat and curry the bay while he arranged all his new gear on the McClellan. Longarm got laughed at, now and again, for favoring such a sissy saddle, but while old General George McClellan had messed up during the Peninsular Campaign, he'd known what he was doing when he designed the cavalry saddle named after him. It had so many brass fittings there was no end to how much stuff you could secure to it, and while the open slot down the center of the seat scared gents who rode with their pants loose, it was easier on the mount than a stock saddle because it kept pressure off the critter's spine and let the heat rise from a sweaty saddle blanket.

He went back to the Western Union office. The Sanderson law had answered his wire, to politely inform him he was full of shit. For they surely had wired all the names and Jessie Starbuck still said they'd stolen her stock, shot one

63

of her riders doing so, and she wanted 'em all hung out to dry.

He hadn't received any reply to his message to Jessie. It was now past noon and that Denver-bound train had come and gone. There was still that last afternoon train, should he manage to straighten this mysterious mess with Jessie out by wire. But he didn't see how he could if she refused to talk to him. The clerk at this end was able and willing to confirm his anxious message had been delivered by a Western Union rider to Lonestar's home spread. Someone there had had to sign for it. Could Jessie be sore at him as well as Ki? Not unless she'd been drinking something more confusing than Maryland rye!

Whatever Ki could have done to vex her, she and Long-arm had parted friendly, with her on top, the last time they'd spoken at all to one another. Something crazy as hell had to be going on. He tried to come up with something halfway possible as he got to work on another telegram blank. The first and obvious way it could work was to have someone kidnap the real Jessie and send mean things by wire in her name. She was always getting in dumb fixes like that, between owning so much property others wanted and her hobby of tracking down other crooks. But if by chance some enemies had waylaid her, how in thunder had they, or could they, get the whole crew at her home spread to go along with the charade? Jessie had a big staff of household help, mostly old family retainers who'd watched her grow up. Her ranch hands came armed, in considerable numbers, and since she'd been pestered by many a crook in the past, any of her riders who didn't stand willing and able to back their boss lady had been weeded out by now. Yet his wire had been delivered to her home spread and signed for. The Western Union rider surely would have mentioned it, had he arrived to find the place shot up, with buzzards circling overhead. There was no damned other way anyone pretending to be Jessie could have occupied the spread, and the main house had been built mighty fortified, in the days

64

Comanche had still been an ever-present danger.

His long message to Billy Vail assured the boss Longarm had accounted for the Panhandle Kid in a convenient as well as law-abiding way. Stalling for time, he threw in the shoot-out with the late Dandy Dunbarton and allowed he might have to stick around for a coroner's hearing. Then he told Jessie's Uncle Billy about the mad way she seemed to be acting and asked Vail to wire her and see if she was mad at everybody for no damned reason he could see. He sent that day rates, too, despite the extra cost, in hopes Vail could get some answers before this day was done. Then, having his choice between the Harvey House, Martha's place, or the saloon, he went to the saloon.

There was hardly anyone there to talk to at this hour. When he started jawing with the barkeep to keep from drinking too fast as it kept getting hotter, the worldly West Texan advised Longarm he was just begging for heat stroke if he went riding south before sundown.

Longarm nodded but said, "I may not have to go at all. If I do, I'll likely ride my mount into the ground in any case, because I got to get there sudden and I'll need every hour in the saddle we can manage."

The barkeep insisted, "You force any mount to carry you more than an hour or so under that hot sun outside and even if it's still alive at sundown you won't get it to carry you much farther. I used to ride this range before I got this more sensible job."

Longarm smiled thinly and said, "I can't say I blame you. But I won't be riding a cow pony. Army horses are picked for more faithful stupidity. I mean to try for half hours riding and half hours leading afoot before and after sundown. My army bay ought to be cheered by the cool shades of evening just as it's getting set to die of the heat. Figuring three miles an hour on foot and six or eight in the saddle I ought to average . . . Right, ten or twelve hours to make her to Sanderson."

"You won't make it," the barkeep assured him cheerfully. "If I was you I'd wait till sundown. You'd still ride in early in the morning, while it was still fairly cool. What's your big hurry, anyway?"

Longarm said, "If I knew, I might not be in such a hurry to get there. Have you ever had a woman just get mad at everybody for no reason you could fathom? I don't mean a gal just getting mad at you for no reason. They do that all the time. But have you ever known one to just cloud up and rain on you, her hired help and such, without saying why?"

The barkeep thought, shrugged, and opined, "Not no lady with all her marbles. It's been my experience that when my old woman is sore at me she talks sweet as hell to the cleaning woman just to rub it in. Of course, I've known women as well as men to just go loco en la cabeza. There was this little old lady up in Redford last year who just shot a delivery boy on her porch and barricaded herself in her attic, yelling about Mex demons coming across the border any second to stick pitchforks or their demon dongs in her. She wasn't yelling too clear at the end. It was a good thing she decided to suck on her shotgun like a sugar cane and pull the trigger with her toe. Made an awesome mess. But at least the town law didn't have to gun the poor old crazy lady."

Longarm ordered another drink. As a lawman, he knew all too well about such cases. Folk did just go loco now and again. But Jessie? Hell, she was young and healthy, and while she might act sort of wild now and again, she'd never yet aimed at the wrong *targets* so grotesque. He started to ask the barkeep if he'd ever heard of folk going mad because of some ague. But he didn't. Longarm knew he read a lot more than most gents of his working class. Reading textbooks from the Denver Public Library was a secret vice, to sort of make up for the fact he'd run off to war before he'd finished school in West-by-God Virginia. He already knew there were bugs that could do funny things to one's brain. The most common cause of madness among country folk, he'd read, was a condition known as pellagra. They couldn't say what caused it. But poor whites and colored folk come down with it a heap. They got all rashy and moody and sometimes took to murdering their wife and kids with anything handy and no sensible reason at all. Jessie was neither poor nor colored. She was blonde as a Viking princess in fact. But what if she'd caught pellagra or some other bug as made one mad, like chewing loco weed did if you were livestock?

He finished his beer with an anxious glance at the clock and went back across to the Western Union office. Billy Vail, bless him, had already wired back, saying he'd just received a wire from his old Texas sidekick's daughter and that things looked simple enough to him. Ki had gotten drunk and tried to rape the poor little gal. She'd licked him good, instead, and chased him off the property. She hadn't known he'd gone all the way bad before Sanderson had wired they were holding Ki with some of her more recently hired riders and a heap of her cows. She told her Uncle Billy she hadn't connected Ki to the gunning of another Starbuck rider and missing beef until he'd been caught with the same and she'd just had to add up the simple figures.

Vail added it was time for Longarm to be getting back to the office. Longarm shoved the crazy message in a coat pocket with a bewildered curse. When the telegraph clerk begged his pardon and asked him to repeat that, Longarm smiled sheepishly and said, "I wasn't out to pick a fight with you. I got enough on my plate. But let me describe a fight to you and see if you think it makes a lick of sense."

As the clerk listened attentively, Longarm said, "Let's say in one corner of the ring we put a mighty athletic but human-sized woman. Let's endow her with as much or more strength as an average man and say she was brung up knowing all sorts of ways to fight, including them tricks they use in Japanese wrestling. Are you with me so far?"

The clerk nodded and said, "She sounds like a lady most men wouldn't want a fight with."

Longarm nodded and said, "She shoots good, too. I just allowed she'd be more than a match for the average man. But now listen to what I'm putting in the other corner. Picture a man about my size with both white and Oriental blood in him. Say he not only knows all them fighting tricks but taught the ones she knows to the much smaller gal in the other corner. Say I've seen him bust bricks with the edges of his hands and spring five or six feet in the air to kick another man in the skull and crush it. Say before he ever came to America to look up his Yankee kin he served a hitch as a Ninja, which is sort of Japanese cross between a hired gun and a Chinese hatchet man. Now say he gets to feeling a mite amorous and decides to just grab the gal across the ring and kiss her. What do you reckon the results might be?"

The telegraph clerk laughed easily and said, "Hell, a man as big as you who knew even more of them tricks than the gal would be able to screw her as well, if that was what he aimed to do. Might have to knock her silly to do it, of course. But that don't sound too tough for a man who busts bricks with his bare hands. You *know* such a gent, you say? I'm glad I don't. He sounds sort of scary."

Longarm nodded soberly and said, "He is. I'm not sure he likes me and I'm not sure I like him. But up to now I've always been able to trust him and we've saved each other's hides a time or more. I'm glad you agree it seems hardly likely the gal I just mentioned could take old Ki on and win, if he was really out to do her wrong. When two friends you can't see lying to you tell two tales, and one of 'em just plain impossible, I reckon you have to go with the other, whether he's a hell of a lot uglier or not. It's been nice talking to you. But I got me some riding to do now."

★

Chapter 5

The sixty-mile shove through dry chaparral was rough on Longarm and damned near killed the army bay. He knew it would be too stove in to ride again for the better part of a week when he finally got it safely stalled at the Sanderson livery, and when the crusty old stable-hand foreman cussed him hard enough to turn the early morning light blue Longarm could only agree that life was hell on horses and that his own ass didn't feel all that great either. He asked how they felt about hiring him the use of another pony while the army bay recovered. The old cuss snapped, "I'd let you ride my daughter first, you infernal cruel rider! Men like you shouldn't be allowed to ride anything. That poor brute back yonder in the stalls with a throwed shoe and mesquite cuts all over his poor hide may forgive, you, someday, but I won't. I'd refuse you any service at all if I didn't fear you'd leave your mount to bleed to death tethered in front of a whorehouse!"

So, under the circumstances, Longarm thought it wise not to leave his saddle and gear in their tack room. He toted it to the hotel near the depot, hired a single with its one window opening to the north, and draped his saddle over the footrail of the bed before he made tracks to the county lockup.

Most of the shops he passed along the way hadn't opened yet. But jails perforce stayed open for business round the clock. So he found a desk sergeant and a couple of turnkeys playing penny-ante blackjack in the front office and, while they seemed polite as well as impressed by his federal badge and credentials, he saw he was in for considerable argument when the county lawman in charge said, "You can talk to them cow thieves if you like, Uncle Sam. As to leaving with even one of the rascals as a federal want, you're going to have to convince the county court about that. Judge Winslow is riding circuit right now, so he won't be at the courthouse for at least a week, Lord willing and the creeks don't rise."

Another county man chimed in, cheerfully, to add, "As soon as the judge do get back we'll be holding a fine necktie party for the sons of bitches. Judge Winslow don't mess around when he's trying a cow thief for murder. It's just zim, zam, thank you, ma'am, and I sentence you to hang by the neck until you are dead, dead, dead, and may God have mercy on your worthless soul, you son of a bitch."

Longarm asked if perchance their hanging judge ever had to cuss the jury, since the Constitution did call for a jury trial for a capital offense. But the desk sergeant snorted in disgust and demanded, "Since when does the damn Yankee Constitution apply to a cow thief standing trial in Texas? Only one of the rascals we're holding can say he's a white man. The others seem to be two greasers and a Chinaman. Which one of the sons of bitches did you come here to talk to?"

Longarm said he reckoned he'd settle for a few words with the one called Ki. So one of the turnkeys got up from the game to lead him up the back stairs. The lockup was built pueblo style with juniper-pole beams sticking out through the two-foot thick adobe walls all about. The county lawmen had obviously heard of prisoners digging out through 'dobe with, say, spit and a spoon and a heap of time. So as they mounted the stairs Longarm saw the inside walls had been plastered thick with Portland cement mortar.

The upstairs cells were lined up along the rear wall of the massive 'dobe. To scrimp on sweeping up and such, all four riders captured in the company of the Starbuck herd had been thrust in one cell together, and if there were only two bunks, tough shit. The tall Amerasian called Ki recognized Longarm through the bars, of course. Young Willy Shepherd apparently didn't recall him, and the two mestizo vaqueros just went on sitting on the floor like a pair of paiute basket makers, waiting to be handed some straw and not counting on that, either.

Longarm addressed Ki in Spanish. Ki shook hands with him through the bars, answering, "Bueno. I don't think any of these unreconstructed rebels understand this language, either."

As if to prove Ki's point the turnkey asked, "How come you're talking Mex to the funny-looking cuss, Deputy Long?"

Longarm said, "You just said he didn't strike you as a good old Texas boy. If you want to know what we're plotting in Spanish it's a jailbreak, of course. Us federal lawmen can't be trusted worth spit."

The turnkey chuckled and said he'd be downstairs if anyone busted out on Longarm. As he clumped away, Longarm dropped back into Spanish, just in case. He knew Ki spoke it better, despite starting out in Japan. Ki was all too right about the way a heap of Texas felt about learning the lingo of what they considered an inferior breed. But a man who aspired to getting anywhere in the cattle trade—and Ki was, or had been, segundo of a mighty big outfit—took the time to learn to talk shop, and no matter how they pronounced

71

'em, half the words of cowboy jargon derived from the Mex vaquero, or buckaroo, who'd invented the business.

Longarm began by saying, "I can see the trouble you four are in. So tell me how you got into it to begin with."

Ki shrugged morosely and replied, "We have no idea. We left the Circle Star a week or more ago with some breeding stock ordered by the Jingle Bob spread in New Mexico Territory."

Longarm cut in to ask, with a frown, "We're talking about Big John Chisum, over in Lincoln County?"

To which Ki replied, with a weary nod, "Of course. He's been expanding and upgrading his herds now that the Lincoln County War has become a matter of distasteful memory. Jessie, as you probably know, has been trying to tenderize her beef with Hereford blood for some time. To get right to the point, these other riders and I were simply driving fifty head of Hereford-cross brook stock by night, because of this heat, when a posse appeared out of nowhere. I explained we'd crossed the Pecos but meant to drive north in line with it to water at the creeks running into the Pecos farther up, where the water's as good and the fords aren't as wide and infested with quicksand. They accused us of being on our way to the nearby border with the beef. The rest you know."

Longarm shook his head and switched back to English to think clearer as he replied, "Not hardly. Is it safe to assume you all had Jessie Starbuck's permit to drive her cows anywhere at all?"

Ki snorted in disgust and asked, "Have you gone crazy, too? Do you really think I'd even pet one of Jessie's cows without her permission? These boys and I weren't eating cow dust just because we felt it would be a change of ranch routine. John Chisum asked Jessie to sell him some breeding stock. She asked us to deliver them, and we would have, if we hadn't all wound up in this trail-town jail, you *baku* lawman!"

Longarm recalled Jessie calling him *baku* one time when

72

she was sore at him instead of Ki. It meant foolish, in Japanese. He told Ki, "It ain't me or any other lawman that's been playing the fool, you rascal. It was the simple duty of them posse riders to ask for an accounting when they came upon strange riders driving strange cows through their range. Didn't they tell you they wired your outfit for verification of your story, or that Jessie wired back that said herd was stolen from her, at gunpoint?"

Ki nodded but said, "They lied. The bastards just saw the chance to impound some good breeding stock at the expense of strangers. You know how out-of-the-way trail towns run by a clique of cronies like to do that."

Longarm shook his head and said, "That was the first suspicion as occurred to me. I've had to clean up a few such towns in the six or eight years I've been riding for Justice. But Sanderson is the county seat, population a thousand and change, with railroad connections to the outside world and at least two rival newspapers. Aside from which, Jessie told the same tale to Billy Vail by wire, and I just can't see the boss marshal of the Denver District Court in cahoots with a far-flung Texas sheriff."

He saw Ki was taking that hard. But he didn't have the time or a way to put things more delicate. So he continued, "Jessie wired my office she'd fired you for getting uppity with her. Then, as she tells it, you must have decided to pay her back by running off some of her stock, gunning one of her more honest riders in the process. How do you like it so far?"

Ki didn't. He started to call young Willy and the two Mex riders over. But Longarm told him, "Don't. This conversation is confusing enough as it is, and I don't need anyone to back your version, Ki. The question before the house is why Jessie would tell such fantastic fibs about you, of all gents."

The big Amerasian's oddly feline features were normally stoic as a mill pond. But Longarm knew him well enough to read the pain in Ki's catlike eyes as he gulped and softly said, "I don't know why Jessie lied about me. I'm surprised that you take my word against hers, considering we've hardly ever been as, ah, close."

Longarm smiled crookedly and explained, "You'd be surprised how close I've been to female fibbers in my time. I swear I'd have bet my life on Jessie Starbuck's word as a lady, and you're right about me liking her better. But I ain't acting sentimental about your Oriental ass, you ugly cuss. I got to take your word because your words make sense and, no offense, on account of I know how mean you are when you're *really* out to do someone dirty."

"I'd never do anything to hurt Jessie, damn it," insisted Ki.

"I just said that. If you'd somehow gone loco and turned on her, she'd be dead, and no man with half your sneaky brains would ever settle for fifty head of even high-grade stock when you could just as easily help yourself to a good part of your victim's fortune, if you felt crooked as well as mean."

Ki hesitated. Then he swallowed and said, "Thanks, I think. I may have misjudged your grasp of logic in the past. Not many men would take the word of a comparative stranger over that of a beautiful lover."

Longarm scowled and said, "Don't you go talking dirty about your boss and my . . . let's say old pal. Jessie Starbuck's morals ain't the problem. It's the way she's acting that's the problem. It only works two ways, Ki. The poor little thing's gone loco en la cabeza, which does happen to the best of us, or else she sent them fool wires under duress, which makes more sense. Let's not waste time squirrel caging our own brains about what's wrong at your home spread before we can get there to find out."

Ki grasped two bars like a big ape in a cage and tried to shake them, to no avail, before he asked, bitterly, "Just how do we plan on riding for the Circle Star right now, then?"

Longarm started to tell Ki. Then that same turnkey came

back to ask if he was all right. Longarm said he'd be down directly and switched back to Spanish as he told Ki his plan. Before he was half done the two young vaqueros were grinning sly but smart enough to just let the brims of their sombreros drop down as if they were dozing against the wall. Longarm finished, cussed them all in English, and turned to follow the local lawman back downstairs, muttering, "Couldn't get them to say word-one about that federal case I'm more interested in. I reckon I'll have to settle for letting you boys hang 'em for us all."

The turnkey said it wouldn't cost Longarm's office a cent. So, downstairs, he shook all around and parted friendly to go do some serious plotting.

Downtown Sanderson was open for business, now. But it was still cool enough to sort of stroll around town and get the kinks out of his legs after all that night riding, should anyone ask.

Nobody did. Lots of folk were just sort of wandering loose and, come to study on it, they didn't look suspicious to him.

It was easy to determine that the back wall of the county jail faced a vacant lot, well shaded by desert willow and cottonwood, both of which sprouted like weeds wherever there was more water than usual in the normally arid soil. The row of shops across the way likely emptied their slop buckets out the back doorways, and the trees didn't care what water smelled like as long as it was wet and tossed out fairly regular.

The roof of the pueblo-like jail was flat, he saw, and any half-assed roper would have no trouble tossing a loop around one of those beam ends sticking out through the 'dobe walls. That was providing he had a rope, of course.

It would have been dumb to be remembered buying throw rope within city blocks of the county jail or courthouse. So Longarm took a stroll across the tracks to a shabbier part of town and, when he spied some Mex vaqueros spitting and whittling in front of a stock-supply shop he went on in.

The fat Mex who ran the shop didn't look too astounded to see an Anglo dressed sort of cow. For despite the manners of some Texas hands of Anglo ways, a lot of good cowhand gear was Mex-made, and the Mexicans were the first to say so. He smiled at the shopkeeper and said he was in the market for a hundred or so yards of manila braid. The Mex smiled back and opined el señor had to be planning on doing a lot of roping indeed, since few hombres carried more than fifty feet of throw rope and some of that was just for show.

Longarm said he was buying for his outfit. The Mex nodded and said, "Bueno. I could not have sold you that much rope in one length to begin with. How does three hundred-foot lengths appeal to you, señor?"

Longarm said that sounded swell, and when the Mex still looked dubious, he offered to pay in advance. The Mex took the money, but said, "I was only wondering what any one rider would do with a hundred-foot coil. I could cut it and fit each length with a honda, if you like. I presume you favor those machine-made brass hondas that seem to be in fashion with Anglo riders?"

Longarm shook his head and said, "Not hardly. Should I want to blind a calf I can poke him in the eye with a stick a lot cheaper. You just give me the rope long and raw and we'll divvy it up and fashion our own rawhide hondas at one end or the other."

So the Mex reached under his counter, hauled out the big bulky coils, and proceeded to bind them with cotton twine for Longarm to carry convenient as he said, in a friendly tone, "I see you must be a true vaquero, despite your gray eyes. I thought you might be when you asked for braided line instead of the cheap but almost as strong manila twist."

Longarm agreed a braided rope threw a lot more accurate and didn't need half as much breaking in. So they parted pals. But as he stepped back outside, one of the loafing vaqueros grinned and observed, in Spanish, "I see it must be true what they say about gringo ropers. They need a lot

76

of rope because they break it when they manage to rope anything.''

Longarm chose to ignore the remark, even though he grasped its meaning. It was true his kind were rougher on rope albeit easier on their fingers when they roped tie-down instead of dally, as most Mexicans did. The Mex vaquero combined skills the Spaniards had learned from the Moors in herding long-horned Hispano-Moorish stock with the tricks they'd learned on the Aztec branch of their family tree. Before the Indians had even seen a horse or cow they'd been wonders at roping wild deer and such to butcher 'em closer to their sunbaked homes. Nobody roped as good as the true buckaroo, and they thought the methods of the gringo roper rough on stock as well as a heap easier to learn.

Longarm could rope either style, being curious by nature. But he didn't want to have a roping contest right now, even though he had won some drinking money that way, easy, in the past. If anyone around here recalled him at all, later, he wanted them to dismiss him as just a fool Anglo who'd needed some throw rope. It was in character for him to ignore a few sarcastic comments in a Mex barrio. Mexicans with a lick of sense ignored comments about greasers in an Anglo neighborhood.

But one of the bored vaqueros must have been banking on the common courtesies of a border town and saw a chance to look big at minimal risk. For he sort of scampered ahead to turn and block Longarm's way with his concho-trimmed chaps spread wide and a mocking grin on his face. In very bad English, he asked, ''Hey, a donde va with all that rope, amigo? Do you have to tie your sister up before she'll let you fuck her?''

Longarm already had the heavy coils over his left forearm. So he half turned to cover himself both ways with a wall to his back as he replied, in pretty good Spanish, ''My sister fucks just about anyone. Does your mother?''

The young Mex blanched. For the rules of the border game of ''tu madre'' called for far more back-and-forth

77

comments than that before anyone's *mother* was mentioned. The Mex was packing his S&W buscadero, in a low-slung side holster. He glanced pointedly at the grips of Longarm's Colt, facing him cross-draw, as he smiled sort of sleepy eyed and softly purred, "Did I hear someone refer to my sainted mamacita just now?"

Longarm said, "You did, and you'd better run home to her now, chico. I haven't time to play in the street with children."

"That is too bad. Because I think I *want* to play with you and I don't think your mother is a saint. What do you say to that, eh?"

Longarm sighed and said, "Have it your own way, then. Your mother sucks the priest and I would piss on your father's grave if even you could tell me who he might have been. So fill your fist or get out of my way."

The young Mex probably would have. Then Longarm heard yet another Mex call out, "Pero *no*, Tomas! I think I know who this one is."

Tomas grumbled, "I do not care if he is the Pope. He just said very bad things about my family and now he dies."

He was closer to dying than he knew. For while Longarm wanted a shoot-out in Sanderson as much as he wanted the clap, he'd long since learned that when a shoot-out was inevitable it was ever best to get in the first shot. But the peacemaker almost sobbed, "You might shoot the Pope and live. But this is the one they call Brazo Largo and, even if you won, you would have his amigo, El Gato, to deal with!"

Tomas looked like he was fixing to throw up as he moved his gun hand well clear of his gun and said, weakly, "I was only joking, Brazo Largo. *Viva la revolucion!*"

Longarm smiled friendly and said, "I was only joking, too, in that case. I keep trying to tell you folk your troubles with the dictatorship down yonder is none of my concern. But you know how dumb some Mexicans feel about my kind."

The others came drifting in to join them, seeing it seemed

78

safer, now. The one who'd spoiled the fun said, with a boyish grin, "We heard you did not get along with los rurales. Are you here for to shoot some more of the bastards, Brazo Largo? If you are, count us in. I am called Jesus Garcia and this is my cousin Tomas and this other cabrone is—"

"Hold it," Longarm cut in with a fond chuckle. "I'm not down here to help El Gato overthrow your government this time." Then he wondered why he'd said a dumb thing like that and added, "I could use some help, though."

Tomas, who'd started out trying to crawl him or kill him, was quick to say, "Name it! We are at your servicio!"

Longarm said, "I'm going to need four saddled ponies and one bareback. I have my own saddle and gear. How much would you want if you could manage as much?"

The one called Jesus looked insulted and said, "Hey, we got plenty ponies, por nada, in the cause of libertad. Just tell us where and when you want them, *Brazo Largo*!"

So Longarm, which meant the same thing in English, quickly came to an agreement with them. He said the alley behind the cantina just down the way sounded swell, if all five ponies were there just after sundown and ready to streak twenty miles without looking back. Tomas laughed and noted the Rio Bravo would be at low water this time of the year. So they all shook on it and Longarm headed back across the tracks. So far things were looking up, backwards. He still had to get those Circle Star riders out before he could ride 'em anywhere, though.

He didn't want to be noticed wandering about town with all that rope. So he wandered into the bushes behind the jail as if he aimed to take a leak and, when nobody seemed to notice, he cached the rope at the base of the wall under Ki's barred window and rolled some handy tumbleweed on top of it, smashing the sticky stems flatter so they wouldn't roll off. Not even kids messed with tumbleweed. It rolled all over the place and the stems were prickly as well as otherwise uninteresting.

Back on the main street he consulted his watch, then strode into a saloon to wet his whistle and stuff some free lunch down his gullet. He hadn't had any sleep since leaving Fort Stockton, either. But he was good for seventy-two hours without sleep if need be, and this was one of those times it just needed to be.

As he consumed pigs knuckles, boiled eggs and beer, one of the turnkeys from the jail came in to join him, saying, "Howdy. You still here? I just got off duty. Figured you'd be gone by now."

Longarm kept his own voice as casual as he replied with truth enough to be checked out, "I jaded my mount bad, riding down so sudden on a fool's errand. He'll need some rest as well as a new hind shoe before he'll be fit to ride back north. Meanwhile I'm a curious cuss. I might stick around for the trial. You know how talkative a man can get in the shadow of the gallows."

The turnkey helped himself to a boiled egg as he agreed that sounded reasonable and asked just what deep dark secret Ki might be holding back on the law.

"It's a long shot," Longarm said. "They might really be telling me true when they say they know nothing about some Indian beef as turned up missing in the same part of Texas. I'm tempted to just chuck it, if my mount recovers before your circuit judge gets back."

Then he got out of there before he had to lie anymore. He found his way to the Western Union in Sanderson. They were all set up the same. He wired Jessie again, in the event she might decide to remember him. Then he wired his old pal John Chisum at the South Spring spread in Lincoln County, knowing it would take some time for a Western Union delivery rider to make it out and back from their office in Lincoln Township. One had to at least try. He didn't wire Billy Vail. Old Billy was going to have a fit as it was. Getting back late was one thing. Riding the wrong way entire was another. Thinking about this inspired him to take back the message to Chisum and change the return address to the Denver office. For that took care of two birds with one wire. It hardly seemed likely he'd still be here when Big John got around to confirming or denying Ki's story. If Chisum had in fact ordered those cows from Jessie Starbuck, Longarm wanted U.S. Marshal William Vail to know it soon as possible.

It was pushing eleven A.M. and starting to warm up good as Longarm stepped back out into the sunlight. His attention was attracted to a string of black smoke puffs rising against the cloudless cobalt sky, down closer to the courthouse. The train tracks were the other way. He drifted toward the mysterious smoke even as he idly wondered why. He'd promised Ki he'd make his play during the siesta hours, the only time the streets of Sanderson would be cleared. For being this close to Mexico, even the Anglo population knew better than to run like mad dogs in the hottest time of day between, say, noon and three in the afternoon. He was still cussing himself for having made such a fool promise. The only thing he'd come up with so far involved those few sticks of dynamite he carried among his possibles in case he needed to blow something up. Dynamite would no doubt do a job on 'dobe. But the noise would leave them mighty little time to work with, after.

As he got closer to the courthouse he saw the wonders of modern science had attracted all the kids and half the dogs in town as well. A heap of grown-ups were watching, too, albeit pretending not to be as agog about the unusual doings as the kids. They were paving the hitherto dust-and-horseshit-paved approaches to the courthouse. Sprinkling a coat of tar mixed with coal oil on a dirt road was nothing new. But here they'd sprung for gravel mixed with hot mineral tar, and the object of all the admiration was a steam-roller a third the size of a railroad locomotive, rolling back and forth to flatten the pungent mixture. Some kids kept trying to toss bottle tops, nails and such just ahead of the big steel roller to see what would happen. What happened most was a gent in tar-stained overalls chasing them with a tarry shovel. He didn't stop the kids from preserving a few small items forever in the new paving, but at least he kept 'em from tossing a dog, a cat or baby sister between the hot tar and massive steel roller.

Longarm leaned against a cottonwood tree to light a fresh cheroot in the shade. The shade wasn't doing all that much good this late in the morning. The paving crew out in the sun were commencing to sweat like pigs and some of the grown-ups and more sensible kids were already starting to drift away. Longarm would have headed back to his hotel for his own siesta under more usual circumstances. But Ki and the boys were in an unusual fix, and Longarm knew that if he took a flop after going so long without sleep he could wind up slugabed past sundown and that wouldn't work. As he stood there smoking, sleepy eyed, he considered how he could get that big steamroller to work for him. It hardly seemed likely the paving crew could be persuaded to help him bust Ki and the boys out. On the other hand, they'd be knocking off for la siesta any minute now, and any fool could see how you steered that slow but powerful contraption. He keenly studied the Italian-looking gent at the controls as the cuss ran the roller back and forth over the heat-softened paving. There was a sheet-iron sunshade above the sprung-steel seat. But since there were no sides Longarm could watch the gent's hands easy enough as they worked the gear levers and bitty steering wheel. Longarm naturally knew how to run a steam combine as well as a locomotive and this machine seemed to partake a mite of both. But driving it wouldn't be half the problem. Driving it without being noticed would. Longarm closed his eyes and just listened and, come to study on it, the contraption didn't make any more noise, or a different noise, than a beer dray passing a siesta-shuttered window might, and the crew would hardly be taking the big machine home to bed with them when they knocked off for a few hours. His mind made up, Longarm turned away to establish some character in that saloon. It wouldn't do to be remembered loitering near a steamroller just before it had been stolen.

Longarm let them shut the bar in his face and waited out the first hour and a half of the siesta in his hotel room before he made his move. As he'd hoped, the streets were bake-oven hot and deserted entire when he slipped out the back door of the hotel and started working his way toward the courthouse in the inky shade of as many arcades as he could work out. The steamroller had been parked around the side of the courthouse. There wasn't so much as a stray lizard watching as Longarm just walked over bold as brass and climbed aboard. The brass rail he first grabbed was hot as hell, and despite the sunshade the steel seat and controls weren't much cooler. It was easy to see why the crew had felt it prudent to knock off in the full heat of a West Texas afternoon. But having no doubt had some sorry experiences with kids in the past, the son of a bitching driver had chained and padlocked the steering wheel. So Longarm had to go to the trouble of picking the lock with a certain blade of his pocketknife he'd had filed funny with just such chores in mind.

Then, having already gone further than he felt up to explaining to its proper owners, Longarm gingerly turned up the oil-fired burner and, having seen there was already some pressure in the boiler, cracked the throttle just a mite to see what might happen.

What happened was that the steamroller started rolling, or rather strolling, about a mile an hour. Longarm figured that was about fast enough. The jail house was only a few hundred yards away, the long way, and silence was more golden than speed just now.

He still felt conspicuous as a naked lady in church as he crept the monstrous machine away from the courthouse and down a shady alley. The backyards on either side were fenced or hedged with prickly pear, and nobody would be taking an afternoon nap in a sunny backyard anyway, even if they were Calvinists. But he still couldn't believe he was getting away with it as he went on getting away with it. He made more noise than he felt he had any right to when he crunched through the wall of dry weeds between the alley and the lot behind the lockup. But all that happened was that Ki peered out through the bars up yonder, looking sort of thundergasted. There were no back windows on the ground floor, and fortunately all the other cells upstairs were empty at the moment. Longarm steered the roller into as much willow shade as he could find, stopped it, and dropped down to run over to the base of the wall. He didn't yell up and Ki had too much sense to yell down. They'd already talked about the ropes, even though neither had known at the time there was a steamroller in town.

Longarm drew his pocketknife again as he kicked the tumbleweeds aside. Then he hunkered close to the 'dobe to do some cutting and splicing. He tied a tight coil of line to one end of a much longer length. Then he backed away, swung the heavy bundle around his head a few times and let fly. Ki missed the first cast with both hands out through the bars. Longarm cussed and tried again. This time Ki caught the far end and hauled it inside. Longarm gave Ki time to unfasten the coil of rope he'd need for his own part of the plan. Then he saw Ki had wrapped the line leading down securely around bars at both sides of the steel-framed window and was giving a thumbs-up signal. One of the things Longarm admired about Jessie's sometimes morose segundo was that he could think fast when faced with surprises.

Longarm jogged back to the steamroller with the other end of the stout manila line and fastened that end to the seat with a clove hitch. Then he reached up to open the throttle just a tad. As the steamroller began to inch away from the jail wall at the speed of cold molasses Longarm waved good luck up at Ki and strode out of the lot looking innocent. He was tempted to run, but he didn't. He just walked back to his hotel, entered by way of the back door, and managed to be sitting in the lobby so as to sit smoking in an easy chair under a rubber plant when all hell commenced to bust loose outside.

As the thunderous roar faded away the hotel clerk came out from the back, buttoning his shirt, to stare groggy eyed at Longarm and ask what was going on. Longarm shrugged and told him, "Can't say. I just came down. Too hot to sleep. Sounds like we might be having another thunderstorm."

The clerk moved over to the glassed front door to peer out and opine, "Don't think so. The sun's shining bright as ever and some of the boys are running about out there like chickens with their heads lopped off."

So Longarm rose grudgingly and followed the clerk out front to watch from under the hotel awning while, sure enough, men ran this way and that, waving six-guns and yelling fit to bust.

One of the lawmen he'd spoken with earlier spotted Longarm despite the shade of the awning and ran over, panting already from the heat and excitement, to gasp, "We're mounting a posse. Want to ride with us, Uncle Sam?"

Longarm smiled agreeably but replied, "My pony's stove in. What's going on? Who are we after?"

The county lawman explained, "Them four cow thieves. They just busted out and you'll never guess how!"

Longarm chuckled easily and said, "I'd rather you told me. I just woke up."

So the other lawman said, "They pulled their barred window clean outa the wall with a goddamned steam engine! They must have had a confederate do it for 'em, I mean. We just now stopped the infernal machine crunching Mizz Tillman's cactus hedge, dragging our jail-house window behind it like a cat with a tin can tied to her tail!"

Longarm smiled at the picture and said, "Well, I swan. I figured that Oriental one might be ingenious. But ain't that quite a jump, with or without bars in the window?"

The other lawman nodded but said, "They lowered themselves on another rope. One of 'em just leant out and throwed a loop around one of the juniper beams sticking out above their damn window. Then all four of 'em just climbed down. The five of 'em, counting their steamroller-stealing sidekick, must have had ponies ready to light out on. For if one of the bastards was still in town we'd have heard the shots by now. We figure they have to be making for the border. It should be easy to trail 'em by broad day. It's a good twenty miles and you can see dust rising father away than they could have ridden by now!"

Longarm nodded and said, "You don't need me, then. I'd be proud to tag along if my pony was up to it. But we'd just slow you down."

The local lawman didn't argue. He was already running for his own mount as, in front of the lockup, others had begun to gather, mounted and buzzing like yellow jackets around a stove-in hornets' nest. Longarm turned to the clerk and said, "I hope this means the saloon will open early. What time is it?"

The clerk looked wistful and said, "Past two-thirty. You're likely right. Everyone ought to be up for good, now. The boys will be drinking late tonight as well. There's nothing like a posse bringing prisoners in to get a party going."

Longarm didn't really go to any saloon, at first. He found a beanery open again, early, and went light on the chili and heavy on the black coffee as he tried to stay alert as well as awake.

It wasn't easy. For though he was just about sloshing with black coffee when he walked, he still had some tedious time to kill. He stopped in more than one saloon, establishing he was still around but meaning to leave as soon as it got dark, if only he could find a mount to carry him. That gave him an excuse to kill more time and build some character. He strolled back to the livery and paid them a mite above the going price to see that the army bay was reshod and boarded there until the remount service up to Fort Stockton could pick it up. Then he strolled to the Western Union to wire the army the same, with his sincere apologies. The clerk took his form with a nod, saying, "We just got a wire in for you, Deputy Long."

Longarm took the yellow envelope with a puzzled frown. For as he recalled he'd failed to tell either Big John Chisum or Billy Vail to wire him in these parts. Maybe Jessie had decided to talk to him after all?

The message was from Billy Vail. The sly old former Ranger was good at following a paper trail. He didn't have to explain how he knew Longarm would be in Sanderson right now, once Longarm read what he had said at a nickel a word.

By sheer luck John Chisum had been in Lincoln, shopping with his niece, Miss Sally, when Longarm's wire had arrived. So Chisum had wired the Denver office right off and Billy Vail had never heard it was impolite to read a deputy's mail. Chisum verified he had indeed ordered that breeding stock from Jessie Starbuck and wanted to know where in thunder they were right now. Billy Vail's own conclusion was that little Miss Jessie was making no sense at all. So Longarm could do what he could to get her falsely accused riders out of jail and see what the hell was going on.

Longarm chuckled fondly. He'd already gotten the boys out of jail as Billy, bless him, had assumed he might before he'd sent such orders. But then Longarm's smile faded as he considered the second part of the order. For while he, Ki, Billy and even Big John seemed to agree, something odd indeed had to be going on. Longarm would be switched with snakes if he had the least notion what *was* going on.

For whether running her Circle Star outfit as the socially sedate Miss Jessica Starbuck or running wilder as Lonestar, Jessie would never turn against her own pals in her right mind. The thought she'd gone loco en la cabeza all of a sudden was too awful to contemplate. But the only other thing that worked was as crazy, since it hadn't worked the first time, and everyone knew it. They'd had to run the story in the Texas papers to clear the poor gal after slickers had tried to frame her by having their almost perfect double pose as Jessie, robbing folk.

Anyone inspired by that story to try and get it right should have seen it just wasn't possible to impersonate a well-known person with a heap of friends, no matter how you coached and messed with the appearance of a carefully selected look-alike.

Yet, as Longarm knew from both experience and other cases he'd read up on, impostors were a popular temptation to confidence crooks in a mushrooming economy where it took hours to check stories by telegraph and photography was in its infancy. Poor old Andrew Carnegie, the steel baron, had been pestered half to death by long-lost kin issuing orders and drawing money in his name. Any spread-out business empire such as Carnegie Steel or Starbuck Enterprises was vulnerable to that sort of flimflam, with half the straw bosses and hardly any of the working staff on personal terms with the big boss. A crook with enough brass hardly had to look exactly like Andrew Carnegie or Jessica Starbuck to forge a check or issue false instructions by long distance. But if that was what was going on at the Circle Star, where in thunder could the *real* Jessie be?

★

Chapter 6

Night fell purple, jasmine-scented and quiet in Sanderson, with most of the able-bodied men in town out searching for Ki and the other ''cow thieves.'' It was even darker after Longarm waited for the first stars to come out and mosied over to the lot behind the lockup with yet another length of throw rope.

For as he'd expected, someone had reached out through the cell window, or rather the big raggedy hole left in the 'dobe wall by the original window being sort of yanked like a tooth, and cut the escape line to leave just the noose and a foot or so of braided manila still attached to the beam end above.

Longarm rummaged around in the darkness of the lot until he found a handy fallen cottonwood branch. Then he busted it over his knee to suit his needs, tied it as a weight to one end of the rope he'd been able to buy openly enough once everyone was chasing his secret pals to Mexico, and whirled it a few times to scale it up and over the 'dobe parapet of the flat roof.

He could tell by the gentle jerks on the line that someone up yonder was fastening the other end to a rooftop sewer vent or something. Then, sure enough, Ki came down the rope first, easy, as he tested it for the others with his considerable size.

As the Japanese-American joined Longarm at the base of the wall he growled, "Remind me never to listen to you again. Have you ever been panfried on a tar-paper roof under a Texas sun?"

Longarm chuckled at the picture and asked, "What did you boys want, eggs in your beers? I waited till the worst heat of the day was over."

Ki said, "Speak for yourself. Where are the ponies?"

"I've been studying on that. Some vaqueros I met up with earlier are supposed to have some waiting for us across the tracks. On the other hand, I was playing 'tu madre' with at least one of 'em earlier."

One of the Starbuck Mexican riders joined them as Ki was saying, "I've always wondered how you manage to make friends so quickly. Do you really think we can trust total strangers who never liked you in the first place?"

Longarm grunted, "I just said that. I'm even less popular in Old Mexico with los federales and rurales, and there's a handsome reward on the hide of Brazo Largo. I grabbed at the chance when I saw it. They've no doubt had plenty of time to study on it since."

By this time the second Mex was down and young Willy was on his way down. Longarm picked up his heavily laden McClellan and said, "Whatever we do, we don't want to stay here. Vamanos, muchachos."

As he led the way—none of the others knew their way around Sanderson at all—he distributed the six-guns he'd picked up that evening. He hadn't had to pay for the ones he'd taken off the Panhandle Kid and Dandy Dunbarton, and the other two had been sold as a brace, cheap, by a hopefully indifferent shopkeeper when he'd allowed he needed a new throw rope as well. As they spotted the moon-lit rails of the yard at the far end of the alley they were easing down, Ki asked how far those waiting ponies might be.

Longarm answered, "Just under a quarter mile on the far side of yon tracks. There's no way to tell what else could be waiting as well. I can think of a dozen dirty ways to double-cross me and I'm not even a border Mex who's mad at me."

Ki grimaced and opined, "If they're for the rebel cause they'd want to ambush Brazo Largo on this side of the border and say no more about it. If they get along at all with los rurales they may prefer to let us ride into a police trap on or near that border."

Longarm said, morosely, "I wish you'd stop repeating me. I just allowed it was too big a boo. Even if them Mex kids are on the up and up we stand too good a chance of meeting up with the Anglo posse, big and spread out between here and the river."

"Then where are you leading us if you think that barrio across the tracks sounds spooky?"

"To the tracks, of course. Did you boys think I spent all my time jerking off while you were sunbathing up on that roof? There was a stack of railroad timetables smack on the counter at my hotel. I helped myself to one without even asking and read it later in my room, discreet. So all we have to do is avoid getting drunk and disorderly a few more minutes, say twenty, and the SP westbound we want ought to be along any time now."

Ki knew better, but young Willy asked why in thunder they'd want to catch a westbound freight when it stopped for water, the home spread being the other way entire. One of the vaqueros, the once called Galvez, growled, "Estupido, they *know* we rode in from the east. Is a good plan. Even if they suspect we grabbed a boxcar out they are more apt to think it was one going the other way."

Longarm saw the boys were still confused and didn't want to have to coach them in their roles at the last minute. So he gathered them close in the dark shadows and explained, "Everyone knows outlaws hop freight trains a lot. That's why we don't want to. You four are hot as two-dollar pistols. But I ain't and I got the I.D. to prove it. So we'll wait down this way, clear of the depot lights, while a passenger varnish, not no fool freight train, pauses for a drink. Then we'll just climb aboard by way of the rear observation platform as five, not four, and I'll do the talking."

The three who'd never ridden with Longarm before told him he was mad as a hatter and that they wanted nothing to do with such a loco notion. Then Ki, who had adventured with Longarm in the past, said, "He's not insane, he just talks uneducated and, if need be, faster than a snake-oil salesman. We're going along with his idea, risky as it sounds, because I, for one, can't come up with anything better on such short notice, and we know how risky it is to stay here. That posse could be back any minute!"

So a few minutes later, when the Southern Pacific Express pulled in, Longarm began by just tossing his saddle aboard the rear platform as if he owned it, climbed on up, and helped his followers aboard. All but the vaquero called Moreno. He insisted railroad travel made him edgy and that if there was a Hispanic barrio attached to Sanderson he thought his chances would be a heap better there.

Longarm saw no way of forcing him aboard that didn't involve more noise than he really wanted to make. Ki growled down at the spooked Mex, "See that you don't get caught, then. And if you do get caught see that you don't remember where the rest of us went. I mean that, Moreno. You know that I know where your family lives, just in case I never track you down."

Moreno swore on his mother's honor that he understood the code of gentlemen on the run. Further conversation was broken off by the train starting up again with a jolt. Longarm waited until they were well clear of the outskirts of town before he told Ki and the two others, "Stay out here and stay mysterious in the tricky light. I'll bring you some beer on my way back."

Then he stepped into the club car, bold as brass. Only one of the passengers seemed to pay any attention and the one who did was a woman, reading a magazine at the bitty table and no doubt wishing some gent would buy her a drink. It was too bad. She wasn't bad looking. Longarm strode past her to the bar and ordered four schooners of beer. The colored barkeep shot him a curious look, but proceeded to pour.

He'd just finished when a portly old cuss in a conductor's uniform came back to the club car with a concerned expression. Longarm knew about the sneaky electrical buttons they had under railroad bars. Trouble was always starting in the club cars. The conductor looked relieved to see it was Longarm who seemed to have come over the back railing without a ticket. Longarm traveled a lot and knew the conductors on most of the main lines. He nodded and said, "Howdy, Sam. I reckon I owe you four fares. They just had a jailbreak back in Sanderson. Most of the boys rode out for the border with the sheriff. Me and the ones with me aim to check out the crossing at El Paso–Juarez."

The conductor nodded understandingly and said, "Let's call it a free ride, then. El Paso ain't far and you've no idea how nice it feels to have four lawmen along in bandit country after dark."

So that was all there was to it. Longarm toted the clumsy cluster of beer schooners back to the observation platform, where they were gladly taken off his hands by men who'd just been through a mighty thirsty afternoon. They drank some more and enjoyed some club-car sandwiches as well before the train pulled into El Paso before midnight. They'd all dropped off and were out of the yards without anyone aboard having a good look at anyone but Longarm, and nobody had any right to be looking for Longarm.

Knowing his way around El Paso, Longarm headed for

a shabby but discreet hotel he knew of, toting his saddle with the others in his wake. But as they strode a dark side street he told Ki, "There's no sense pushing our luck further than we just did. I have more freedom to move cross-country. You and your riders will be safer holed up here in a town I don't see how you could have gotten to, while I get on over to the Circle Star and see if I can find out what's wrong with Jessie's head."

But Ki shook his own head, firmly, and said, "I'm going with you. I agree traveling light is our best bet. So we'll leave Willy and Galvez here and—"

"Hold on," Longarm cut in. Choosing his words carefully, he went on, "There ought to be a more delicate way to put this, Ki. But since there ain't, I'll just say I could get about easier with either of these old boys, or both, under my wing. No offense, but you're a sort of head-turning individual. You know how strangers stare at you, trying to figure out whether you're a squint-eyed Texas rider, a Chinaman dressed like one, or something even more disturbing."

"I can pass for white when I want to," Ki growled.

"A man as big and mean looking as you can no doubt pass for the Czar of all the Russians if he insists on it. But that's not saying folk who address him as Your Majesty won't recall him, should anyone ask. You just busted out of jail, goddamn it. Speaking from six or eight years experience with the law I can promise you there's an all-points out on you alerting the law far and wide to look for a sinister Oriental bigger than any laundryman has any right to grow."

Ki growled, "Damn it, my mother wasn't Chinese. She was a high-born Japanese lady of the Yamoto Class."

"Hell, I knew that all along," Longarm said. "But most folk in these parts can't tell and don't want to know the difference between one breed of foreigner from another. We both stand out in a crowd, Ki, and I'm pure Anglo-Saxon. I know you're anxious to confront Jessie about the mean things she said about you. I want to hear it from her own

94

lips as well. But neither of us figures to hear anything from her if we get caught on our fool way to see her, can we?''

Ki insisted, ''I can get you through to the home spread better than you might manage on your own. It's a big spread in the middle of big country. Nobody knows the approaches better than I do. They're sure to have most of the ways in staked out.''

Longarm shifted the saddle to his other side to rest the arm it had tired as he said, ''Hell, I wasn't planning on pussyfooting in no back doors, Ki. Jessie and me are old pals. We used to be, at any rate and, even if she's mad at me, too, she still has to know I'm a federal lawman.''

Ki nodded but said, ''That's if she's really there, and acting of her own free will. I've had more time to think about that than you, Longarm. I watched that girl grow up. I just can't buy her going mean and crazy on us. Surely not *both* of us. And even a madwoman would know better than to lie to Marshal Vail about Big John Chisum, damn it!''

Longarm grimaced and said, ''I've never been able to guess what crazy folk might or might not do. That's how come they spook me. But try it another way. What if Jessie's been sending such crazy messages as a message? She knows she can trust you and her Uncle Billy Vail. I hope she knows she can trust me. So what if some mysterious *they* have the drop on her and she's pretending to go along with 'em?''

Ki brightened and said, ''I like that a lot better than any hint of madness in the Starbuck family. I taught the girl to use indirect moves in a tense situation. Anyone less subtle, holding her, would be inclined to want her to dismiss any questions as quickly as possible. They wouldn't want her communicating with the outside world any more than she just had to. So, sure, they let her answer wires from distant lawmen, in as few words as possible. But if she knew that they didn't know much about the way she ran her business, she could have sent those crazy messages to alert us all that something mighty odd was going on!''

''In that case they'd have to be in the dark about Starbuck

Enterprises indeed. She never answered me at all. She may have tried to. But in all due modesty I'm sort of well known among crooks. You'd think they'd find out who she might have working as her segundo, though, before they let her wire both Sanderson and a U.S. marshal in Denver that some missing stock had been stolen by disgruntled employees. What if *everyone* there is a might touched?''

Ki suggested, ''If we're dealing with a not too well organized gang, she could be allowed to reply to messages by some and not at all by others. The point is that we're not going to find out by just guessing. We have to get back there, Longarm. I can get you to the home spread and, better yet, inside the house by way of a foray tunnel built back in the wilder Comanche days.''

Longarm smiled grimly and decided, ''I like it. For I'd just love to pop out of the woodwork like a magic rabbit and ask old Jessie and anyone with her who's gone loco or not!''

Once all the escapees but Ki had been safely stowed away it was not, in fact, all that difficult for Longarm and Ki to wend their way discreetly to the Starbuck home spread. They rode in late at night, tethered their ponies over a mile from the main house, and moved in the rest of the way Comache style.

The house was dimly and ominously lit as they approached. The sky was overcast and it was so dark Longarm knew he'd have never found that trapdoor under a sticker bush without Ki, even if Ki had drawn him a map. The long crawl through the long-out-of-use foray tunnel was more uncomfortable than spooky. Even with Ki in the lead, Longarm wound up with his face and mustache all fuzzed up with cobwebbing. He could only console himself with the thought that Texas tarantulas weren't web spinners. Of course, black widows were, so it tended to even out.

He suddenly bumped Ki's ass with his nose. Before he could say he didn't go in for that sort of bullshit with other

96

men, Ki hissed, "We're there. Have you got your gun out?"

Longarm growled, "Why, no, I never draw my gun in advance of a bust-in. Ned Buntline says in his wild West magazines that it's against the code of the West."

Ki didn't think that was funny. He said, "All right, listen tight. We'll be coming out of a Spanish cupboard in the dining room. At this hour there shouldn't be anyone there. Don't bet our lives on it, though. I'll cut to the right and flatten against the wall on that side. You do the same to the left and after that, good luck, agreed?"

Longarm said, "Bueno. Get your ass out of my face and let's just do it!"

So they did it. The dining room was dark as well as empty. So once they'd stood there a time, listening to their hearts beating, Ki silently pointed with the muzzle of his six-gun at the dim lamplight painting the floor through an open doorway, and took the lead.

Longarm knew the big Amerasian had to be leading him somewhere important when a woman screamed and he heard china smashing to the floor. But Ki held his fire, and as Longarm moved into the parlor after him they both stared back at the Mexican maid who was staring back at them as if they were ghosts.

Ki broke the silence to demand, "Where is la patrona, Maria?"

To which the maid replied, in a less terrified tone, "*Quien sabe?* She did not tell me when she left this afternoon. Pero she had on her fine clothings, such as she wears when she goes east on business."

Ki introduced Longarm as another man to be trusted before he questioned the maid further, with Longarm chiming in with some questions of his own. They quickly established that no, there had not been any recent visitors, with or without guns drawn, and that the maid well recalled taking many telegrafo messages in to Jessie, who'd been spending some time alone in bed, as if she might be feeling poorly. The maid said la patrona had sort of cussed when she'd torn the wires open to read. Then she'd quickly written replies for the Western Union rider having cake and coffee in the kitchen, and that was all Maria knew. She read neither English nor other people's mail. The two tall men exchanged puzzled stares. Longarm knew the way to Jessie's bedroom well enough, but he thought it more polite to let Ki suggest that and lead the way, with the little Mex gal tagging after them.

There was a bath attached to the bedroom of such a rich young lady. Longarm went in there as Ki looked under the bed and went through closets and drawers. So it was Longarm who found the odd bottle in the cabinet over the sink. He knew said cabinet of old, since he'd had to leave his shaving kit somewhere as a house guest with bedroom privileges, and he knew Jessie Starbuck never took, or needed, sleeping tablets. But that was what the label on the blue glass bottle said the two tablets left had to be. He carried the bottle back into the bedroom to show the others. Ki said he'd never known Jessie to order such medication. Maria said, "Oh, I think she bought those in town the last time she went shopping there. I remember that blue bottle from when I helped la patrona open her packages."

Again the two men exchanged thoughtful looks. Longarm asked the maid how long ago all this had been going on. Maria thought and said, "Monday, I think. Is important for to know for sure?"

Longarm grimaced and told her, "A day or so either way hardly matters. The label says to take no more than one a night, and there had to be a lot more than seven pills in a bottle this size!"

He held the label up to the light for another reading before he whistled and added, "Jesus H. Christ! This allows there had to be two hundred and fifty sleeping pills in this bottle when she bought it and that all of 'em contain tincture of opium!"

Ki took the bottle from him, saying, as if he might know, "Nobody could consume that much opium in less than a week and then get dressed up to go back East or anywhere else! Jessie's tough for her size, but she's simply not big enough to consume that much opium in such a short time, unless they're just using a lot of hot air and a trace of the drug to sell sleeping pills to unsuspecting women.''

He shook one of the remaining pills out, bit through the coating, and spat the results into his palm to sniff them. Then he shook his head and said, ''There's no opium in these pills. Once you've smelled the real thing you never forget the stink.''

Longarm treated the remaining pill the same way. He had to taste the white innards and he still wasn't dead certain. But he said, soberly, ''As a lawman it's been my opinion for some time that it just ain't right to sell such strong drugs without a prescription. If I'm right about this being cocaine mixed with cornstarch, it's a mighty queer prescription for a *sleeping* potion!''

Ki had to confess he knew more about opium, hashish and other Oriental drugs. Longarm said, ''It's small wonder. Cocaine is pure American. South American, leastways. It don't damage the Indians much, just chewing the leaves for pep. But of late some fools have commenced to refine it to pure danger. Nobody takes it to have sweet horny dreams, like opium users. Cocaine wakes you up more than anyone has a right to be woke up and it's a painkiller as well. I had a mighty grim encounter with a gunslick on cocaine a year or so back. He'd commenced as an honest young puncher, using cocaine just to keep him awake on the trail. Next thing anyone knew he went bad entire, and you've never seen a man draw until you've seen him do so full of Peruvian pep! I thought I was a gonner till I noticed he couldn't shoot worth a damn with the stuff messing up his poor brain. He sure shot a lot though. Emptied his wheel in my general direction in the time I took getting off the one shot that was important.''

Ki scowled down at the mess in his palm to say, ''Jessie has no need for medication to outdraw and outshoot anyone human. I taught her to fight almost as deadly bare-handed and, damn it, why does the label say these were sleeping tablets if they're some sort of crazy pep pills?''

Longarm suggested, ''They could have been mislabeled, and that would sure account for many an odd mood indeed. What if a lady suffering insomnia for any reason took wake-up pills for sleeping pills, and then maybe took even more when they didn't seem to be working and she kept getting more sleepless and edgy by the minute?''

Ki made a wry face and said, ''Ouch! But Jessie hardly ever uses any medication at all. Surely she'd have sense enough to see something was wrong when even one pill worked in reverse. You'd have to be awfully stupid to take anything one after the other when the label warned you to only take one, right?''

Longarm shook his head soberly and said, ''Wrong. I just told you I've dealt with dope fiends in the past. They don't know they're acting fiendish. The dope scrambles their brains and makes them feel smarter than the rest of us. They may decide their own mother is out to do 'em dirty or that some total stranger coming the other way is a devil from hell as needs killing. But they never doubt their own twisty logic. Like I said, there ought to be a law.''

Ki muttered, ''I can't believe anything would affect Jessie that way. Not even if she took the whole bottle.''

But Longarm pointed out, morosely, ''She just did. Even saying she only swallowed a dozen or so at a time, that'd be enough cocaine to cloud the judgment of a saint, and Jessie would be insulted if anyone accused her of sainthood. We know she turned on you, of all people, and I sure wish you hadn't taught her all them Oriental ways to bust folk up, bare-handed, should she feel any call to do so.''

Ki swore and stepped over to a nearby closet. As the maid bitched, Ki commenced to throw Jessie's wardrobe out on the rug, as if searching for something more important.

He was. When he got down to some empty clothes hangers and the shoes lined up under them, Ki turned back to stare at Longarm thundergasted as he said, "Her gun rig's missing. So is the Stetson with the throwing star she wears. She hasn't gone back East. She's gone hunting!"

Longarm asked the maid if the lady had left the house with any baggage. Maria nodded and said, "Si, two bags full. For why do you ask?"

Longarm turned back to Ki and said, "Hunting sneaky, if she lit out dressed sedate with her gun and star carried sly. Unless and until that drug wears off, there's just no telling what she might do. Cocaine don't affect your co-ordination, just your head. So she can still go after folk like a well-oiled killing machine, and we don't even know who she might be after!"

Nobody with a lick of sense would search for a segundo who'd been fired at the spread he'd been fired off. So at sunrise Longarm rode into town alone. Maria had no idea where La Patrona had bought those mixed up sleeping pills. But there were only half a dozen drugstores in town, so it would have been easy, if only one recalled selling Miss Jessie Starbuck anything at all in recent memory. She was well known in town, of course. She owned a heap of it. But as one druggist observed, wistfully, she kept some first aid supplies for her help and that was about it.

He had better luck at a sidestreet drug store where the pretty female pharmacist didn't recall a Miss Starbuck at all. It was easy to tell she was new in town. When Longarm asked her to look the empty bottle over, anyway, she said, "We don't carry this brand. I know opium is lawful to sell, but I don't approve of it in patent medicines or teething lotions."

Longarm said he didn't, either, and told the firm jawed but otherwise sweet-faced little brunette, "I have reason to suspect this bottle contained something else entire. I know it's empty, now. But as you can see there's still a lot of dust from whatever on the bottom. Is there any way a good druggist could prove what it might or might not be? The

U.S. Government will be paying for such an assay, of course.''

That inspired her to allow she'd sure try. He asked how long it might take. She told him to come back in an hour. So he promised her he would and went next to deal with another important chore, at the nearby Ranger station.

Unlike Billy Vail, who'd once ridden with Captain Bigfoot Johnson before the war, Longarm got along with some Texas Rangers less than he did others. For, like Canadian Mounties, a heap of Rangers seemed to feel that when the Good Lord created the first of 'em, He'd thrown away the mold and never bothered creating any other lawmen. But the captain in command, here, turned out to be a sensible cuss. That was likely how he'd made captain. He knew Longarm by rep and seemed to feel there were enough crooks to go around in this wicked world. So he offered Longarm a seat and a cigar in his back office and began by saying, ''I was just about to send a rider out to the Circle Star to question Miss Starbuck.''

Longarm didn't want any Ranger doing that, so he said, ''She ain't home. I just came from there. Her help says she went east on business. What did you want to question her about?''

''Same thing you just tried to find out about, I'll vow. We just got a wire from your boss, Marshal Vail, a man whose memory is honored in these parts. He claims Jessie Starbuck told a big fib about her segundo, that big Chinese or whatever. She told us, too, that this Ki jasper had lit out for New Mexico Territory with some of her beef. Billy Vail has double-checked the version her riders gave when they were picked up with said beef near the Pecos. The New Mexico rancher who'd ordered the cows not only confirms he ordered them from her fair and square but has a money order receipt from the U.S. Postal Service to prove it. As you likely know to your own chagrin, Marshal Vail ain't a man to accept anyone just saying so. He was Ranger trained.''

Longarm grinned with the cigar gripped between his teeth and said, "He sure can be picky about my expense account. Let me guess. Billy naturally wired the postmaster in Lincoln?"

The Ranger captain nodded and said, "Here, too. The money order was sent by John Chisum to Miss Jessie Starbuck. She in turn had to sign for it, at this end, when she cashed it. Her bank confirms she deposited said money with 'em the same day. So there's no getting around the simple logic of that Ki gent's story. Nobody before him delivered head-one of Starbuck breeding stock to Chisum. He was driving the right number, the right direction, when the law in Terrell County questioned his driving of the same and got told a big fib."

He leaned back expansively, enjoyed a drag on his own big smoke, and asked, "How do you reconstruct it? Lovers' quarrel? They say she and that Ki jasper have always been mighty close, and you know how some women can act when a gent two-times 'em or can't one-time 'em oft enough."

Longarm said, soberly, "I've been told by both that they're platonic. Miss Jessie sort of inherited Ki from her late father. If he had criminal tendencies, they'd have surfaced long before she was old enough to accuse him of anything but child molesting, and I can't see her big tough daddy standing for that."

"Yeah, but her daddy's dead and buried and they've been out there, living under one roof, ever since."

Longarm's eyes narrowed coldly as he said, "It's a waste of time arguing with a natural gossip. Whether their relationship is pure as they both say or whether she's been posing for French postcards since she was a baby ain't the question before the house. There's no federal law covering fornication and Texas laws only cover adultery between married folk, which neither is. So what charges might Texas still have against my pal Ki?"

The Ranger captain said, "You left out rape, criminal or statutory, and we don't hold with some of them freak shows

103

they put on in Galveston cathouses, neither. But as for the charges regarding stock stealing, there ain't none now. You can't expect the Texas Rangers to punish a false-hearted or impotent lover, damn it. It's agreed he couldn't have stole those damned cows off her. If I didn't know she had half as many damned lawyers as riders I'd be tempted to charge *her*, not *him*, with making the law look foolish!''

Longarm agreed domestic arguments were a pain in every lawman's ass. Then, though he didn't want to, he had to ask where Ki stood with Texas about that cowhand somebody must have gunned. The Ranger captain sighed and said, ''Let's just forget anyone ever said that. Like I said, lots of expensive lawyers and no real harm done.''

Longarm raised an eyebrow to comment, ''Well, I've heard you good old Texican boys don't consider Mexican lives important.''

But the Ranger captain scowled and said, ''Bite your tongue, Denver boy. This man's outfit upholds the Constitution as fair as anyone seeing a heap of Southerons signed and ratified it before our little falling out with the north. You ain't allowed to gun a greaser and just forget it in these parts. But as far as anyone can figure out, no such shooting occurred. I sent one of my Rangers to record the delicate corpus to no avail. The ranch hands he questioned hadn't heard word-one about any of 'em being shot and dying dolorous. All they could recall was their foreman cutting out some brood cows and driving 'em off the spread with four other riders. When he went to the main house to ask Miss Jessie about it she allowed she had an awful headache and may have got it wrong. She said one of her help had told her a rider had been gunned. But she disremembered his name, or just who'd told her. My old woman can get like that when she's got the rag on and I come home late on a sultry evening with heat lightning brewing.'' He smiled wistfully and added, ''Lord, I sometimes wish I had the luck, and manhood, to perform half the wonders my old woman has accused me of in a rage. There's this one young neighbor woman . . . Never mind. Suffice it to say you can't always go by the word of a woman who's been feeling poorly.''

Longarm knew Ki would be asking a heap of delicate questions out at the Starbuck spread. So he agreed he'd noticed as much in his own time as a lawman and they shook on it and parted friendly.

He went next to the nearest Western Union to wire the boys at that hotel in El Paso it was safe to come on home and suggested they pick up Moreno along the way if it wasn't too much bother.

Then he wired the sherrif at Sanderson, lest the boys run into more trouble there. The Sanderson law had no way of knowing he'd had any part in that jailbreak, and any county sherrif who didn't take the word of both the federal government and the state of Texas would have to be mighty uppity.

Longarm hesitated before he wired Billy Vail up in Denver. He knew Uncle Billy shared his mixed feelings about the rich and ever unpredictable Jessie. His boss had in fact ordered him not to shake her tree no more, whether out of concern for the pretty young gal's virtue or in hopes of keeping his senior deputy out of jail. For when Jessie was riding herd on someone her notions of rough justice could shock even Longarm, and he was always catching hell for bending statute laws a mite in the interests of what he might consider the greater good.

But as Longarm pondered the lesser evil he decided he'd best level with his home office just this once. Things were confused enough with Jessie suddenly telling fibs or refusing to even stay in touch. Hoping he was doing the right thing, and knowing Billy Vail would be worried about him as well as "little Jessie," as Billy persisted in calling a grown woman just because he'd bounced her on his knee a few times when they'd both been a lot younger, Longarm brought Vail up to date on the little he'd learned so far, said he was looking to find out more, and didn't offer any return address, lest old Billy reply to the contrary.

Then, since that hour was about up, Longarm went back to that drugstore where his pony still stood tethered in the shade of the far side of the street. But when he got to the door he saw the curtain had been drawn down behind the glass door and that the druggist gal had hung a sign behind the glass saying she was out to lunch, which was the way Anglos described la siesta in this part of Texas. He didn't think she meant him, so he knocked. When nothing happened he knocked some more, but still nobody responded.

That was something to study on, more ways than one. The gal had told him to come back in an hour. So she must have figured he might, and it was way too early for anyone to knock off for "lunch," as fancy folk had started to call noon dinner. An old gent across the way was repairing a picket fence just a few yards from the tethered pony Longarm had picked up since leaving El Paso. The pony was a surefooted but sort of high-strung bay with a white blaze and socks. It was flinching each time the old man hit a nail off center with his unsuited ball-peen hammer. As Longarm strode across to the shady side, the old gent shot him a wary look and said, "I'm almost finished, mister. I didn't come out here to spook your mount. It's just that the infernal kids will walk a picket fence when little gals are there to admire 'em."

Longarm smiled down at the old gent to assure him, "Your fence was here before my pony was. I've never ridden a pink-hooved critter who wasn't a mite shy. I refuse to ride a white pony with pink *eyes* at all."

The old-timer laughed, more easy minded now, and allowed Longarm had to know something about horseflesh, despite the Colorado crush to his Stetson.

Longarm nodded and said, "You're right. I'm a stranger in this neck of the woods. Maybe you can help me. I can't help noticing the drugstore across the way is closed, despite it being on the shady side of eleven. The young lady as runs it told me to come back about now. So I did. Only she don't seem to be there.''

The old gent hit a nail head a good lick, muttered, "That ought to hold you," and rose to his full height, or about to Longarm's chin. Then he said, "That would be Miss Doc. Or Alice Dumas, to be precise. She's all right. Come out here a year or so back to help her uncle, Doc Westwood, run the place. He died and so she runs it now. We don't care. They say she got a degree in mixing drugs back East, and she charges fair. You might try knocking harder. She lives in the back. Does her own cooking, and never closes entire at noon as a rule.''

"I did knock more than once. Sort of firm. Anyone inside a frame building that size should have noticed.''

The friendly neighbor decided, "She ain't in, then. Folk in this part of town know Miss Doc don't mean them when she's closed if they really need some medicine. Maybe she had to go deliver some of the same. She's all alone in there since the delivery boy she used to have run off to be a cowboy.''

Longarm glanced up at the sky, saying, "Well, I don't mind waiting as the sun climbs, but this pony has already been standing a spell with no water.''

"Hell, Colorado, you can leave him with my carriage team in the back, if you want. There's a water trough in every stall and my old swaybacks will enjoy the company. They never get to talk to anyone but one another and—''

"Only if you let me pay you," Longarm cut in. "I ain't trying to insult you, but . . .''

"Then don't insult me," the crusty old Texan insisted as he moved to untether the pony. "I'll lead him about to our carriage house. Wait here and I'll take you inside for some coffee and cake while you're waiting for Miss Doc to get back. I'd say to just go on in, but the last time a stranger tried that my old woman hit him with her broom. It's ever best to introduce a gent to old women more formal.''

Longarm laughed and said, "I've heard of Texas Hospitality. I've even enjoyed some before. But to tell the truth I've other errands to run, as long as I'm at this end of town. So while I'd be a fool to turn down your invite to my pony, I'd best pass on your other kind offer."

The old man told him to suit himself, adding he didn't know what he was missing and that he'd first decided to court his old woman at a cake sale at First Methodist. Longarm chuckled and said he'd noticed his new friend was sort of potbellied, no offense. Then they parted friendly and Longarm got well out of sight before he found a gap in the storefronts and worked his way to the alley behind the drugstore, taking out his pocketknife and opening the lock-picking blade, muttering, "Damn it, Jessie Starbuck. You're sure getting me in Dutch with all this nonsense. I'm supposed to be the law and here I go breaking and entering after engineering a jailbreak."

Miss Doc's backyard was fenced high and no second-story windows overlooked her back door. So Longarm just strode up to it, opened the screen door, and gave it a few good licks. Nobody answered them. He hadn't really expected anyone to. He tried the knob. The back door was locked, too. But of course it only took him a few seconds to get it open. He stepped into the small, nice-smelling and neatly kept kitchen, calling out, "Anybody home?"

Nobody answered, but he heard something scraping down the far side of another door just off the kitchen. It was where one was apt to find a linen closet. The sound had been that of stacked linen falling from a shelf and working its way down. Mice hardly ever messed in a linen closet half that noisy. Longarm drew his .44-40 and eased over silently on the balls of his booted feet to grab the knob with his free hand and yank the door open, snapping, "Freeze, you rascal!"

But the stark-naked brunette he'd exposed to broad-ass

day did no such thing. She let out a yell to wake the dead and grabbed for a sheet to wrap her moist curves in, sobbing, "I was taking a bath, you horrid brute!"

Longarm was sure she couldn't be armed with so much as a corset stay, so he stepped back, reholstered his gun, and politely asked Miss Doc if she bathed a lot in linen closets.

By this time she'd wrapped herself in the sheet to resemble a mighty pretty Roman senator. She stepped out, barefooted, to explain, "I'd just gotten out of the tub when I heard you picking my back lock. I feared you were one of those murderers, so—"

"Back up," he cut in. "What murderers might we be jawing about, Miss Alice?"

She sniffed and said, "The ones I fear you've involved me with, of course. A *gentleman* would have *respected* the sign I hung out front. I was hoping you'd just go away and leave me be. I want no part in a federal investigation of a murder plot!"

He frowned down at her and said, "It must be tempting for a druggist to sample some of his or her own wares. Would you kindly sober up enough to tell me what this is all about?"

"That bottle of so-called sleeping pills you asked me to analyze for you. I want no part of it. You have to take it back!"

He followed as she led the way, not up front behind her counter as he'd expected but into a dinky bedroom. The sheet she'd wrapped around her wet derriere left little to the imagination as she dropped to her hands and knees to rummage under the bed for the bottle, explaining, "I was so afraid someone would come in asking about this if you were followed to my poor innocent doorstep!" She got the apparently empty blue bottle out and sat on the bed to hand it up to him, saying, "The cornstarch wasn't as hard as the *conium maculatum* with even more *hyoscyamus*, both deadly enough to do the job alone! No licensed pharmacist ever filled *this* prescription! You might try the Borgias, if any of them live in Texas these days.''

Longarm whistled as he pocketed the mysterious bottle, saying, ''We figured them pills had to be strong stuff. All I could taste was cornstarch and something bitter and leafy, like cocaine.''

She grimaced and said, ''I hope you didn't taste much of that nasty mixture. You'd probably translate the Latin as poison hemlock and henbane. I don't understand the recipe at all. For as I just told you, either would kill a person on its own.''

Longarm felt wobbly legged at the thought of another pretty lady swallowing such pills in the mistaken belief they'd help her get some rest. He sat down beside the sheet-wrapped druggist gal to insist, weakly, ''A friend of mine was taking the pills for at least a few days and nobody noticed her dying. The household help said she did look sort of sick, and she has been acting out of sorts. But since she don't seem to be dead, what could I be missing?''

Miss Doc shrugged her bare shoulders and decided, ''It would depend on the dosage, I suppose. Don't ask me what a fatal dose of either hemlock or henbane might be. No doctor would ever write a prescription calling for either. There were traces of sucrose—that's sugar, to you—so I assume the pills were made up with cornstarch filler and a mighty thick coating to hide the bitter taste indeed. I've read about so-called witches in the old days sipping infusions of henbane. I've always assumed they had to be mighty weak, if any foolish old woman managed to get her henbane down, with cream and sugar. It's more bitter than quinine and has a nasty odor. Nasty to humans at any rate. It's called henbane because chickens go for it the way cats go for catnip, only cats just get silly on catnip and chickens drop dead, fast.''

Longarm frowned down at the rug, muttering, ''I'm sort of a country boy. My folk kept chickens. But to tell the truth we never had any act like that.''

Miss Doc explained, "Neither henbane nor poison hemlock grow wild on our side of the ocean, praise the Lord. Henbane is a pernicious weed in northern Europe. Hemlock is what they used to poison Socrates that time."

"In other words, somebody had to go to some trouble putting together such a witch brew. I heard about that Greek philosopher's execution by poison. What might hemlock have done to old Socrates if he hadn't taken quite enough to kill him?"

She shrugged again and said, "About what it did to him, only less so. Hemlock was popular with suicides in classic times because of the way it affects the human body. It starts as a calm pleasant feeling. Then the flesh goes numb and one can't feel pain. Hemlock would make a swell anesthetic if it wasn't so dangerous. Anyhow, starting at the fingers and toes and working up, the body just goes deader and deader until the hemlock hits the heart and lungs and that's the end of it. I don't see how your friend could have gone anywhere at all with a fatal dosage of hemlock in her. You say it's another *woman* they were out to poison? You've no idea how comforting that is to me right now."

Longarm put a reassuring arm around her shivering shoulders, assuring her, "I'm sure they were out to steal more than a drugstore, if that's the motive. The lady they seem to have switched pills on has had rascals out to grab her cattle and trading empire before. She must have been too tough for the hemlock they fed her in them pills and wound up simply feeling sort of numb and fuzzy headed. Tell me about henbane, ma'am."

Miss Doc tried. She said, "There's even less in the professional literature about *hyoscyamus*. Not even the Borgias saw any need for it. Its effects were discovered by half-cracked spey wives during the witchcraft craze between the Black Death and more common sense. A fatal dosage, whatever that may be, will leave a human dead as any chicken. The deluded old women who thought they were practicing witchcraft didn't want to die. They wanted to fly. Apparently a sublethal dosage of henbane gives one a lightness of being, combined with hallucinations. Confessed witches reported some mighty odd sights at their midnight affairs with you know who. They obviously suffered, or enjoyed, repeated orgasms. I find it harder to believe they climaxed high in the moonlight with half the odd creatures they thought they were, ah, fooling around with.''

Longarm nodded and said, ''I've seen the pictures in some of the old books on the subject. I don't see how even an ugly old gal would want to carry on like that with a really horny cuss all covered with scales, tails, and bat wings. But I thought all them witch trials were just hysterical, on the part of loco church elders, I mean.''

''A lot of them must have been. Everyone at the time was awfully superstitious, but they should have seen how impossible some of the confessions were. But at least some confessions of consorting with Satan must have been sincere. The inquisition did find solid evidence now and again in the form of corpse-wax candles, inverted crosses, buried infants and, ah, odd sexual devices. In fairness to the Inquisition, *everyone* believed in black magic, then, and it stands to reason at least some people sought to improve their lot in a closed society by resorting to the same. We know respected philosophers were trying to turn base metals into gold, discover the secret of eternal life and so on. We modern druggists owe a lot to the ancient alchemists. They did lay the foundations of modern chemistry, if only by discovering what didn't work, or blew up in one's face. The even more dubious spey women discovered a lot of herbal remedies as well as worthless spring tonics and some deadly poisons. Anyone who took henbane, more than once, would have to think she was a witch and enjoy the feeling. You have to consider the logic as well as the painful methods of the Inquisition. The Bible does say one should not suffer a witch to live and includes a passage about Saul and the witch of Endor. So they sincerely felt they were saving the world from the forces of Satan and, by their logic, they were.''

Longarm smiled thinly and remarked, ''I take it you'd be of the Roman persuasion?''

''French Canadian Catholic, of course. That's why I feel qualified to say Joan of Arc was guilty as charged, even if she was French and they made her a French saint, later, to please Napoleon.''

Longarm stared at her dubiously, saying, ''Oh, Lord, I only wanted the dregs of this bottle assayed and now we're accusing Joan of Arc of witchcraft! Are you sure you didn't sample some of the stuff just now?''

She turned her face to his, indignantly, to snap, ''I most certainly did not! I don't *want* to fly high in the sky and get naughty with a flying fiend. The effects of henbane have been recorded well enough, thank you very much, and every French girl knew Joan of Arc was guilty before the Church cleaned up her record for political reasons!''

Interested in such an odd notion, despite himself, Longarm said, ''I'll bite. The way I read the story, Miss Joan led the French army against the redcoats, got captured, and they went and barbecued her even though they didn't want to eat her.''

He added, ''She was framed.''

The French Canadian gal replied, flatly, ''Bull. A modern court would no doubt find she was insane and just have her put away as a lunatic. But you have to remember her judges didn't see madness as a mental illness. They just took her at her word, and her own words condemned her as an evil sorceress or a liar who fibbed about the Lord, which in those days was considered worse.''

Longarm insisted, ''Aw, come on. The poor little gal was court-martialed by the English as a French general in skirts.''

''A lot you know,'' Miss Doc said. ''To begin with she was a six-foot strapping country girl who fought in pants under her armor. That alone was against the law in France

113

as well as England in the fifteenth century. Are men and women allowed to dress up like one another, even now?"

He shrugged and said, "Well, the most a strict judge might give a bloomer gal is a fine. He wouldn't burn her at the stake or even hang her, just for wearing pants."

Miss Doc said, "Maybe someday folk will feel we were sort of strict about dress codes in our own time. But that was the least of the charges against Joan of Arc. She only got to lead the armies of France by telling everyone she'd had a vision. She said she had it personal, from Mary, Queen of the Angels, and a squad of angels as well, that if France put her in command of the French army she'd lead it to victory over the English."

Longarm opined, "Well, you can't say she didn't try."

"Trying isn't good enough when you're selling the word of the Mother of God. She didn't beat the English. They beat her, and she was taken prisoner. They never charged her with fighting for her country. They wanted to know just what sort of spirits she'd been consorting with. It still works, if you buy spirits at all, that Saint Mary and real angels wouldn't come down from heaven with a false message for anyone. But the message she said they'd given her *had* to be false. The English had won, after her spirits told her she would, and a lot of men had been killed on both sides. That left her stuck with either having to admit she'd made the whole thing up, or that it had been evil fibbing spirits she'd been messing with, so—"

"Never mind," Longarm cut in, wearily. "I've never to this day been called on to testify in court about spirits, good or bad, except for some sold to Indians, and that's different. I got a more important worry on my mind. I'd like you to tell me, as a druggist gal, whether it's possible anyone could take such a hellish mixture as hemlock and henbane, over a period of some time, and just feel crazy as hell instead of dead."

Miss Doc nodded soberly and said, "If each pill held a

less than lethal dose and she was awfully strong as well as lucky.''

He tried, ''Say she liked the effects, or felt too stupid to fully savvy 'em, and just took another each time the floating painless effects began to wear off. Could she still have put away as many as were in that bottle in the space of a week?''

Miss Doc shook her head and said, ''Impossible. Not if there was enough hemlock and henbane in one or even two such pills to affect her much to begin with. Assuming there were two hundred or so effective doses to begin with, that would come to around two dozen a day and—''

''She must have emptied the bottle into a handier container as she was packing,'' Longarm cut in. Suppressing a shudder he added, half to himself, ''Say she only takes one at a time, to keep floating. She's got enough to float a hell of a ways, and I've already seen her float up in the air and plant two boot heels in a grown man's face. You say that henbane figures to make an already healthy gal horny as hell, too?''

Miss Doc nodded soberly and said, ''Judging from the, ah, witch toys the Inquisition recorded, ladies on henbane must feel mighty passionate. The hemlock would of course have a contrary effect, leading to Lord knows what sort of perversions. Some of those poor witches confessed to astounding crimes against nature. Most of them just disgusting and some . . . sort of interesting if they really worked.''

Then she blushed everywhere her flesh was exposed, adding up to considerable blushing, and murmured, ''Heavens, is this any way to be talking, alone with a man who's seen me stark naked?''

He grinned and said, ''I didn't see nothing any gal should feel ashamed of. I've often suspected it was saggy older folk who must have invented clothes. I don't buy that story about fig leaves in the Garden of Eden, considering nobody else was around and they'd already got to know one another so well. But we've argued enough about religion. So I thank

115

you for your help, Miss Doc, and now I'd best get it on down the road.''

"Where are you going?" she demanded in a worried tone. "I'm still frightened! What if they come after me as well?"

He held her a mite closer, assuring her, "Nobody has any reason to suspect I brought that bottle to any drugstore for an assay, Miss Doc. They likely think my missing, ah, friend still has it. She's sure been acting like she has. As for where I aim to go, you sort of got me. Another pal is asking other questions out at a cow spread, even as we speak. He may or may not have figured which way the half-poisoned gal headed. So once it cools a mite, out on the range, I'd best ride out to ask him.''

"Don't leave me until then. I'm still scared, and if it's a drink you want I can serve you better, here, than any old saloon in town could hope to.''

She was right. Medicinal alcohol laced with mint flavoring tasted swell as well as strong. She got a couple of such drinks ahead of him as they reclined in her bedroom out of the noonday sun, jawing about all sorts of this and that. When her sheet slipped a second time to expose her perky little cupcakes, and she didn't bother to pull it back up, he suspected she just paid no mind because she didn't care. She hadn't really had that much to drink, but he'd noticed it had been her suggestion to hang up his coat, vest and gun rig to get comfortable, and she was the one who kept bringing up the subject of odd things witch gals might have done to themselves, or had done to 'em by someone just as wild. So the next thing they knew he was showing her how it might have worked on the altar at a black mass, albeit they only had her bed to work with and he didn't have any devil mask on. Once he had it in her that way, with her confessing sort of clinical that the old-fashioned way made a lot more sense, he just shucked the rest of his duds and they just went loco for a spell in the position Adam and Eve likely started out with.

After he'd assured her they were only doing this out of

116

pure scientific curiosity, she let him in on some other curious notions she'd read up on in medical tomes about sex maniacs. They didn't try anything anyone could see had to be painful, but some sex maniacs sure had worked out mighty queer positions. Some of 'em felt sort of nice, once you managed to get it back in.

When Longarm at last had to pause for a smoke and his second wind, being only superhuman, Miss Doc told him she had more than one love potion, out front, guaranteed to restore his full manhood. But he said, "Not hardly. I've always figured when a man can't get it up he's had it up long enough. Another doc told me, when I was younger and more worried about such things, that it was safe to come all you could, as long as you stuck to coming natural. It's artificial stimulants that does in so many old men with young lover gals."

He blew a smoke ring at the ceiling and held her closer to his naked chest as he added, soothingly, "Don't fret about it. I ain't done, yet. I'm just resting up for another scientific experiment."

Meanwhile, out at the Starbuck spread, the man called Ki was having a similar conversation under similar circumstances with Maria, the house maid. They were resting up in her dinky bed in her quarters. The maid's room was nice enough. Jessie Starbuck had always treated her hired help decent. It had simply never occurred to la patrona that her bitty Mex maid would need a bed big enough to hold her and a man as big as Ki.

The tall and muscular Amerasian had never been in it before. He was too smart to wagtail where he worked, as a rule. But Ki was cool and skilled in all the martial arts, including this one, and there was nothing like a little skillful screwing to loosen the tongue of a woman not too bright to begin with. Maria was of course just delighted to find herself the object of the handsome segundo's affections, at last. For little Maria was shy as well as pretty in her own

117

peon way, and she'd included Ki in many a fantasy in the past, never dreaming the day would really come when the usually friendly but firm segundo would prove her lack of imagination by making love to her in ways she had never imagined.

In this case it had been Maria who begged for a breather, since Ki could keep going indefinitely when he set his mind to it and didn't really care if he came, himself. He'd found Maria inspiring enough to remain halfway between pleasure and detachment, even a touch of distaste, as the poor little bundle of brown-skinned frustration had gone loco under him with more animal enthusiasm than skill. As they lay there, now, perforce in cozy closeness on the rumpled sheets of the tiny bed, Maria crooned that she had never been so happy before in all her days. Ki skillfully made her happier with a fingering trick taught to him by a no-longer-young geisha girl who liked young boys, when he'd been one. She gasped, "Pero no! I do not wish for to come all the way, this way!"

He said, soothingly, "Relax and enjoy life while you can. Who can say what may happen, should la patrona return. I think she may fire me. She keeps telling others she already has."

Maria protested, "Oh, no! For why would she wish for to do such a cruel thing to both of us?"

Ki sighed and said, "I don't know. Nothing she's said or done the past few days makes any sense. Are you sure she didn't tell you where she was going? The two of you must have exchanged at least a few words as you helped her pack, no?"

Maria kissed his bare chest and answered, "No. I did not help her do anything that day. She did not even let me brush her hair when she got out of her bath. I don't think she even took a bath. Not that morning. Not for many mornings before. I mean no disrespect to la patrona, she did use a lot of perfume toward the end, but there are limits to what

118

perfume can do for a woman who has not been bathing during a Texas heat wave.''

Ki grimaced. He saw no need to confide in the servants, but if he had he'd have been able to inform Maria that if there was one bad habit Jessie Starbuck had, it was an almost obsessive cleanliness, for an American girl, at any rate. Partly raised by Japanese help her late father had brought back from the Orient after picking up some bathing habits there, himself, Jessie not only bathed more often than most American girls of her era but insisted on a tub too hot for most to climb into. Even out in the field, where hot tubs were few and far between, Jessie never passed up a chance to take a nude dip in a prairie pond or icy mountain stream.

Ki didn't want to think about Jessie's naked body, washed or otherwise. By tacit agreement, it had long been established that there could be nothing of a carnal nature between the beautiful cattle queen and her faithful samurai, as Ki preferred to think of himself. For although the marriage of his high-born mother to a Yankee barbarian had forever made Ki an outcast from her warrior clan, the Japanese code of Bushido, or the chivalry of a Japanese aristocrat, had rubbed off on him, growing up in Dai Nippon as a poor relation nobody liked to talk about.

Privacy as Victorian Americans knew it simply didn't exist in the Orient because it couldn't. So samurai were trained not to notice when an indiscreetly ajar wall screen offered a glimpse of one's master or mistress enjoying a bath or perhaps someone they really weren't supposed to be doing that with. He smiled thinly as he recalled how even Jessie had been shocked the time he told her how servants avoided bursting in on the lady of the house when she was, let's say, instructing her gardner how to plant his root. Well-staffed Japanese mansions were provided with lots of peepholes. Everyone knew they were there, but, officially, they weren't. So when a house servant wanted to dust or straighten up any room in the joint, he or she peeked in before entering and naturally didn't enter if anyone

119

was up to anything naughty. There was never any gossip, because officially no mere servant would ever admit peeking. When Jessie had asked how come they didn't simply knock, he'd had a hard time explaining that, as his mother's people saw it, that would just lead to all kinds of embarrassment and even fibbing. What was the lady of the house to say, should someone knock on her screen while she was acting sort of bawdy while her husband was out chasing bawds? That she wasn't in there? That she was alone and didn't want to be disturbed by servants who usually scrubbed her back? Nice little Japanese children were taught not to lie, and never did, if they thought they'd be caught at it. It was much more comfortable for all concerned if they simply relied on those peepholes and nobody had to say anything about anything. Jessie had said it would make her feel mighty awkward to be in bed with even a husband, knowing someone might be watching her every move through a hole in her bedroom wall. Ki accepted that as only natural. She was, after all, not a true daughter of Dai Nippon.

Aware his mind was wandering into uncomfortable waters, Ki asked the girl he was in bed with to tell him more about the recent activities of their boss lady. Maria said, "In truth there is little more to say. I told you she had no overnight guests while you were away, and that none who dropped by in the daytime were strangers I had never seen before. She was alone every night and much of every day. I do not think she got much sleep. Every time I came for to wake her in the morning with her usual breakfast she was already up, pacing the floor. Sometimes she was as nice as ever. Other times she looked at me most strangely and asked who I was. It was most frightening when she acted that way. Her hair hung down over her eyes and she stared out so wildy from between its long blonde strands."

Ki muttered, "It doesn't make sense. She never took dope or even drank enough to worry about. Try it another way. Since we agree she wasn't acting like herself, how can you be sure it *was* herself?"

Maria asked what he meant by that. So Ki explained, "You only came to work here a few months ago. Meaning no insult to your own raza, Anglo Texans find it easy to confuse one Mexican, or one Oriental for that matter, with another. To you, one attractive Anglo girl with long blonde hair might look a lot like any other, even if she was neatly groomed instead of dirty and disheveled."

Maria gasped and demanded, "Are you saying I am estupido? Do you think I would mistake some mad impostor for my own patrona?"

Ki insisted, "It happens. What if she was only acting crazy, to keep you from getting near her? I know it sounds fantastic. But I find an impostor pretending to be Jessie Starbuck at least as sensible as the Jessie Starbuck I know suddenly turning into a dope fiend and trying to have me hung for murder!"

Maria agreed it sounded most strange, both ways. But then she spoiled it all by asking, "If the woman pacing that floor so many days and nights was not la patrona, then where could the real patrona have been all that time?"

Back at the drugstore, Longarm hadn't started to worry about that grim point, yet. Taking the house servants at their word, he simply assumed Jessie had been acting mighty queer of late and, thanks to Miss Doc, he could see how any gal could be off her feed, ingesting a mixture of hemlock and henbane any time at all. To clarify the exact effects of the barely sublethal mixture, he blew another thoughtful smoke ring and told the hot-natured lady druggist, "I want you to study some before you answer, Miss Doc. Despite your scientific detachment towards what we've been up to in recent memory, you do have your own religious notions, which can't be the same as them devil-worshipping old gals your church was so annoyed at. This pal of mine I'm worried about is neither a Roman Catholic nor a would-be witch. I ain't sure you could call her a Christian, in fact. I mean, she seems a nominal Protestant of some sort, but she might have been influenced a heap in her girlhood by the Oriental notions of her dad's servants and even her dad. The Starbucks came out to Texas before it was Texas, and getting in on the ground floor didn't hurt 'em none. Aside from cattle and cotton they got into clipper ships out of Galveston, Corpus Christi and other Texas ports. Trading between the Lone Star State and the Far East made Starbuck Enterprises sort of odd as well as rich. So we're talking about a gal who might have at least a lukewarm interest in both Christian and the three or more religions of the mysterious Orient.''

The warm-natured brunette began to take more than a mild interest in his semi-limp or semi-erect organ grinder, stroking it gently as she yawned and said, ''I don't see what difference that could make to anyone sort of sleepwalking about on hallucinogenic nonprescription drugs.''

He said, ''I asked you to study on it. Whatever was wrong with Miss Joan of Arc, she saw angels when she was having visions. The old crazy ladies who wanted the devil to make 'em young and pretty, or at least powerful, saw demons as Christians tend to imagine demons. This other gal has been raised on other mythology. I don't think Confucius ever mentioned angels or demons. The time they asked him about the hereafter he just shrugged and told 'em he was having enough time trying to figure out life and that he'd worry about death when he was in a better position to study it. The Taoists, as near as I can figure from Chinese I've talked to, talk so confused nobody can rightly say if they rate any angels or demons. Buddha never mentioned anything spooky, no more than Jesus did, but that didn't stop either Buddhists or Christians from coming up, later, with a whole mess of awfully spooky notions. Aside from dragons and fu dogs that look half lion and half dog, they got a real mess of mighty wild visions I'd sure hate to see, cold sober. As for what a gal full of henbane might or might not see staring out at her from dark corners, I've been pondering what they might tell her to do!''

Miss Doc began to twirl his dong between both palms,

like she thought it might be an infernal fire stick, saying, "I don't want her demons telling her to do this. I saw you first."

That, of course, was far from true and Longarm felt a pang of guilt as he considered what he was allowing another gal to do to him right in Jessie Starbuck's own county. He said, "You're twisting too hard, unless you're out to discourage me. I ain't worried about anyone getting horny. It's a free country. But I read someplace about folk being mesmerized, and how you can't get most folk to do anything in such a spell that they wouldn't do if they was awake. Them crazy old witch gals would have been mean-hearted and dirty minded when they started to screw the prince of darkness, a goat, or whatever. Miss Joan of Arc would have wanted angels to tell her how to whip the English, her being French and all. Do you see what I'm getting at?"

Miss Doc didn't answer. She likely thought it impolite to talk when her mouth was full. Longarm leaned back to enjoy it, as any man would have, but even as he let her his mind kept gnawing on the same bothersome bone. He couldn't see how Jessie, even possessed by a dozen devils, could accuse poor old Ki of trying to rape her. For anyone could see the poor half-breed was too cold-natured to mess with any women at all.

★

Chapter 7

Far to the north, in the club car of a Denver-bound express, two whiskey drummers were staring with interest at the stunning young blonde seated alone at a table across from their own. She seemed a little travel-worn in her wrinkled mauve duster, and most ladies kept their hair pinned up under a hat in public, instead of riding bareheaded with their hair down over their shoulders like that. There were wash-rooms attached to all the Pullman cars and the porter had just confirmed, for a nickel, that she was traveling alone in her own compartment. But she seemed content to just powder her pretty face ever more instead of washing it. One of the drummers confided to his pal, "I don't know, Saint Lou. She's mighty pretty, but a man has to consider his health on the road, and she don't look like she's had a bath in a month of Sundays."

The drummer working out of Saint Louis chuckled low and dirty before he half whispered, "She ain't no whore.

It just come to me who she is. That there gal is the one and original Jessica Starbuck of Starbuck Enterprises. I know because my outfit supplies the string of high-toned saloons she owns, personal. She owns all sorts of things, from clipper ships to cotton mills, and if she's wearing a whisper under that thin poplin duster I'm no judge of titties!''

His more cautious fellow traveler murmured, ''I noticed. Nice ass, as well. But why would such a rich and handsome gal be traipsing about half-bare-ass and stinky? Lord have mercy, I can smell her armpits clean over here!''

Saint Lou grinned dirty to reply, ''That ain't her armpits we both smell, and I admire a gal who keeps her crotch natural. I can always wash my old ring-dang-doo-rod clean as ever, after. She's drunk, of course. Looks like she's been soused for days. Trust a whiskey drummer to spot a heavy-drinking woman, and you've no idea how many times I've been next to one. Just watch me pick her up. Lord knows I'd never get next to anything that high-toned if she was sober. But she ain't. So here's my chance.''

The other drummer made a wry face and muttered, ''I dunno, it sounds sort of dirty, Saint Lou.''

But the would-be Romeo just chuckled and replied, ''Of course it's dirty. I like to get dirty with gals. What do you get dirty with, boys?''

With a smirk he rose, went to the bar, and told the barkeep to offer the little lady a drink, with his compliments. Then he sat back down with the other drummer, saying, ''You learn how to be smooth working out of the big city.''

A few minutes later the barkeep sent a colored waiter over with the drink to the sort of sullen-looking beauty. She looked at the glass as if it were filled with live bait. Then she glanced across at the drummers as if they were wriggle worms, too, when the attendant explained where the free drink had come from. She curled her upper lip in a way to make at least one of the whiskey drummers sure he never wanted to kiss her. Then she got to her feet and flounced out. But when the one drummer laughed, Saint Lou said,

"She's just being delicate. Can't you read an invite when you see one?"

As he rose to follow, his fellow traveler warned, "If that was an invite I'd sure hate to see her refusal. I'd pass, if I was you, Saint Lou. You can't win 'em all and that's one mean gal."

But Saint Lou was already on his way, knowing he had to catch Jessie before she could make it back to her compartment if he meant to catch her at all. There was nothing like a little kiss to soften a gal *before* she could slam a damned door in one's face. So he was moving fast as he stepped out on the open platform between cars. Then something chopped the side of his neck, just under his left ear, and as the starry night closed in about him, Saint Lou felt himself lifted from the platform by the back of his jacket and seat of his pants. He just managed to moan, "No! Don't throw me off!" before he was thrown not off but down the narrow slot between cars to land on his head and enjoy the small mercy of complete unconsciousness before the wheels chewed him into bloody sausage slices.

A few moments later, as a Pullman porter was passing one of the compartment doors, the door slid open and a feminine voice called out, "George? Come in here for a moment, won't you?"

The middle-aged gentleman of color was not named George, but he knew white folk seemed to think all porters were, so he began to join the white lady in her compartment. Then he froze in the doorway when he noticed she was not only young and pretty but had tossed her travel duster aside to stand there scandalous in her mighty short shimmy shirt!

The porter gulped and asked, "Is there anything I can do for you, Miss Starbuck?" She replied, matter-of-factly, "Yes. This train won't reach Denver in less than an hour and I feel sort of passionate. Come in and shut the door, George. I've always wondered what it would be like to fuck a darkie."

The porter turned and ran for his life. He was almost fifty

years old and he felt he owed getting that old, at least partly, to the fact that he'd never messed with white women. He'd only been liberated after reaching the age of thirty-five as a house servant, and that crazy lady back there came from *Texas*!

He ran the length of two cars before the white conductor stopped him, asking, "What's got in to you, Jim? You look as if you just seen a ghost and it's still broad daylight."

The rattled porter gasped, "I ain't half as scared of haunts as I am crazy white ladies! You know I wouldn't mess with no passenger lady of any color, don't you, Cap'n?"

The conductor soothed, "Why sure I do. You've been working this line a good ten years and nobody's ever had a bad word to say about you, Jim. Calm down and tell me who you think might be crazy, for land's sake."

Jim hesitated, knowing he could be in for it either way. But he knew the conductor had served with the Union and treated colored folk fairly. So he said, "I swears to God I was never alone with her one minute, Cap'n. If she accuses me of messing with her she's just out to spite me cruel for some reason."

The conductor's eyes narrowed thoughtfully as he asked, quietly, "Are you saying some white woman aboard this train tried to mess with *you*? Who was it? She's getting off at the next jerkwater. It ain't that I don't respect you, Jim, but you know the rules on miscegenation as well as I do, right?"

Jim nodded and said, "I surely do, Cap'n. Even if I didn't, I got my own sweet Cindy May waiting for me in Denver. I mind there was this high yellow boy back home who messed with a trash-white gal one time, and she was *willing*. I seen him after the Klan was done with him. It was awful."

The conductor said, "Never mind all that. Who was the white woman on this train who flirted with you?"

"That Miss Jessica Starbuck in Compartment H. Only

127

she didn't flirt with me. She asked me right out to *fuck* her!''

The conductor blanched. He started to accuse Jim of being drunk, crazy, or both. But he knew his crew. Jim had never lied to him yet. He decided, "We'd best forget all about it, then. I feel sure it was all some sort of mistake and, even if it wasn't, this child ain't about to take on a lady with a controlling interest in this here railroad!"

Jim asked, in that case, what he was supposed to do the next time Miss Jessica Starbuck asked him to fuck her. The conductor laughed despite himself and said, "I reckon you'd *have* to. But I have a better idea. You go on up to the dining car and steady your nerves with some coffee. We can get by without Pullman service, or any other kind of service, between here and Denver. We'll be there within the hour and, all in all, I feel it's best if we just let Miss Starbuck detrain and go fuck anyone she aims to, as long as it's not on railroad property, hear?"

So that was how they worked it out, and if the oddly dressed blonde noticed railroad employees whispering about her as she strode through the Union Depot in Denver bold as brass with a six-gun on her hip and a silver star in her Stetson, she didn't seem to give a damn.

Female or not, Jessie Starbuck made for an imposing if not downright powerful image in her Justin boots, split riding skirt, and wicked weaponry. Henry, the sort of prissy young gent who played the typewriter in the front office of Marshal Billy Vail, knew this. But what surprised him most when the wild-eyed gal barged in on him was the silvery steel star that went buzzsawing past his right ear, close, to thunk into the oaken door of Vail's inner sanctum, deep, as she shouted, "Howdy, Henry. If Longarm's not here I reckon I'll settle for my Uncle Billy!"

Henry gulped, tore his gaze from the wicked ninja weapon stuck in the marshal's door, and said, "Longarm's out in the field, Miss Jessica. I thought you knew that. He went to Sanderson to straighten out that misunderstanding with your Oriental segundo. Then he headed for your place. We just got a wire in from him that says so."

"Damn. Just my luck. Nobody fucks like that big moose and I'm not home! What about your boss, Henry?"

The clerk gulped again and replied, "Marshal Vail just left for the day, Miss Jessica. Is there anything I could do for you?"

She looked him up and down, thoughtfully, before she decided, "Well, you're a mite puny, but it might help your pimples if I made you come a heap. Let's go in the back and get down and dirty on Uncle Billy's chesterfield!"

Henry gasped, and his voice cracked as he asked her, "Are you . . . all right, Miss Jessica? No offense but you look sort of, ah, ill?"

She insisted, "There's nothing wrong with me that a good fuck wouldn't cure. What's the matter, Henry? Don't you like gals?"

Henry's confusion began to give way to indignation at the taunt to his manhood. He knew he looked sort of sissy. In school the bigger boys had called him a queer and thrown his hat up on the roof as often as they could. They'd have no doubt thrown it up there more often if he hadn't learned to just bunch up his puny fists and wade in, getting the shit kicked out of him a few times before they decided, as his dad had told him they might, that it was more fun to pick on puny boys who never fought back.

He said, "I reckon I can handle women good as most, Miss Jessica. I reckon I could show you a thing or two on that old leather chesterfield, if I was sure the boss wouldn't be back and . . . Ah, you sure smell funny, no offense. Are you sure you ain't sick?"

She laughed, wild and sort of frighteningly. Then she shrugged and said, "Aw, you wouldn't have much to offer if you did manage to get it up, and I haven't time to waste on pimple-faced pansies. I'm bound for the Peace River, to do right by a skunk who done me wrong. I was hoping to

129

find Longarm here and take him along. For we make one hell of a team, in or out of a bedroll. But, shit, if he's in Texas, I'll just have to forge on alone. It's been nice talking to you, Henry. Next time you kiss a cavalry trooper, give him my regards as well!''

Henry protested, ''Wait, Miss Jessica! You can't go off to Canada without even saying why! Both Longarm and Marshal Vail want a few words with you!''

But she was already gone. Henry started to get up and chase after her, then he noticed that steel star still stuck in Billy Vail's door and remembered she was packing a six-gun as well. Henry was a lot braver than he looked, but not that brave. He'd been opening the many wires coming in about that Starbuck gal, and she'd just now convinced him she had to be in a mighty strange mood.

He went back to his typing. Just as the wall clock told him it was about time to quit for the day, Marshal Billy Vail grumped in on his stubby legs, muttering, ''Forgot that fool wire from the Texas Rangers.'' Then the short, stout, middle-aged lawman spotted what was sticking in his door, turned to Henry with a puzzled scowl, and demanded, ''Has that crazy Ki been paying us a visit?''

''No, sir. It was the lady he rides for, Jessica Starbuck. I don't know why she flung that thing past my poor head. She wasn't making much sense. She said something about heading for the Peace River, with Longarm. Only he's at her home spread in Texas, right?''

Vail scowled harder. Neither Henry nor Longarm had ever been able to fathom how, no matter how hard he was already scowling, their boss could always manage to look even more pissed off. Vail said, ''That just plain makes no sense, Henry. I know Canadian stockmen have commenced to graze the Peace River range of late, but Starbuck Enterprises don't have no beef up yonder. Didn't she say how come she had to go up yonder?''

Henry shook his head and replied, ''No, sir. She wasn't

making any sense. If I told you half the things she said you'd think *I* was drunk, too.''

"You say she looked *drunk*, Henry?'' Vail asked with a more puzzled than angry scowl as he moved over to pluck the ninja weapon from his door panel. It didn't pluck easy. Vail was glad it wasn't stuck in his skull as Henry said, "She sure looked and acted drunk, sir. Rolling-in-the-gutter-full-of-pulque drunk, if you ask me. Her hair was all stringy and she smelled as if she'd been herding codfish clean from Texas, even if she was all smeared with perfume and face paint.''

Vail grimaced at the picture and said, "What Longarm wired about her being on dope, whether on purpose or otherwise, must be right, then. I'll send him a night letter bringing him up to date. Meanwhile, do you recall that Canadian mounty that Longarm gets along with better than most?''

Henry nodded and said, "Crown Sergeant Foster, up at Fort MacLeod. But wouldn't it be easier to stop her here in Denver before she leaves?''

Vail stared soberly down at the wickedly sharp throwing star in his pudgy palm as he grunted, "On what charge? She's always been a determined young lady, even with her head screwed on correct. It sounds safer to wire Fort MacLeod and let the mounties know she's headed their way, likely without a permit to cross their border. The MacDonald Administration up that way don't get along with us too well, and they've been mighty proddy about their fool border since the Red River breeds have been acting up. We'll warn Sergeant Foster our sweet little Jessie might be sort of loco en la cabeza. Foster's an old pro. He'll ask her why she wants to invade his country, and if that don't work he knows how to take folk gentle. If Longarm's right about them pills she's been taking we got to get her off 'em, pronto. I can't see her swallowing none in the guardhouse at Fort MacLeod. By the time I get Longarm up yonder to take her off Canada's hands, she might be making a heap more sense.''

Henry nodded, but asked, "What charge can Longarm use to extradite her from Canada, sir?"

"Hell, I just told you Longarm and Sergeant Foster was pals. If push comes to shove we can always charge her with giving false information to the law, and then drop it once she's safely home and making some sense. You know how to handle the wire to the Mounties. I got to go over that message from the Rangers some more and see how much I ought to wire Longarm. I'd best just tell him to get in contact with the Ranger post at Galveston and the hell with it."

Henry blinked and asked, "How did Galveston get into this odd case? I mean, if Miss Starbuck's headed for Canada, and our Longarm is at her Texas spread—"

"Jessie must have passed through Galveston on her way up this way," Vail cut in. "I know it's out of her way, but we've all agreed she hasn't been making all that much sense. One of the Starbuck steamers just put in at Galveston with a load of tea and silk and such from Nagasaki. According to a mighty confused sea captain, Jessie Starbuck ordered him to take it out in the gulf a ways and throw it all overboard. When he told her she was instructing him mighty strange, she kicked him in the balls and stomped him silly. When he woke up he reported it to the law. They say he'll live. But the Rangers would still like to hear her side of the story." He looked away, muttering, "Poor little gal. I wonder if she even knows she did it."

Night letters were Western Union's pragmatic answer to folk cussing about their nickel-a-word day rates and threatening to spring for a two-cent stamp. Direct wires naturally went direct as possible. If you could hold your horses Western Union would send a lot more for you, a lot cheaper, late at night when their business was slow and their wires were still up, anyway. Night letters got there when they got there. They were still a lot faster than the U.S. Mail and, as luck would have it, it was a slow weeknight and the Western Union delivery rider overtook Longarm on the wagon trace out to the Starbuck spread. Being no fool and knowing the trail led nowhere else, the delivery rider hailed Longarm in the moonlight to ask if he might be headed out to the Circle Star. When Longarm allowed he was, the Western Union man told him he had a delivery for a Deputy Long, care of Miss Jessica Starbuck, and got a dime tip as well as a shorter ride out of being so smart.

Longarm couldn't read Vail's night letter in the saddle. The moon wasn't that bright. He stuffed it in a coat pocket and rode on, too morose to lope his mount. He'd run out of notions regarding Jessie or that drugstore gal and he was feeling sort of blue about behaving that way, now that Miss Doc had sated him considerable. The sneaky little brunette had tricked him that afternoon. When he'd said he just had to get it on down the road she'd agreed she had to open her shop again in case anyone needed cough medicine or liver pills. Then she'd suggested he catch just a few winks before risking sunstroke in the full strength of a Texas afternoon and he, like a fool, had gone for it, only to wake up after dark with Miss Doc on top and the shop closed for the night. In the end he'd had to sneak his pony out of that nice old couple's carriage house, like a thief in the night, and he'd wanted to hand the lady of the house some chocolates, at least, by way of thanks.

So here it was, pushing midnight, and him feeling like a low-down dirty dog. It wasn't that he'd taken a favor without even offering a proper thanks, and it wasn't that he'd been messing with another gal behind Jessie's back. They'd long since settled that they were both young and healthy and that just because they could never get hitched was no call to moon about it celibate. Meeting up with Miss Doc should have been every man's daydream come true. A no-strings roll in the feathers with a natural gal who just loved to roll in the feathers with men and made no demands on the same. But he'd have enjoyed it more, he knew, if all the time he'd been making love to Miss Doc his mind hadn't kept wandering back to a prettier gal, and greater lay, he was really

133

worried about. He'd given up trying to tell himself it was only her looks and the way she could move 'em that made him pine for Jessica Starbuck at the damdest times. Longarm was a man who preferred to face up to facts, no matter how grim they might be. So he was willing to admit that someday he was going to die, and that like it or not he was in love with that infernal Jessie. It felt better thinking about dying, someday. He'd come to terms with that by deciding death couldn't hurt him, either way. If there was anything after death, like the Good Book promised, he figured to be pleasantly surprised. If there was nothing at all, once you were dead, well, you wouldn't know you were dead when it happened, so why be scared of nothing?

Being in love, though, was a real pain in the ass. For you didn't get to go on to something better and the feeling was still there, even with your eyes shut tight and even in the arms of another. A couple in love had to either give in and marry up or just settle for feeling frustrated and miserable until they up and died or managed to get sore at one another.

He didn't want Jessie to die. That had happened to poor old Roping Sally and it had hurt like hell, even though he hadn't been as much in love with her as he was with Jessie. They hadn't had near as much time together. Maybe that had been a good thing, in the end. For with most gals, a man loved 'em less as time passed by. The bitter joke attached to the term "honeymoon" was that most gals did start to get on a man's nerves after just about a month, as many a married man had no doubt discovered to his chagrin. Any decent-looking gal was just grand, at first, and if a man wasn't mighty careful he could be trapped for a fool by soft words and hot bouncing. Women had some sort of union rules that denied them the right to say they had a headache or demand a man change his habits and get a better job before they'd been awfully nice to him a month or more. It was when you'd spent that month or more with a sweet loving gal that you knew it was the real thing.

He muttered aloud in the moonlight, "Damn it, Jessie. If I told you once I told you a thousand times that I like my job and that it's all I know. It would never work out if I made a settled woman of you. You'd either wind up fretting as I rode off after owlhoots, knowing we didn't really need the money, or, even worse, you'd wind up a widow gal, hating me for getting killed when you'd told me over and over I didn't have to!"

The other alternative was just as unthinkable. He knew his own restless nature too well. It would only take him a year or so as a rich gal's lap dog before he took to snapping. He'd spent some time with rich gals, even before he'd met Jessie. Lazing about with all the good food and drink one might want, along with a willing woman at one's beck and call, sounded a heap better than it really felt. To take his mind off the temptations of here and now he let his mind wander to that sort of honeymoon up to Bitter Creek with the lovely Kim Stover, and when that wore thin he asked himself if that society gal he'd spent that time with back East had married up by now, and with whom. It just made him want to bust the no doubt prissy dude's head. He laughed at his own jealousy, knowing how unfair it was. He still didn't ever want to catch Jessie or even old Kim in bed with another gent. The one time he'd told Jessie that she'd laughed and accused him of having a double standard. He'd said he didn't care. Bees were supposed to buzz from pretty posie to pretty posie. The other way around sounded wanton. She'd assured him he'd never catch her buzzing from bee to bee, at least while he was around, and they'd sure had fun making up that night.

As he rode into the dooryard of the Starbuck spread a fool dog started yapping and a Mex kid came out to take care of his mount for him. So he wasn't surprised to find Ki waiting for him in the parlor, buttoning up his pants. Longarm asked the big Amerasian if he'd gotten him out of bed. Ki shrugged and said, "I wasn't asleep." So Longarm took out the night letter and sat down by a coal-oil lamp to read it. Once he had he sighed and handed the message to Ki. As the segundo scanned it, Longarm got out a cheroot and lit up. Ki sat on a sofa across the cold fireplace from him, looking sort of sick. He said, "This is just insane, Custis. Starbuck Enterprises has nothing brewing up on the Peace River range."

Longarm said, "I had them pills assayed in town. The druggist tells me Jessie's been taking hemlock and henbane. Either can drive you crazy, if they don't kill you outright. How do you like that sea captain in Galveston getting kicked in the nuts?"

"I don't even understand it. Captain Wilson has been working for Jessie for years. He's trustworthy as George Washington and Jessie knows it. Why on earth would she want him to jettison valuable cargo in the gulf? It makes no sense at all!"

Longarm nodded soberly, blew smoke out his nostrils like an annoyed bull, and said, "I wish you'd pay attention. I just told you she's been taking crazy pills. As I understand it, henbane makes you see things or maybe suspect things that just ain't there. So Lord knows what Jessie might have thought that poor old skipper had brung home from Japan. *I* wouldn't want anyone unloading a cargo of mad dogs or even puppy-dog tails on the Galveston docks, would you?"

Ki frowned thoughtfully and asked what hemlock did to one's mind. Longarm frowned back and said, "I'm still working on that and I just can't get it to work. Unless the druggist I spent all that time with is lying, and I fail to see why, hemlock just plain numbs you to death."

"I don't see what's so confusing, then," Ki said. "Obviously Jessie was given poison by some person or persons unknown. I've questioned all the servants who could have possibly been anywhere near Jessie's medicine cabinet. Their stories match up and none of them have any logical reason to murder such a fine employer. It's not easy for a Mexican or Oriental to get a decent job in this part of Texas. They certainly don't stand to inherit any part of her estate.

136

I've read the Starbuck legacy. Nobody without the combination to Jessie's office safe could have.''

"There you go," Longarm said. "Somebody dabbling in herbal witchcraft could figure anything might happen if they poisoned la patrona. Only I don't buy anyone with a Mex or Far Eastern background switching pills on her. Henbane and hemlock don't grow in *their* old countries. It's the infernal mixture I just can't fathom, damn it!''

Ki asked why, pointing out the mixture seemed lethal enough to him. But Longarm insisted, "If they wanted her dead, why did they feed her henbane instead of just more hemlock? The druggist told me hemlock kills gentle and pronto. Most American doctors could hardly know much about such an exotic herb. Had the maid just come in one morning to find Jessie stone-cold dead, that would be that. So why did they put in that henbane to drive her loco? I mean, along with the other stuff. They could have drove her even crazier by feeding her henbane alone, see?''

Ki shrugged and said, "Well, I'm glad to know she was not in her right mind when she tried to have me hung. We'd better get on up to Canada and make her stop taking those pills, right?''

Longarm shook his head and said, "Not hardly. Billy Vail was mighty slick to wire ahead to Fort MacLeod. I know Crown Sergeant Foster of old and he's slick, too. The first time we met we was fighting over a prisoner. Since then we've ridden on the same side. Either way, Foster always gets his man, or woman, in this case. Jessie won't get past Foster if he's between her and the Peace River, expecting her. If she's really headed Foster's way he'll have caught her and taken away them pills before we could ever hope to catch up with her. So I vote we head for Galveston.''

"What for? She just passed through Denver on her way to Canada, damn it!''

Longarm nodded and said, "I know. You said Starbuck Enterprises has no serious business interests up yonder. Don't Jessie own a heap of Galveston?''

"Certainly, but if she's not there—"

"Somebody *else* might be," Longarm cut in. "Unless we assume Jessie was out to poison herself, which hardly seems likely, she was poisoned by somebody else and, like the French say, search for the gal, and if that don't work, search for the *money*. Unless the skunk behind all this is just plain loco, he, she or it has to be out to rob our Jessie, and they likely know as well as we do that she ain't in Galveston right now!"

Ki objected, "Neither is a substantial part of her money. As you know, her father was a canny cash-and-carry businessman of the old school. So much of the trouble Jessie inherited along with Starbuck Enterprises was a lot of tempting cash on the barrelhead, along with a portable fortune on the hoof or floating on sea water. But old Alex Starbuck educated his only child in bookkeeping as well as the fighting skills he'd used to build up Starbuck Enterprises, and we live in changing times."

"Get to the point," Longarm prompted.

Ki explained, "She's surpassed old Alex as a canny businesswoman. Money that's tied up is not only harder to steal, it draws interest. Her trading vessels out of Galveston and Corpus Christi are insured to begin with, and title to them is tied up in holding companies. I don't know all the details, but I know she's taken business loans, putting up her herds and other business interests as security, then reinvested the money in a way to really shuffle the deck. Old Alex was killed by that big European cartel that hoped to just pick up the pieces from what they took to be a single, weak and feminine heir. With the help of friends like you and me Jessie showed them what a dreadful mistake they'd made. But it does get tiresome playing King of the Hill against all comers atop a pile of ready cash, so—"

"She's made sure the cash ain't all that *ready*," Longarm cut in with an understanding nod. "I ain't sure how it works, neither, but I know other rich folk and they seem to agree money is best kept working for you than under the mattress.

138

I can see how tough it might be to peddle beef or cotton that a herd of big-shot bankers had a business lien on. I don't know where I'd sail a ship that was owned on paper by a complicated holding company, either. I always said Jessie was smart. She's set things up so nobody can just bump her off the catbird seat and take over her business empire. They'd have to get her, or someone who could pass for her and sign her name in front of a heap of witnesses to even fake a bill of sale for one cow!"

Ki nodded and said, "That was why we were herding those brood cows to the Chisum spread with no bills of sale. She'd sent the legal forms to be notarized by her law firm and forwarded to Chisum's bookkeeper. Big John is getting hard to steal from too of late. As I just said, we live in changing times. The bad old days of grab and git are fading fast."

Longarm smiled thinly and said, "I've been running into enough grab and gitters to keep myself busy, but I follow your drift. So let's study on how someone might still feel tempted. I have noticed in my six or eight years as a lawman that some crooks just can't seem to resist a challenge. As fast as Yale comes out with a new lock or Mosler invents a new safe, some sly-faced son of a bitch sits down with pencil and paper to figure a way to bust in. I don't need a pencil to point out the weak link in Jessie's paper chain of signing, co-signing and such. No matter how she's set things up, she has to be able to get at quick cash, herself, should she really need it. Have you forgotten that gal the cartel recruited that time to act as Jessie's double?"

Ki grimaced and replied, "How could I? She almost got the three of us killed. It was one of the first things I considered when Jessie began to behave so oddly. The house servants, here, all agree it was Jessie, acting odd indeed, before she lit out for Canada full of funny pills."

"By way of Galveston, where she acted even odder," Longarm pointed out. "That other gal who pretended to be

139

Jessie acting odd, that time, was accepted as the real McCoy by lots of folk."

Ki nodded but said, "She wasn't an exact double, and they had to go all the way to England to recruit and coach a girl who came at all close. Jessie is a striking beauty, and even *ugly* green-eyed blondes are rare. The plot was too wild to work the first time anyone came up with it, and we taught them that, to their everlasting sorrow."

Longarm shrugged and said, "I don't know how sorrowful dead folk feel. I do know they did find a double for Jessie, once, and I do know the Jessie Starbuck I know ain't evil, even if she's sick in the head from poison. I never knew her to take patent medicine to begin with, come to study on it."

"Her maid, Maria, saw her take pills from that blue bottle just before bedtime," Ki insisted. "Give me credit for at least as much imagination and, well, almost as much knowledge of her personal habits. I knew she wasn't behaving as herself before you did. There's nothing like a few nights in jail to concentrate one's mind. So, sure, it occurred to me at once that someone might be playing If-you-don't-succeed-at-once. But we more than proved that time they tried to send in a ringer for Jessie that it just won't work! It caused us trouble, true enough, but as you pointed out yourself, the plot was too full of holes to work."

Longarm stared into the cold fireplace, musing, half to himself, "I know. I'm trying to figure how a really smart plotter might have stopped up the holes. The first dumb thing they done that other time was have that gal who looked like Jessie lead a gang of bank robbers. Not even the Rangers could figure, once they calmed down, why in thunder a lady with millions in the bank would want to rob any bank to begin with. The real Jessie could have just *bought* some of them country banks she was supposed to be holding up. When I pointed out to Jessie later that they'd have just murdered her and slipped her double in her place, if they'd had a lick of sense, it was Jessie who pointed out why that wouldn't have worked. Aside from the fact that any number of old retainers, like you and me, might have seen through the resemblance, the odds on finding a double who not only looks like a gal but happens to be skilled enough at forgery to sign heaps of business papers for her, with honest employees watching, are just plain astronomical.''

Ki nodded and said, ''I always felt sort of sorry for that poor barmaid they found and trained, then trained some more to pass for Jessie at a glance. There isn't any way to plug up the holes in such a wild plot. Even if the girl who kicked poor Captain Wilson in the groin was someone other than Jessie, and even if they've done something to the real Jessie I just don't want to think about, it's not going to work. There's simply no way on earth anyone but Jessie Starbuck, sane and sober or crazy as a loon, can transfer funds worth mention. They'd be just as well off if they simply murdered her and contested her estate, for example.''

''Not with me investigating said murder,'' Longarm growled ominously. Then he said, ''I've been wondering about that, too. The druggist I, ah, talked to, told me them pills should have done in anyone who took 'em. Jessie must be even stronger than we thought, and I never figured her for a sissy. We'd best get on down to Galveston and see who gets a slice of the pie if Jessie should wind up poisoned entire!''

★

Chapter 8

The Texas seaport of Galveston was laid out skinny on an offshore barrier island of sand that might have shifted more if it wasn't sort of nailed down with sea walls, docks and such. It was named after a former Spanish governor, and formed the main port of call for ships doing business in and out of Houston. They kept jawing about a shipping channel to let seagoing ships put into Houston more direct, for anyone could see Galveston figured to be swept away by the restless waters of the Gulf one of these days. But in the meantime, Texas made do with the sandbar town of modest dimensions and wide-open manners. Longarm had never been to Port Said or Singapore, but he was willing to accept as fact that Galveston was just as wild. He'd been there after dark before and had the grim memories to prove it.

It was broad day when Longarm and Ki crossed the lagoon to get out to the Texas version of Port Said, so, knowing they faced more talking in circles than anything else until they might stumble over a lead, they split up to tend to chores each might be better at. Ki was to interview business associates of Starbuck Enterprises on the island while Longarm checked with the law and scouted for witnesses to the attack on Wilson along the waterfront. They agreed to meet at the hospital just after sundown so they could talk to Wilson, together, during the evening visiting hours.

Galveston had its own police force as well as a Ranger station. Starting at the top, Longarm discovered the Rangers were mighty vexed with Miss Jessica Starbuck, knowing she'd acted sort of wild in the past, but that they'd gotten their recent charges against her secondhand. The local waterfront police had responded when old Captain Wilson had wound up down in the hold with his nuts all swollen. So Longarm reminded the Rangers it hadn't really been Jessie robbing banks that time, and went to see what the Galveston P.D. had to say about it.

The desk sergeant sent him back to the squad room to jaw with some plainclothesmen. They were even madder at Jessie than the Rangers. For when they'd first gotten word of the attack and been given the I.D. and description of said attacker, they'd of course tried to seal off all routes to the mainland. But to no avail. One of the Galveston lawmen opined Miss Starbuck had to be hiding out somewhere on the island. It was bigger by far than the town itself, and there were all sorts of palmetto jungles a crazy lady could hide out in, even if no whorehouse would have her.

Longarm snubbed out the last of a cheroot with an expression of finality, and told them, "Whatever her present state of mind, the last report I got on her from my Denver office puts her way up yonder, throwing shurikens at our typewriter player."

He saw how blankly that inspired them to stare back and told them, "I never heard of a shuriken before I met up with her, neither. Miss Jessie was raised sort of odd by her dad and some Oriental servants he brought back from Japan to the Circle Star. She got to play with funny toys as a little kid. A shuriken looks like a big spur rowel, and you ought to see how she can wing one at someone she don't like. She must not have been really mad at old Henry. He says she missed his head by at least an inch. She left it stuck in Marshal Vail's door. I hope it was the only one she had on her.''

The chief detective growled, ''We've established the gal is lethal. She turned on poor Captain Wilson like a mad dog!''

But Longarm said, ''I doubt she was really out to kill him. If she had been, he'd be dead. She was likely just fooling around with him, like she was with our clerk in Denver, only she don't know her own strength right now. Somebody poisoned her with pills that make her act a might queer in the head, see?''

Another Galveston dick said, ''That's for damned sure. But we're much obliged to you for telling us we can call in the dragnet for her here. None of our boys was looking forward to encountering a crazy lady with a six-gun. How come they let her get away in Denver?''

Longarm shrugged and said, ''You just said yourselves she moves unpredictable. She may be headed for the Peace River range. If she is, I'm expecting a wire any time now from the Mounties. A crown sergeant I know up yonder is more used to dealing with sudden moves than our clerk-typist. Did anybody see which way she went after she kicked her own skipper into the hold?''

The chief detective shook his head and said, ''No. The crew on board said it was over before anyone noticed she was having an argument with her skipper on the well deck. Our uniformed men naturally canvassed the neighborhood, if that's what you'd like to call a rabbits' warren of warehouses, gin mills and worse near the docks. Nobody saw nothing. They never do. It does seem sort of odd, though, that a pretty gal dressed so cow could get past so many hard-up seamen without even one noticing.''

Longarm shrugged and said, "She grew up playing hide-and-seek with an older playmate trained in ninja scouting. A ninja is a sort of Japanese sneak, half armed retainer and half cat burglar. They both run across rooftops a lot at night when they don't want others to notice 'em. She must have sensed she'd been a mite naughty and lit out discreet."

Another local lawman said, "We've heard she hangs out with a mysterious Oriental. Do you reckon he could be with her, backing her mad play?"

Longarm shook his head and said, "Nope. He's with me, backing mine. Her segundo, Ki, is as worried about her as the rest of us. You might spread the word he's all right. I wouldn't want any of your boys needlessly bent out of shape."

They shook on it and Longarm tried the U.S. Customs House next. He started to explain his problem to an old gent in an airy office overlooking the docks. The customs agent headed him off by saying, "We know all about the incident. The attack is a Texas matter. We're only interested in the cargo manifests of ships putting in from foreign ports."

Longarm asked what they could tell him about the cargo old Captain Wilson had gotten into such an argument with Jessie over. The customs agent shrugged and said, "I don't have a complete copy of the manifest here. But I recall it well, for we naturally went over that Starbuck steamer with a fine-tooth comb when we heard the owner had beaten up the skipper."

"And?" asked Longarm.

"And everything was in proper order," the customs agent assured him. "We checked the contents of each cargo net as it was swung to the dock. The tea they unloaded matched the tea on the manifest, to the leaf. We made them unroll the bolts of silk, knowing how smugglers like to roll things up in such a handy hiding place. There was some novelty chinaware, cute but inexpensive and, oh, right, a couple of gross of Japanese paper parasols, very popular with Texas belles in summertime. We even patted down the crew as they came ashore. Nothing. There was simply no sane reason for the owner to order the skipper to jettison such an innocuous cargo. There was nothing at all dangerous aboard. It was all stuff Starbuck Enterprises has been dealing in for years.''

Longarm nodded and said, ''Her segundo tells me Captain Wilson sailed for Alex Starbuck years ago on the bridge of an all-sail clipper. He must have found her order sort of confusing. I'd like to talk to some of his crew. Could you aim me at their ship, sir?''

The customs agent shook his head and said, ''I fear you got here just too late, Deputy Long. The S.S. *Jessica* put out to sea for Hilo and points east on the tide before last, carrying Texas cotton, hides, bonemeal and canned goods. A vessel makes no money for its owner in port.''

Longarm frowned thoughtfully and said, ''I can see that. But its owner didn't seem to want it in port to begin with, and who might be in command if the skipper's in the hospital?''

The customs agent replied, ''First Mate Cunningham is on the bridge right now, with the blessings of the Starbuck shipping agency here in Galveston. Before you ask, Cunningham's an old salt who's been with the company for years. Fine seaman. I know him personally.''

Longarm didn't follow up on that. He knew Ki would be a better judge of his fellow employees, and they'd be meeting soon enough to compare notes. There was no sense questioning the customs agent on the honesty of Jessie's shipping agents here in Galveston. If U.S. Customs thought they were crooks, they'd have said so long before now.

Back down on the street again, he saw the sky out over the Gulf was turning brassy, which meant they were either going to enjoy a hurricane or a sunset any time now. But it was still way too early to meet Ki at the hospital, so he went scouting for some supper while he had the time.

The customs house had been neatly whitewashed, of course, but most of the buildings this close to the docks seemed a mite disgusting. He didn't want to get sick on strange grub in a strange town. He knew unwisely prepared seafood could get a man sicker than trusting the cream in a border-town café. But he didn't get a crack at fresh-caught snapper and such in Denver, and the salt air off the Gulf had inspired a craving for something more fishy than chili con carne. So he asked an old coot in a doorway if there was a seafood joint in the neighborhood it was safe to eat in. The old coot advised him to try the Jolly Roger on the far side of the block, saying it was a swell place that served entertainment as well. So that was where Longarm went for supper.

It was sort of gloomy, rather than jolly, inside. But he didn't want to go through all that again, so he sat down at a corner table, and when a bored-looking but otherwise pretty waitress advised him to try the seafood sampler special if he didn't know much about fishing he said that sounded swell as long as he got a schooner of beer with it.

As he lit a cheroot and leaned back, waiting for his order, a piano started up in the smoke-filled gloom and someone lit a limelight to beam it on a bitty stage he hadn't noticed up to now. A funny-looking little squirt in baggy pants stepped into the limelight and commenced to tell jokes that weren't funny. They were just dirty. The other patrons laughed at them, though. Longarm could see better, now. Everyone at the other tables looked more oceanic than cow. The comic went into a really disgusting tale about a traveling salesman that Longarm hadn't enjoyed the first time he'd heard it, in Dodge, maybe ten years or more ago. He was tempted to try somewhere else. Longarm enjoyed a *funny* dirty joke as well as the next man, but the notion of eating food with someone talking about pulling hairs out of an old man's asshole just didn't sound at all appetizing.

But then the waitress brought his beer and seafood sampler, and both smelled grand. So, seeing he'd have to pay no matter what, he dug in. The food was decent enough, so he tried to pay no attention to the dirty show across the way.

Until they brought out the gals, that is. That part of the show was even dirtier. But Longarm was no prude and it was fun to watch nice-looking gals dance hootchy-kootchy as one chawed breaded shrimp, oysters, and Lord only knew what, washing it down with mighty fine draft. Anyone could see the law in Galveston turned a blind eye on such forms of entertainment as the show kept getting worse, or better, depending on how much bare female skin a man liked to look at. The gals kept shedding stuff as they danced ever more bawdy. He wondered just how far they'd be able to go before somebody called the law. When all the sailors assembled let out a whoop of delight at the sight of naked titties bouncing literally abreast, Longarm ordered dessert. It seemed sissy to leave just as they were working themselves down to nothing at all. He knew they'd likely put out the limelight just as the gals dropped their last shreds of modesty, but he knew he'd wonder, later, whether they had or had not, for certain. So he dallied over his lemon pie, and just as he was sure they meant to show no more of their charms, the piano got louder and they did.

It was sort of a letdown to see five gals let down their drawers all at once, seeing as you couldn't do a thing about it. So after he decided the sassy brunette second from the right was the one he'd want if there was any way to have any of 'em, he asked for his tab, left a dime on the table for the waitress, and left.

He swore softly when he got back outside, for he'd told Ki he'd be at the hospital around sunset and the sun had already gone and set, thanks to that last infernal slice of pie and sassy brunette. There was nothing he could do about it now but get on over to meet Ki and say he'd been held up by dropping drawers, cuss his curious nature.

He knew that the hospital, like most everything else of importance in the skinny city, lay fairly close to the waterfront. So he legged it along the cobblestone quay in the gathering darkness, more intent on making up the lost time than on noticing his immediate surroundings. Then a familiar voice behind him yelled, "Longarm! Duck!" So he did, just as a length of lead pipe whipped viciously through the space his Stetson had been traveling through so innocent.

He naturally hit the cobblestones rolling and came up a few yards away, gun in hand, facing back the way he'd just come. But as he did so Ki stomped the figure on the paving between them again. So Longarm moved in, reholstering the gun he saw he'd have no use for as he said, "Thanks. I take it you came looking for me when I was a mite late?"

Ki growled, "More like an hour late, and I deserve your thanks, you idiot. I spotted you, and what was following you, just in the nick of time!"

"Aw, don't rub it in. Roll him over and let me have a look at him. I never forget a face." But when Ki did so with another kick, Longarm stared soberly down at the awful mess and said, "Forget what I just said. That was unkind of you, Ki. How in thunder am I supposed to I.D. an old boy after you've stomped him faceless as well as dead? What the hell are you walking around on, steel-rimmed Dutchboy shoes?"

Ki had already hunkered down to go through the shabby duds of the man he'd downed. He said, "The cobblestones did that. I was just dancing light as a fairy on the nape of his neck. Next time I'll just let you get clobbered." Then Ki said, "Not one bit of identification. He must have been a professional."

"Or poor and desperate," Longarm pointed out. "This is a tough part of one tough town. He might have only been after my wallet. Like a fool I just flashed some money in a seafood joint full of shabby strangers a few minutes ago."

Ki said, "He must have wanted your wallet bad, then. He wasn't winding up to just knock you out."

"Either way, we'd best depart sudden. I've already talked to Galveston P.D. all I want to."

So Ki grabbed the corpse by the ankles, swung the con-

149

siderable weight as lightly as most men might a length of cordwood, and sent it flying over the edge of the quay to hit the water with a mighty splash.

Longarm chuckled fondly and said, "I always heard Japanese folk were neat. Let's go."

So they went, but not to the hospital. Ki had already spoken to Captain Wilson, and visiting hours were nearly over. Longarm said he'd take Ki's word on the conversation, so they found a dinky saloon, took a booth in the back, and compared notes.

After Longarm had Ki up to date on his own dead ends, Ki told him, "I can't say I did much better. Jessie didn't visit any of her associates here. According to Wilson she just showed up on the ship her father named after her, storming at him to put back out to sea and throw all the contraband overboard before he got her in trouble with the law. When he asked what on earth she was talking about, he wound up down an open hatchway, fortunately atop some bails that broke his fall, with a pair of busted balls. He's really in bad shape, Custis. She couldn't have done that kneeing him. I'd say she half turned away, as if in dismissal, and lashed out with a boot heel. He'll be lucky if he doesn't end up singing falsetto."

Longarm looked pained and said, "I feel for him. But I'm sure glad I didn't have to feel it. Did you follow up on my suspicion about someone trying that old chestnut with a double?"

Ki nodded grimly and replied, "I did, feeling foolish even before Wilson called me an asshole. He's been working for Starbuck Enterprises since before Jessie was born. He first met her at the age of four when Alex Starbuck brought her aboard the clipper Wilson skippered for him then. He said he never would have expected such a sweet little girl to grow up half as mean. Before you ask, of course Jessie's been aboard, a lot, since then. She got to christen the steamer named after her as a teenager. He saw much more of her after Alex was murdered by that cartel and she had to take over running his business empire."

Longarm sipped at the drink he'd ordered, muttering, "U.S. Customs vouches for the rest of the crew, and Jessie would have never won if Uncle Sam had teamed up with that cartel. But, even driven a mite loco with them pills, Jessie must have had *some* damned reason for ordering Wilson to jettison that cargo!"

Ki said, "Granted. But who's to say what might strike someone full of henbane as a sensible reason? You say it causes hallucinations. Who's to say what she might have imagined she saw down in that dark hold, or what she thought Wilson was when she, well, defended herself?"

Longarm repressed a shudder and said, "I read this book about folk getting drugged up and seeing things. It said a loving husband could attack his own wife under the distinct impression she was a burglar, or throw their baby out the window because it sure looked like a bomb. She knew who Henry was, lucky for Henry, so she might be getting better. Or maybe it was time to take one of them nasty pills again. I hate to consider what she might feel like when she finally runs out of 'em. She won't be able to buy more. Not by that brand name, for sure. I asked Miss Doc what the aftereffects might be. She said she had no idea, since she'd never in her career mixed henbane for anyone."

He saw Ki was looking sort of sick to his stomach, so to change the subject he asked who else the big segundo had jawed with. Ki shrugged and said, "I told you. Mostly people who could hardly know as much as we do. Everything seems to be running smoothly here in Galveston. Jessie's a smart businesswoman, when she's herself, and knows how to delegate authority."

"How much authority, and to who?" asked Longarm, suspiciously. "Not enough for anyone to steal from her without the books showing it. All important checks and legal documents have to be signed in front of witnesses and her Galveston lawyer."

Longarm grimaced and asked, "Since when have you started trusting *lawyers*? Haven't we caught more than one such naturally larcenous rascal trying to crook her?"

Ki nodded but said, "We live and learn. How many times do you think you'd hire an untrustworthy law firm if you were Jessie?"

Longarm smiled thinly and said, "A heap, if I was worth half as much and trying to run half her empire and most men took me for a foolish young female. Money and power attract crooks the way shit draws flies and, as we know, lawyers who never tried to cheat a client before have gone gaga once they saw a chance to cut into a pie like Starbuck Enterprises!"

Ki sighed and said, "Jessie knows that, now. Her attorney of record, here in Galveston, is a man her father knew before she was born. Better yet, he didn't want the job. He knew about her many enemies and said he didn't feel comfortable with that much power over that much money. He'd heard about us having a few more-ambitious lawyers defrocked by the Texas Bar Association, I imagine. Anyhow, Jessie finally persuaded him. You know how persuasive Jessie can be. His name is Pomerance and he only agreed to oversee her legal affairs here in Galveston. At his own insistence he has nothing to say about Jessie's herd, cotton gins, or even her ships putting out of other ports."

Longarm said, "What a crooked lawyer could steal from her in Galveston has to be worth more than the wallet I just came close to getting killed for. Do you trust him yourself?"

"No. As Jessie's segundo I can't afford to trust anyone on the payroll. But I have checked Pomerance out and I mean to check him out some more. As you said, people have been murdered for less than the value of one cargo, and Pomerance gets to oversee a lot more than that changing hands."

Longarm said, "Bueno. Let's hope you don't catch him with his hand in the till. Crooked lawyers are getting tedious, and even when you catch 'em they can put up one hell of a fight in court. So it's always best to gun a crooked lawyer. What say we check with Western Union to see if Billy Vail has more on Jessie's curious trip to the Peace River? Then, seeing we're done on this fool island, let's get off it.''

Ki said, "I'll walk you to Western Union. I'm not done here yet. As I told you on the way here, Jessie bought a tidy little hotel here in Galveston for the use of her seamen when they're in port. I'll give you a business card and they won't charge you for a room and bath.''

They finished their drinks and headed for the telegraph office. On the way, Longarm said, "I can't argue about the price, even if I wind up lonesome, but where might you be spending the night if you don't mind my asking?''

Ki smiled softly and said, "With Pomerance's stenographer. I don't think she's high enough on his payroll to stand up under torture for him. But as she types for him and opens up his mail, she might know things he might have held out on me.''

Longarm blinked and started to ask a dumb question. Then he recalled that the cool-headed rascal knew how to torture a lady within the letter of the law, although he'd never gotten to watch Ki question a suspect right on the razor's edge of orgasm, and had no real desire to know how Jessie knew that. He hoped it was just because Japanese, or Nihogo, as they called it, was a franker lingo than Victorian English. He knew French folk were allowed to say *merde*, or shit, in mixed company because they just didn't have dirty and delicate words for the same things. Jessie had told him that in Dai Nippon, as the Japanese called their own country, folk thought nothing of bathing bare-ass with total strangers of the opposite sex and that it was all right to ask a gal for a piece as long as you used proper grammar. It was considered shockingly rude to ask right out if someone wanted another bowl of rice or a good screwing. You were supposed to ask a guest, or a pretty gal, if their honorable selves might find a second helping, or a good screwing, desirable. Then they got to call you honorable and say alas, they couldn't take you up on your gracious offer, without slapping you silly. He had to allow Queen Victoria had a lot to learn about fancy manners. Jessie had told him even a white gal could get used to sitting in a hot tub, bare-assed, with strange Japanese men, once she learned they hardly ever asked and only asked polite when they did. He sometimes wished he savvied the lingo when Jessie and Ki were going at it, calm as anything, even when he suspected they were talking about matters that might faint poor Queen Victoria dead in her tracks.

As they were crossing over to the Western Union he asked Ki if they put on dirty stage shows in Japan. Ki said, "It depends on what you mean by dirty. My mother's people enjoy bawdy jokes as much as my father's people do. They just don't laugh at the same things. If you're talking about the hootchy-kootchy shows they put on here in Galveston, a show like that would fall flat in Nagasaki. Everyone knows what a naked woman looks like. Our whores tend to get tattooed if they want to surprise a customer with something he wasn't expecting to see."

Longarm laughed and said he'd always found a tattooed lady sort of surprising, albeit hardly stimulating if they'd overdone it.

At the telegraph office they found that Billy Vail had indeed wired Longarm, and the news wasn't so good. Track walkers had found a mighty mangled body along a quarter mile of the Denver & Rio Grande right-of-way, about fifty miles south of Denver. The gent had been identified as a whiskey drummer who'd been aboard a train Jessie Starbuck had booked a compartment on. It got worse. Western Union wouldn't put dirty words on its wires, but of course Longarm and his boss had a sort of code of their own. Longarm deciphered Vail's message and turned to Ki, ashen faced, to murmur, "A porter on Jessie's train says she asked him, pungent, to come into her compartment and throw the blocks to her. I don't know what she might have said to the white gent someone seems to have thrown down between the

154

wheels. Billy says he doubts anyone could charge her, either way, but he's sure upset and that makes two of us!''

"You mean three of us," said Ki, soberly. Then he shook his head and said, "That couldn't have been Jessie. Maybe you're right about them sending in a ringer, dumb as it was the other time.''

"Henry says it was her at our office. She's been there before and, ah, it seems she propositioned him as well.''

Ki snorted in disbelief and demanded, "Are we talking about that skinny pansy out in the reception room?''

"Henry ain't a pansy, but I'll allow he ain't most gals' picture of a matinee idol. I doubt he'd lie about a thing like that. Henry's always been truthful as well as skinny and shy. So how do you read it?''

"I don't. I can't. Even if there was Spanish fly in those pills, and even if Spanish fly worked, no woman half as attractive as Jessie would have to proposition Pullman porters and pathetic simps like your Henry. She'd only have to sit alone in a taproom a few minutes and let nature take its course.''

Longarm shrugged and said, "Assuming she was thinking halfway natural, you mean. The pal who identified the run-over traveling man says the victim tried to pick Jessie up in the club car, just before he was never seen alive again. And there was nothing in the hold of that ship to scare or enrage anyone with eyes working sensible. What if she don't see things, or men, the way they really look?''

Ki grimaced and growled, "Let's hope she runs out of those pills fast. Any news from Canada?''

"Not yet," Longarm replied. "She's barely had time to reach Havre by rail, and from there she'd have to hire a mount to go on up to the Peace River. It's open prairie and the border was being closely watched before Billy wired Fort MacLeod to watch for anyone distinctive as Jessie. Metis gunrunners have been crossing sort of regular this summer.''

He saw Ki didn't follow his drift and added, "The Metis,

or Red River breeds, are in rebellion against the MacDonald administration up yonder. Can't say I blame 'em. Mac-Donald's a real pain in everyone's ass. But border troubles work in our favor as far as Jessie's concerned. Are you sure you never heard her mention the Peace River before?''

"Oh, she's mentioned it in passing, of course. Anyone in the cattle industry takes some interest in new range opening up. But the Peace River is one hell of a way to drive Texas cows, even if we had any reason to. As you said, it's hard for us Americans to do business in Canada with a Yankee-hating government in power."

Longarm knew Ki liked to consider himself American, and Jessie didn't mind being called a Yankee in the sense Ki meant that. He put the wire away and said, "Well, don't let me keep you from torturing that stenographer gal. Lord knows how I'll torture my fool self. It's too early to turn in and hootchy-kootchy ain't no fun unless they let you get in on it."

Ki warned, "If I were you I'd go straight to the hotel and read a magazine or something. Galveston's a tough town and you already gave them one crack at you."

Longarm smiled crookedly and muttered, "Look who's talking. I just said I had no local gal to torture. I've read all this month's magazines, and that cuss you treated so mean was likely just a footpad, out to get some drinking money at the expense of my fool skull. Now that I know drunks are so ornery in these parts I'll watch 'em closer."

"I'm pleased to hear you have eyes in the back of your head. No fooling, Custis, I won't be there if they try for you again."

Longarm said, "That sounds fair. You'll be on your own if that stenographer gal decides to beat you up. And who's this *they* you keep talking about? Are you implying we might not have this island all to ourselves?"

"Isn't it obvious?" Ki asked. "We know nobody on our

side ever slipped those mind-bending pills to Jessie. They have to know we're on *her* side. Add it up. It has to be some sort of fiendish plot, and fiendish plotters tend to run in packs."

★

Chapter 9

Ki had been right about the small hotel Jessie had bought for the use of her seamen in port. It had no need to advertise. Longarm passed the doorway once before he saw it was the only numbered doorway on the side street big enough to go with a business establishment. He went in, handed Ki's card to the old gent behind a dinky counter, and got a key instead of an argument. Longarm's saddle and possibles were reposing in the railroad checkroom in Houston. He went up, anyway, to see what sort of room they were charging him so much for.

It was on the second floor and surprisingly pleasant. The bed against one wall was way bigger than any bunk aboard a ship, and the wallpaper Jessie had picked out was a restful shade of sky blue with white ivy vines growing up it. But it was too early for bedtime, so he went back down and asked the old desk clerk if there was a decent drinking establishment within easy walking distance.

The old-timer said, "Well, it's more like three city blocks unless you want to drink with riffraff gents and gals no man with any interest in his health would touch. Try Blacky Morgan's to your left as you step out yonder door. They charge fair for liquor that won't blind you for life and the gals working there ain't outright whores. So don't buy drinks for any of 'em unless you just enjoy conversations with ladies that don't get you nowhere serious."

Longarm chuckled, said he knew a couple of places like that in Denver, and left to see how much trouble he could get into on this side of midnight. He didn't want to get in much. He felt it would be sort of shitty to bring a gal back to sweet little Jessie Starbuck's own hotel. Knowing she'd decorated the room would likely make him feel too guilty to enjoy sharing it with another gal. He knew better than to go anywhere else with a strange gal in such a seedy neighborhood. There could be worse things waiting for a man than a dose of clap if he strolled the primrose path in a town as tough as Galveston with anyone he didn't know mighty well.

Blacky Morgan's was easier to find than the hotel. It had a gaslit sign out front. Inside, it was more brightly lit and better smelling than the Jolly Roger had been. Most of the other gents bellied up at the long bar or seated at the bare tables seemed to be seafarers. More than one had stripes on the cuffs of their jackets, so Longarm figured the place catered to a higher toned crowd. An upright piano was tinkling "Aura Lee," more as a conversational background than an encouragement to foot stomping. Longarm decided he liked the place well enough to take a corner table and order a pitcher of suds with a clean tumbler. None of the few gals in evidence came over to pester him. They'd no doubt found beer drinkers slim pickings in the past. He didn't care.

When a man was just window-shopping he could look over the gal of his dreams better at some distance, and many a dream had been shattered by a gal having bad breath and

159

missing teeth. He could see they didn't serve decent neighborhood gals in Blacky Morgan's. The four gals holding down the bar with their bare elbows and the one leaning against the piano wore their skirts so short you could almost see their kneecaps, and they had their bodices cut so low you could almost guess the size of their nipples. Places that did serve neighborhood gals almost always did so in a back room with a side entrance, anyway.

Longarm was working on his second tumbler of beer, wondering when if ever they meant to put on a show, when a dapperly dressed young squirt came in with a handsome gal his own height clinging to his left arm. Longarm made note of the six-gun he seemed to be packing, low slung, under his checked frock coat. A second mate at another table hailed the newcomer as Blacky and asked where he'd been. The obvious owner of the joint smiled pleasant and replied that he'd been over on the mainland overseeing his joint in Houston. That seemed to satisfy the seaman. It didn't satisfy Longarm. He was sure he'd seen that young gent somewhere in the past. Longarm had trained himself to remember faces. He ran that one through his skull in the short time he had to study it. Then Blacky and his gal had passed through the beaded curtain of a corner archway. Longarm's first notion was that the squirt was likely going upstairs with the good-looking gal. He knew *he* would, if he'd been away a spell and she was welcoming him home so friendly. But then he noticed a couple of other gents get up to follow them. So he decided to do the same. It hardly seemed at all likely Blacky let other men watch, if that was all he meant to do upstairs.

He'd paid in advance for his beer—it was that sort of joint—so he just picked up pitcher and glass to head for that beaded curtain. He'd almost reached it when the brassy blonde leaning against the piano hissed, "You can't go up there, stranger!"

But Longarm told her, "Sure I can. I ain't too drunk to walk up a flight of steps."

But at the top of said steps he found his way blocked by a big ape dressed like a man. It said, "Members only, friend. You just go on back down and behave yourself, see?"

Longarm replied, "It's all right. Blacky and me are old pals." So the ape told him to wait on the landing and ducked through a more solidly built door for a spell. Longarm pretended not to notice, or care, when a peephole popped open to stare at him a few thoughtful seconds before it shut again. The ape came back out to say, "Sorry, Mr. Long. I was only doing my job. Blacky says you're all right. Go on in."

So Longarm did. He'd thought he recalled that sort of sissy face from some damned where. As he stepped into the brightly lit upstairs room he saw it was a gambling hall. Almost as big as the main room downstairs, it was furnished with a crap table, a roulette layout, and a wheel of fortune, or real sucker trap, against the back wall. Card tables were set up elsewhere, still empty. The evening was still young and there were only a handful of players upstairs as yet. Blacky Morgan had removed his frock coat to preside over the roulette layout. Longarm had been right about the low-slung side arm. It was an ivory-handled single-action Remington, likely a .45, with that particular frame. A man had to be mighty self-confident or just showing off to pack a single-action these days. You could get off the first shot just about as fast with a thumb-buster, but unless you finished the fight with your first round, you could be in trouble. Most gunslicks now packed double-action and tended to throw a heap of lead back at you, even going down.

The suckers who'd gone upstairs ahead of Longarm were gathered about Blacky's layout. The handsome young owner shot a nod of recognition Longarm's way and commenced to spin the wheel. Longarm nodded back, went to an empty corner card table and sat down there with his beer to study the young but obviously ambitious businessman. Longarm *knew* they'd met somewhere before, but try as he might he couldn't place that face. Morgan's nickname was obvious.

His greased-back hair was black as the ace of spades, and though he'd obviously shaved his swarthy face in recent memory, his jaws were that shade of blue you noticed on men who shaved twice a day without much luck at appearing cherubic. The squirt's features were distinctive. He looked sort of baby faced and awfully tough at the same time. So who in the hell was he and where had they met before?

The young gambler was short enough to qualify as shorter than average, like Kid Antrim, Billy the Kid, or whatever else you wanted to call that other little bastard. But Blacky was obviously not Billy the Kid, and there were only so many wanted men who fit that particular pigeonhole. Longarm had learned, when logic failed, to go with instinct. If he'd ever been sore at anyone who looked like Blacky he'd likely still want to plant a fist in those delicate features. He didn't. As he studied the young squirt and let his feeling just drift with the tide, he found himself feeling sort of friendly. So they'd likely met sometime, casual, under friendly circumstances. That made sense. Longarm was friendly by nature, when folk allowed him to be, and he seldom bothered to file away friendly faces not in trouble with the law.

The same pretty gal Blacky had come in with downstairs had changed to a more shocking red dress somewhere in the back. He still had no trouble recalling her face, or figure, when she came right to his table, a fresh deck of cards in hand, to sit down uninvited and commence dealing. But before Longarm could ask what the table stakes might be, or what they might be playing, she said, "Keep still and just listen as I go through the motions. Blacky told me to tell you this is no night for a lawman to be up here with the suckers. We're fixing to have a police raid any time now. It's just pro forma for the ladies of the Galveston W.C.T.U., of course. But how would it look if the one and original Custis Long's name appeared on a police blotter?"

"Embarrassing," he replied with a grin. Then he said, "I'm glad Blacky knows me well enough to treat me decent.

I think I like him, too. But I'll be switched with snakes if I recall where we might have met before. I know it wasn't here in Galveston. After that my mind goes blank. Did he ever spin a wheel up Colorado way, or maybe in Dodge?''

The fancy gal said, ''I can't say. I've only known Blacky since he opened this place a couple of years back. It's funny you should say what you just said. Blacky just said he knows you're a lawman of some kind named Custis Long and sometimes known as Longarm, but he can't recall where he knows you from.''

Longarm decided, ''Well, it's a big country and we both seem to get about in it, if he's only been here a couple of years. If I stick around a spell it may come back to me.''

''Are you crazy? I just told you the police are getting set to raid us.''

He nodded and said, ''I know about pro forma raids. So does yonder boss gambler, since he don't seem to be shutting down. If he knows they're coming he's made the usual arrangements with the precinct captain. They go through the motions, he pays the modest fine, with a separate envelope for the right Galveston fixer, and that'll be that until it's his turn to get raided again. If anyone in this town but the W.C.T.U. was serious about sin they'd never let ladies dance naked in the Jolly Roger. Them gals are dancing more sedate when it's their turn to get raided, right?''

She smiled knowingly and said, ''No girl wants to ride in the paddy wagon in her birthday suit. Some of the boys on the force can be awfully fresh. What do you want me to tell Blacky?''

He chuckled and asked, ''About him or naked ladies? Say, if you must, that I'll just sip some more suds and be on my way in a few minutes. Town law can talk fresh to us federal men as well. I just want enough to drink to get some sleep without counting too many sheep. As a former cowhand I don't admire sheep in really big flocks.''

She nodded, gathered up her cards, and said, ''You'd best leave by way of the back door. Out through the kitchen,

163

downstairs. The police always enter through the front door so the reporters can watch 'em doing their duty.''

She rose and left to stroll back to the wheel of fortune and stand by it, smiling. She smiled grand. A sucker would need some encouragement to bet against a wheel of fortune. They were a lot easier to rig than a roulette wheel.

More suckers were crowding in up here, now. As other card tables were occupied Longarm could tell at a glance which man at which table was playing for the house. Maybe the suckers could as well. Men who frequented gambling halls were a lot like men who went to whorehouses. They knew all the others were being taken, but believed they were special and hence apt to be taken care of better by the hired help.

He saw the table he was holding down with a beer pitcher was not apt to make any money for old Blacky, so he got up to head on down and out with his beer. As he passed the roulette layout Blacky Morgan nodded and smiled a good night at him. He nodded back just as polite and went on down the stairs. He placed the tumbler and still half-filled pitcher on the top of the piano for the professor and fancy gal there, in case they wanted it. Then he stepped into the kitchen, nodded at the sort of surprised-looking colored folk working there, and just went on back to the alley door. The alley was a heap darker, but he hadn't had much to drink, and beer inspired him to piss more than it did to get lost, anyway. So he got his bearings and headed for his hotel by way of the dark alley. It didn't seem quite as dark, now that his eyes had adjusted. Then he saw more than two black forms, outlined by the street light at the far end of the alley, step out to block his way. He must have been an even blacker blur to them. For one asked, cautiously, "Longarm?"

Any man who answered such a question with two men facing him in uncertain light, guns drawn, would have been suffering suicidal tendencies. So Longarm dropped silently to one knee as he got his own gun out. When both their guns flashed as one to whiz hot lead through the space he'd just been standing in, he sensed he'd made the proper response.

He fired his .44-40, better, to send one of them reeling back out of the alley. Then another shot rang out, *behind* him, and Longarm knew he was dead until the second rascal went down.

Longarm spun on his knee to throw down on whoever the hell had fired back yonder. But he held his fire when he recognized the white sleeves and dark vest of Blacky Morgan. He said, "That was mighty neighborly of you, Morgan."

His benefactor replied, modestly, "It was nothing. All I needed was a famous lawman ambushed in the alley behind my place. Meg, standing lookout by the piano, told me your departure via the kitchen had drawn considerable attention on the part of two strange toughs at the bar, who'd whipped out the front door directly after, without paying. I figured I'd best see you got off my own block, at least. Who were they and how come?"

Longarm said, "I ain't had time to study 'em. That gunplay should draw any copper badges within a mile and they may be able to help us out, if we just dropped two local boys."

Blacky Morgan put his smoking six-gun away, muttering, "Speak for yourself. I prefer to only talk to coppers on my payroll. So I'll just sort of crawfish back to my kitchen door if it's all the same to you."

Longarm said he understood the young gambler's views, but he still had to ask, "Before you go, would you mind telling me where we've met before, Blacky?"

Morgan said, "I've been trying to figure that out, too. Have you ever been to Leadville, Colorado?"

Longarm said, "Sure, I get up there regular. Is that where you think we might have met?"

"Must have been. I was dealing faro up in the Colorado mining country before I came here to Galveston."

165

Longarm decided, "Maybe. Leadville ain't all that big a town, and I thought I knew it well. Where might you have dwelt before you worked in Leadville?"

Blacky laughed and said, "You name it and I've been there at least once. Before I discovered I had clever hands I was trying to make a living with my clever feet. Used to trod the wicked stage as a soft-shoe dancer. I was born to a show-business family, so it took me some time to discover how lousy dancing pays, next to betting with the house."

They both heard the dulcet tones of a police whistle coming fast, so Longarm suddenly found himself alone with two dead gunslicks. Their guns lay close by on the paving. Longarm kicked them well clear, just in case, before he hunkered down to see what he and Blacky had wrought. He'd been right about them both being dead. The Texas voting cards they'd likely picked up to I.D. themselves out of vagrancy charges told him one had been known in life as Jones and the other had answered to Johnson. They hadn't struck him in life as original thinkers.

Both bodies were dressed half cow and half seagoing, with high-heeled Texas boots and riding-tight jeans under pea jackets and billed seamen's caps. As Longarm was getting back up a lost looking copper badge appeared to be crossing the intersection to his right. So Longarm yelled, "Over here, officer!" as he put his .44-40 away.

The uniformed Galveston lawman approached gingerly, stopping entire when he spotted the bodies on the walk, to cautiously ask if they were dead or drunk.

Longarm replied, "They might have been drunk. Now they're both dead. I'm U.S. Deputy Custis Long. These other gents were laying for me. I know this because one used my name in vain, with the results you can see for yourself."

The local lawman replied, "We heard you was in town, Longarm. You're sort of famous, all over, and I for one am sure glad we're on the same side!"

So Longarm knew it was safe to get his gun out again

and reload as the copper badge moved in for a look-see. When they both heard another police whistle in the distance the one with Longarm put his own to his lips and chirped an ear-splitting reply. Then he turned back to Longarm to ask, "You say these jaspers *called* you, by name, and then tried to outdraw you?"

"Nope. They were waiting in the mouth of the alley with their guns already drawn. That might have given them a false sense of confidence. They couldn't see me as well with my back to the darkness and must have wanted to be sure it was me and no harmless drunk they gunned."

The uniformed lawman whistled softly and said, "It was still mighty dumb. They must have had a mighty serious reason, or been paid a heap, to go up against the likes of you!"

Longarm put his fully loaded gun away again, saying, "I've never seen either of their ugly faces before, so I'd say it was a cash transaction. Did you ever get the feeling that for some reason you just weren't popular in certain parts?"

Next morning over breakfast in the dining room Jessie owned as well, Ki managed not to say, "I told you so!" as Longarm brought him up to date on events since they'd last talked. So it was Longarm who got to say, "You were likely right about that other one you tossed in the drink. When he never returned with good news about me they sent more serious workers to finish the job right. I don't mind telling you the hours I spent over at police headquarters were tedious. But in the end we established the two who tried to waylay me in that alley had modest records here in Texas. They'd both done time for assault and battery. If they ever gunned anyone before they tried to gun me, they got away with it. I don't much care if I nipped them in their buds as serious killers or not. They'd both beat men, and women, sort of dreadful in their time. The one who liked to be called Johnson put a whore in Houston on the streets

167

by busting up her face too bad to ever work in a parlor house again."

Ki grimaced and said, "Then he must have been working for a pimp or worse at the time."

"There's nothing worse than a pimp. But I follow your drift. I suspect they just worked freelance. According to Blacky Morgan, who should know, the vice lords of Galveston have the law paid off. So I can't see any of 'em sending killers after me. Even if some local pimp or brothel madam in town was afraid of getting arrested, serious, they'd still have no call to fret about my federal badge. A U.S. deputy don't have jurisdiction in such petty local matters."

"I've always wondered how you know so much about the lowlife of the west," Ki said. "Run that Blacky Morgan by me again."

"There's nothing much to run. To the extent I recall him at all I recall him friendly and he proved he liked me well enough, last night. He sounded free and open enough when he allowed he'd been a dancing man and then a gambling man. When gents make up life stories they tend to describe themselves as ex-Confederate colonels or railroad engineers down on their luck. I doubt a man would admit to having a tinhorn gambling or show-business past if he was worried about folk thinking he was unrespectable. I've hardly ever had anyone send two killers after me and then save me from them. Like I said, the ones after me here in Galveston are more likely trying to *hide* the fact that they ain't as decent as they're letting on. How did you make out with that lawyer's stenographer gal?"

Ki smiled softly and replied, "Unless a woman of her limited intellect can lie and beg for it at the same time, I'd say old Pomerance is clean. She drops all the office mail in the box on her way home, so she'd have noticed if her law firm was sending out many letters she hadn't typed up herself. She opens the office in the morning. Pomerance usually gets in no earlier than nine, by which time she's

168

opened all the incoming mail and put anything needing his personal attention on his desk. Everything else goes to the lawyer's personal secretary or law clerks, depending on what it might be. Most law firms get a lot of routine paperwork the boss doesn't want to bother with.''

Longarm objected, ''If you consider the stenographer gal sort of dumb, who's to say for sure what she might allow past her without suspicion?''

Ki smiled modestly and said, ''I questioned her in depth. She may not be bright, but to take dictation a girl has to have an almost photographic memory. She assured me Pomerance has only been dealing in routine local matters for clients he had before Jessie hired him. I know all too well how subtle some crooks have been in the past, though, so while she was sleeping the sleep of the well sated, I took the liberty of making a wax impression of her office key. A very discreet locksmith I've dealt with in the past only needed a few minutes to make me a duplicate key. It's in my pocket now, so we can get in any time we want to go over their books in more detail.''

Longarm chuckled, but said, ''I hate to paw through dusty old legal briefs, even when I know what I'm looking for. Pomerance would have to be mighty stupid as well as crooked to leave a paper trail across his own office. The U.S. Mail is delivered to home addresses as well, and anyone with a modest amount of sneaky blood can write personal love letters in code. If you think the stenographer gal is honest we'd best assume the rest of the office staff is too. Crooked gangs don't hire honest innocents to tend to their incoming and outgoing mail. But that still leaves Pomerance, and I've yet to meet a lawyer that I trusted entire. Since you and Jessie seem to, though, let's let him simmer on the back of the stove for now. It hardly seems possible old Pomerance would try to have me killed and let you screw his office help at the same time, if he was the mastermind with a guilty conscience.''

''I don't think Miss Tillie's boss knew I was that interested in her," Ki said. "But you have a point. I'm well known here in Galveston as Jessie's segundo. So why do I have the feeling I'm being left out? What on earth could anyone be afraid *you'd* find out about that I don't already know?"

"If I knew that," Longarm said, "I could make a more educated guess as to who we're dealing with and what in thunder they're up to! Assuming Pomerance to be honest, just for laughs, nobody's gone after him or even his office staff, except for you, you horny rascal. The only associate of Jessie that's been attacked worth mention here was that Captain Wilson who worked for Jessie, and he says it was Jessie herself who kicked him in the balls."

Longarm stuck more ham and eggs in his mouth, swallowed, and asked Ki, "You're sure he was sure it was her when you talked to him last night?"

Ki looked impatient and said, "I'd have told you if he'd said it was one of the James-Younger gang. I tried to shake his tale of woe, damn it. He insisted that once a lady kicked you in the groin you'd never forget her and, as I said, he's known Jessie since she was a little girl."

Longarm ate some more, washed it down with black coffee, and decided, "All right. We'd best take his word on that. I've been studying the travel time involved. It's possible, but just barely possible, to get down here from the Circle Star, kick a man in the balls, and get up to Denver and scare Henry with a throwing star in the time she had to work with. But not if she wandered about in a daze worth mention. She'd have had to move direct, missing no rail connections and knowing exactly what she was up to. So what in thunder could she be up to?"

Ki said bleakly, "That's another question we can't answer before we know more. I don't understand her scaling that shuriken from her hat at your clerk and then leaving without it. She's always worn it on her hat as a sort of last-resort weapon. I should think that even on drugs she'd recall the many times that shuriken most men take for a hat ornament

170

has saved her after everyone thought she'd been disarmed. And you say there's a lot of trouble up in Canada this summer?''

Longarm nodded and said, ''The Metis have risen before and the Mounties expect them to rise again, any minute. But look on the bright side. At least we know she can't go throwing that wicked ninja weapon at anyone she mistakes for the boogy man.''

Ki stared soberly across at him to say, ''She could have more than one spare shuriken on her, and even if she'd left her .38 special in Billy Vail's office, she's still a trained killing machine, sane or otherwise, armed or bare-handed. This isn't the first time I've wondered if I ever should have instructed her in the martial arts of the Orient. You see, unlike me, Jessie's always waited until she was *angry* at someone before she really went after blood.''

Longarm sipped more coffee and said, ''I've noticed that on occasion. Seems to me you'd have to be sort of vexed with someone before you mistook their head for a brick and busted it with the edge of your palm.''

Ki shook his head and said, ''That is not the Bushido way. A true warrior should kill without a trace of passion. Rage can dull one's fighting skills and, aside from that, it's considered uncivilized to kill in anger by my mother's people.''

Longarm shrugged and pointed out, ''Jessie and me belong to your daddy's race. Our Good Book says to turn the other cheek and, if someone slaps that one, too, stomp the shit out of him. But we ain't supposed to kill cold-blooded, we're supposed to do all we can to avoid killing at all, and then—''

''I want to tell you a story,'' Ki cut in. ''I have told it many times to Jessie. Each time I do she says she understands and promises to remember. But, like you, she's too American to kill unless she's at least a little annoyed.''

Longarm finished his cup, put it down, and got out an after-breakfast cheroot as Ki continued, ''Once upon a time

171

a *damio*, or feudal lord, was assassinated. His samurai, or knightly retainer, searched high and low for the killer. At last they met, alone, and after a furious swordfight the killer was disarmed. So the samurai raised his blade to strike. The wounded and desperate killer cursed him, cursed his honorable parents, and spat at him. The samurai became very angry."

Longarm nodded and said, "Well, wouldn't anybody? What did he do, then, to the ornery son of a bitch?"

Ki said, simply, "Nothing. He sheathed his sword and turned away. You see, it was his duty to kill the assassin to avenge his damio's death. It would have been *wrong* to kill for *personal* revenge."

Longarm chuckled, lit his smoke, and said, "Remind me to spit at you if we ever have a fight. Wasn't it just as dumb to let the rascal live, seeing he was still the murderer of that there samurai's boss?"

"Oh, he killed the man, later, about a year later, after he'd sought spiritual peace and could hack his enemy to bits with a calm smile. Bushido teaches that anger leads to excess and atrocity. That is why common people have never been allowed arms in Dai Nippon. Since the recent overthrow of the shogunate, some commoners have been allowed into the armed forces of the Emperor. I approve of democracy, of course, but I still shudder to think what Japanese soldiers might do if they are ever allowed to fight in *anger*. As I said, the true warrior fights with a cool head, striking neither harder nor softer than the situation calls for."

Longarm blew smoke at Ki and dryly observed, "I've noticed how you pull your punches. Had you left a face on that one with the lead pipe last night, I might have been able to connect it up to my Wanted list. As things now stand, I haven't a clue as to who's out to kill me, or why. I'll likely just have to let 'em keep sending more until I recognize one, or wind up dead."

Ki said, "I've a better idea. We know that whatever might be going on here in Galveston, Jessie must be somewhere up on or about the Canadian border. So why don't we get out of here and go searching for her in a land of fewer dark alleyways?"

Longarm shook his head and said, "You're talking a heap of land, and the Mounties know it a heap better than we do. If Crown Sergeant Foster can't round Jessie up it'll mean she's working at it, and if she's acting even half as smart as she can all three of us together would have a tough time finding her. That little gal can vanish behind a grass stem when she sets her mind to it."

He reached in his pants for some change for the waiter as he added, "Nobody up Canada way switched them pills on Jessie, and I just can't see even Prime Minister MacDonald hatching a plot against a Texas cattle baroness. The skunks behind all her present troubles have to be somewhere closer. They wouldn't keep trying for me and only me if they didn't think I was getting warm. So you ride up to the Peace River range if you like, but I'm staying here in Galveston till I see someplace better to search for the sons of bitches."

They got up to leave, but they were met in the doorway by one of the Galveston lawmen Longarm had talked to in that squad room. The dick said, "I was hoping to find you somewhere around this hotel, Longarm. You know that crazy lady you was talking about with us?"

Longarm scowled as he replied, "I never said Jessie Starbuck was crazy. I said she'd been fed brain poison."

The local lawman shrugged and said, "Whatever. She's sure been acting crazy. The vice squad picked her up in a dawn raid on a house of ill repute just this morning. They found her hiding bare-ass in the basement, raving like a wolf giving birth. They got her over to the hospital now, in the mental ward, of course."

Longarm and Ki exchanged stricken glances. It was Ki who said, "Thank her gods and mine she's safely under medical supervision. We were so worried she'd get hurt, or hurt somebody, before she could be found!"

As the three of them stepped out into the bright morning sunlight, the Galveston lawman said, awfully cheerfully, when one studied on it, "Oh, she hurt somebody good enough to kill her. We got a gal on ice at the city morgue with a busted neck. The other whores working the cribs upstairs swear they can't I.D. the dead gal. But it's pretty obvious who killed her, bare-handed."

Longarm said, "Hold on. How could poor little Jessie wind up accused if she was being held prisoner in the cellar?"

The other lawman snorted and replied, "Who said anything about her being locked up? The basement door wasn't locked. She'd just run down there when the raid commenced. The other whores all say she was *running* the damned place, see?"

★

Chapter 10

The mental ward at Galveston General was on an upper floor. A doctor and a burly matron had joined the two lawmen and Ki on the way up, so they made quite a parade as they filed on through the open ward to the padded cells down at the far end. Most of the more harmless loonies paid no attention to their passing, but one old gray-faced geezer in a hospital shimmy shirt snapped to attention and saluted, cackling, "The Union forever and I'm being held against my will by the damned old Texas Rebs!"

Nobody paid any attention to him. The matron produced her key ring to open one of the solid wooden doors, saying, "Careful, gents. She's wearing a straitjacket, of course, but she sure can kick!"

Then the door was open and Jessie was standing there wide eyed and haggard in another hospital shimmy. A crumpled canvas straitjacket lay at the base of one mattress-padded wall. The matron gasped and stepped in, snapping,

175

"How did you get out of that jacket, you naughty girl?" as she made a tentative grab for her more slightly built patient.

Longarm and Ki both shouted, "No!" without waiting to consider who they were trying to caution. Then Jessie had the matron by one outstretched wrist and then the big old gal was flying ass-over-teakettle at them. Ki caught the screaming matron before she could land on her head and managed to deposit her safely on her fat rump, still screaming. Longarm stepped in, soothing, "Now, Jessie . . ." and then she was in his arms, her own arms hugging him like a frightened huggy bear as she sobbed, "Oh, Custis! Help me! Help me! Wake me up from this nightmare!"

As he held her the doc jabbed Jessie in the rump with a mean-sized needle as Ki held the now enraged matron in the doorway. Longarm snapped, "Hold on, Doc, what do you think you're doing to this lady?"

So the man with the needle quickly explained, "Trying to calm her down, of course. It was just a mild dose of morphine. It won't put her under. She's been on opium at least a month, judging from her symptoms, and you can't take them off it just like that if you don't want them acting just like recent!"

Longarm shook his head, holding Jessie so tightly it wouldn't matter if she'd wanted to climb any walls or not. He told the doc, "It wasn't opium and I doubt she was on it that long. Some rascal fed her henbane. A druggist told me it don't make you sleep and dream like opium, it makes you see things, wide awake."

The doctor shook his own head, saying, "Nonsense. I just examined her when they brought her here, disoriented and barely able to see who she was trying to kick and scratch. I'm familiar with the effects of henbane, morning glory seeds and such. I tell you this young lady has been on opium, or maybe morphine derived from the same."

Longarm felt Jessie relaxing in his arms as the effects of that last shot calmed her. He disengaged one arm and reached in his coat pocket for the mysterious blue bottle. He held it up so both the doc and the girl he was holding could see it. He said, "She bought this bottle as it's labeled. Only someone had put crazy pills in it. Right, Jessie?"

She yawned and said, "If you say so, dear. I don't remember ever having seen that bottle before. It's pretty, though."

He frowned down at her to say, "Jessie, we found this in your medicine cabinet at the Circle Star. If you didn't put it there, who could have?"

She snuggled closer and murmured, "I don't know. Didn't I just tell you I never saw it before?"

Longarm stared sternly at the man who still had that infernal needle in his hand, saying, "You gave her too much. But a lady ought to know what ought to be in her own medicine chest. This bottle's empty, as you can see. But I had a druggist assay the pill dust that's left and it seems the contents had henbane and, oh, yeah, hemlock poison and cornstarch in it."

The medical man took the bottle from him with a sniff, saying, "We'll just run this through our lab and see about that. Why on earth would anyone put such a voodoo mixture in a bottle of mild sleeping pills?"

Jessie yawned and murmured, "Sleeping pills? Why would I want any sleeping pills? I can barely keep my eyes open as it is."

Longarm said, "Don't close your eyes just yet, honey. Are you saying you *never* take sleeping pills?"

She answered with another yawn, "Why should I? I hardly ever have trouble falling asleep after a busy day and, when I do, I like to read in bed, as you well know, sweetheart."

Longarm felt his ears redden as he shook her gently to open her eyes some more, saying, "Stay with us a minute, pard. Your maid, Maria, says she helped you unpack that blue bottle after you'd come back from town. Are you saying she told us a big fib?"

177

Jessie said, "I don't remember coming back to the Circle Star from Galveston. Aren't we still there? People keep telling me this is a hospital in Galveston."

He assured her, "It is. Tell us what you do remember, honey."

She lay her head against his chest, murmuring, "Before things got so scary I was having tea with these two ladies. They wanted me to help them with some charity. Then, all of a sudden, I seemed to be on the floor and they were talking French. I can speak French when I'm wide awake, but it was all so blurry and then I was having awful dreams. There was this one awful face looming over me a lot. I knew it was someone I knew too well to be scared of, but she scared me, anyway. Then I was running from the iceman and other killers from that cartel that orphaned me and they were scary, too, but not as scary as that one white-faced gal who kept grinning down at me. She was, let's see, blonde and sort of nice-looking with familiar features and . . . Oh, Lord, I think she looked like *me*! Maybe that's why she scared me so. It feels so odd to have yourself being mean to you!"

In the doorway, Ki let the now calmed down matron go as he said, soberly, "The police found another woman in that house of ill repute. We'll want to question the surviving bawds as well."

The girl in his arms didn't seem up to much more questioning at the moment, so Longarm gently lowered Jessie to the padded floor. He saw he'd made the right move when she just rolled over and fell into a peaceful sleep. He picked up the straitjacket. He rose and held it out to the matron, saying, "Don't use this on her no more. I mean it. We'll be back directly with her lawyer and a writ of habeas corpus, hoping to find you all alive and well. The little lady ain't loco, she's just been poisoned with henbane, opium or whatever."

The matron glanced at the doc, who nodded, but told Longarm, "I fear it's going to take more than a writ of habeas corpus to get her out of here. We're holding her on a murder charge and her best plea would be criminal insanity!''

The city morgue wasn't far, so the city lawman tagged along. The stiff attendents weren't about to argue with two lawmen and a mighty big Oriental. They wheeled the sheet-covered cadaver out to the viewing room and pulled down the sheet. Longarm had seen Miss Doc naked before, albeit not so bruised and wiry necked. As he stared down at the dead brunette's face he nodded and said, ''Things are starting to fall into place at last. She told me she was French Canadian and Jessie heard the two of them jawing in French right after they drugged her.''

He got out his notepad to write down the dead girl's full name and drugstore address for the Galveston law as Ki asked, ''How can you be sure this one had any part in that? Don't you think we ought to let Jessie have a look here?''

Longarm said, ''There's nothing sure but death and taxes. But I'd only put a sick and worn-out lady through this as a last resort. This gal spoke French. She seems to have lied to me about medical matters. What cinches it, for me, is that she was found on the premises when the vice squad raided the same. So add it up.''

Ki did. He said, ''Jessie couldn't have done it if they found her semi-conscious in another part of the house. If they used this recent druggist as a tool to feed you misinformation, they might not have wanted her changing her story after being picked up by the law, knowing you were in town and on good terms with the local detective squad.''

Longarm turned to the nearest member of the same to say, ''I'd like you to consider such matters ain't federal before you tell me whether that vice raid was random or tip-off?''

The Galveston dick shrugged and said, ''I'm too decent to work with the vice squad. But if you want an off-the-record guess it would have been a tip from some informant.

The place they raided was being run sedately, up a side street. They usually hit gaudy joints when it's just for show. I can find out for you, if you think it's important.''

Longarm nodded, but said, "That falls in place pretty good as is. They wanted Jessie Starbuck to be found, bare naked and full of dope, but alive. This gal on the slab had outlived her usefulness or, just as likely, wanted out and came there demanding traveling money. I scared her when I asked too many questions and she had to come up with answers, fast. Like I said, it's starting to fall together, partways, at least.''

Ki said he still couldn't make any sense of it. Longarm told him, "That's because you don't work on the side of the law half as much as I do. Jessie was here on a business trip. Two nice charity ladies lured her to tea and spiked her cup. Whoever may be behind the dastardly plot didn't want to kill her entire. I have to work on that part some more. They carried her to that cathouse and they've been holding her a prisoner all this time by giving her just enough dope to keep her too groggy to get loose. This dead druggist gal here could have told 'em exactly how much to give her, and how often.''

Ki objected, "Then how did they get Jessie to go back to the home spread, let Maria see that blue bottle, and mope about sort of odd before she lit out again to act wild and woolly?''

Longarm snorted in disgust and said, "They never. It wouldn't have worked. Maria just saw another blonde Anglo lady wearing la patrona's duds and bossing the household help about. When you and those other riders were stopped near Sanderson with the cows Jessie told you to herd over to South Springs, it was the same impostor who wired back all those mean things about you. Then she came down here to put Captain Wilson in the hospital before she headed for the Peace River range, or tried to make us all think that was where she was going. I reckon they wanted me to chase up there after her. That's why she acted so odd at my home office.''

Ki shook his head and growled, ''Come now, not again! It didn't work the first time they tried to use a double to discredit the poor girl, damn it!''

Longarm said, ''I doubt it's the same them. We got that bunch. We've already agreed it's hard as hell to find a look-alike that can pass for anyone to their close friends. But back up and just reconsider what we know about this confusion. *You* never got to lay eyes on the sham Jessie. Neither did her business associates in Galveston, except for Captain Wilson, who got kicked in the crotch and thrown down a cargo hold after dark. Maria was the only one she had to brazen it out with enough to matter, and Maria's new help, a mestiza who might have some trouble telling one blonde Anglo gal from the other and—''

''What about that clerk up in Denver?'' Ki cut in.

Longarm explained, ''Aside from being shy around all women, poor Henry's only seen the real Jessie now and again, passing through on her way to old Billy Vail's office. He might have caught on, given time enough to study her. But she just barged in, with her face overpowdered and her hair, or wig, dangling wild. Then she scared him and shocked him by skimming a steel star at him and talking dirty long enough for him to recall the visit, and then she was gone. She and her pals could have made sure Billy Vail would be out of his office at the time.''

Ki brightened and said, ''That shuriken left in his door was a mighty artistic touch! Even if Henry told Vail he wasn't sure it was the Miss Starbuck he remembered, the two of them would have had a time coming up with anyone else it might have been. The crooks lost tabs on you, of course. You were supposed to be sent after her to Canada while I was languishing in jail or worse. When you showed up here in Galveston, instead, their first thought was to take you out of the picture and, when that didn't seem too easy . . . Right, they simply changed the last act of their drama by having Jessie found, in a state that would explain all the mad actions of their impostor. Then . . . Damn, that's where I get stuck, too!''

The Galveston dick, who'd been following intently and had a head on his shoulders to follow with, opined, ''There can't be many ladies on this island as look just like that one I just saw in the hospital. We'll put a dragnet out for the sneaky bitch!''

Longarm said that was a grand notion, but added, ''I doubt the other gal looks all that much like Miss Starbuck. All pretty young gals look *sort* of alike, dressed and made-up much the same. But if the gal who's been acting so wild was a dead ringer she might not have had to act so wild. By now she'll have changed back to her own duds, hairstyle and maybe even color. She could likely pass us on the streets and we'd no more than whistle at her. Add up all the gals on this island with regular features and a swell figure, then consider she might not even be out here anymore, and, no offense, your dragnet has some holes in it!''

Ki said, ''Wait. The police report has Jessie, or someone who resembles Jessie, running that cathouse she was found in. Might that not be the best place to start scouting for sign?''

Longarm asked the Galveston lawman how soon the whores arrested by the vice squad figured to get out on bail. The dick said, ''Surely you jest. Arrested on whoring alone they'd already be out. But Galveston P.D. has *some* rules. Knowing they're material witnesses to a homicide, and knowing how flighty such gals are by nature, they ain't about to get out on bail before we get a handle on the killing of this here dead lady!''

Longarm said, ''Bueno. There's no hurry to question them, then. They'll no doubt swear their madam was Jessie or a mighty close match. None of 'em would have been invited to supper by their boss, and ladies running whore-houses are inclined to wear a heap of face paint while they drink alone. Our best bet regarding that mysterious house of ill repute will be the city clerk's records. You can't buy even a whorehouse without recording the transfer of property with the city clerk, right?"

The Galveston lawman asked if Longarm would like him to cover that lead. Longarm said, "I wish you would. My boss, Marshal Vail, enjoys paper chasing a heap more than I do. What say we all meet again this afternoon, at the hospital. Me and Ki have to get over to Miss Starbuck's law firm."

They shook on it and split up outside. Ki knew the way to the office of old Pete Pomerance. As they got there Ki pointed out a stout elderly man coming at them in a snuff-colored suit and said, "That's Pomerance, now. I've heard of showing up at the office late, but this is ridiculous!"

But as Ki introduced Longarm to the lawyer near the entrance of his business building, it seemed they'd misjudged him. For Pomerance said, "I heard. I just came from the hospital. I told little Jessie I'd do all I could for her, and she seems a bit calmer now."

Longarm asked what her lawyer was doing for her and Pomerance admitted, with a sheepish smile, "I lied. I naturally applied for a writ of habeas corpus and the judge naturally turned me down flat."

Ki scowled and said, "Damn it, Pete, the right to habeas corpus is in your own Texas constitution as well as the federal bill of rights!"

Longarm, who had to study up on law more than even a good segundo, explained, "Habeas corpus is Latin for how come you're holding the body, meaning the body arrested, in this case. If it meant nobody *could* hold nobody, judges like Isaak Parker up to Fort Smith would never get to hang nobody. Before they wrote the bill of rights, royal lawmen had the habit of picking up anyone who mentioned any kind of rights and just holding them, without any particular charges, until they got good and ready to let 'em go, if ever. So a writ, or court order of habeas corpus, really means the law can't hold nobody unless they can show just cause.''

Lawyer Pomerance nodded and said, ''They never put it clearer at Harvard Law, albeit they took more words to say it. They're holding Jessie on two serious charges. One is manslaughter. The other is dangerous lunacy. I wish I only had to defend her on manslaughter. I don't know how in hell you prove someone's sane after they've acted mighty crazy!''

Longarm said, ''We've got most of that figured out. It wasn't Jessie running about so wild. She likely spent the better part of a month in a cellar, drugged silly but harmless. I see what you mean about the manslaughter charge. No witness who saw her even fuss at that lady druggist has come forward. Since the other gals abiding in that house say they never even saw the dead gal before the copper badges found her dead, I doubt anyone will have the gall to bear witness against the other victim of the real villains.''

He reached absently for a cheroot as he asked the portly lawyer, ''Can't we get Jessie off on being loco if she just acts sensible?''

Pomerance nodded but spoiled it all by saying, ''Of course. But she'll still have to face a sanity hearing. I'll be representing her, of course, along with more than one local physician who can certify her sane. But, until we can set a date for such a hearing I fear there's no way to get her out of that awful place!''

For a gent who gloried in tales of ice-cold samurai, Ki sure needed calming down. So when Longarm hauled him back to the hotel dining room only to discover they couldn't serve drinks without sit-down meals, Longarm hauled Ki the rest of the way to Blacky's. The downstairs was even quieter by daylight, and Longarm didn't care what might be going on upstairs. They took the same corner table and ordered a pitcher of beer. While they were waiting on it Longarm reminded Ki of his trouble on an earlier visit here. Ki said,

"Never mind all that. We already knew someone was after you in Galveston. We have to round up a herd of character witnesses for Jessie or, failing that, we have to bust her out of that damned hospital!"

The waitress in a shocking knee-length skirt put the pitcher and two glasses on the table between them and murmured, "Gee, thanks, sport," when Longarm told her she could keep the change. Ki made a mental note to leave a quarter on the table when they left and then insisted, "Jessie's well known here in Galveston. We ought to be able to find a lot of people who don't work for her and still think she's perfectly sane."

Longarm nodded but said, "Simmer down and let's study on the whole bucket of sheep dip. To begin with, unless Pomerance just plain throws the case, and he'd better not, he won't need a whole parade of character witnesses to prove the obvious. Jessie's well known all over Texas and lots of other places as a canny young businesswoman with a good head on her shoulders. You don't have to prove you're sane to stay out of a loony bin. Somebody has to prove you're loony. We got an impartial medical report allowing the poor gal was brung in doped to the gills by a person or persons unknown. I've arrested folk on dope. The results was sort of distressing. Once someone's been taking it for a spell, willingly or otherwise, they get sick as hell if they're forced to quit cold. So she's better off under treatment at that hospital. They can wean her off that opium gentle by giving her just enough to keep her from feeling wiggle worms under her hide as they cut down the dosage each time. Aside from her needing more medication before she leaves, where in thunder were you thinking of taking her after you busted her out informal, Patagonia?"

He poured for both of them, explaining, "You're so right about Jessie being well known, all over. If word got about that a possibly dangerous lunatic had broken out of the Galveston mental ward, the Rangers and U.S. Cav, if need be, would have the Circle Star surrounded within hours.

185

Until she could be caught her whole business empire would be placed in receivership by the courts to protect her creditors and . . . Hmm, that does lead to some mighty interesting motives, doesn't it?''

Ki sighed and said, ''You're right. Whether listed as an outlaw or a lunatic, Jessie would lose control of Starbuck Enterprises. I think I'd better go over the books again, starting tonight with unannounced visits to our various offices in this port and Pomerance's files. Once we figure out who stands to be placed in control of her affairs if she should be proven incompetent—''

''We won't know shit,'' Longarm cut in. ''You likely know more than me about business, Ki, but trust me on the way court judgments work. You do get a feel for it after they let a heap of skunks you've arrested off for nit-picking reasons. I have dealt with more than one murder or accidental death of a plutocrat, so I know how the courts try to tidy up. Should they declare Jessie incompetent to do her own business chores, temporary or worse, they'll start by naming an executor. That may well be you, unless somebody else with a say in the matter objects to your doing so, and that could as easily be racial malice as serious theft. Seeing there has to be all sorts of money in the pipelines, both ways, they'll likely impanel some sort of committee to manage her empire for her. The fact that someone's on it won't mean all that much. I've seen gents appointed to settle a complicated estate kicking harder than a cardshark trying to avoid jury duty.''

Ki grumbled, ''You speak as if Jessie was already dead, damn you!''

''She would be if the mastermind behind all this figured to just step in and pick up the reins. So that's a clue. We're looking for someone who stands to gain *not* from the probate of an estate but from Starbuck Enterprises being left in a neither-nor state of confusion.''

Ki thought for two swallows of beer before he asked just how that might work. Longarm finished his own sip and replied, "If I knew for sure we wouldn't be having this bewildering conversation. I'd go arrest the son of a bitch. I can think of too many ways a crook could benefit from putting Jessie halfway out of business, starting with simply stealing some business that might otherwise have gone to Starbuck Enterprises and working up to wheeling and dealing on the stock market. Say you're dealing in beef futures, betting on the price of the same come this fall's roundup, and whether the Circle Star herd will be shipped or not is sort of misty."

Ki brightened and said, "I see what you mean! If Jessie was her old self this fall, anyone dealing in beef futures could predict she'd send the most profitable amount of beef to market she could work out. If she was simply dead, it would be safe to predict there'd be no Circle Star market herd to worry about before her will had been probated. But with her sort of floating in a business limbo, we're talking about one hell of a lot of beef that's sort of in limbo as well!"

Longarm nodded but said, "She ships cotton and imports all sorts of Oriental produce as well. So for all we know the son of a bitch could be out to corner tea leaves."

Ki sighed and said, "I wish you hadn't said that. Cutting the right suspects out of all the business rivals who stand to make money on Jessie's discomfiture is not going to be easy, or even possible, damn it!"

"There's another way to slice it, if we can count on Pomerance having any pull at all with the local courthouse gang."

Ki said, flatly, "He does. A lawyer who can't pull strings isn't worth his retainer. I'm fairly sure we can trust him. But to do what?"

"To get Jessie's sanity hearing moved up," Longarm said. "The crooks who got her in such a fix know she ain't crazy, and they know that given a fair hearing she's sure to be declared competent to manage her own affairs. So they're working to some devious timetable. They let her be found when they did because they were ready to make their next move. They figure they have time to make their next move, whatever it may be, in the time it usually takes to get their victim off opium and on the court docket. The wheels of justice grind fine, but they grind exceedingly slow, as a rule.''

Ki smiled thinly and said, ''I think you got that old saw backward, but I see what you mean. It can take months, even years, to get some cases heard. You're saying that speedy justice just might throw someone's devious plot out of gear, right?''

Longarm nodded soberly and said, ''It might be sort of interesting to note who might or might not want to contest Jessie's sanity. They may feel obliged to, if Pomerance can get her a sudden walk through. For, unopposed, that's all it'll amount to if Jessie shows up bright eyed and bushy tailed to just tell 'em she feels fine. You and a few other employees of Starbuck Enterprises may be called on to opine she's been running things just fine since Alex Starbuck was killed. That doc ought to be able to convince the other medical men on the panel that she was just a mite dazed from opium, not crazy, when they found her. If an uncontested hearing takes a full hour I'll be mighty surprised. If Pomerance can get her case heard just before noon dinnertime it ought to go even faster.''

Ki asked, ''What about that murder charge?''

Longarm grinned and said, ''Hell, that ain't the business of a sanity hearing, and suspicion of homicide is why habeas corpus was put in the bill of rights to begin with. You can't charge nobody with a killing just for being on the premises at the time. You got to come up with material evidence. The police report already shows Jessie was in the cellar, naked and semi-conscious, when they raided the place. Any of the other gals they found on or about the same premises works as well and even better as the killer. I doubt they'll want to hold all them whores as suspects all that long. Where would the Galveston entertainment industry be with all that fun-for-a-fee flesh out of circulation?''

Ki nodded knowingly and might have made his own observations on a wide-open sin strip had not a burly gent in a pea jacket come over to lay a heavy hand on Ki's shoulder and demand, "Hey, are you a damned old Chin-Chin-Chinaman?''

Ki turned in his seat to regard the intruder coldly as he softly replied, "I happen to be part Nihongo, and get your hand off me, fast!''

The drunken waterfront bully did no such thing as he snarled, "I knew you was some kind of infernal furriner.'' So Ki just reached up, grabbed the lout's forearm in both hands to hold the unwelcome paw tighter against his shoulder. Then he shrugged the shoulder and broke the bully's wrist.

As his annoyer fell to the sawdust-covered floor, wailing in sheer agony, Ki rose gravely, tossing his chair lightly aside, to ask, mildly, "Anyone else?''

There seemed to be two more. As they moved in, demanding to know what he'd done to their pal, everyone else in the place commenced to edge the other way. Longarm shifted his weight to rise from his corner seat. Ki sensed the movement without looking back and said, "Stay out of this, Custis. Two to one seems just about fair.''

So Longarm called him a spoilsport and settled back to watch. One of the hoodlums glanced thoughtfully at the gun rig Ki would have felt undressed without in Galveston and muttered, "We ain't armed, you heathen son of a bitch.''

So Ki unbuckled his gun belt, tossed his rig on the table, gun and all, to purr, "Neither am I.''

They'd lied, of course. They both produced bowies as they moved in, grinning. Ki nodded, half to himself, and then pulled a little surprise of his own. He dove headfirst at the floor instead of at them, to land on his horny palms and finish the unexpected move with a forward flip, planting a heel in each of their startled faces.

189

Longarm had seen Ki fight before, so he wasn't as surprised by the way they both went down as he was by the way Ki wound up standing over them instead of down in the bloody sawdust with them. They were both out like lights, if they were still alive. The one with the broken wrist was still raising a fuss on the floor. So Ki kicked him in the head to stretch him out to dream some in the sawdust before he rejoined Longarm at the table, poured himself another drink, and asked, "Now, where were we?"

Longarm laughed and said, "I'd say we were just about to leave. Do you always sit with your back to the crowd right after you've put some of it on the floor?"

Ki grinned boyishly and replied, "Sometimes it's more fun that way. You're covering me under the table, aren't you?"

Longarm said, "Sure. But you've proven your point and it's tedious to drink with a gun in my good hand. Put your own gun back on and let's get out of here."

Ki didn't argue. But as he was buckling his gun rig back around his hips the beaded curtain across the way parted to let Blacky Morgan out, with his own gun hand resting casually on the grips of his .45. He noted the carnage on the floor near their table, recognized Longarm at the same time, and came over to mildly ask what was going on.

Longarm said, "This funny-looking jasper is Ki, the segundo of the Circle Star. We were enjoying a quiet drink together when one of them gents on the floor objected. They ain't gunshot, just busted up a mite."

Blacky nodded and snapped his fingers. That inspired some of his hired help to come closer and drag the three unconscious ruffians out the back way to the alley while Blacky sat down with them, muttering, "It's up to me and my help to decide who drinks here and who does not. That one old boy, Hook Daws, is sort of noted as a barroom brawler. So you two may have saved us some trouble, later. What did you do, Longarm, pistol-whip 'em?"

Longarm nodded modestly at Ki and replied, "Nope. My

190

pal, here, didn't need no help. He just kicked the three of 'em gally west all by himself.''

Blacky stared at Ki with renewed interest, asking, "Oh, might you be a practitioner of *la sabot*?"

Longarm explained, "He means logger-style foot-fighting."

Ki replied with a sniff, "I know about la sabot. They say the French navy brought some of the more cunning kicks back from Indo-China. Might you be interested in such skills, Morgan?"

Blacky said, "Not hardly. But as a former dancer I've found it sort of interesting to watch. We had this little French female impersonator on the Orphium Circuit with us one time who may have served a hitch in the French navy. He liked gals just fine when he wasn't dressed up like one. But small-town roughnecks would call him a queer on occasion." He helped himself to some of their beer, sipping from the side of the pitcher, before he added, "They never did that twice. Lord, most ballet dancers couldn't kick that high without winding up on their butts. It was the balance that fascinated me, from my own professional perspective. I could never figure how he kept his center of gravity in place, kicking gents in the jaw so fine."

"You just missed a performance," Longarm said. "How did that raid you was expecting go, last night?"

Blacky frowned uncertainly and said, "It never came off. The boys got a tip on a real den of sin, they tell me. Some new gal in town was running wide open, without even paying a courtesy call on the powers that be. That's no way to run a whorehouse. Heard they even found one of her soiled doves done in by some john. How did your, ah, police interview go last night, by the way?"

Longarm said, "Oh, I'm allowed to sin, in my own way, without having to make payoffs. I took credit for both of 'em. I hope you don't mind."

Blacky shot a warning glance. Longarm nodded and said, "It's all right. I told you Ki was a pal of mine. We're working on the same case. He seems to think someone here in Galveston wants me off it. You'd have heard, I hope, if there was any open bounty on my head?''

Blacky nodded but said, ''I'd have heard for certain. Only I never. I wish you hadn't told me that, Longarm. As anyone can tell you, I've always done my best to get along with the law. But I'm trying to run a nice quiet establishment here, and it does seem every time you drop by things get sort of noisy, if you follow my drift.''

Longarm nodded, politely, and said, ''We'll be moving on as soon as we finish our beer, if that's all the same to you.''

Blacky said he never liked to rush anyone who didn't need some rushing and got up to leave them to sort it out. As he vanished behind the beaded curtain, Longarm asked Ki, ''What did you make of him? I'm dead certain, now, I've met up with that squirt before.''

Ki shrugged. ''I've seen that face before. But it stands to reason I would have, coming here to Galveston as often as I have to. I've never had trouble or even words with him before, though. His face was more familiar than his voice or mannerisms. It's this place he runs I find more interesting. He seems friendly enough, in a hard-boiled way, and he had his chance to back-shoot you, last night, and didn't. But don't you find it odd that first you, then I, seem to get picked on so much in the same surroundings?''

Longarm grimaced and said, ''Great minds run in the same dumb channels. But I dunno, Ki. You could still be being left out. I didn't make them three bully-boys as trouble-for-hire. I fear they come at you for free. I don't mean to be unkind, but we did have them Chinese riots all through the '70s. An idiot labor organizer called Kearney started 'em on the Frisco waterfront for some fool reason. He was never too clear on whether he was afraid some oriental was after his job or his sister.''

Ki muttered, ''Tell me about how welcome anyone of even vaguely oriental appearance can be made to feel in most parts of the west, now that the Cantonese finished building the railroads at starvation wages. I could tell you some sad stories. But just as I was about to pack it in and go back to fight with my much smaller relatives some more I ran into Alex Starbuck, who'd known my father when they were both trading in the Orient after Japan opened her ports to the outside world again.''

Longarm said, ''I remember. I was just old enough to read when Perry steamed his black ships into Tokyo Harbor and convinced the young shogun of the error of his ways. Do you mind if I ask a personal question, Ki?''

Ki stared at him dubiously, but didn't say not to. So Longarm said, ''Well, I know it's none of my business, but you do allow your daddy was a Yankee trader and your mother was a highborn lady of Japanese persuasion. So I just have to confess I've often wondered how you managed to get born so sudden. I mean, if no outsiders were allowed to come courting any kind of Japanese gals before the trade treaty of fifty-four, and one has to allow some courting time as well as the usual nine months—''

''Watch it!'' said Ki, coldly, before he shrugged and allowed, ''I'm younger than you, in years. Which of us has been through more fights is less certain. You haven't known prejudice before you've been ganged by a mob of pure albeit lower-class Nihongo. I was able to take on a grown man by the time some decided I was a pretty little boy in the slums of Tokyo. Less-degenerate ruffians were kind enough to help me polish my skills in the martial arts. Perhaps I picked up a little more polish, along with some education, from kindly but dangerous masters of Zen and Shinto. Shinto is a sort of silly religion but never mess with their monks.''

Longarm said he hoped he'd never have to, but insisted, ''In other words, you can't be much older than Jessie, mean as you look, next to her. So how come she looks up to you as a sort of big brother, you young squirt?''

Ki smiled despite himself and said, ''I came to the States as a teenager. It was that or settle for becoming a mere ninja, or a fighting man of outcast social rank. It didn't take me long to find out breeds can have a tough time in the land of the free. But, as I said, I was lucky enough to be taken under the wing of Alex Starbuck. It's true I was only a couple of years older than his only child. But years are longer when you're young. To an adolescent girl, a boy who's begun to shave is a grown-up, whether he's quite old enough to vote or not.''

Blacky Morgan came back down again to scowl their way from the beaded curtain. Longarm caught the eye of the waitress and ordered more beer, even though they hadn't finished their first pitcher. The gesture wasn't wasted on the owner. He came over to say, softly, ''I thought you boys were just leaving.''

Longarm said, ''We was. I don't like to be pushed. Are you pushing me, Blacky?''

Morgan gulped and said, ''Oh, for Christ's sake, I only wanted to see if you were still here, is all.''

Longarm said, without expression, ''We are, and it's hot out. I told you I understood your problem. But are you trying to be my problem, Blacky?''

Morgan muttered, ''Oh, shit,'' and turned away to leave them in peace. Ki asked, quietly, ''Are we trying to start another fight here, Custis?''

Longarm said, ''I ain't sure. It might be sort of interesting to find out. Your life story ain't as interesting as I'd imagined. Let's get back to Jessie.''

Ki said, ''She's at the hospital and it is getting later as we sit here. Didn't you tell that other lawman we'd meet him there this afternoon?''

Longarm nodded and said, ''That was before I began to get the distinct impression I wasn't welcome here at all. I'm keeping tabs on the time. Let's just give Blacky a few more minutes to decide on peace or war. We were talking about Jessie.''

Ki shrugged and said, ''I suspect you know her as well as I do. You were there when she avenged the death of her father. Before that she had a privileged but rather unusual upbringing. Old Alex wanted his daughter to grow up a young lady of refinement and education, but, perhaps sensing she might someday have to fend for herself in a still untamed west, he made sure she knew how to take care of herself as well as any son he'd had might have managed.''

Longarm said, ''I wasn't concerned about all that. She's often bragged on that special .38 her father had made for her on a .45 frame, even though she ain't really weak wristed enough to shoot sissy with a .45-60. I know about her being taught Japanese by an Oriental nanny and French at that fancy finishing school. She showed me how you and her father taught her shooting, roping, and busting bricks with the edge of her palm the first time I asked, sort of terrified. I'm more interested in what she's been up to that I might not know as much about. For as you know we've mostly got together when one or the other of us was in trouble.''

Ki said, softly, ''You know damned well you could stay with her till death do you part, you stubborn fool.''

Longarm shushed him with an impatient wave of his hand and insisted, ''That's neither here nor there. The folk out to get her declared a helpless idiot ain't interested in mush. When I say I want to know what she does when I might not be around I mean her more sedate routine, between roundups and chasing crooks.''

Ki shrugged and said, ''I'm not sure I know what you mean. As both the mistress of a business empire and a lady of refined ways, she leads a fairly sedate life, when she's allowed to. She serves on local charity committees and donates to others on a fairly regular basis. Her father brought her up with a set of good social values, as well as marksmanship. Having the money to do so with, she's interested in education for orphans and minority children. I know she funds at least three Indian schools and donates considerable money to Booker T. Washington, the Negro educator.''

Longarm frowned thoughtfully, and as if he'd read his mind, Ki told him, ''As a Texan, Alex Starbuck naturally backed Texas, and the south, in that stupid war you had. But slavery was never the issue in cattle country. Please don't ask me to explain States' Rights. Suffice it to say, Jessie was raised by her father to divide the human race into good and evil, rather than along the more usual lines. Apparently Washington is starting, or has started, a Negro college back East. Are you suggesting the *Klan* could be behind all this skulduggery?''

Longarm curled his lip to reply, ''The Klan that's left ain't got enough sense to plan a simple stickup. The original Klan disbanded after President Hayes had the good sense to end the so-called Reconstruction. Nobody but trash ass-holes with nothing better to do are night riding in their bed linens, now. I knew Jessie did some charity work, if not as much as you say. I don't see how anything like that could account for her present troubles, though.''

Ki asked, ''If someone were to get power to sign for her, could they give away any large amount of her money in the name of some fake charity?''

Longarm muttered, ''I just told you that couldn't work. Anyone handling her money as a trustee would have to keep mighty neat books for the court. Can you see your average Texas judge sitting still for anyone giving good money away to educate colored kids or even white kids? The trustees would perforce stick to rock-bottom business in Jessie's name. They couldn't even give a party on her loose change. Any trustee controlling the purse strings of a minor, a lu-natic, or other ward of the court is supposed to do so tight-fisted as a miser. Anyone out to collect Jessie's money in the name of a charity or religious sect would be left out in the cold.''

He sipped a few more suds, glanced at the wall clock above the distant bar, and decided, ''Nobody seems up to throwing us out, and a man can only consume so much beer at a sitting if he likes to walk straight and piss regular. We'd best get on over to the hospital. I want to check in with Western Union along the way as well.''

Ki nodded agreeably and they left the extra pitcher of beer untasted to step out into the bright sunlight. As they strode off side by side, Ki muttered, "I wish I could place that Blacky Morgan. Didn't we have trouble with a Mormon called Morgan over in Utah that time?"

Longarm nodded but said, "Blacky don't look at all like old Morgan Welch and their names are on backward. Morgan is the Welsh version of Murphy, which is the most common Irish name I know of. I think they both mean something like *seaman*. I doubt Blacky could be a Mormon. Most folk with Welsh last names tend to be Methodists. I fail to see how either sect could hope to profit by having Jessie declared incompetent to contribute one dime to either. But I'm glad you reminded me of that time some crooked lawyers tried to frame Jessie so fake relations could claim Starbuck Enterprises after Jessie was executed on fake murder charges. For I'm sure now that wherever I've seen that Blacky Morgan it was more recent. Have you ever had a name or face sort of hanging on the tip of your tongue but just refusing to click in place?"

"Of course. As we were talking to him I felt sure I'd seen his features before, but oddly skewed, as if he'd maybe worn a beard or had different colored hair the last time we met."

As they neared the telegraph office, Longarm said, "You could be right about face hair. The hair on his head is the black hair he was born with, though. In my line, you get good at spotting wigs, fake whiskers or even dyed hair. I sometimes wonder why so many gals go to all that trouble. I know this wandering piano-playing gal, Red Robin, who has her head dyed another shade every time we meet, and I still know for a fact she's a natural brunette."

"I'm sure you would," said Ki, dryly. Recalling Ki was his one true love's segundo and confidant, Longarm dropped the subject of gals who only dyed the hair on their heads as the two of them entered the Western Union office. Billy Vail never sprung for a nickel a word unless he had something important to say. But Crown Sergeant Foster had wired all the way down from Fort MacLeod, even though he didn't have all that much to say, either. The Mounties had been watching the border so sharp that Foster felt few jackrabbits with sinister intent could have slipped by them. Mounty posts up along the Peace River had nothing to report, either. When he let Ki scan the wire Jessie's big segundo muttered, "We know full well Jessie never went up that way. She just woke up here in Galveston. But might that not be a lead to consider, Longarm. That dead druggist told you she was French Canadian, and with all that separatist business going on up there the girl pretending to be Jessie could have had better reason to head north."

Longarm said flatly, "She never. The whores at that parlor house Jessie was being held in claim they saw a madam who looked sort of like Jessie more recent than poor Henry got scared by the same. I don't know Miss Doc was French Canadian. She lied to me about lots of things. She may well have been French French. She did go on about Joan of Arc, who wasn't a saint or even important in France when the first French Canadians arrived back in the sixteen hundreds. Someone just making things up about Canada might just grab the Peace River out of her hat. It's on even rough-scale maps of Canada."

Ki said, "You mean the impostor, then, not that French girl they just murdered. Wouldn't that make the one they frightened Henry with a fake French Canadian as well?"

Longarm snorted, "How should I know? They could have a whole squad of fake Jessies traipsing about just to confuse us."

As Longarm picked up a telegraph blank Ki told him, "You're wrong. Don't you remember the last time someone tried to pull a fast one by impersonating Jessie? They had to go to a lot of trouble to come that close and, even then, she wasn't an exact double to anyone who knew the real Jessie well."

Longarm started to block letter his message as he replied,

even while writing, "Nobody who really knows the real Jessie has ever seen one or more doubles, this time. So, like I just said, they could have a whole squad out. Most any gal with a trim figure, blonde hair and wearing an unusual outfit could pass as well if she just said she was Jessie Starbuck. Hold still and let me finish this wire to Chicago."

Ki did. But when Longarm had finished and handed it across the counter, saying, "Day rates, pronto as possible," Ki naturally asked who they wanted to get in touch with in Chicago.

Longarm said, "I learned a mite about show business and French show folk while bodyguarding Miss Sarah Bernhardt one time. So I'd like to hear from the Orphium Circuit's midwest booking office."

He saw Ki was having a time following his drift, so he went on to explain, "The Orphium Circuit is a chain of vaudeville houses all across the country. Blacky Morgan told me he used to be in show business. I thought I'd see what show business might recall about him and another critter he mentioned in passing. He said he once knew a female impersonator of French extraction, remember?"

Ki smiled incredulously and started to say something dumb. Then he nodded more soberly and said, "Right. That little French druggist might well have been killed by an expert at la sabot, and Captain Wilson was *kicked* down that cargo hold as well. But seriously, now, a *man*, fooling Henry in broad daylight at close range?"

Longarm shrugged and said, "Henry don't kiss nearly as many gals as you and me, and a man who made a living pretending to be gals would have to be sort of convincing, dressed up like one in smeared makeup and a bedraggled wig as he, she or it threw steel weapons about the office. You're right about it being tough to find a gal with Jessie's features, and not even Henry would have been fooled by a downright poor match. But as soon as you allow for pretty boys as well as pretty gals the field *doubles*! So who's to say whether a gambling man here in Galveston who'd noticed Jessie in passing might or might not recall a sissy boy from his past with the same general features? Female impersonators don't just walk on stage pretending to be themselves as a gal. They imitate a string of well-known ladies by changing their hair, walk, makeup and general appearance. So much a sly gent who'd had time to study the real Jessie might well be lots better at imitating her than your run-of-the-mill crooked lady.''

Ki nodded and said, ''I wish you'd brought up that suspicion sooner. Why did we just walk away from that place? Let's go back and hammer some facts out of Blacky Morgan!''

Longarm shook his head to point out, ''Blacky don't look like a cuss who hammers easy. Whether I'm on the right track or just grasping at straws, I doubt he'd fess up before we killed him or vice versa. You got to eat the apple a bite at a time, you cool-headed samurai. We got to have more on him than a wild guess before we take on him and his gang of bouncers.''

As they left to go on to the hospital, Longarm added, ''I hope Chicago assures us Blacky's a good old boy and that his French female impersonator is touring France. For Blacky did save my life that time and, I don't know, I just can't help liking the little squirt. For I'm still sure we met somewhere before, a heap more friendly. He ain't old enough to be an old school chum or army pal. But I still feel we used to be on good terms and I know for a fact he couldn't have been called Blacky Morgan, then.''

★

Chapter 11

The doc who was treating Jessie up in the mental ward met them in the hospital reception room. The Galveston lawman hadn't shown up yet. Longarm naturally asked how Jessie was coming along and her doc replied, "Remarkably well, considering all she's been through. She must have a fantastic constitution, and of course it helps if one's not what we call a natural addict."

Ki asked what that meant. The medical man explained, "As you may have noticed in the company of drinking men, some can stop when they've had enough and others can't. We think it's more a family trait than willpower. Naturally, normal people are affected much the same way by drugs or drink. Real drunks and dope fiends seem to be able to tolerate more before either has an effect on them, as a matter of fact. People who are not meant to become addicted to anything tend to feel worse instead of better when they have too much served to them. So it's possible Miss Starbuck didn't absorb as much opium as we first feared. She recalls some nightmares, but not the pleasure fantasies of the true opium addict.''

Longarm said, "Her father, Alex Starbuck, was neither a drunk nor a dope fiend, Doc. Could you sort of get to the point?"

The doc looked a mite hurt and explained, "All right, in sum, she just refused her last mild dose of morphine, upstairs. She says she feels terrible, but that she'd rather tough it out."

"Can she?" asked Ki, who'd had some experience with narcotics in the Orient.

The expert on the subject replied in a tone of admiration, "Fifty-fifty. We told her withdrawal would be quicker as well as a lot tougher if she tried to do it her way. She seems a very determined young lady."

"Either one of us could have told you that," Longarm said. "How soon will she get better, hanging tough?"

The doc said, "Much sooner, naturally. But she won't be her full self for at least a week or more. In addition to keeping her sedated all that time they didn't feed her too well, and of course she lost some muscle tone, flat on her back in a dank cellar. We have to hold her under observation until her sanity hearing in any case. Not in that padded cell, of course. As soon as she began to make more sense we moved her to a private room of her own. She should be up and around, at least around this hospital, by this time tomorrow.''

They asked if they could go up to see her, of course. The doc said he had no objection. But just as they were about to head as one for the stairwell, that Galveston dick came in. He didn't seem too happy. As he joined them, he said, "Well, I fear I have bad news from the hall of records. You'll never guess who they have registered as the owner of that house of ill repute!"

Longarm sighed and said, "No, I won't. Crooks hardly ever leave their own names on record, and they went to some trouble to make the whores at that whorehouse consider themselves employees of Starbuck Enterprises. Anyone who could make him or herself up to pass for Jessie worth mention could surely sign her name to a property deed. Proving forgery will be a snap, though.''

The Galveston lawman shook his head and said, ''They never. The property was seized in the first place for back taxes a couple of years ago. It wouldn't have been smart for a madam by any name to sign any legal papers. So the whole deal was done through a local law firm. The only signature on file in connection with the property goes with a Peter Pomerance, Esquire.''

Longarm and Ki exchanged stricken glances. Ki groaned, ''By the balls of Buddah, not again! Isn't there one honest lawyer in this country?''

Longarm smiled thinly and said, ''If there is I've yet to meet him. But this does read raw, even for a lawyer.''

Ki growled, deep in his throat, ''You go on up and comfort Jessie. She'll be expecting you at this hour. I'll deal with that two-timing two-bit crook!''

But Longarm said, ''Calm your nerves of steel, you ice-cold samurai. There's nothing two-bit about what's going on around here. I figure two-bit crooks easy and I'll be stomped by an elephant if I can figure what's been going on. You run on over to that law office before it closes, only recall your own advice on fighting cool. Sweet-talk Pomerance or torture his stenographer out of the one thing we need right now, a clear signature in his own hand. Meanwhile I'll run over to the hall of records while it's still open and beg, borrow or steal a copy of that whorehouse deed.'' He turned to the medical man, who was staring mighty confused by now, to ask if they had a microscope anywhere on the premises. When the doc allowed they had more than one Longarm told Ki, ''There you go. A banker gal I met up with one time told me how to spot most forgeries, magnified. We want to make certain Pomerance signed them papers before we do anything mean to him. So don't be

203

mean to him, and what are you waiting for, a kiss good-bye?''

Ki said he was on his way and proved it by dashing out into the oncoming sunset. Longarm turned back to the doc to ask, ''Could you tell Miss Starbuck I'll visit her later, and will I be able to?''

The doc nodded and said, ''She's in a private room. I'm sure the guard posted outside her door will let you in when you show him your own badge.''

Longarm cocked an eyebrow at the Galveston lawman, who just shrugged and asked, ''What do you want, egg in your beer? If the gal's neither a lunatic nor a murderess she's still a material witness, and the boys have orders not to pester her. You may need me along if they close the hall of records before we can get there. I can still get you in past the night watchman.''

Longarm agreed that had picking locks beat by a country mile and told the doc he'd be back directly. The doc explained, ''You may not find me here. We're about to change shifts. But just tell Dr. Chambrun who you are and that I said it was all right.''

They shook on it and Longarm left with the detective. The doc went back to the staff's wardroom to kill coffee and time until his night-watch replacement showed up.

Meanwhile, upstairs in her private room, Jessie Starbuck was sitting on the edge of her steel-pipe hospital bed regarding the golden light through her barred window without enthusiasm. It would soon be getting dark and she wasn't looking forward to it at all. She knew she'd never be able to sleep, as tense and itchy as she felt under her thin hospital gown. Her common sense told her the gown was soft clean cotton. Her skin kept saying it was filthy and gritty. She was tempted to take it off and just go naked. But she knew she'd still itch, and that nice young doctor had said he'd be stopping by with her night-shift sawbones before he went home to his wife and children. It would never do to have them both catch her acting off. Maybe if she let them give her just a little medicine, to help her get some rest . . .

"Get a grip on yourself!" Jessie snapped, aloud. In any frame of mind she was still, by God, the daughter of Alex Starbuck, a man who'd licked more than a little discomfort to forge his Texas empire with no help from anyone but his stern Lord and nary a lick of self-doubt or pity. Jessie knew she'd never have her father's utter self-confidence. She wasn't sure she wanted it. It had gotten him killed. But he hadn't raised her to feel sorry for herself. So she tried not to. They'd warned her it would be rough on her to just quit cold after all that opium those mysterious rascals had forced on her. But they'd also told her she'd get over it a heap faster if she didn't baby herself. So she didn't intend to, but, Lord, she wished they hadn't fed her supper so early. Sunset was always the most lonely time of day when one was this alone and . . .

Jessie brightened hopefully when she heard a tap on the door. For right now she'd be pleased as punch to talk to a door-to-door peddler. Without waiting for an invitation to enter, her caller opened the door and stepped in as Jessie rose from the bed to stand there barefoot and sort of waiflike in her too short but baggy gown.

Her visitor was wearing a matron's seersucker uniform, and if it had been possible Jessie would have taken her for even uglier and tougher looking than the one she'd flipped back in that padded cell. The staff worker had a familiar blue dress over one arm and was carrying Jessie's go-to-town summer bonnet and high-button shoes as well. She smiled as sweetly as a gal that plain could manage and said, "Your friend, Ki, sent me to sort of slip you out a side entrance during the change of shifts. Get dressed, fast. We don't have much time."

Jessie took her things automatically and shucked the hospital gown to slip the silk dress on over her nude form without any underwear. The expensive silk still felt itchy as wool and the girl inside it sensed her dress was trying to tell her something, if only her head felt clearer. As she

205

was buttoning it she asked her rescuer where Ki was waiting. The matron said, "Out back, with a buggy and team. He says they'll be expecting you to light out for the Circle Star astride, in your cowgirl outfit."

Jessie nodded and murmured, "Good thinking." Then she thought, and said, "Wait a minute. This isn't going to work. I can't go back to where I get all my mail if the law is after me, and why would Ki want the law to be after me? That nice police officer posted just outside told me, less than an hour ago, that they were keeping an eye on me as much for my own good as anything else. Pete Pomerance has been trying to get me out of here the lawful way. I haven't done anything wrong, so why should I run for it?"

Her burly visitor shrugged and said, "I'm only following your own segundo's orders. He paid me well to do so. I don't know what his plans are. You'd better get cracking with your hat and shoes, honey."

Jessie sat on the bed as if to do so. Then she said, "You didn't bring my stockings. I don't understand this at all. What about that lawman posted just outside?"

The matron said, "Don't worry about him. Just get yourself presentable, damn it. We can't walk you through the halls bareheaded and barefoot, even when they're crowded."

Jessie stared up soberly to say, "I'm not going anywhere before I get some answers that make sense. Why would Ki want me to break out of here as if I'd already been convicted of some crime? Where did you get this dress of mine? It wasn't the dress I wore to Galveston. The last time I saw it my maid had just pressed it and she was hanging it in my wardrobe at the Circle Star!"

The matron sighed and said, "Well, it would have worked a lot better if you'd come along like a good little girl. But there's more than one way to skin the cat."

Then she tried to kick Jessie's head off with one of her own stout and thick-soled high-button shoes.

It would have worked, on anyone else. It caught Jessie

206

Starbuck by surprise and she rolled with the kick just in time. And then she had her attacker's ankle in her own strong hands to come up, twisting it, trained in the martial arts of East and West.

But the much bigger stranger in the matron's uniform had obviously been trained to fight in a most unladylike fashion. For when Jessie spun her around on the one foot still on the floor to send her crashing into a far corner, the thick-set matron broke the fall with firm palm slaps and rolled to pop back up, obviously still full of fight.

So it was a grand fight while it lasted. Jessie caught one sabot kick with a shoulder that spun her around to crash into the wall. But as her attacker sprang high in midair to plant both high heels in the small of Jessie's back, Jessie wasn't there anymore. The vicious attempt to break her spine left two deep heel marks in the painted plaster, yet the adept at la sabot failed to wind up on her broad behind, as anyone bound by the laws of gravity was supposed to. Using the wall as a sort of floor, the murderous matron pushed hard with both heels to back-flip and land upright in the center of the room, grinning at Jessie from a fighter's crouch to mutter, "You're pretty good, girlie. Now let Momma show you how it's done."

But Jessie knew how it was done, and she had her attacker's style figured better, now. So as the foot-fighter did a little dance to make it hard to judge which big foot would be coming at the smaller girl's head, next, Jessie stepped inside the range of foot or fist to just grab the big bitch, plant a hip just under the massive torso's center of gravity, and send her crashing through the door, upside down, to land out in the hall amid a shower of splinters. As her now somewhat dazed attacker struggled to rise, Jessie stepped out of her room, picked up the empty chair of the guard that was supposed to be there, and sweetly asked, "Are you still there?" before flattening her attacker total with the bentwood chair. It didn't do the chair much good, either, but at least splintered wood couldn't bleed.

Naturally, the racket had attracted considerable attention. So as staff members approached from both ends of the hall a more ladylike Jessie Starbuck tossed the remains of the chair aside to say, pleasantly, "I cannot tell a lie. I chopped her down with my little chair. I couldn't find a hatchet."

The doctor who'd been so nice to her up to now stared ashen faced at her, reaching in his white smock for something as a rather stunning redhead in a similar smock dropped to one knee to examine the patient on the floor. She looked up bleakly to murmur, "Dead. It's going to call for a postmortem to say why for certain. This poor thing sure seems covered with lacerations and contusions. Who was she? I don't recall seeing her on duty here before."

The doctor Jessie had thought on her side up to now said, "I don't know her, either, Dr. Chambrun. Miss Starbuck, I don't want to hurt you. So if you'll just be good this isn't going to hurt a bit."

But Jessie backed into her demolished doorway, protesting, "I don't want another shot. I don't need another shot. It was that woman out in the hall who was acting crazy! She came in my room to kill me and . . . Look at that wall, there, if you don't believe me!"

The one with the needle kept edging closer. But his red-headed associate said, "Wait, Larry. There's more than meets the eye at first glance, here. Miss Starbuck never left those heel marks in the plaster, barefoot, and how come she seems to have a dress on? Didn't you tell her police guard she wasn't supposed to receive packages from outside without your approval?"

Larry, if that was his name, lowered the sharp shiny dose of morphine to his side as he replied thoughtfully, "That copper doesn't seem to be anywhere around, and I've never seen that dead matron before. What's been going on here, Miss Starbuck?"

Jessie looked relieved but said, "I only wish I knew." Then she filled both doctors in on her recent grotesque adventures.

When she had them up to date they stared soberly at one another. The redhead broke the silence by saying, firmly, "I've seen our mental patients do some mighty weird things. But this one seems lucid enough and there's no way she could be making all that up. That guard had no call to leave his post, and no staff member had any right to come in here and dress a patient in her street clothes without even mentioning it to anyone else on the staff!"

Before anyone she'd been talking to could answer, a Mexican orderly came shyly to the door to clear his throat awkwardly and say, "We have trouble in the broom closet just down the hall, señor y señoritas."

Dr. Chambrun turned to the orderly impatiently to say, "We're having trouble, here, Hernan. Can't it wait?"

The young Mex replied, cheerfully enough, "Si, I do not think he is going anywhere. He is just sitting there among my mops and push brooms, dead as they are."

The one called Larry gasped and demanded, "A dead man, in your broom closet? Who is he, Hernan, do you know him?"

The Mex nodded and said, "Si, at least I did, when he was alive. Is the lawman who was sitting just outside this door, when there was still a door."

Jessie started to follow as the two doctors tore out. The male member of the team snapped, "Back inside. We're not at all satisfied with your story, yet!"

But the redhead said, "Oh, let her come along, Larry. There's simply no way she could have done in *this* one. She was locked in her room. That strange matron who attacked her wasn't. Add it up."

They'd found a more secure room for Jessie and were working over both bodies in the basement autopsy theater by the time Longarm and his helpful Galveston lawman returned with a copy of the sinister deed to the house of ill repute. There was now a heap of other local lawmen on the premises, of course, so Longarm had no trouble finding out what was still going on, as mysterious as it seemed. The lawman with him said he'd seen some postmortems before and didn't really cotton to watching two at once. So Longarm swallowed a deep breath and tiptoed in on his own. It was worse than he'd been braced for. Two naked and cut-open gents lay side by side on twin slabs as the doc he knew, helpers he didn't, and a strange redhead any man had to admire went on tearing both cadavers apart with professional cheer.

One of the forensic team told him to back right out. But the one he knew said, "It's all right. He's the law, and this one that came in disguised as a woman might be on some Wanted list."

Longarm gingerly moved closer, staring down at a totally strange dead face as he said, "They told me upstairs about Miss Starbuck winning a fight with a matron who'd apparently kicked in this other gent's skull, first. Are you saying this ugly mutt was trying to pass himself off as a female?"

The redhead casually pointed at the dead man's rather large male organ with the wicked blade in her rubber-gloved hand as she replied, calmly, "We're not all young and pretty. He only had to pass for a heavyset ugly woman long enough to kill a few people. He only got to kill that poor policeman on the other table because Miss Starbuck turned out tougher than she looked. He was probably over-confident. He finished off the seated and unsuspecting Patrolman Muller with a kick to the solar plexus and a stomp on the neck when he fell to the floor. We've just decided none of the internal injuries inflicted on her mysterious attacker by Miss Starbuck would have called for more than a light diet and plenty of bedrest for a few weeks. It was the seat of that chair slicing into his mastoid and then some that finished him off. Since she had every right to, I'd say all the law has to worry about now is the *identity* of this brute."

Longarm stared harder. He shook his head and decided, "I'd remember a face like that, had I ever noticed it before. He has to be a hired thug, and I have a way-out-in-left-field female impersonator on my list of just possibles. This one was sure impersonating a female. But I don't know. The gent I had in mind was supposed to be convincing in a wig and dress, and French besides. This old boy don't look too French to me.''

Dr. Chambrun shrugged and asked, ''Just what is a Frenchman supposed to look like? It so happens I'm of Cajun descent, and a lot of people take me for Irish.''

Longarm looked at her more thoughtfully, it didn't hurt, and decided, ''I can see why. You do look sort of Irish. But I've met pure blond Spaniards. I'm talking about typical French.''

She looked annoyed and demanded, ''Are my people supposed to be stamped out by a cookie cutter? The French are a nation, not a race. Don't go by music-hall French comics or exotic dancers, half of whom are Lord knows what. France is a big country with a long history. The Burgundian French are long-lost Germans. The Norman French used to be Vikings and still look it. I happen to be a Breton, so if you want to be technical I'm a Celt.''

Longarm grinned sheepishly and said, ''I said you looked Irish. This ugly mutt who attacked Miss Starbuck could pass as Irish as well, come to study on it.''

The redhead shrugged and said, ''Thank you. I'm glad you never called him a Breton. Actually, the people of Brittany are more closely related to the Celtic Welsh. I don't even speak decent French. But I understand that in the old country Bretons and Welsh could talk to one another in their old Celtic dialects.''

Longarm frowned down thoughtfully at the dead man to observe, ''I never heard of Irish or Welshmen fighting scientific with their feet. So, no offense, is there any outside chance this rascal *could* have been a Celtic Frenchman with more opportunity to learn the skills of la sabot?''

The redhead grimaced and said, ''I certainly hope not. I've always felt proud of my heritage, and I assure you I never heard of any Breton with such disgusting habits!''

He nodded and said, ''I just hate it when a West-by-God

Virginia boy goes bad. But it happens. When you all get done here is there any way I could borrow one of your microscopes? I'm in no hurry. I'm still waiting for some of the evidence.''

She assured him they were about done and that she'd be happy to help him out as soon as they stitched the bodies up to bury more neatly.

Almost as if that had been his stage cue, Ki came in with a puzzled frown, saying, ''They told me you'd be down here, Custis. What have we here, anyone we know?''

Longarm said he knew for sure about the dead copper badge but that he was still working on the other one. They stepped outside so Longarm could smoke as they repaired the Y-shaped incisions with butchers' twine. Once you were dead it was more important to make sure stitches didn't let you pop open in the middle of a warm-weather funeral than it was to sew neatly.

Longarm brought Ki up to date on recent hospital events, then asked if and how he'd gotten something Pomerance had signed for sure, without arousing the lawyer's suspicions. Ki smiled and said, ''He was pleased to see me and hand me a writ for Jessie's release from police custody. He got a judge he no doubt drinks with to let us post bail for her, pending the outcome of that sanity hearing we know she'll pass. He says the local law has dropped the murder charges, thanks to the same medical opinion that called for the damned examination of her poor little head. The staff here gave Pomerance a statement to the effect that she was simply too doped up at the time they deem that other girl was killed.''

He took out the writ signed by Pomerance and handed it to Longarm, who in turn produced the deed to the whorehouse and held them up to the uncertain gaslight for comparison. They looked a lot alike and he said so. Ki growled, ''All right, let's get back to the son of a bitch and see what he has to say about buying whorehouses in Jessie's name!''

Longarm said, ''Not yet. We got enough worms wriggling in this bait can. I wish Jessie hadn't inherited such a complicated business empire. Everyone who sets out to rob her gets complicated as a steam-driven Jacquard loom. I wish old Alex had just stuck to cows. I'm good at tracking cow thieves. Don't even tell Jessie, but I confess I'm in over my head on this one. It was tough enough when crooks were only out to kill her so fake heirs or made-up business partners could take over Starbuck Enterprises. Why anyone would want to buy and run a cathouse in her name, hold her prisoner there, and then make sure the law rescued her, alive, is way the hell over my poor head!''

Ki suggested, ''The only other time anyone tried to use an impostor they were out to discredit Jessie by making everyone think she was a crook, remember?''

Longarm grimaced and growled, ''All too well. It was close. But I doubt this is a second try at a plot that never worked so good the first time. There are only so many ways to plot against a rich lady who packs a gun. So we may be following a primrose path someone *wants* us to follow by using just one ruse of a plan that failed. Nobody's imitated Jessie with half as much sincerity, this time. I suspect they were only out to throw the *time* out of joint, to give themselves time to do something else and, if you ask what that might have been, I swear I'll bite you on the leg.''

Ki said he'd chance that. So Longarm swore at him and said, ''Let's work backward, since working forward has me all fucked up. We know, and they must know, that Jessie won't wind up in any bughouse. In just a day or more she'll be alive and well to run her business as she sees fit. So they must not care. As we take one step backward, it must have been the mastermind who tipped off the vice squad so they could take Jessie off their hands, alive. Why murder important gals who drink tea with the first lady if you don't really have to?''

Ki nodded and said, ''Right. They simply wanted to keep her out of sight a time while her double . . . did what? I mean, sure, she acted wild and confused us all, but I don't see how anyone could have made a profit at that.''

Longarm said, ''They were making a profit at something else. The confusion was meant to distract you, me, and of course Jessie and all her other friends and business associates while they did something we might have otherwise noticed. Had I fallen for the prank they played in my office, leaving that steel star behind lest me or Billy doubt poor Henry's eyes, I'd be way the hell up in Canada now. You'd be searching all over Galveston for her and . . . Now, that *is* sort of odd, when you study on it. Why did they want to even hint Jessie might be held on this island after they went to all that trouble to convince us she'd run off to the Peace River range for some fool reason?''

Ki suggested, ''They wanted to lure *me* here?''

Longarm shook his head and said, ''They lured both of us here. And it's me they've tried to put out of the game, more than once. Neither you nor any other business associate here in Galveston has been attacked. Maybe they were upset at me for not being up in Canada?''

Ki said, ''Well, they must know a lot about Jessie to even imitate her crudely, and you are a professional lawman, with skills they might not think the rest of us have.''

Longarm said, ''Aw, mush. They'd have to know you had a hand in tracking down Alex Starbuck's killers, and you have to know way more than me about Jessie's business dealings. Even Henry, up to Denver, has me skunked at paperwork. They had to be worried about me spotting something here that they didn't fear you or Jessie might, even though you both come here more regular on company business.''

Ki sighed and said, ''You're right. It's a can of worms.''

The forensic team began to file out from the autopsy room. When Longarm tried to take up the matter of Jessie's release with her male doctor, the doc shook his head and said, ''Take it up with Dr. Chambrun, here. I'm way late as it is and my wife will be sending the bloodhounds out any minute now.''

The redheaded Dr. Chambrun nodded and said she was the one on duty until dawn. Longarm said, "In that case I'd like to borrow your microscope before I argue with you." So the good-looking sawbones led them both down the corridor to another lab. As she struck a match to light the gaslamps above the long table, she told Longarm to help himself. She didn't sound as if she thought he knew what he was doing. Her expression changed as Longarm put his hat aside and perched on a stool in front of a double-field microscope, saying he'd hoped they'd have one. As Ki and the redhead watched with interest, Longarm placed the signatures on both papers between glass slides and tried to fumble them into focus.

The redhead told him to let her do it, whatever they were doing, and bumped him aside with a shapely hip to take his place for a moment. She fiddled with a mirror above the bench to shine more light from the overhead lamps on the subject. Then she adjusted the twin knobs carefully and decided, "There. That's the best I can manage and you'll see it's not much. At that magnification it's impossible to get a full letter, let alone a signature, in position to examine this way."

Longarm thanked her and changed places with her, peering down through the lens at the not too brightly illuminated partial loops of ink on paper that sure looked a lot rougher than bond, right now. He didn't see what he was looking for, at first. But thanks to Doc Chambrun having shown him the ropes he was able to follow the ink lines without losing them as she shifted both samples. So as he counted the barely wider spots where the pen had pressed a mite harder, he decided, "Lawyer Pomerance is off the hook. There are way more pulse beats to his signature on the property transfer."

Ki and the girl exchanged glances. Ki had learned Longarm tended to talk sort of strange at times. So it was the doc who asked, "What are you talking about? Everyone has a pulse. Are you suggesting those two signatures were signed by people having different pulse rates?''

Longarm began to put things back in order as he answered, ''Not that different. Most folk sign their names in less time than it takes their heart to beat more than twice or thrice. You have to write, or trace, mighty slow to get a pulse jiggle or more to every letter. Pete Pomerance in the flesh had no reason to sign this one paper half that slow. It was done for him by someone taking much more care to get his signature right.''

Ki started to smile and wound up looking even more puzzled. He said, ''Wait. I told you we use Pomerance because he's a well-connected lawyer with lots of pals in the local bureaucracy. That's how he gets things done in a hurry for Jessie. Wouldn't they be taking a big chance by having some forger pretend to be *him*, as well?''

Longarm got to his feet and reached for his hat, saying, ''Nope. Trust me on courthouse gangs. They chose a big-shot lawyer, maybe from the city directory, because they knew some lowly clerk from his office, or someone who said he or she was, would never be questioned as they went through the dry routine few lawyers bother with themselves. They had to have somebody sign this fool deed. Not wanting to sign themselves, they just made a bid on the property and let their lawyer, they said, take care of the paperwork. You and Jessie would have noticed, a good two years ago, if they'd paid with a Starbuck check. So they must have paid cash, and I reckon that's the end of that particular paper chase.''

Ki scowled and demanded, ''Do you mean this gang we just learned about planned this wild whatever two years in advance?''

Longarm said, ''That does sound wild, doesn't it? Try her another way. Say they just grabbed Starbuck Enterprises off the front of your Galveston offices and warehouses the way they grabbed lawyer Pomerance out of the city directory. Even though ladies are present, we all know what they really meant to use the property for.''

The redhead said, "You're wrong. I read the police report. It goes with my job, ladylike or not. That property would have never been raided if it had been established long as that kind of place. It had obviously been used as . . . a house of assignation just a short time before it was raided. What if the people behind Miss Starbuck's troubles learned somebody *else*, perhaps no more than a slum lord, had bought the property in the name of less shady people and then, knowing what you just found out, they used that against her as well by taking over the property and, you know."

Longarm and Ki both smiled at her. Ki said, "That works a lot better. Even though it doesn't really explain what on earth their real motive is, or was. For if this was all a charade to pull something while we were all mixed up, they may have *done* it by now!"

Longarm nodded and then, while everyone still seemed in such an agreeable mood, he decided this would be as good a time as any to slap the lady doc with Jessie's escape clause. The redhead scanned it, shrugged, and said, "It was the law, not us, who might have been holding Miss Starbuck here against her will. But if you want my medical opinion, another night's bedrest won't hurt her. That exercise she had earlier this evening may have helped flush out her system but it left her mighty fatigued as she calmed down. Won't you just let us keep her under observation one more night?"

Longarm glanced at Ki, who nodded, before he told the redhead, "Can't hurt. Might help. We'd like to go up and visit her, now."

The lady doc said that was jake with her. But Ki cleared his throat awkwardly and said, "You go on up to Jessie's room if you like, Custis. I thought I'd visit old Captain Wilson, as long as we're here. He does work for us and—"

"Are you talking about Caleb Wilson, the sea captain?" the redhead cut in. She shook her head and said, "He was

217

discharged today at noon. Didn't they tell you? His wife and son came to take him home."

That went over better with Longarm than with Ki. Jessie's segundo blinked in surprise and said, "Wilson has no family here in Galveston! He's married to a Nihongo girl in Nagasaki and lives alone when he's in port at this end!"

Longarm whistled and said, "I sure hope you know where he lives. We'd best go see if he's alive!"

But Ki said, "It's early to get that excited. I naturally know his Galveston address, but it could excite him needlessly if we barged in on him and some girlfriend I didn't know about with our eyes blazing. Why don't I just run over and scout the place? It isn't far and Jessie's no doubt been expecting company all day."

Longarm considered, then said, "All right. But don't bust in on your own if things seem spooky. I doubt anyone would be dumb enough to kidnap a man and carry him home to his own digs. If you can't make sure by pussyfooting, come right back and get me."

They agreed and split up downstairs. The redhead went on up the stairs with Longarm. On the way she asked a heap of questions about Ki. A lot of women seemed to find the good-looking cuss sort of tall, dark and mysterious.

Longarm left the chore of dismissing the police guard in the hall to the lady doc and went right in to give old Jessie a big kiss. He could tell by the way she kissed back that she was not quite her old self yet. As they sat on the bed together he asked how she felt and Jessie murmured, "Horny, now that you're here. But don't take me up on that. For even if that door locked on the inside, I feel sort of awful as well."

Longarm took her hand tenderly in his and assured her he wasn't always a raging bull. She smiled at him wistfully and said, "I know, dear. From the first time we met there's always been something more than good clean lust between us, even though I've sure enjoyed that part when I've felt up to it. Sometimes, when we're just talking like this, I feel

218

even surer about the way we really feel about each other."

He said he knew what she meant and reached absently to rub away a speck of soot that seemed to have settled on her cheek. She said, "It won't come off, dear. I noticed when I was washing up after that fight. It's ground-in grit. We both got bounced off the walls a mite. Is it true that was a man dressed up as a hospital matron I was fighting. An orderly told me that. But it sounds so wild."

He assured her the whole case was mighty wild and brought her up to date on the little he and Ki had managed to find out.

She said she was even more puzzled. For first they'd let her be found, alive, and then they'd tried to get her back, apparently with murderous intent.

He said, "I've been studying on that. It works best as a falling out among thieves, with one faction more murderous or maybe more scared than the other. I suspect the master-mind hired a gang of habitual crooks to take you out of some action he or she was up to, without direct orders as to your final fate. As things got more complicated some members of the gang commenced to panic. That lady drug-gist wanted out. Nastier members of the gang sent her out of the game for keeps. At least one of 'em thought killing you as well was just begging for too much trouble, knowing me, Ki, and even the Rangers would never stop hunting until they brought such important killers to justice. So he, she or it tipped off the vice squad, got them to raid the place you were being held, and the rest you know."

Jessie shook her head and said, "Not by half. Why do you keep saying he, she or it, dear?"

"Hell, Jessie, you just wiped out one female impersonator with a chair. The gang has a French flavor. They may be a sort of Franco-American criminal clan, and I know of at least one French dude who can pass for a pretty gal and fights with his feet a lot. The gent who came after you this afternoon in a skirt may have been as inspired by the tale, but having seen him in all his glory I doubt he ever went in for that on the wicked stage. I wired a booking agent in Chicago to see if they could locate me a more convincing cuss who fits better as a sort of deadly imitation of your own sweet self.''

She grimaced and said, ''Talk about long shots. Why on earth would anyone go to so much trouble, dear?''

''Good question. What have you been up to of late that I might not know about and that someone else might want you to cut out?''

She sighed and said, ''I've been sitting here in this itchy shimmy racking my brains about that. You know Ki and I got the last of Dad's killers quite a while back. Thanks to the housecleaning after malcontents working for me tried to frame me on that murder charge in Utah, Starbuck Enterprises has been just about running itself for me, smooth as a top. I've had no labor unrest to deal with, the books are all in apple-pie order, and we're neither suing nor being sued by any business rivals.''

He kissed her hand just for practice and asked, ''What would you be up to right now if you weren't sitting here so pretty in your hospital room, honey?''

She thought and told him, ''Not much, really. I took care of a few minor business chores here in town just before I was lured to that tea party and knocked out a spell. Had that not happened I suppose I'd be lazing about at the Circle Star right now. It's too early in the summer to worry about either roundup or harvest on any of my holdings. I might have entered some prize stock in the Fort Worth State Fair, which is just about over, but surely nobody would go to all this trouble over a blue ribbon or two. I hadn't even decided one way or the other when all this nonsense started.''

He frowned down at the floor, saying, ''It sounds too expensive for pure nonsense. Even if I double 'em in brass we're talking a fair-sized gang, and gangs don't work for free. The gals who invited you to that poison tea party might have been the druggist gal and the female impersonator. That would account for Miss Doc being so edgy when I barged in on her, asking awkward questions she answered mighty ingenious as well as scared stiff. But neither fits the description of them two gun waddies me and old Blacky took out, so—''

''Who's Blacky?'' she cut in.

''A suspect I can't pin down sensible. Owns a gambling hell near the waterfront. You wouldn't know him. Nice ladies don't frequent that part of Galveston and . . . Suffering snakes! That *would* account for my getting picked on ever since I came to Galveston!''

She asked what he meant. He kissed her before he got to his feet, saying, ''They had you stored on ice, or opium, leastways. They left Ki alone because they knew he didn't like to prowl strange neighborhoods, looking sort of odd and more likely than me to get in trouble just minding his own beeswax. But I was a loose cannon on the deck. Aside from being a lawman with a rep, I was likely to turn up anywhere in town, cuss my adventurous soul. They wanted to take me out before I spotted something they didn't want spotted. So let go my fool hand and let me go see if I can spot it!''

But as she did so he stuck it in a vest pocket to take out the two-shot derringer clipped to one end of his watch chain. He handed it to her and reached for a few extra rounds of man-sized round for the bitty weapon, saying, ''You were wrong about the door lock. Keyholes work both ways, and with the guards off duty we'd best switch the key to this room from the outside to the inside. With a locked door and that gun between you and the outside world it ought to be safe for you to try and catch some shut-eye.''

As he popped the door halfway to transfer the big key to the inside Jessie rose from her bed to join him there, standing on her bare toes to wrap both arms around his neck and plead, ''Don't go prowling such a tough little town alone, Custis. Wait till Ki gets back. He knows Galveston better than you.''

He kissed her, good. But when they came back up for air he told her, "If Ki knew *all* the sights of Galveston that well they'd have been shooting at him all this time instead of me. Let me go, lover. I got to get it on down the road."

★

Chapter 12

At this hour Blacky Morgan's was going full blast. Nobody in the crowd downstairs seemed to pay Longarm much mind, but when he got back up to the second-floor landing the same trained ape told him, "You'd best find somebody else to pester tonight. I got personal orders from Blacky. He don't even want you causing trouble for us down in the taproom."

Longarm drew his .44-40 and tried, "Pretty please?"

So a few moments later the handsome owner joined them both on the landing, wearing a scowl and that same .45, to growl, "Damn it, Longarm, I'm trying to run a respectable place here!"

Longarm smiled thinly and asked, "What do I look like, a wild Indian? Would you like to see my badge and credentials?"

Blacky snorted in disgust and said, "You know what I mean. How in tarnation am I supposed to see to the comforts

223

of my customers with a moving target drifting in and out so unpredictable?''

"That's one of the things I've come to discuss with you," Longarm said. "Play your cards right with me and I just might lose interest in this particular port of call. Try to deal me a hard time and I just may reshuffle the whole joint, starting with you and your bouncer here.''

Blacky shrugged, indicated yet another door opening onto the same landing and said, "All right. In there. But can we make this short and to the point? I got a lot of action going on inside.''

Longarm didn't answer. But Blacky still opened the door and, as he stepped into the blackness beyond, told the husky bouncer they didn't want to be disturbed by the devil incarnate or any other pests. Then he struck a match to light a gaslamp sticking out of the wall near the door and Longarm followed him in.

The room was small and furnished as a spartan business office. Blacky moved to perch his rump on the edge of the rolltop desk as he nodded at the one chair. Longarm remained standing. He still had his gun out. Blacky raised an eyebrow at it to ask if Longarm was worried about rats popping out of the baseboard at his boots. Longarm said, "I don't mind them kind of rats. I just left Miss Starbuck at the hospital, feeling proddier than before after an unusual hospital routine. I'd tell you more about that if I wanted to bore you with tales you may already know. On the way here I stopped by the Western Union. The Orphium Circuit's booking office in Chicago never heard of a dancing man called Blacky Morgan.''

The namesake a lot closer than Chicago shrugged and casually replied, "Did I say Orphium Circuit? It was a long time ago and booking agents come and go, you know.''

"I thought you wanted me to get right to the point," Longarm said. "I might be able to, faster, if you'd listen tight. I still got to put a few cards on the table, faceup, before I offer you a mighty fair pot. To begin with, it's

224

been my experience that there are four main types of fibbers. Folk who ain't at all good at it dummy up and try to change the subject when I ask questions they ain't up to answering. Folk who fib natural but dumb spout fantasy fibs about all the wonders they've seen and done. Anyone drinking with 'em, even drunk, can usually see right through 'em by the time they get to how they told Lee to just hold on a mite longer, only he just wouldn't listen. But there's a gabby fibber who's harder to catch in a lie as he or she answers mostly true and just lards in a few fibs here and there. A lady living down a shady past, for example, might just say right out she used to play piano in a house of ill repute without mentioning she went upstairs with the other gals when the herds were in town. That keeps her from being caught by some gent who met her one time in such surroundings, while it still preserves her more delicate virtues.''

Blacky sighed and asked, ''This is getting to the point?''

Longarm nodded and said, ''The fourth kind of fibber is the one too good to trip up at all. So who's to say how many there might be? You're the third kind. Knowing any of your many patrons might recall you from your checkered past, you say right out you used to be a wandering entertainer and just skew what you really did on the wicked stage a mite. Most figure nobody would lie about a detail or more about life upon the wicked stage, once he'd owned up to being that wicked.''

Blacky shrugged and said, ''All right, I was never on the big-time Orphium Circuit.''

''Shut up. Don't bury yourself with your glib tongue before I get to the deal.''

So Blacky did and Longarm continued, ''You told me you'd once trod the boards with a bitty French female impersonator who was mighty handy with his feet in a fight. Chicago remembers *him*. It was pointed out to me recently that some nominal French folk are Breton Celts who talk the same lingo as the Welsh across the channel. So Morgan

225

could be a Breton name as easy as it could be the Welsh name I first took it for. A mite later, as I was trying to scrape some ground-in dirt off a lady's cheek, it came to me how much it looked like a couple of close-shaved beard roots. She's never yet had to shave, of course. But as soon as I sort of pictured Jessie Starbuck with blue jowls, heavy black brows and short black hair, it struck me why you both looked so familiar to me. The resemblance ain't at all re-markable as I study on it in the here and now, but, yeah, it could fool some who might not know either of you all that well."

Blacky gasped incredulously and brazenly demanded, "Are you trying to say *I* was the one who impersonated the Starbuck girl, keeping *girl* in mind, you blamed fool?"

Longarm said, "I ain't trying. I'm saying. But hear me out. To save you the trouble of saying it, I know I can't prove it. The bill of rights would likely prevent me from hauling you into any federal court wearing a blonde wig and a skirt, and anyone can see how manly you look wearing pants and needing a shave. I ain't sure I could pin a federal rap on you in any case. I wish you'd let the real Jessie's riders drive them cows across a state line before you wired that accusation to a Texas sheriff. But what the hell, none of the purely local deaths were serious. So far, all the folk we've done in, between us, would seem to have been crooks as bad as you."

Blacky was breathing funny now, and Longarm waved a casual gun muzzle at the dapper squirt's gun hand trying to sort of snail-crawl along the edge of the desk to warn, "Don't. If I was out to gun you I'd have done so by now, you little shit. I told you I came to deal, not fight."

Blacky asked, very quietly, "Just what did you have in mind?"

Longarm said, "Correct me if I'm wrong, but you and your own are just the spawn of a no doubt ancient criminal clan. You ain't done nothing any other professional criminal might not have done for love of money and no hard feelings.

As a peace officer I can't just let it go at that. But as a federal officer I can give you a few hours lead, say sunrise, before I just have to tell the Rangers how ornery you've been acting.''

Blacky decided, ''You're bluffing. You're trying to trick me into saying something you could use against me. You know you don't really have anything on anybody.''

Longarm nodded agreeably and said, ''I don't need anything I can use against you, Blacky. I'll leave scum like you to the Rangers as I fry bigger fish, provided you answer me some more serious questions. Am I getting through to you at all? Would you like me to draw pictures on the blackboard for you, punk?''

Blacky heaved a defeated sigh and quietly asked, ''Twenty-four hours?''

Longarm shook his head and said, ''Giving you till sunrise is a hell of a bargain and you know it. I got a heap of answers figured without your help. To show you how smart I am I'll tell you I know you were hired to take Jessie Starbuck out of the game with no particular instructions about her health. As is the case in most kidnappings, you got to arguing amongst yourselves on whether it might be best to keep her alive, avoiding the fuss of a mighty serious murder investigation by all the serious lawmen who still recall her father so fondly, or just making sure she'd never be found and never be able to testify against you. Since she was recovered alive and almost well, who was it that wanted to kill her, my old pal the lady druggist?''

Blacky shrugged and said, ''You're pretty slick. We all agreed you had to go, when you first showed up. I don't mind telling you I almost shit my pants when we met face to face outside. Then I saw you hadn't recognized me at first sight after all, and you likely know it's not considered professional to kill a lawman if and when it can be avoided.''

Longarm nodded and said, ''You'd already sent them boys out to lay for me. When you saw a chance to get in good with me and have fewer to share the spoils with, you

227

blew them away and let me have all the credit. You're all heart, Blacky."

The two-faced crook smiled boyishly and said, "Consider the alternatives."

Longarm smiled despite himself and said, "I sure like it once all the cards are on the table. Only we're still missing some. Who hired you to kidnap Jessie and how come? Why did they order you to make everyone think she'd gone loco by dressing up like her and scaring folk, you mischievous kid?"

Blacky said modestly, "That was my own grand notion. You were right about it being risky to either kill her or have her on our own hands any longer than we could help. I recalled that time some other gang tried to get Miss Starbuck in trouble by using a double. The people who wanted her on the shelf for just six weeks or so never said how to keep her there. I figured she could do them no more damage in the nuthouse than locked up in that cellar. I knew you'd come looking for her, and I sure didn't want to ever have this conversation we seem to be having. So I figured if only I could get you to look for her up Canada way—"

"This conversation ain't going at all well," Longarm cut in. "Cut the bullshit. Your story has more holes in it than dirty wool socks left to the moths a whole winter. You were hired because you were a female impersonator who could pass for Jessie at a quick glance. You were fed information about her and her close friends you never could have got from the riffraff you usually play with. Try her another way. Try that poor scared druggist gal, knowing she was one of the two ladies who'd lured Jessie to that treacherous tea party, and that I, for one, might remember her face if Jessie didn't, tipped off the vice squad to raid that whorehouse so's to end the fool game before it could get worse. That would sure account for her dying so sudden as you, made up as the madam, were on the way out to let the law pick up the pieces."

Blacky shook his head stubbornly and said, "You're

228

really reaching into your guess bag now. I'd love to hear you try and sell such wild ravings to a judge and jury."

Longarm said grimly, "You may get to. I came here with a damn fine offer and you keep trying to deal from the bottom, you poor fool. You're under arrest or you want to talk straight? It's your move. And it's my last offer."

Blacky hesitated, sighed, and said, "All right. They warned me you were good and that I'd better take you out if you sat in. I should have listened. The razzle-dazzle was to establish Jessie Starbuck as sort of loco before she was found, dead by her own hand, full of dope, at a time and place not even you could have pinned on her real enemies, since they'd have perfect alibis proving they'd been nowhere near her for some time. You must have known poor Alice, or Miss Doc as you call her. She was willing to put knockout drops in Miss Starbuck's teacup, and of course a druggist was able to procure all the opium we needed earlier in the game. But after she felt you getting warm, both ways, she started turning chicken on us. It wouldn't have mattered if she hadn't called the law before she came to warn me I had maybe five minutes to vamoose."

He looked away to add, absently, "I was always fond of cousin Alice. She was great in bed, as you doubtless know. You know the rest."

Longarm said, "Not by half. Why did you kick Captain Wilson in the balls, pretending it was Jessie?"

Blacky shrugged and said, "I was out to kill him. But he sure was a tough old buzzard."

Before Longarm could ask why the mastermind behind all this wanted Wilson dead as well, he and his gun went flying headfirst across the bitty room with the big door and at least six or eight big men doing all the shoving!

As he wound up in one corner with his legs pinned by the pileup, Longarm pistol-whipped the nearest head to give himself some breathing space. He was about to hit another when he saw it was old Ki, tangled up with Blacky's baboon pack. So he shot off the face of the one trying to crush

229

Ki's skull with a length of lead pipe as Ki, in turn, sort of twisted inside his own skin like a badger being worried by hounds to bite one rascal's ear off and drive forked fingers into the eye sockets of another. The poor bastard sure hollered for a man who'd been no more than blinded for life.

Now that he had a better grasp of what on God's earth might be going on, he commenced to use his six-gun on anyone who didn't seem to be Ki. As the crowded room commenced to fill with gunsmoke and a mist of blood and brain tissue, the pack lost interest in both Longarm and Ki, albeit it wasn't half as big a pack as it all tried to tear out of there at once. Longarm got one on the way out but saw he'd wasted a round when his target went down with one of Ki's throwing stars imbedded in the back of his skull. Longarm kicked the door and the bodies aboard it off his legs as he tried to locate Blacky among all the confusion. But the dapper little killer had vanished from view and, as if that wasn't enough, the place seemed to be on fire. Longarm had sort of wondered where all that thick black smoke near the ceiling could be coming from. Gaslamps were never intended for small rooms filled with a free-for-all. Ki helped Longarm to his feet, grinning like a mean little kid who'd been eating strawberry jam as he said, "I figured you'd be here."

Longarm quickly reloaded, growling, "Here might not be here all that long. Help me find Blacky Morgan in the fleeing crowd. I'll tell you why after we catch the bastard!"

But they didn't, that night, albeit they'd sure put the squirt out of business between the fire they'd started in his office and the gleeful efforts of the Galveston volunteer fire department to flatten everything at all smoky with their axes and fire hoses.

The local police, Rangers, and half the men and boys on the island came running to add to the total chaos as Longarm and Ki tore through the crowd trying to spot one familiar face among so many, weirdly illuminated by the roaring flames of the two-story den of iniquity and a couple of smaller dens to either side. After he'd been stopped and questioned by a dozen other lawmen, answering with big fibs, of course, Longarm told Ki, "He'd be dumber than us if he was still within a mile of here by now. The little shit got away. Come on. I'll buy you a beer and tell you all about it. But first wipe that blood off your face, you heathen."

★

Chapter 13

The Galveston law tried. The Rangers tried. The customs and coast guard even tried. But by morning it was generally agreed that Morgan had either made it to the mainland or was passing for a sweet old woman with a tabby cat in her lap by this time. Most felt better about a total escape. Longarm and Ki agreed that seemed likely. But just in case, they agreed the best place for Jessie would be forted up on her own secure home spread. So they woke her up at the hospital to tell her so. She said she'd just love to go home. But as Longarm and Ki waited out in the hall for her to get dressed to travel, Ki told Longarm, ''I've been thinking about Captain Wilson.''

Longarm nodded and said, ''Blacky confessed he'd been out to kill him, just before you and all them other big apes came to join us so rude.''

''That was their idea. I just asked to be shown in to you and the next thing I knew, well, you were there. Jessie told

232

me you'd gone slumming when I got back from Wilson's place. He wasn't there. I can't come up with any sensible reason he should be involved with Jessie's kidnapping, can you?''

Longarm shook his head and said, ''Morgan could have been just stalling for time. So we got to take everything he told me with a dose of epsom salts. But if Blacky and his gang were just hired by someone bigger, and I can't see any way a gang of waterfront rascals could have known as much about her on their own, we'll ask 'em about Wilson when we catch 'em.''

''Don't you mean *if*?'' asked Ki.

''Nope. They're already in too deep to just back out discreet. We may have gotten Jessie back ahead of their timetable. If so, they may not have set up their iron-bound alibis yet. So one trail I aim to sniff once Jessie figures out who her serious rivals might be, is which such serious rivals seem to be planning a trip back East, a big wedding with all the Rangers invited, or something along them lines. I wired Billy Vail I was staying on this case until I cracked it. I didn't ask him. I told him. I doubt he'll be sore enough to fire me. Alex Starbuck was a pal of Billy's in their salad days.''

Ki suggested, ''All right. Why don't you take Jessie back to the Circle Star while I scout Galveston some more?''

Longarm raised an eyebrow and observed, ''I noticed you and that redhead working here at night seemed to hit it off.''

Ki never blushed, but he had to smile sort of sheepishly as he said, ''Her name is Yvette Chambrun, M.D. But I really do want to find Wilson, or at least his part in all this. We agreed Morgan took some risk in pretending to be Jessie here in a town where she's so well known. In pants or riding skirt he must have had a reason for wanting to kill Wilson, right?''

Longarm pursed his lips and decided, ''Maybe. But the skipper got to talk a lot when he survived that dive into the cargo hold. You said yourself he's long been a trusted employee of Starbuck Enterprises, and both your company books and the U.S. Customs agree he was neither stealing nor smuggling worth mention. Why would a man half that honest cover for a gang that had just tried to kill him?''

Ki said, "He might not have known that. He might have thought that good swift kick in the balls was meant as a less than fatal warning. Please don't ask me what he wasn't supposed to tell us, Custis. I have to catch up with him before I can ask. With Jessie recovered and the gang scattered he might feel a lot more free to tell us, right?''

So they shook on it and Jessie said she didn't really mind if she had to go on back to the Circle Star with Longarm, alone. By the time they got there she was kissing him much more often and said she'd about recovered from her short spell as an opium fiend. But he told her to hold the thought until they could feel sure they wouldn't be interrupted in a helpless as well as embarrassing position.

They drove into the dooryard in one of Jessie's go-to-town surreys with his old saddle and possibles and her new hatboxes in the back. It had been sort of awkward, helping Jessie with some last-minute shopping to replace things she'd likely never see again. Longarm seldom shopped in such places and, when he did, they expected him to pay cash instead of just waving an airy hand and telling snooty-looking folk to just put it on the tab.

He became even more aware of the differences in their stations when Jessie held court in her big old parlor, seated like a sort of friendly queen in her dad's old easy chair while her considerable help filed in, hats in hand, to assure her she didn't seem to be missing a cow or even a jar of preserves from the larder. Longarm asked some questions as he leaned against the fireplace, smoking one of the fancy cigars Jessie had insisted on bestowing upon him. He figured Jessie and her household staff would best know about breaking and entering while she'd been away, but he had some sharp questions for the hand who handled her stock and got to ride farther out. They all assured him la patrona was ahead two calves that had been dropped late in the season. Nobody had messed with her remuda. There wasn't even a pony on the place missing a shoe nail. Nobody had been spotted skulking out on the range, even though Jessie owned a lot of range to skulk on. Her boys patrolled it regular, most of 'em packing guns. Longarm said he wanted 'em *all* packing guns until further notice and warned one and all to be on the lookout for . . . well, just about anything. He added, "Don't let any gal who could be taken for la patrona get within pistol range of you. Get the drop on her with your saddle guns and call me, pronto!"

He saw that had them mighty confused indeed. So he explained, "Miss Jessie here won't be riding in her usual outfit, with or without me along, and her Texas hats are dismissed until further notice. I doubt they'll try it this late in the game, but they do have a gang member who can pass for Miss Jessie at some distance, and you don't want such a sneak getting *close*! If I knew for sure what they meant to try next I'd be able to tell you better what to watch out for. But, like I said, they've been acting mighty mysterious. So I want you all to keep an eye out for anything the least bit unusual, and should you gun a tumbleweed by mistake I'll back you. Meanwhile, don't none of you ranch hands come busting in here without knocking. I'm on the prod for mysterious movement as well, and I got five in the wheel and two in my belly gun."

One and all who heard this lecture assured him and Jessie they savvied tight. Most of the gun hands had been with both Jessie and her late father in other uncertain times. As the last rough-looking but tested rider filed out, Longarm told Jessie, "Now all we got to do is set tight until Ki gets here."

She replied with a radiant smile, "Bueno. How tight do you want me around our mutual desire, you sweet horny thing?"

He chucked the fancy cigar in the cold fireplace and got out a three-for-a-nickel cheroot as he muttered, "As I told

235

you, or tried to tell you all the way here, Jessie, we got to study some on that. You know I'll always want you, that way. But we both agreed, the last time we got up to dress, that the warm feelings between us are just cruelty to animals. We both knew, right from the start, that we weren't meant to be. When Billy Vail sent me to look into the death of your father he told me, as if I had no eyes of my own, that you were too rich for my blood, and I should have been whipped with rattlesnakes for forgetting myself and seducing you when you were feeling so lost and alone.''

Jessie sort of switched to her more earthy self as she smiled archly up at him to say, ''You flatter yourself if you think you were taking advantage of an innocent child, cowboy. Didn't anyone ever tell you we women are the ones who decide who's really the seducer or seducee?''

He grinned sheepishly and recalled, ''You have wound up on top now and again. But you called the shot true when you called me cowboy. I may have risen a mite, social, since I was riding drag and eating dust in my Dodge City days, but I'll always be just a country boy at heart. The only thing we got in common is that we seem to be sort of in love, at least when we're together. After that I smoke cheap cheroots and never let 'em put anything more fancy than bay rum on me, come haircut time. This outfit I got on was bought cheap and ready-made in a shop you'd never darken the door of, Jessie. It still cost more than I could really spare from my drinking money. I'll never be more than a working man who'd only embarrass you in front of your real friends.''

She rose to her feet to soberly take him in her arms as she almost sobbed, ''I guess I know who my real friends are, and for God's sake I'm not asking you to escort me to the White House. I just want you to lay me, you sweet fool!''

So he picked her up, carried her to her familiar bedroom, and did. He was only human, after all, and any man who'd refuse a daylight orgy with a blonde Venus who'd out-and-

236

out asked for it was carrying modesty to pure insanity.

So they both went insane together for a long sweet spell and, even though he'd already known there was nobody better, it seemed every time he entered her lovely welcome-home body it was still an awe-inspiring surprise to find anything human could make love so much like an angel suffering from sex mania.

They didn't have to speak when their bodies just seemed to agree it was time to change position. They just went right on kissing, passionate as teenagers who'd just found out why boys and girls were built different, as they sort of wound up in some mighty wild positions on and off the bed. But after she'd climaxed the fifth or sixth time, seated in an armchair with a white thigh hooked over either padded arm and him doing his best not to tip it over backward, all the way, he noticed a tear running down one cheek. He kissed it away, stopping the other ways he'd been comforting her, to ask, in a tone of concern, "What's the matter, honey? Have I got it in too deep?"

She sighed and replied, "You know that'll be the day. How often do I have to tell you I like tall men? Go on and finish, darling. Don't mind silly old me."

He did no such thing. He picked her up, carried her back to the bed, and gently lowered her to the rumpled linens as he soothed, "Somebody has to mind silly you, little darling." So she smiled up tenderly and told him to put it back in. But he said, "We'd best take a breather. The sun ain't even set yet, and I wasn't planning on taking you to no opera. What's the matter? I told you before we came in here that I'm no damned good."

She began to cry in earnest then, holding him close to her naked breasts as she sobbed in his ear, "Oh, darling, you know how good you are, in every way a woman really values. I knew who and what you were from the beginning. Uncle Billy never would have sent anyone but a true gentleman of the old school to my rescue, that first time."

He kissed the part of her hair as he caressed her back,

saying, "Uncle Billy's often said he never should have, and we ain't in any school, old or new. This is the real world, Jessie. Outside these cozy bedroom walls, leastways."

She murmured, "I know. I sometimes wonder, thinking of you at the damndest times, whether that might not be part of the magic. For desire made flesh lasts such a little while, and maybe we can only feel true love to what we know we can't ever really have."

He nuzzled her neck, muttering, "You've picked up too much philosophy from the Far Eastern sages you and old Ki carry on so much about. I don't know whether love is best described as a wet dream made real or something so complicated you can destroy it by examining it too close, like a flower or a swell clock. I know a flower ain't much to admire after it's been torn apart, and even if you manage to put a clock back together it might not chime so sweet to you, once you know where the bell song is coming from. I used to worry about feelings I couldn't fathom, honey. Only, instead of going up on a mountain to stare into space for the answers, I learned to deal with the world as I found it and play by the rules of a gent raised decent by plain but upright country folk. The man who said nobody should ever watch laws or sausages being made was right. Philosophy's for the weak who can't take their world straight, the way it's poured."

She chuckled fondly, holding him closer, as she murmured, "That's one of the things I love most about you, Custis. I know that I or anyone you're not really mad at can always count on you to treat them decently, by your own stern-but-just Old Testament code."

He hugged back harder and said, "I don't recall a word in the Good Book telling me to treat you half this sinful. But I'll just take my chances with Hell if you'd like to let me back in Heaven, now that we got our second wind."

She was willing and he was right about it being Heaven. For once she'd had her fool cry, women being like that at times for no sensible reason, they busted a heap of rules in the Good Book and a couple of statute laws of Texas as well, since the moral codes of their era had been put down on paper by old fusses who felt a heap more moral speaking to the voters than they might to the gals in the parlor houses most of 'em visited regular.

But by the time the sun began to set, they'd just had to stop a spell and, knowing one another of old, they knew it would take 'em at least a warm supper and a few hours' rest before either would be up to that interesting armchair again.

So they just lay sated in each other's arms a spell. Then Longarm's belly rumbled and Jessie laughed and said, "Me, too. Let me up and I'll see what Maria's made for us in the kitchen. I told her to just leave it on the counter."

He smiled and asked if she'd been planning that far ahead. She told him, "Of course. Weren't you?"

He studied on that, smoking in bed, as Jessie slipped into a robe and left him for the moment. He blew a thoughtful smoke ring and told it, "Well, you might have known how weak natured I am. It would have hurt just as bad if we'd held out as it's going to hurt, now, when we have to part once more."

The smoke ring never answered. Longarm knew the answer. He reconsidered what Jessie had said about love hurting more when one knew one couldn't have it all. He'd left many a gal still sleeping, in his time. Saying adios could be a real pain in the ass, and he'd sometimes suspected they'd been just as happy to wake up alone, after a whole swell weekend with all the stories told and all the experiments repeated more than once. He found himself wondering if parting with Jessie would be such sweet sorrow if they ever gave in and just got it over with.

He was surer he'd been right the time he told an otherwise swell widow woman up on Denver's fine Sherman Avenue that if he ever took her up on her standing offer to settle down with her and let her serve him a life of ease as well as her great body, they'd just wind up hating each other,

239

once she saw she was stuck with thinking up new things to serve him, three times a day, and he found himself not winking back at new barmaids at the Parthenon or Black Cat. But it was hard to think of him and old Jessie ever fighting about anything, even if she served his eggs cold and spilt the coffee on him. They already *knew* each other's stories and jokes and she still made him laugh. If only she was just as rich as Kim Stover, up on the Bitter Creek range, and really *needed* a man to help her manage things for her.

As if to prove great minds ran in the same channels, Jessie came back in with a tray of grand-smelling Tex-Mex grub, along with real Arbuckle coffee, brewed cow-camp black. As she put down the tray and stripped, Jessie said, "I've been thinking about when you . . . finish, here."

He said, "Don't. Thinking ahead can gloom the hell out of the here and now." He nodded at some envelopes tucked under the edge of a plate of tamales wrapped in corn husks to stay warm and, not really caring, asked about 'em.

Jessie didn't seem much more interested as she reclined across the bed on the far side of the tray to pour their coffee. As she did so she said, "Just some mail that came while I've been gone. Nothing that seems important. I was thinking that, once we find out who's been causing all this trouble, we might get Uncle Billy to give you, say, a month off. It'll be cooler up in the Front Range west of Denver at this time of the year, and I own this little patch of mining property up there. The lode bottomed out about a year ago, but the couple I kept on as caretakers keep saying they'd like to move on. What if you and I were to just ride up there among the aspen glades and spend a while in that dear little log cabin? It's been kept free of pack rats and spiders, and there ought to be plenty of provisions just the two of us could share, away from the madding crowd, see?"

He sipped some coffee lest the cup spill over on the tray before he said, "Sure I see. We'd be rustic as Adam and Eve, on land you owned. How do you feel about shacking up with me for a spell in an abandoned sod house I know of, northeast of Denver near a prairie-dog town? We could pack in some oats for our ponies and, well, prairie dog ain't bad, grilled over a cow-chip fire.''

She didn't get it. Or maybe she didn't want to get it. She stared soberly at him with her big green pussycat eyes and sort of purred, ''If that's the way you'd like it, darling.''

He bit into a tamale, washed it down with coffee before it could eat his tongue away entire, and said, ''That ain't the way anyone with a lick of sense would like it. My dingy furnished digs on the unfashionable side of Cherry Creek have a soddy or even a likely leaky log cabin beat hollow, and I know how you'd enjoy living my usual style, Jessie. I don't make enough to keep a refined waitress in the style she'd like to get accustomed to, even if I was dumb enough to make any woman risk early widowhood.''

Jessie looked away and murmured, ''All love stories end as a dirty joke or a tragedy, Custis. My mother and father stayed true to one another and had some good years together while it lasted. It was she, not he, who died early and unexpected. Once you face the fact that has to be the way true love simply has to end, in the end, who's to say how long either of us might last?''

He smiled thinly at her and said, ''Well, you being wilder by far than most women, you may have a point. But just hush and eat your supper now. With any luck, the rascals after you will kill us both and we won't have to talk so morose at suppertime.''

★

Chapter 14

They spent two glorious days alone at the Circle Star. The nights weren't bad, either, and try as they might, they just couldn't seem to get tired of one another. He even found Jessie's mail interesting as she read it aloud to him in bed, even though it had been in truth sort of dull. Rich folk sure got a heap of begging letters as well as bills. He knew she wasn't worried about paying her bills, and there was nothing sinister as such in progress reports on a colored college being built back East or an invite to sit on the judging committee at the state fair, seeing the Circle Star didn't seem to be entering any show stock this summer. She'd answered all her mail by the time Ki rode in one noon and they just had to get dressed.

As Maria fed Ki in the kitchen, smiling shyly at him a lot for some fool reason, the big segundo filled them all in on his own last few days in Galveston, leaving out the nights he'd shared with a certain brunette stenographer and a few stolen daylight moments with a redhead who worked nights at the hospital.

Ki said, "Captain Wilson's dead. Some crab fishermen just pulled what was left of him off the bottom of Galveston Bay. The crabs got to keep some of him."

Jessie blanched as Ki went right on eating, to say, "Shed no tears over the skipper, Jessie. I'd worked out what he'd been up to before I was sure he was dead."

Jessie protested, "Caleb Wilson couldn't have been crooking Starbuck Enterprises. Not unless I need new book-keepers and no doubt a new law firm in that seaport!"

Ki wolfed down more frijoles, swallowed some tea Maria had made special for him, the way she knew he liked it, and explained, "As a matter of fact it was Pete Pomerance who put me on to what the skipper had been up to. Pomerance seems to be honest enough for us to use without being a prude about it. He's been in with the Galveston machine a long time and gets to ask questions many a more sissy lawyer would have a tough time getting answers to. Wilson wasn't stealing a dime from you, Jessie. He carried out his duties to you to the letter. You paid him well to do so. I won't say you spoil your help, being one of them, but nobody can say Starbuck Enterprises pays starvation wages. So Wilson had the extra cash on hand to go into business for himself on the side."

"Doing what? And stop trying to talk with your mouth full of beans," Longarm demanded.

Ki went right on eating as he told them, "Real estate. Old Wilson was buying odd lots and condemned buildings cheap, with an eye to the future. As you'll recall, Jessie, your late father used to tell us that in the long run land just had to increase in value, land being finite and the human race breeding like rabbits."

Longarm growled, "In the long run we'll all be dead, and old Wilson was more than halfway there. Keep your breeding habits to yourself and tell us what he was doing that was at all *crooked*, Ki. There's no law saying a man can't invest in real estate, even on an infernal sandbar swept regular by hurricanes.''

Ki delicately sipped some tea and said, "I never said he was wrong to buy up cheap property, even if he did go to a lot of trouble to keep it a secret. He may have thought we'd slash his salary if we noticed how rich he was acting. He may have just spent too much time on the bridge, dreaming a miserly old man's convoluted dreams. Anyway, as Pomerance was able to find out, once I showed him he seemed to be the owner of record on slum property deeds he couldn't recall signing, Wilson had been buying and paying the taxes on mostly vacant lots and some few buildings by tracing an important local lawyer's name and just filing as a humble and unrecorded messenger boy, or dirty old man. Nobody pays much attention as long as the papers seem in order. Can we get off the petty details of his murky real estate empire, please? All that's important is that you'll never guess who the real owner of that parlor house they were holding Jessie in might have been.''

They both gasped "Wilson?" as Ki sipped more tea, looking just a mite smug, as he had every right to be. He nodded and told them, "That house along with the bigger tinderbox Blacky Morgan ran as a saloon cum gambling hall. As Pomerance, the police and I put it together, shady characters don't like to actually own much they can't pick up and run with. So Blacky was just renting. Lawyer Pomerance was mighty surprised and chagrined to find Starbuck Enterprises seemed a silent partner, and he'd signed for that when the fire marshal looked him up in the wake of that grand conflagration.''

Ki smiled up at Jessie to add, "Pomerance got it straightened out with city hall. There's a lot to be said for a lawyer who's in good with the boys.''

Jessie still looked hurt as she shook her head and marveled, "I never would have suspected old Caleb Wilson of betraying us like that.''

But Longarm said, "I doubt he was. Like Ki says, he

was just more secretive than sensible about business on shore. He surely couldn't have been plotting against anyone, personal, when he bought said property at least a few years back." Then he shot a look at Ki to ask, "Didn't you tell me one time it was sort of tough for outsiders to buy land in Japan, Ki?"

The part-Japanese segundo nodded and said, "It's flatly impossible. Even the U.S. Embassy is forced to rent from a loyal subject of the Chrysanthemum."

Longarm started to ask a dumb question, recalled from past conversations that the fool Japanese called their emperor a damned old potted plant, and decided, "Wilson was likely just acting as sneaky about land he owned in Texas as he might have been about property in Nagasaki. It's too late to ask him just what was on his old seawater-rusted mind. So skimming over his odd real estate notions, it's still safe to assume that as Blacky Morgan's landlord or semi–business pard, he'd have understood some about his high-toned boss lady and filled Blacky in about Starbuck Enterprises."

Ki had about demolished Maria's cooking, but he poured himself one last cup of her tea as he scowled at it and asked Longarm, "I thought we'd agreed Blacky must have been working for someone more important. The Galveston law had him down as a high-rolling gambler it wasn't safe to owe money to. He didn't seem to be involved in anything all that subtle."

Longarm nodded and explained, "The mastermind who hired him and his gang might not have given such subtle orders about our Jessie, here. But Blacky had been a female impersonator and high-kick artist in his misspent youth. So when he scouted Jessie, already knowing more about her than he should have, and noticed how close they were in size, he came up with his own sneaky angle. He likely hugged his fool self for thinking so slick. The jails are full of clever crooks who did things the slick way when the simple way may have worked better. His orders were to just have Jessie vanish. The ones paying may not have cared how or whether she lived or died, as long as she was out of the way a spell. We can assume, since she's still alive, that at least some of the gang balked at outright murder but were willing to go along with a kidnapping. As our recovering Jessie alive just proved, it's a heap harder to hold a well-known lady prisoner in the very town she vanished from. So old Blacky first turned that one house Wilson owned into a house of more ill repute, figuring such a place would be the last place anyone might expect to find Alex Starbuck's daughter.''

Jessie said, ''They had the place fixed up more sedate when those nice ladies invited me to tea. I'm pretty sure, looking back on it, that it must have been the same place.''

Longarm nodded and said, ''It don't really matter. Blacky didn't want nobody looking for you *anywhere* in Galveston. So he put on that wild impersonation, making sure he never met up with anyone who knew you too well, to convince us all you were not only acting gaga but tearing off across the country anywhere but Galveston. When I commenced to get warm, despite the way they upset old Henry up in Denver, Blacky came up with the mean notion of having you die by your own hand full of dope. I'll ask him when I catch him if that had been his plan all along and poor Miss Doc figured it out, or whether he was just playing by ear as the scenery shifted. He showed us the other night he can think fast on his dancing feet.''

Jessie said, ''I still don't understand where poor Captain Wilson fits in. I can't believe he'd be party to my abduction.''

Ki said, ''Neither can Pomerance or anyone else who worked more closely with him. Wilson never would have gone along with Morgan on that. Pomerance suggests, and I agree, the old man may have tumbled to the fact that Blacky had converted his property to a parlor house while he'd been out to sea a good while. He would have naturally raised a fuss. But when Blacky came close to killing him aboard his own steamer—''

"I doubt it was Blacky or anyone dressed up as Jessie," Longarm cut in. "Now that you raise the likely reason for a scared old man's silence, the tricky timetable seems a heap less tricky. Blacky lied when he said it was him trying to kill Wilson. But I've noticed he likes to speak in half-truths. He sent one of his baboons to shut Wilson up. Wilson lived in spite of being kneed and thrown down the hatch at his age. If he hadn't heard Jessie was acting crazy he'd have no doubt turned to her for help. But convinced he could be in trouble with he couldn't say whom, he just made up a wild story and did his best to get better.''

Ki grimaced and said, "Damn. Wilson's wild tale about being attacked by Jessie could have been a twisted cry for help! Had I or even Pomerance questioned him closer, alone—''

"What's done is done," Longarm cut in. "The old man just dealt himself a hand by the overly complicated rules of his own devious game and lost when Blacky stole him from that hospital to shut him out of the game for good. The question before the house is still said *game*! For we'll never figure out who's sitting in until we figure the table stakes.''

Jessie saw Ki was finished and that Longarm was getting tired of standing with his back against the kitchen wall. So she told Maria they'd all like some tea in the parlor before she led the two men in that direction. Longarm didn't care. Tea was better than nothing and he knew both Jessie and Ki had been sort of brung up on the stuff.

As they all sat down more comfortably by the fireplace Ki had already decided, "Whatever the game might be, nobody can get at Jessie here on her own spread. If we leave her forted up here, and go out after them together, Custis—''

"You won't catch anybody," Jessie cut in. "Whoever might be behind all this, the game has to involve my sitting it out. If they'd felt they could get away with whatever it

247

is with me just running the place as usual, they'd have never gone to all that trouble."

Longarm nodded and said, "I've been wondering ever since I noticed you hadn't really gone loco why they didn't just bushwhack you to begin with."

Jessie grimaced and said, "Please don't try to cheer me up while I'm thinking, Custis. They didn't want me dead as a matter of public record. They just wanted me out of sight and out of mind, both ways. So what might I have been doing all this time if I hadn't been down in that cellar?"

The two men exchanged glances. Ki shrugged and Longarm felt obliged to point out, "You'd know better than us, Jessie."

She frowned thoughtfully and insisted, "I wasn't planning on doing anything unusual. As I told you before, things are slow out here in midsummer. The business I would have been doing mostly by mail leads nowhere serious. The only social event this side of fall is, or was, the fair over in Fort Worth, and that's about over. I wasn't planning on going this year in any case."

Longarm pointed out, "You did get an invite, though. So who might have been able to say, for sure, whether you'd be there or not?"

She said, "Anyone who knows me and my stubborn Starbuck pride, for openers. The prize bull we'd planned on entering in the stock show died on us this spring, eating larkspur, the sissy dude. I get tired enough, watching Colonel Upjohn win year after year, without having to watch."

Before Longarm could ask who they were jawing about the Mex maid came in with the tea tray, set it down in front of Jessie, and nervously murmured, "Permiso for to speak, la patrona?"

Jessie nodded with a pleasant smile and Maria twisted at her apron nervously as she confessed, teary eyed, "I know is not my place, but I have been listening and, oh, you must find me so estupido. For I should have known that other woman was not you, now that you are yourself once more.

248

But in God's truth she made me so uneasy I never looked her in the eye, even when she made me brush her hair, and it just occurred to me that when I first came here to be your personal maid, you told me you did not wish for anyone to help you with your hair or for to get dressed!''

Jessie smiled up at the little mestiza to say, ''That's all right, Maria. The mean thing had a lot of people fooled.''

So Maria curtsied and would have ducked back out if Longarm hadn't stopped her with, ''Hold on, Maria. While that fake patrona was out here, fooling you and everyone else with that sick or loco act, did he, she or it have any visitors?''

Ki said, ''I already asked. Maria wouldn't know the neighbors as well as most of the help, of course. But I asked them while I was at it. Maria missed a few Anglo names, but she was able to describe anyone she couldn't name. So it seems Blacky got away with that as well as letting Maria brush his wig, not knowing any better.''

Maria shot Ki an adoring look and said, ''Si, was all nice people who have dropped by in the past. Few came by at all before just last week, when more than one asked la patrona, I mean that other one, if she was going to the fair. The evil person pretending to be la patrona pretended to feel bad and got rid of them poco tiempo. All but one couple, who stayed for supper.''

Ki said, ''That would have been Jimmy Upjohn and his new bride, from Maria's description of them. You remember Colonel Upjohn's younger son, don't you, Jessie?''

Jessie looked even more peeved as she curled her lip to say, ''I wish I didn't. The old man's puffed up enough about his so-called war record under the Stars and Bars. My dad told me when he thought I was old enough to know the facts of life that Colonel Upjohn never made it past brevet lieutenant in the Texas Cavalry. But who's going to be picky with a rancher that rich?''

Longarm cocked an eyebrow to ask, ''Then these neighbors of yours could be counted as enemies?''

Jessie laughed dryly and said, "Heavens, no, they'd have to grow brains, first. The old man is just a blowhard. A harmless blowhard, according to Dad, who surely knew men as well as he knew horses. The Upjohns had two sons. The eldest was almost intelligent, but not smart enough to get out of the way of a stampede years ago. Jimmy, the one left, might qualify as a half-wit, cold sober in church, if he ever went to church, drunk or sober. He's more often drunk. The thing I admire least about him is the high opinion he's always had of himself. It must run in the family. He got fresh with me years ago when I was still too young to understand just what he wanted, but I slapped him silly, anyway. Blacky must not have known how I felt about the fools if he let them stay for supper, even faking a headache."

Ki nodded and started to say something else. But Longarm shushed him with a look and demanded, "How come you said fools, plural, Jessie. Ki just said the pest stopped by with his *new* bride."

Jessie shrugged and explained, "She's new as far as marrying Jimmy Upjohn goes. She's not new in these parts. I didn't think much of her when we were kids, either. She was smarter than Jimmy Upjohn—our *ponies* were all smarter than Jimmy Upjohn—but she . . . Hortense, I think her name was, was a stuck-up little snob with nothing to be stuck-up about, save for being white, I suppose. She and her parents came west after the War Between the States. She worked after school in their notions shop in town and didn't like it much, to hear her whine about the big plantation and all the darkies they'd owned in one of the Carolinas. Do we have to go on about such tedious folk, Custis? I neither know nor care much about Jimmy and Hortense Upjohn, and they don't possess the brains between them to mastermind a fence cutting."

Maria was still standing there. But since she hadn't even been able to recall the Upjohns by name, Jessie dismissed her with a nod and turned back to the menfolk to say, "All those neighbors on the way to the state fair just gave me an idea. As I said, it's almost over by now. Whether I'd meant to go or not I missed the serious judging. So by now they'll be down, or up, as they see it, to the awards, social gatherings and such that the fair's really a sort of excuse for. If we hurry, we can still make it to Fort Worth before everyone sobers up to go home and sleep with their own wives for a change.''

Ki said, ''But, Jessie, you just said you hadn't planned on going this year.''

''I know,'' she answered with a sardonic smile. ''I don't like to get drunk and sleep with flirty wives. But what if someone didn't know that? What if someone was afraid I might show up? What if I do show up, after all?''

Ki shook his head and said, ''It'll be a waste of time if you just guessed wrong, and too risky if you guessed right!''

Longarm nodded and said, ''I hate to have to agree with this rascal, but he's making sense for a change. We don't have the least notion who might not want you there, Jessie. You'd be walking into a considerable crowd as a moving target!''

She shrugged and said, ''Well, you boys will be there to sort of watch my back for me, won't you?''

★

Chapter 15

The rival Texas towns of Dallas and Fort Worth didn't want
to declare an all-out war, so they sort of alternated holding
state fairs. Since they were only a few miles apart nobody
else in a mighty big state cared, and both towns perked up
considerable as folk came in from all directions to admire
one another's wives and other livestock. They only handed
out blue ribbons for critters allowed to be seen in public
with no clothes on. But it was widely held that had they
awarded prizes for multiple adultery, many a rancher who
lost out in the stock showings would surely go home with
blue ribbons and literal loving cups.

By the time Jessie showed up, riding sidesaddle as the
better known and more social Miss Jessica Starbuck of
the Circle Star, they were already starting to take down the
stands out at the fairgrounds. But the winners and losers,
along with the tinhorns who followed such action across the
country, were still whooping it up in and about Fort Worth.

For in a time and place where next-door neighbors might see one another that one time a year, given the size of Texas spreads and the slow growth of that new Bell telephone notion, from the way some neighbors flirted with one another's spouses, having ridden hundreds of miles in some cases for the chance, it was likely just as well they didn't see as much of each other down home.

For whether Victorian, urban or rural, they had been brought up with odd if not downright impractical notions of proper behavior. The old queen, herself, could have never managed to become the grandmother of half the crowned heads of Europe by acting so sedate *all* the time. Whether old Vickie insisted not even a piano could have *legs* but persisted in calling them *limbs*, she must have spread her own a time or more to the late Prince Albert, as snooty as he looked in his officious tintypes. So, being mostly country folk at heart, who got to watch stock rutting, and even helping 'em do so when the neighbors fifty miles away weren't watching, the duded-up ladies and gents of Texas high society reminded Longarm of mean little kids all dressed up in their Sunday best, with their mammas watching, just dying to kick up their heels and whoop like Comanche full of firewater.

He paid a courtesy call on the town law while Jessie rustled them all a suite in a hotel she owned an interest in. At the Fort Worth lockup he learned more than one old boy had whooped indeed, and there'd been one shooting over the wrong wife being caught in bed with another lady's husband. It had been the other wife, an obvious spoilsport, who'd done the shooting. But, so far, nothing unusually sinister had taken place at the fair just ended. Not even a prize leghorn had been stolen. There'd been no more than the usual cussing when the prizes had been handed out. Nobody but a total idiot would have wanted to steal ribbons and silver-plated cups of no real cash value, so nobody had. The real money in entering stock in the big state fair came afterward. Prize stock sold for a heap more after it had won

253

some prizes. Such selling as had taken place, up to now, had been too orderly for the local law to record on their complaints blotter. They said they'd surely let Longarm in on it if someone stole a champion show horse or robbed a breeder who'd just been paid handsome for any sort of critter.

They shook on it and Longarm headed back to the hotel, dragging his feet a mite. For the livery he and his friends had stabled their mounts in was so fancy he'd felt sort of ashamed of storing his beat-up old McClellan in their tack room and, while he'd often fussed at Billy Vail for making him report to work in his sissy tweed suit, it had been cheap tweed to begin with and he'd rolled around in it some since last it had been cleaned and pressed. His hat could have used a blocking as well, to sort of flatten down those few bullet holes.

He stopped at a neighborhood tailor shop to ask the old gent behind the counter what they might be able to do about his duds as he waited. The old tailor raised an eyebrow and asked, "You want the truth? Burn it! I can sell you a new suit, as cheaply made as that one, for no more than I'd have to charge you for the invisible mending alone. So tell me, how did you manage to live through that train wreck?"

Longarm said it had only been a few fights and falling off a few ponies before he said, "I reckon I'll just have to settle for having my boots shined and hope nobody notices."

The tailor sighed and asked, "Broke? So what was it, a card game or a jealous husband? Look, take off the hat and coat, and go next door for a shine in your pants and vest. I'll see what I can do for six-bits, all right?"

Longarm agreed. The old colored gent shining boots next door was mighty dubious about his scuffed-up army boots. But he said he'd give 'em a try in memory of the army that had set him free. It took the old pro some elbow grease and cussing, but in the end Longarm was so pleasantly surprised by the results he tipped the old gent an extra dime.

Meanwhile the tailor had worked his own miracles on the

hat and coat. As Longarm admired himself in the cracked full-length mirror he told the old tailor he considered him a genius. The tailor said, "I know. In this business, in Texas, I have to be. In full sunlight you're still a mess. Indoors, you may be able to convince them you're a poet."

As Longarm reached for his money he caught sight of his coat cuff at a better angle and said, "Hold on, you *did* do some sneaky mending, and nobody but me would have ever been able to tell. So how much do I really owe you?"

The tailor shrugged and answered, "You're the one they call Longarm, aren't you?" To which his customer could do nothing but own up. The old tailor nodded and said, "It came to me while you were next door. I knew I'd seen you before. I used to work in Denver. So wear it in good health and let's not argue about mere money."

Longarm studied the older man's features as he smiled sheepishly and said, "On what I make I can't afford to. But, no offense, I don't recall meeting up with you before, amigo."

"You didn't. My niece pointed you out to me one morning as we passed you on our way to temple. You wouldn't remember her, either. She was just a girl some cowboys were teasing in a rough neighborhood when you made them stop, escorted her to where she had to make a delivery, and then you waited until she was through and walked her back to Colfax."

Longarm thought. "It must have been a long time back, then. I don't recall the young lady at all."

"She wasn't pretty," said the tailor. "Maybe that's why she remembered you addressing her as Ma'am and tipping your hat to her once you'd escorted her to safety. So go, gratis, and for God's sake get yourself some decent clothes!"

But Longarm didn't think he looked all that bad as he caught glimpses of himself in store windows on the way back to the high-toned hotel. The mood vanished as he entered the same to wade through red velvet carpeting that could have used a mowing.

It got plusher as he rode up in the hydraulic lift that resembled a gilded birdcage and was run by a snooty young squirt dressed more expensive than he was. Even the door numbers on Jessie's floor were gold-plated. When the sweet little gal opened up he saw she had her golden blonde hair pinned up under a sort of hummingbird made of jewels, real ones, and her summer frock of blue brocaded Japanese silk was gathered in the latest fashion. But she sounded human as ever as she said, "Bueno. I'm glad you've made yourself more presentable. Ki went out to scout around the stock chutes for big money changing hands we don't know well indeed. It's going on half past noon and my usual routine, at times like these, calls for me to dine in the restaurant downstairs. So shall we go, dear?"

He said, "Not if you mean that eating place I just passed on my way in. Can't you have grub sent upstairs?"

"Of course. But I *came* to Fort Worth to let everyone know I'm here. How are they going to see me if I hide out with you up here? Can't you wait until sundown, just this once, you passionate fool?"

He laughed and gave her his arm as she stepped out in the hall, asking, "Don't you want to lock up, honey?"

She told him, "No. The chambermaid wants to freshen the rooms up and there's nothing of value in there right now. I even put my six-gun and some throwing stars in the hotel safe, and I've a few dollars and a derringer in my garter. I'll show you later, if you like."

So they went downstairs to grub fancy. Jessie couldn't tell him in front of the snooty lift operator, but just before they got to the dining room she whispered, "You're supposed to order for both of us, in case anyone's watching. When our check comes, just sign it. I own the joint."

He said that sounded fair. He still wished Ki had tagged along. For at least all the snooty-looking folk seated at the other fancy tables as they entered might have spent more

256

time trying to figure out what on earth Ki might be than wondering where Miss Jessica Starbuck had found such an unlikely escort. He could tell some of 'em knew her as she smiled and nodded at stuck-up folk in passing. The place was too fancy to let you pick your own place. A gent dressed like a butler walked ahead of them and even held Longarm's chair for him as he sat down across from Jessie. The snooty cuss asked if they'd like something to drink before they ordered. Longarm caught the warning look in Jessie's eye just in time to call for mint juleps instead of a draft with a needle of rye in it.

Another dude entire brought their drinks and two menus that looked like they were bound for a library, and Jessie murmured, "Oh, Lord. I hope they don't see us! Don't turn around, but Jimmy Upjohn and that bitch, Hortense, just came in the street entrance. I hope they have their own reservation and . . . Good grief, they don't. That fool, Jimmy, thinks you can just walk into a place like this off the street and, oh, *no*!"

But Longarm could hear the trilly female call "Yoo-hoo, Jessie!" without turning his head. Knowing he was really in for it now, he got to his feet as the other couple bulled their way through other tables to join them, uninvited. Once he got a look at them, he saw they didn't seem quite as awful as Jessie had described them. Jim Upjohn looked more comfortable in his prissy gray suit than most cowmen might have and his wife, Hortense, was a nice-looking little brunette who could have passed for sweet if she hadn't smiled so foxy. Her husband had at least the common courtesy to suggest their old pal, Jessie, might prefer to eat more private. Hortense said, "Nonsense, we're all old friends and I'm famished!" as she plunked herself down in one of the chairs the help seemed to pull out of hats at such awkward times. Jim shot Longarm an apologetic look as he took his own seat at the table. Longarm decided he might not be so stupid, after all. It stood to reason that any growing boy at the gal-grabbing stage would have made a grab for the then-

257

younger Jessie before he went after a sheep.

After they'd ordered the same juleps for the newcomers Longarm saw he was supposed to do something about rustling them up some grub. He had no trouble reading the menu, he just didn't savvy what half the fancy words meant. As the waiter stared down as if expecting at least a funeral oration, Longarm sidestepped by asking the others what they felt like, and when old Jim said he'd have the poached salmon as well, bless his hide, Longarm smiled up at the waiter and said he guessed they'd all have the same thing. But even Jessie looked sort of worried when a cuss with a big brass key hanging down the front of his vest brought the wine list and presented it to Longarm. As Jessie prayed silently, Longarm studied the list poker-faced. Then, just as the bitchy Hortense nudged her husband with a sly look at poor Jessie, Longarm decided, "Well, seeing we're all having seafood, the Riesling seventy-four looks interesting."

The wine steward nodded humbly and murmured, "An excellent vintage, sir." Then he tucked the list under his arm and scooted off to fetch whatever in thunder Longarm had just ordered, as both women stared at him sort of oddly. Old Jim likely knew what Riesling wine might be.

It turned out to be a white wine that sure went swell with fish, like he'd said. Longarm had been so worried about making a fool of Jessie—he wasn't worried about himself—that he hadn't paid much attention to the smalltalk between the two gals. Old Jim was sitting sort of quiet over his own grub. Then Jessie asked Jim, if only to shut Hortense up, if the Upjohn's champion he-brute, as bulls were called in polite society, had won first prize as usual, this year. Jim just nodded. His wife said, "We got a grand offer on old Attila, too!"

Jessie frowned and asked, "You're *selling* that grand animal, Jim? Why, I thought your father would sell *you* before he'd part with Attila!"

There was an awkward silence. Then Hortense said, "The

colonel passed away this spring. Didn't you get an invite to the funeral? Jim was wondering why you didn't show up.''

Jessie put out an impulsive hand to touch the wrist of a man she'd really never liked, saying, "Oh, Jim, I'm so sorry! I really didn't know!"

He shrugged and said, "I figured some notices got lost in the mail. A lot of folk never showed up. As for old Attila, well, he ain't getting any younger, either, and the colonel did stick us with some debts to settle. We've had to sell off as much as we can get by without."

Hortense sort of whined, "Even *land*. Far be it from me to speak ill of the dead, but the colonel might have shown some consideration to his only heirs."

Jim muttered, "Shut up and eat your damned fish!" So that silence got awkward indeed. Longarm started to tell a joke, but he decided it might be too dirty in front of a lady he didn't know better. So he just polished off his own fish, and when Jessie suggested they eat a mousse for dessert he just ordered four. As it turned out, the waiter knew she meant a sort of fancy custard.

As they had coffee Jessie quietly asked Jim Upjohn if there was anything she might manage for him in the way of a loan. He looked surprised and murmured, "I'm sure glad you said that, for old times sake, Jessie. But, no, thanks, we'll manage."

Only Longarm saw what Hortense was doing to Jim's floating rib with her sharp elbow. He tried to pretend she wasn't there. Longarm figured most men would have to learn to do that, unless they had the balls to kill the ball-breaking little bitch.

Having eaten and jawed enough for now, Jessie asked Longarm if he'd like to ask for the check. He did, crossing his fingers. For he didn't have enough on him to pay for two such meals, let alone four. But when he scrawled his John Hancock across the awesome tab and wrote in ten percent extra, hoping he was doing that right, the waiter just thanked him and they got to leave without anyone calling the law on them.

As Jessie pecked cheeks with her old pals in the archway to the lobby, Longarm found himself closer to the wine steward. So he stepped closer to mutter, "Thanks, pard. I never would have gotten away with it if you hadn't put that check mark by the wine I was supposed to order. You had me figured for cow all along, didn't you?"

The wine steward answered, pleasantly, "We cater to a lot of ranchers in Fort Worth, sir, and, to tell the truth, I used to ride for the Jingle Bob."

He decided to tell Jessie later, after she just begged him to tell her how he'd gotten so couth of a sudden. As they were going up in the lift she told him, "Jim's grown up a lot. I guess he had a lot of growing up to do. What did you think of dear Hortense?"

"The first part of her name fits her pretty good," he replied with a smile. "I'm glad we got rid of 'em. Now you don't have to fence with her until this time next year, right?"

Jessie smiled and said, "If then. Apparently the old colonel left a heavy burden of debts for his estate to pay off. They may sell off entire and start over out California way. It takes a heap of range to keep one cow, and Jim's heard you can put a heap of California orange trees on one acre. It's funny how I misjudged him. I'd have expected him to leap at that offer I made him. To give Hortense her due, she seems to have settled him down a lot more, well, mature."

As they got out on her floor Longarm said, "Well, randy young goats seldom think straight as a married man who's getting even a good-looking bitch fairly regular. But as long as we're on the subject, are you sure they was them?"

Jessie paused as he opened the door for her to demand, "Was that Jimmy Upjohn and Hortense Whatever just now? Good heavens, Custis, I never forget a face I never liked."

Then she proved it. For as they stepped into her suite she

260

nodded sweetly at the Mex-looking maid who'd turned to face them near the window. Then, moving casually as the wealthy part owner of the place, she reached casually up as if to take the hummingbird pin from her hair, and then she threw it, hard, by its long golden tail to drive the long needle beak into the other woman's heart, as deep as the bird's ruby eyes.

The maid still managed to get off one derringer shot from her wad of dust rags as she went down, losing her black wig in the process. As the maid hit the floor Longarm kicked the door shut and got out his gun for a closer look-see, muttering, "Damn it, Jessie. You just said *I* had a suspicious nature!"

But as he hunkered over the figure sprawled on the floor he saw who she'd just killed. So he said, "Well, so much for Blacky Morgan. He sure was a persistent little bastard. How did you recognize him, Jessie? I didn't, with the light behind him and made up as another lady entire!"

Jessie bent down to recover her expensive lethal weapon, saying, "Oh, that was easy. I told you I owned a share in this hotel. It was at my insistence they hired colored girls and only colored girls as chambermaids. The poor dears have such a time finding a steady job in Texas. I noticed right off she, or he, wasn't the maid I'd spoken to earlier. But his big mistake was that derringer hidden under a wad of dust rags."

Longarm asked, "Do tell? I didn't spot it. He had his gun covered pretty good." He picked the weapon up to add, "Four-shot .32, the sneaky squirt. You say you *saw* it, despite all his sincere efforts?"

She said, "I saw the way he was moving it, at the last, but the real tip-off, once I saw he wasn't one of the regular help, was what he'd been up to, all this time, with *dust rags.*"

He looked blank. She waved a manicured hand at the nearest tabletop to insist, "Look at the dust all over this place! How could that be, if someone was supposed to be dusting up here all the time we were downstairs?"

Longarm chuckled down at the dead face of Blacky Morgan to say, "Well, you may have been able to convince men you were a woman, old son, but you made a hell of a mistake trying to convince a woman, didn't you?"

Fort Worth was willing to take what was left of Blacky Morgan off their hands without too many questions. Galveston had put out a want on Morgan in connection with the murder of Captain Wilson at least, and who knew how many others for sure.

Jessie said they were still stuck with the Hunt Club Ball. They were in bed, later that afternoon, when she sprung that on him after he'd just been so nice to her. So he kissed her sweet nipple and said, "I give up. What do they hunt at a hunt club, each other's wives?"

She chuckled and asked, "Why did you think I was trying to wear you halfway faithful? I think they had fox hunting in mind when they built the first such club, back East. But Texas feels entitled to anything the tidewater swells ever had, so they built one here. It's generally used just for get-togethers of the landed gentry, Texas style. The one this evening will be the last grand bash of summer, and anyone who can't make out tonight will have to wait on the Harvest Ball."

He kissed her some more and murmured, "Let's hold out for fall, then. Why would I want to go to a party with strangers when I got old pals here to party with?"

She said, "Ooh, let me get into a better position. We have to go because it will be our last chance to see all the important people I know, and we've agreed rascals behind all my recent troubles are afraid I'll meet or see someone or something I'm not supposed to, right? Ooops, that's the wrong place, you sweet silly thing."

He got in her right and, as she hissed in pleasure, told her, "I doubt we'll ever know the whole story, now. Thanks to the neat way the real maids cleaned up in the next room,

262

the game could be over, as a draw. It happens that way sometimes.''

She pleaded, "Custis, are you out to make love or conversation?" So he started moving in her nicer. But then, of course, even as she was thrusting back with combined skill and familiarity, she had to ask, through gritted teeth, "What do you mean by a draw? Couldn't you see they sent that disgusting little female impersonator to ambush me, if not both of us?''

He had to pant a mite now, as he replied, "Blacky was more than a crook who liked to dress up sissy. He was likely the queen on their chessboard. You do play chess, don't you?''

She sobbed, "Faster! Of course I play chess, and Japanese Go and, oh, go, go, go!''

He did. As they were getting their breaths back, letting it just soak friendly, he said, "The mastermind never would have played with Blacky and them other pawns if he or she had been man enough to fight you halfway brave. In a chess game the queen is the piece that makes all the best moves. Nobody in the gang with the possible exception of that lady druggist who wound up just as dead ever struck me as halfway clever. They just did what Blacky told 'em to. As you just saw, Blacky made most of the more serious moves himself, and he just today made his last one. I used to know a chess hustler who rattled his prey by letting 'em take his queen and winning with his other pieces while they were trying to figure why he'd made such a stupid move. Most chess players just want to fold when they lose their queen. If the mastermind who hired Blacky sees things the way I do, he's likely to just back away from the table, calling it a draw, before anyone can figure what the infernal game was being played for. For he or she must see, now that he or she can't take you sneaky, that it's time to just forget all about it or come out in the open, with you backed by Ki and me, and just proving you could see through and take out the best of his bad boys!''

She sighed and said, "Let's see if we can roll over and let me lie on top without taking it out. I don't like this at all, darling. I don't mean this this, I mean the game some mean thing started, if I don't get a fair chance to win."

He smiled up at her to observe, "Consider the alternatives. If the sneak wanted to give you a fair chance, he or she would have fought fair to begin with and . . . How do you get it so tight like that, speaking of sneaks?"

She wriggled teasingly atop him as she asked, "Why did you think I wanted to get into this position? But seriously, darling, I just plain don't want anyone to get away with all the mean things they've done, even if they're willing to just drop it. And how come you keep saying he or she? You can't suspect poor Hortense Upjohn, of all people! She hasn't the brains of a gnat!"

He said, "Gnats bite. But she'd be more likely to sink her fangs in the leg of a poor poodle who outbitched her at being a natural bitch. I say he or she all the time because from time to time I've wound up arresting female crooks. It's a plain fact that women who kill tend to kill more treacherous than men. Men use guns more often than poison, for instance."

She started to inspire him more by somehow stroking the shaft inside her without moving the hips she held pressed against him as she insisted, "But that nasty Blacky Morgan was a man. A sort of man, at any rate. Wouldn't a cowardly man be as apt as a girl like me to act sly and dirty?"

"Just keep moving dirty, you sly little gal. I'm hoping your secret enemy is running scared for, all right, *its* own hide. I ain't sure I want to come this way, honey, but if you don't cut that out and let me finish right I'm likely to and . . . Jeeezusss! I am! Let me up! Oh, hell, I did!"

But they still wound up with him on top, on the floor, and there was a lot to be said for soft expensive rugs when you got to roll all over 'em entwined with a beautiful naked lady. A man could sure get used to living this lush. But, of course, when they wound up trying to recover in a corner he never said so.

They just lay there a spell, enjoying the soft floor. Then she sighed and said, softly, "I think we'd best go back to bed now, darling."

"Just let me get my wind back and I'll carry you all the way to Powder River!"

"And let her buck," she replied with a dreamy smile, albeit she'd told him he was being rude the first time he'd ever yelled that as he was coming in her. Then she said, "I meant to get some rest, darling. We still have that Hunt Club Ball to go to and, well, I'd like to be able to show up walking less like I'd just carried the Pony Express mail all the way to Sacramento."

He yawned and said, "Well, only on condition you save the last dance for me."

"I might even invite you up for just one drink after I let you walk me home, cowboy."

So they just lay there, wondering if getting up to go to bed was worth the effort. Neither knew, as they calmly murmured about that last dance that someone feeling a lot less calm at the moment was planning they'd never finish that last dance at all. For Jessie wasn't the only one who still wanted to win, and Longarm had been right about the game getting down to desperate.

★

Chapter 16

Like a lot of things west of the Big Muddy, the Hunt Club had been transfigured to something neither-nor by moving so far west. Longarm had traveled all over the west in his six or eight years riding for the Justice Department, so he knew Texas was where things could get mighty transfigured.

There was the size of the place, for one thing. Even had they tried, Texas folk couldn't have settled on being standardized as, say, New Englanders or Tidewater Dixie, and they didn't seem to want to. The first Texans had been Comanche, Cado and such. Then Mex rancheros had moved north into the wide uncertain spaces with their longhorned Hispano-Moorish cattle. But they'd barely gained a foothold before the newly independent Mexico, worried about the expanding and mostly Protestant south, had granted land to a handful of Roman Catholic gringos, hoping in vain that they might form a buffer between old Mexico and the infernal Union. Everyone knew, now, what a poor notion that had been. Faced with fighting over religion or fighting Comanche and Mexicans side by side, the Anglo Texican had been born, to adapt just as sudden to the new conditions of a new land, helping themselves to anything the Mexicans and Indians might know that worked. In the end the mostly cowfolk attending the ball that night were just as much a blend of pragmatic notions as the clubhouse built with flat-saddle fox hunting in mind to begin with, but designed a heap more Tex-Mex, with a wrap-around veranda and Spanish tile roof and adobe walls. One side faced a carriage drive while the other faced a big patch of open grass they said they meant to turn into a golf course, one day, if any members ever learned that eastern notion. Inside, the music was provided in turn by some good old hoedown boys with one not bad on a Cajun fiddle and, when they got tuckered, a posse of Mexicans took over with a lot of brass and a marimba. The folk who'd come to the big shindig danced as well, or as badly, to any old music. For it was widely held that any cowman who bothered learning more than the good old two-step was likely more interested in showing off than he was in cows.

It being such a warm night, Jessie had settled for a black-lace Spanish mantilla over the big comb stuck in her piled-up blonde hair. It looked more wicked to Longarm than that hummingbird, but, then, nobody else at the ball had ever seen her unpin her hair so murderously. He was sorry he'd worn his coat once they were inside the crowded ballroom, and he got to sweat while Jessie howdied all sorts of odd-looking rich folk he'd never met and wasn't sure he wanted to. They caught up with Ki at the refreshment stand, as they called the bar where lady members got to drink with the boys. Longarm had been to church socials at least half as refined, so he knew how to signal the colored help passing out the punch and soda pop for less sissy drinks. The one spiking their so-called punch shot Jessie a dubious look, but since Texas folk knew her rep, few men wanted to argue with her. She tasted what she was served, grimaced, and asked Ki if he had anything new for them.

The big breed shook his head and murmured, "No. You two had all the fun at the hotel. I watched the cattle sales and then I looked into the horse sales. A lot of money changed hands. A lot always does. I didn't notice anything unusual."

He sipped his own drink, wrinkled his nose, and muttered, "You people even put sugar in tea. Oh, I did notice the U Bar J had that bull up for auction. You know the big purebred that put us in second place last year?"

Jessie looked even more grim jawed as she nodded and said, "The year before, as well. We ran into Jim Upjohn and his snippy wife in town. He told me he was in deep debt and had to sell poor Attila off. I wish I'd known earlier. I'd have bid on him myself. Who got him, in the end?"

Ki said, "Old Pirate Peterson, of the Lazy P. He's all right. Mean as hell, but old Pirate and your father had their fight and shook on it, years ago."

Longarm found that interesting and would have gone into it more with Ki if Jessie hadn't shaken her head and said, "Ki said he was all right, Custis. We know him of old, and if there's one thing I can't see old Uncle Pirate up to, it would have to be sneak fighting. I recall his dispute with Dad, now. Dad always found it amusing. They call him Pirate because he will stretch maverick law a mite. They used to say that if Pirate Peterson spotted one of your kids on the way to school, not branded yet, your kids could wind up with Lazy P on their dear little rumps. Dad caught some Lazy P riders branding a fresh-dropped Circle Star calf. They settled it without a killing. Dad knew how to get along with Comanche, too. He always told me the way you treated such gents was fair but firm."

Longarm said, "I've noticed. But your dad ain't with us no more, Jessie."

She shook her head and said, "Pirate was one of Dad's old friends who backed me when the Circle Star estate was

268

disputed, first in court and later, as you know, with guns. I've already been kissed on the cheek tonight by a mess of folk I trust less than Uncle Pirate."

As if to prove her point they got yoo-hooed at in that same unpleasant shrill, and Ki had the sense to slip away as Longarm and Jessie were joined by the infernal Hortense and her dumb husband. Hortense asked, "Aren't you two going to dance? The music's started and, my, ain't that a lively tune, and I don't mind if we do, Mr. Long."

So before Longarm knew it, he was twirling across the dance floor with the fool gal, her leading. He tried to see what his own companion might be up to in this crowd, but Jessie wasn't at the bar anymore and, Jesus . . . Then he spotted her lace mantilla atop its high comb and saw she hadn't been kidnapped again, after all. She was dancing with old Jim Upjohn over yonder. Longarm hoped her old admirer wouldn't try to feel her up this time. He was watching out for more serious trouble than a fool flattened by a dancing partner.

As if she was a mind reader as well as dance teacher, the partner he seemed stuck with smiled up at him, sort of dirty, and cooed, "Jessie's in good hands, Custis. May I call you Custis? She might have told you she used to be sweet on him. But I can assure you no man born of mortal woman would dream of cheating on *this* hot momma! Do you like hot mommas, Custis? You surely seem to, but it's really a little early and . . . Oh, that isn't a gun I feel down there, is it?"

He laughed despite himself and assured her, "It surely is, and I'd be a freak if I had anything else that hard bumping your hips at such an unusual angle."

She laughed, too, and asked, "Why don't we go out on the veranda so you can show me what you have, Custis."

But he took the lead and danced her closer to the hoedown band, saying, "I never show nothing I don't intend to use, Miss Hortense. It ain't that I don't find you as hot a momma as I've danced with, recent. But your man is almost as big

269

as me and I couldn't help noticing, when we first met, that he packs a tied-down six-gun under his coattails."

She thrust her pelvis closer, as if searching his fly for weapons, as she snickered and said, "Pooh, I learned on our honeymoon how much ammunition he's got, for all his size. I suspect he must have hurt himself down yonder, riding horses too hard when he was just a tike."

Longarm stared out across the sea of bobbing heads for some sign of Jessie's mantilla as he told the tease in his arms, if she was teasing, "I started riding early, too. I'm sorry your honeymoon ended so soon, but, no offense, do you always come out with such secrets so bold?"

She giggled and confided, "Not as a rule. But this is our last night in town, we're all staying at the same hotel and, well, Jessie's one up on me and I'm just a mite jealous if you want to know the whole truth."

He doubted that could be the whole truth, but now he could see those Mex musicians in their fancy charro outfits filing in behind the hoedown band. So knowing this particular dance was nearly over, he asked his current dancing partner what might have given her the impression Jessie had more notches on her bedpost, adding, "For one thing she ain't half as bold and, for another, I feel sure she and Jim were never quite that fond of one another."

She sniffed and said, "A lot you know. My Jim had just about every gal in the county before he decided on me. I never understood why Jessie busted up with the only heir of Colonel Upjohn until we went on our honeymoon together. For had I been to bed with him before I married him, I never would have married him, rich daddy or no! I can see why Jessie dropped him, and I notice she hasn't dropped you. So why don't the two of us get even? If you could say you'd had both gals Jim has had, and I could say I'd had both men Jessie gave it to, wouldn't that make all of us even?"

He muttered, "I suspect at least one of us would be left short a conquest and, speaking of your husband, this dance

270

is about over and we'd best track him and Jessie down to swap partners for the hat dance or whatever comes next."

On the far side of the dance floor, Jessie was thinking the same thing as the Mex band started climbing up on the podium with the hoedown boys. The rustic with the Cajun fiddle seemed sort of confused by the intrusion. He'd likely lost track of the time and seemed to be saying so as he went on fiddling. Then Jim had twirled her back to the band and she couldn't see what was going on. It hardly mattered, as long as they finished this infernal dance so everyone could change partners. She hadn't been having the problems with Jim Upjohn that Longarm was having with Jim's wife, unbeknownst to anyone on this side of the dance floor. But while he'd apparently outgrown his jackass youth he still failed to strike her as a good dancer or interesting conversationalist. So she was repressing a yawn when her dull dancing partner trod on her instep, threw her flat on the floor, and went for his gun, yelling, "Everybody duck!"

Some did. Some didn't. For when in the course of human events an octet of gunslicks dressed as Mex musicians commence to fire into a crowd, two-handed, the confusion as well as casualties should be predictable.

But this was a Texas crowd, and Texans gloried in not being predictable. So while most of the women and some of the men ran aimlessly as decapitated chickens, a good many of the men and at least one woman fought back. Those begged, borrowed or stolen outfits turned out to be an easy way to crash a party and a mighty poor way to shoot it out with Anglo Texans. For despite the noise and thick gunsmoke, as soon as one old boy shouted, "Remember the Alamo!" most of the others at least agreed on the general direction one should blaze away.

Longarm had an even better notion. He made for the rear veranda doors, hopscotching over heads and rumps of males and females hugging the waxed floor. For he'd seen two of the bastards going down already and suspected he knew where any survivors might be heading. As he tore out the

271

back he was just in time to spy three others vaulting the rail up the veranda to his left. One lost his big Mex sombrero on the way down to the grass. Then all three were running for the distant ponies tethered in the clump of oak across the open space. Longarm blew one who was still wearing a sombrero out from under it. But as he drew a bead on another he saw the rascal stop, stagger backward and fall, just as he was set to pull the trigger. The third and last acted the same unusual way before Longarm could shift his aim. He rolled over the rail to go see why. He knew why when, halfway there and moving in wary, he saw Ki step out into the moonlight from the inky shade of the oaks.

As they met above the three sprawled bodies, Ki asked if Jessie was all right. Longarm said, "I reckon so. These old boys seem to have made one hell of mistake, whoever they might have been."

Ki dropped to one knee to take back his two tantos, or throwing knives, wiping the blades clean on the dead men's duds as he said, "I know who one of them was. Before he was holding their ponies for them, over among those trees, he was tending bar at Blacky Morgan's in Galveston. He told me, as I was sort of teaching him the art of origami, that they were out for revenge."

Longarm asked Ki to speak English. So the martial arts master explained, "You begin the lesson by folding the paper, or the pupil's spine, with delicate firmness. Just before his spine snapped he assured me he hadn't wanted to come along but that the boys were mighty riled, as he put it, over some sort of double cross."

Longarm began to reload as he nodded soberly and said, "Well, we all agreed on where the getaway ponies ought to be waiting. The shooting back yonder has ceased. We'd best go see who won."

They did. Jessie met them on the veranda, her own garter .32 in hand, to sweetly say, "Five gents down who don't look half as Mex as their outfits. One real musician leg-shot and another hurt worse but still alive. They're still counting the dead and wounded who only came to dance. Jim Upjohn got shot in the head. But it seems just a graze, and whoever would have thought it!''

Longarm shrugged and observed, ''Me. Those murderous rascals seemed to be blazing at one and all in there.''

But Jessie said, ''He saved my life by spotting what was going on in time. He threw me down and stood over me, blazing back, and it was over before I could get this gun out with some fat lady across both my legs. I forgave her when I noticed she was dead. Their first volley seemed aimed at that side of the room.''

Longarm said, ''It's no mystery who they were out to shoot serious. Ki, here, stopped at least one who worked for Morgan down Galveston way. We'd best have a look at the others inside.''

As the three of them stepped back into the Hunt Club it looked more like a dressing station, near the front, after a modest battle. Women were sobbing, men were cussing, and a couple of docs who'd come to the ball were directing the clubhouse help and other volunteers as the wounded were comforted and the dead were covered over with tablecloths. Nobody had done a thing for or about the fake Mexicans sprawled on or about the podium. As Longarm rolled one over on his back with a boot kick, someone shouted, ''Don't mess with them outlaws. We've sent for the law and they like to start from scratch.''

''I am the law,'' Longarm announced. ''I generally start by seeing who might be dead.'' He kicked the big sombrero off another dead man's face, grimaced, and muttered, ''This one was the ape you had to get past to gamble upstairs at Blacky's joint. I can see how he might have felt chagrined to lose both the place he worked and then the boss he worked for.''

He turned to Jessie to add, ''Lucky for you, Jessie, this one never struck me as bright when he was alive and acting nicer. If he was Blacky's right-hand man, it's over. If he

273

wasn't, Ki made sure nobody got away. So it's still likely over.''

She frowned and asked, ''Aren't you forgetting the mastermind the whole gang was working for?''

He replied with a weary expression of experience, ''No mastermind ever sent these wild-eyed gun waddies after anybody, and I'd say they were after you. Ki got one to admit they were mighty displeased, and the most displeasing little thing I can think of has to be the lady who killed their beloved leader with a hummingbird.''

Ki objected, ''He said they'd been double-crossed. None of *us* could be said to have double-crossed them. It was their idea to make us fight for our lives, not deal cards to them.''

Longarm nodded, but said, ''You have to savvy the criminal mind. The Missouri Pacific never did a thing to the James and Younger gang, before they started robbing trains so regular. The line don't run through their native Clay County. But that's never stopped 'em from justifying their stopping of the Glendale train as revenge on lying city slickers. From your average crook's point of view, refusing to hand over your money can be taken as pure treachery. They feel they have to be in the right and that anyone who fights back has to be the true villain.''

One of the colored gents who used to ladle out punch came over to ask Longarm if he was the lawman in charge right now. Longarm said he had to be until someone else with a badge showed up. So the club employee told him, ''We just found some more dead gents in the crawl space under the south veranda. Eight Mex gents, wearing nothing but their underwear and all killed the same way, with their throats slit.''

Longarm and Ki exchanged glances. Ki nodded and said, ''Any other way would have made a lot of noise before they were ready to serenade Jessie, here, with their sixteen six-guns. The Mex band would have been loafing down that

274

way between dances when they were jumped, stripped, and murdered in cold blood.''

Only the club attendant was dumb enough to ask how Ki knew they'd been stripped before their throats had been sliced open. As Jessie was patiently explaining about needless laundry problems a trio of Texas Rangers strode in, impatiently demanding a full account of all this carnage. As Longarm identified himself and began, the Ranger in charge snapped, ''This ain't no federal case and I'll have you know that I, Captain Fred Fulton in the flesh, am in total charge here!''

So Longarm assured the Rangers they were welcome to crawl under verandas all they liked and, taking Jessie by the elbow, muttered, ''Let's go, Jessie. The ball is over and I'd say it was just about bedtime for all good little gals.''

★

Chapter 17

In his own luxurious but lonely room at the hotel, Ki lay awake in the dark, running through all the recent events in his mind as he tried not to dwell on that redheaded Cajun M.D. down in Galveston. For to state she was innocent would have been an insult to her warm nature and love of experimental slap-and-tickle, as his fellow Texans seemed to call it. But wild as she'd been in bed, or against the wall, for that matter, Doc Chambrun hadn't been involved in anything Ki ever wanted Jessie to know about.

Ki yawned and tried a yoga breathing trick to put confusion from his mind, for now, and replace it with sleep, as Ki called the short almost catatonic naps he indulged in, lest he waste the six or eight hours most humans seemed to need to sleep in such a busy universe.

He had himself almost under when he heard the door latch click in the darkness. Ki never slept too soundly to hear a door being opened after he'd just locked it. He lay still, not changing the pattern of his breathing as he opened his eyes just a slit. The intruder seemed to be making no effort to creep closer in the ninja, or almost undetectable manner. He or she simply seemed to be climbing into bed with him.

Ki let the intruder slide under the top sheet beside him before he pounced. There were ways to kill and there were ways to pin an opponent painlessly. Ki was glad he'd chosen the latter when the naked lady in bed with him gasped, giggled, and whispered, "Oh, Custis, you're so masterful!"

Ki had of course gone to bed naked and, being no fool, he waited until he had her in an even more helpless position with two wet fingers where they might inspire the two of them most before he said, politely, "I fear you have the wrong room, miss. May I ask how you got in?"

She stiffened in his grasp to demand, "Who are you? What's going on, here and . . . Oh, unhand me, you monster!"

But even as she protested her hips were beginning to move in time with Ki's skilled fingering. So he fingered her faster as he replied, "I'll ask the questions for now. It wasn't my idea to sneak into your bed. I was only trying to get some sleep while you were getting through my locked door."

She sighed and said, "I only borrowed a passkey from the chambermaid. I told her we were old friends and it only cost me a teeny weeny bit. What are you *doing* to me? Don't you want to do it right, now that you seem to have me in your power, you big brute?"

Ki had her figured, now. Few women Jessie knew had such an obviously dirty giggle. He went on petting her, knowing how to keep a woman right on the razor's edge, as he said, "A man in such a delicate position has to be delicate, Mrs. Upjohn. Does your husband know how much you admire Custis Long?"

She moaned, "He's out for the night with a plaster to his head wound and a bellyful of sleeping powders. Not

277

that he cares all that much when he's wide awake, the uncaring fool. Please don't keep me dangling like this, whoever you are."

So Ki raised her shapely thigh to thrust his hips in under her on that side and stimulate her with just a little more than his mere two fingers. She sobbed, "Oh, I know what you're trying to do and I wish you'd do it, you big sweet thing. I don't care what your fool face might look like right now. But as long as we're getting so friendly, do I know you at all?"

Ki purred, "Not in your biblical sense, yet," as he gave her no more than two or three inches of it. From the way she was twisting about on it, he suspected she didn't think it was near enough. He asked, conversationally, "Might the sleeping pills you fed your man come out of a blue glass bottle, Miss Hortense?"

She whimpered, "What are you talking about? I told you he wasn't going to bother us, awake or asleep. Did you think I left a note telling him where he might catch me in the act of . . . goddamn it, are we or aren't we?"

"We were talking about blue bottles," Ki insisted.

She sobbed, "You're crazy! Jim just took some medication the doc left him. The sleeping powder comes in bitty paper envelopes, out of a bitty pasteboard box and . . . Jesus, do you mean to let a lady come alone?"

That would have been discourteous, in the Far East or Far West. So Ki thrust home to the roots in her quivering love-gushed passion pit and, just as he'd known she would, Hortense climaxed around his shaft, convulsing with sheer delight. And so, not wishing to feel left out, Ki mounted her right, spread her now weak thighs to their limit, and proceeded to satisfy himself as well.

It wasn't a bothersome chore. For despite her lewd foxy smile when one had to look at her, and her annoying voice, even in the dark, Hortense had a beautiful body and all the skills that went with a natural little two-timing bitch. She had not, in fact, been as interested in orgasm as stealing another woman's man when she'd first tiptoed in to seduce Longarm. But Ki's almost painfully skilled lovemaking had her convinced that whoever she was with, she'd certainly come in the right bedroom. Then, as she came again, and wondered how often this was likely to keep happening, she suddenly gasped and said, "Oh, Jesus! I bet I know who you are! They told me Jessie Starbuck had hired this whole end of the hall and . . . you can't be that big Chinese she has riding for her!"

Ki went on moving in her, skillfully, as he said, "I've never ridden anyone I work for like this. Does it really matter?"

She wrapped her legs around him and dug her nails into his bare back as she moaned, "Of course it does. I'm a white lady. Do you think I'd screw an infernal inferior?"

He asked if she wanted him to stop. She gasped, "Christ, no! It don't feel half as inferior as I've ever been taught! Do all Chinamen screw so fine?"

He told her he'd never screwed a Chinaman and showed her a yoga position more often reserved for meditation that felt even better with a full erection probing one's inner being.

So by the time she just had to tiptoe back to her poor husband lest he wake up lonesome, Ki had probed her in every way, and if she'd been lying while he was laying her she was an even better liar than cheat, and she cheated mighty fine.

Not even a Japanese gentleman was supposed to kiss and tell, and Ki was half-American. But when he joined Jessie and Longarm in the morning to share breakfast in Jessie's suite, Ki waited until she was dressing in another room and quickly let Longarm in on where he'd gotten his information. Jessie came in to catch the last of it, dressed for riding, now. She knew Ki never questioned her about what kind of a night she'd had, so she didn't ask how Ki knew as she

279

sat down with them to ask, "Why are we talking about the Upjohns, boys?"

Longarm said, "Letting 'em off the hook, most likely. Colonel Upjohn was the only business rival of your late father that was still around and important enough to sound dangerous if he felt like it. But he's dead, even if he was so mean nobody came to his funeral. His daughter-in-law, Hortense, only seems out to make trouble for her man, and Jim Upjohn couldn't have had murder on his mind when he saved your life last night."

Jessie said, "I fail to see how even his father could have. He wasn't so much mean as an old windbag, unpopular in the county because when he wasn't telling big fibs about the war he liked to lord it over everyone by claiming he was the King Midas of the cattle industry. What on earth ever possessed you to even begin to suspect the poor old windbag, Custis?"

Longarm said, "Two things. The timing fits. He died just before you were abducted in Galveston. So let's say he laid out a mighty devious plan, dropped dead, and left things in the mess we found 'em, with the gang divided as to what came next?"

She looked dubious. He went on, "The second reason is that he wasn't half as rich as he bragged. He died deep in debt and his son and daughter-in-law have been having a time setting his land-rich and dollar-poor estate straight. It could have galled such a proud blowhard every time he thought about how rich his old rival, Alex Starbuck, had left his daughter, and—"

"I can't buy it," Jessie cut in. "His rivalry with Dad was a friendly rivalry. Dad was one of the few men he knew who didn't laugh right in his face when he got wound up about leading Picket's Charge or getting drunk with Stonewall Jackson, who never drank. Even if he was having financial problems, I fail to see how all that razzle-dazzle down Galveston way could have done him a lick of good. He knew he could have just asked me for a business loan or, failing that, simply helped himself to some of my beef. Our herds graze intermingled and not too closely guarded on open range, between roundups.''

Longarm nodded and said, ''I noticed his son, Jim, was too proud to take you up on your offer to help them out. You're likely right and I was likely grasping at straws. I hate to drop a case with strings left dangling, but we seem to have wiped out the hirelings, and I'll be switched if I can come up with any suspects better that a dead windbag. If the cuss who hired that gang has the brains to keep his horns drawn in, we'll likely never even know what the infernal plot was supposed to accomplish, and I don't mind saying that riles me considerable.''

The girl who loved him asked, quietly, ''How soon will you want to head back for Denver?''

He had to answer honestly, ''It ain't what I want. It's what I just got to do. There's a limit to even your Uncle Billy's patience, Jessie. Me and Ki got you out of that mess in Galveston and Ki can see you safely on home.''

He rose to his feet, putting on his hat, as he added, ''I got some chores at the telegraph office down the way. I'll ask my boss to extend me the time to see you home, at least. If he lets me have it, I'll be right back.''

She didn't ask if he'd be back if Uncle Billy said no. They'd both long since agreed mushy farewells were mighty tedious.

The sun was bright that morning. It was shaping up to be a real scorcher. So he was striding down the shady side of the street when he heard his name called from the sunny side. It was that nice old tailor, waving from the open door of his shop.

Longarm crossed over to join him, saying, ''You were right about this coat getting by in dim light.''

The tailor said it was far too bright where they were standing, so Longarm followed him inside with a curious smile. The older man glanced about as if to make sure his empty shop was empty before he confided, ''Two other

281

customers may have been talking about you, yesterday afternoon. I wasn't paying attention. Who pays attention when he's pressing pants? But after I heard about the gunplay at the Hunt Club, later, I began to put things together. You still work out of Denver, don't you?''

Longarm nodded and said, ''I just got sidetracked down this way on a case that's lead to a dumb dead end. What's Denver got to do with that Texas shoot-out last night?''

The tailor said, ''They were talking about Denver Boy. You know how friends talk in a sort of code? Well, the one who needed his pants pressed in a hurry was naturally sitting in the back, behind those gray curtains. His friend was leaning against the jamb outside, talking through the curtains to him as I pressed his pants, see?''

Longarm nodded and asked what they'd looked like. The tailor shrugged and replied, ''What does a Texan in a big hat look like? The one getting his pants pressed looked human. His friend looked like an ape wearing a ten-gallon hat. He was the one who growled the most like an animal. The one inside in his underpants was trying to calm him down. He said as long as someone called Blacky took care of the Lone Star State it didn't matter about Denver Boy. He said Denver Boy wasn't even warm and to leave it all to him and this Blacky. Does any of this make a bit of sense to you?''

Longarm nodded soberly and said, ''It sure does. But are you sure of the time? Late afternoon won't work.''

The tailor thought before he shrugged and said, ''*Late* afternoon, no. Maybe one or two o'clock?''

Longarm nodded and decided, ''Cutting it close, but not too close to fit tight. That could account for the remark about a double cross, too.''

He saw the helpful older man was curious as well as confused. So, not wanting to be rude or waste time, he quickly explained, ''A gang I've been hunting has been divided for some time on the best way to deal with me and a lady. As I piece together what you just told me, the ape

I have reason to suspect I no longer have to worry about was trying to persuade his pal, or boss, to play rougher than he wanted to. I can see how the rougher faction could have taken it as betrayal when a member called Blacky failed sort of miserably at taking out anyone. A gent planning to attend a ball that evening would have been likely as me, yesterday, to require the services of a while-you-wait tailor. Can't you describe him any better to me? You may well have pressed the very pants of the mastermind I'm hunting!''

The tailor sighed and said, ''A big Texas hat, a business suit with the smell of horse to it. When you press you notice. To tell the truth they made me nervous. Even though I didn't know what they were growling about, it sounded tough. So I kept my own eyes down and didn't stare hard at either as they paid up and left. When I first came west I looked more. Good old boys with rotgut on their breath were always asking what in thunder I was staring at. So who stares? I'm sorry, Longarm. I really wanted to help.''

Longarm held out his hand to shake as he assured the timid tailor he'd helped a heap. Then he went on to the Western Union to wire Billy Vail he'd need at least a few more days because he was getting warm, albeit in truth the sidewalks of Fort Worth were getting hotter as he strode all over town, and likely in dumb circles, trying to fit things better by questioning all sorts of gents who couldn't tell him half as much as that one local businessman had.

At the stockyards he learned only that neither Pirate Peterson nor the big prize bull he'd bid on were not to be found and that nobody had seen either this side of dawn. He asked an old stockman if anyone could say where Pirate banked. He was told, ''Drover's Trust, like everyone else. I know because I've done business with Pirate in the past. Never let the cuss near your fresh unbranded beef, but otherwise he's honest enough. He's yet to bestow a rubber check on any of the boys.''

It was even hotter, now. So gents he might have wanted to question had vacated the streets of Fort Worth in favor of the Anglo version of siesta. Longarm had sense enough to know it would be cooler back at the hotel. So that was where he went.

As he entered the cavernous and cooler lobby the desk clerk called him over to say, "Your, ah, things have been stored in the baggage room for now, Deputy Long. Miss Starbuck left a note for you as she was checking out."

Longarm felt a dull punch under his breastbone as he took the envelope to open it. It always left him sort of sick and numb to part with Jessie, even when it was his notion to do so. He wondered if she'd been feeling half as bad as she'd written her short and to-the-point message. It was neither cold nor mushy. She'd simply let him know she'd likely be out at the Circle Star if ever he passed this way again.

He shrugged and put her note in a coat pocket, not wanting to tear it up and throw it away in front of the hotel help. As he turned from the counter he spied Hortense Upjohn lurking in a big chair in a grove of potted palms. She yoo-hooed at him, so he mosied over.

At closer range he saw she'd done her best to cover over a black eye with face powder. It wouldn't have been polite to ask if she'd walked into a door on her way back from Ki's room. As he ticked his hat brim to her she asked, "Have you seen my fool husband? We're checked out and all set to head on home. But I've been sitting here over an hour."

Longarm leaned against a lobby pillar, saying, "I'm feeling abandoned right now myself. Everyone seems to be leaving town this afternoon. Did Jim say where he was headed when he set you down here to wait?"

She nodded and said, "Just to the bank and back. You don't think he's really sore at me this time, do you?"

Longarm hauled out his pocket watch to make certain as he said, "All the banks in town will be closing soon. What bank might he have headed for, and why should he be sore at anyone?"

She answered, "We bank with Stockman's Savings and Loan, like everyone else. We only had a little spat, earlier today, and I was sure we'd made up. You know how it is, once the honeymoon is over and a girl tries to pep things up with just a little spice."

Longarm kept his face blank, even though he knew the best reason for leaving married women alone was that all too many of 'em who liked to screw around didn't consider themselves properly screwed until they'd tearfully confessed to their husbands. Revenge on a man who failed to satisfy just wasn't complete unless and until one let the poor simp know his frustrated woman had to turn to other, better hung, temptations.

As a peace officer Longarm was more familiar than most with her risky marital problems, if that was what was keeping old Jim right now. He chatted with her a spell to keep her company. Then he got out his notebook, tore out a page, and wrote a short note of his own. He put it in the envelope Jessie's note had come in and handed it to Hortense, saying, "I want you to head for the Circle Star with this, not your own spread. Miss Jessie will see you're kept safe from harm for now. I doubt Jim left for home without you. So until I find out where he went, you figure to stay healthier forted up with Jessie and old Ki."

She stared up at him thundergasted to demand, "What are you talking about? Are you saying something's happened to my Jim?"

He told her soberly, "I hope I'm wrong. If I am, old Jim ought to be able to find you at the Circle Star sooner or later and sober. But I just have to say they might have got him. Didn't you tell Ki old Colonel Upjohn had gone heavily in debt to some high-stake gambling men?"

She looked away to fluster, "Never mind what I might or might not have mentioned to the hired help. It was supposed to be a mighty private conversation!"

Longarm smiled thinly and softly said, "You shouldn't have mentioned it to your husband, then. I got to go see about a train now, ma'am. If your man ain't boarding it he's likely just drowning his sorrows somewhere. Either way, you'd best get on out to the Circle Star until things calm down.''

She said she would, seeing that nice Mr. Ki might want to listen to her sad story. So Longarm went back out into the hot Texas sun, walking fast despite the heat. For his job let him travel so much by rail that he had the timetables of the main lines fixed better in his head than many a railroad man, to hear folk bitch about the service.

But he made the nine blocks to the Texas & Pacific depot on Lancaster Street in plenty of time to scout high and low, even in the gents' room, without catching sight of the cheating wife's missing husband. Railroads paid no attention to the climate, run as they were by distant dudes. But thanks to the heat the crowd waiting for the afternoon train was thin. Too thin to miss anyone the size of old Jim among the sunbonnets and Stetsons as they all got aboard. A few minutes later the train clanged on out toward Dallas to leave Longarm standing alone on the platform. He lit a cheroot thoughtfully as he reconsidered. Then he shook out the match and muttered, ''Of course. That's the only way it still might work!''

Stuck in Fort Worth on his own money, Longarm checked into a seedy little hotel near the stockyards. He could have managed a somewhat better place to bunk if he'd had anyone in town to bunk with. But he just didn't have the heart to scout up such companionship this soon after leaving Heaven. Next to Jessie Starbuck, most of the gals frequenting the places he was nursing his nickels at night looked like painted boys. Tough ones.

He spent more on telegraph messages during his tedious daylight hours, knowing Billy Vail would never in this world pay a federal agent back for wasting so much time and money on a purely Texas State investigation, serious as this one was shaping up to be. Longarm wasn't guessing about this. Every morning he got a night letter from his home office, ordering him to cut the crap and hand the can of worms to the infernal Texas Rangers. Longarm would have, had he thought they'd buy such a fantastic criminal conspiracy. But he knew they wouldn't, and he owed it to his pals at the Circle Star to just hang in there for the final showdown. So he did.

On the third day he rose, strapped on his gun rig, and got to the Stockman's Savings and Loan before it opened. He scouted up and down out front, saw the coast was clear, and entered that morn as their very first customer. He flashed his badge at the old uniformed bank dick, explaining he wasn't exactly a customer, and demanding to see someone more important.

He was led back to the manager's office. The fat bald cuss in charge of that branch calmed down a mite when Longarm assured him he doubted anyone was out to stick the place up. As they talked, Longarm ignored the seat he'd been offered to stay by the door, holding it cracked open just enough to peer out as he explained his suspicions to the manager. As anyone else in Texas might have, the manager told him his notion was mighty wild, but got out some ledgers to scout up the figures the tall federal deputy had inquired about. He'd just said, "By gum, we do hold a second mortgage on the Upjohn property, lock, stock and barrel!"

Then Longarm told him to hold the thought and keep his head down, for Jim Upjohn had just come through the front door, packing a big carpetbag and that same big gun. He stopped at the first teller's cage to slide a savings account booklet under the brass bars at the teller. Longarm couldn't see the teller's face from his own vantage point, but he wasn't surprised when the teller headed back to the manager's office instead of handing over that much money in one bunch. Longarm stepped clear to let the teller into the office, waving the bankbook around as he told the manager, "Mr. Upjohn wants to withdraw his whole account. I don't have enough in my till. Do I have your permit to get into the vault, Mr. Blake?''

Before the manager could reply, Longarm told them both, ''I'll take it from here. You boys just remember, in court, how much a customer was out to withdraw all at once.''

Then he drew his .44-40 and stepped out to stride over to the other tall gent at the teller's window, saying, ''Morning, old son. Were you planning on catching the ten-fifteen westbound?''

The man he had the drop on stared green gilled at the weapon in Longarm's hand, but tried to sound calm as he replied, ''Howdy, Custis. May I inquire why you're pointing that gun at me?''

Longarm said, ''You're under arrest. You know how come.''

But his arrestee laughed lightly and insisted, ''You must have the wrong man. I'm only here to withdraw my own money and not one penny belonging to anyone else. Since when has that been a federal crime?''

Longarm said, ''Put down that bag and then place both hands on the counter. I've been laying for you three whole days and I just don't feel like bullshitting with you. Save your fibbing for the judge, you sneaky bastard.''

Then Jim Upjohn, or whoever he was, showed just how sneaky he could be by dropping the bag, turning as if to put his hands on the counter, and kicking the six-gun from Longarm's right fist to the pressed-tin ceiling!

Longarm didn't have time to cuss as he went for his backup derringer in a vest pocket. He knew, numbly, that he just wasn't going to make it as his foe dropped back into a gunfighting stance, going for his easier-to-get-at six-gun in that goddamn tie-down rig. But a man had to try. So Longarm did, and then the killer's gun was clear and rising to fire point-blank, and then there came a wet thunk and Longarm had his derringer out, with his watch dangling on the far end of the chain as his foe dropped his own weapon to clutch at his gun arm with a wild look of astonished pain

288

in his staring eyes as Longarm, wanting to deliver him alive and ever willing to repay a favor in kind, kicked him in the balls and sent him writhing to the marble floor.

Then he said, "Thanks, Jessie," as Jessie came all the way across the bank to pluck her silvery throwing star from the triceps of the gunslick she'd crippled. As she hunkered down in her riding skirts to wipe two points clean on the gray coat of the moaning crook between them, she murmured in a hurt tone, "You might have included this in your hasty note. As it is, I had to figure all by myself that it would take three business days for that last big check he got for Attila to clear."

Longarm replied, "Well, I wasn't sure I was right. For whoever mentioned the tangled webs we weave when first we practice to deceive was on the money. They just told me in the back he'd mortgaged every last fence post the Upjohns owned, and had he not been so greedy he'd have been gone by now. But I reckon he hoped for top dollar from that one fine bull and the rest you see for yourself."

Jessie rose to her booted feet again, putting the sort of decorative star back on her hat as she replied, "Not by half. How on earth did you know this wasn't the real Jim Upjohn? He had me and all the other neighbors fooled!"

Longarm shrugged and said, "Well, fooling one's neighbors ain't as hard when they live forty or more miles apart. Neither the colonel nor his real son met up with anyone all that often, and when they did nobody liked 'em enough to study 'em hard. You said you'd known him best when you were kids, and he'd gotten fresh with you. Am I correct in assuming you never invited him to any birthday parties after that?"

She stared down at the semi-conscious victim of their mutual efforts as she grimaced and decided, "Right. I barely spoke to him a dozen times since I decided when he'd have been about fourteen that I just plain didn't want him around me. But how could an impostor have fooled the colonel,

289

the other hands working out yonder, and even the real Jim's own wife?''

The bank dick, who'd missed the swell ending to the fight, came back in with two Fort Worth copper badges in tow, yelling, ''The one on the floor. The one standing over him is the law. I don't know who the cowgirl might be.''

Longarm walked over to pick up his gun, saying, ''You boys just carry this rascal to the Ranger station and we'll be along soon enough. Me and this little lady have some catching up to do.''

★

Chapter 18

It took Longarm and the Texas Rangers just two more days to tidy up all the loose ends. To say the three nights that gave him with Jessie were heavenly would be to allow honey was a mite sweet. But all things good and bad must end and so the time came, back in Denver, when Longarm had to settle accounts with the usually peppery and now downright irate Billy Vail.

As Longarm sat across the desk from his boss, flicking just enough tobacco ash on the rug to take care of possible carpet mites and without enraging Vail much more than he already seemed to be, his short pudgy superior thundered, "You were gone longer than I could ever spare for my own honeymoon, and what does this office have to show for it, in the end? Not a goddamned thing, you wandering vagabond lover!"

Longarm took a drag on his cheroot and observed, "I hardly ever make love to vagabonds, and I did my duty when I turned the complicated case over to the State of Texas. All the crookery took place inside the lines of that one considerable state, you know.''

Vail growled, ''So my old Ranger pals informed me when they told me to just call you on home. I've *been* calling you on home for weeks and I still don't know what in the name of the great horned spoon you've been up to. What's all this bullshit about a theatrical clan gone crooked posing as all sorts of folk they were never even related to?''

Longarm flicked more ash on the rug and said, ''I'd be proud to tell you if you'd just hush and listen. It's hard to tell such a convoluted tale when folk keep butting in with questions. It took me more than one night to explain things to Jessie Starbuck's total satisfaction.''

Vail grinned despite himself and growled, ''I wish I'd been there, you satisfying cuss. But go ahead and I promise I won't kiss you in the middle of a sentence.''

Longarm laughed and said, ''You don't know how relieved I am to hear that, boss.'' Then he said, ''In the beginning there was this rich but unpopular old cattle baron, the late Colonel Upjohn. He was honest enough in business but couldn't tell the truth about his heroic past when the truth was in his favor. He had a son who took after him. We all create our own myths a mite, but the late Jim Upjohn would have got more of the boys to drink with him if he'd just settled for being a tolerable cowman of average albeit sort of bucktoothed looks. He was widely recalled, if at all, as a sort of goofy grinning young asshole who liked to talk dirty about all the gals in the county, even though he'd likely never had any of 'em. Keep that in mind. The real son kept saying he'd been Jessie Starbuck's lover, everywhere he went.''

Billy Vail looked as if he was busting to ask something, but he just nodded. So Longarm said, ''Like most useless young brags, Jim Upjohn found he could impress folk more away from his home range. He liked to hang out down in Galveston, where nobody ever calls you a liar as long as your money holds out. He didn't have half as much pocket money as he liked to let on, of course. He was the colonel's sole heir, but the old man was tightfisted and no doubt had to be, bragging he was so rich. As I wired you from Galveston, this clan of theatrical drifters, all Franco-American and likely related, had drifted into Galveston to take up more sinful entertainment for more fun and profit. Junior Upjohn fell in with Blacky Morgan, playing for high stakes at the gambling hall run as a sort of family business before me and old Ki burnt it to the ground.''

''Where does Starbuck Enterprises and that sea captain working for them come in?'' asked Vail.

Longarm looked annoyed and said, ''I asked you to hush and just listen, Billy. Nobody in Galveston but the Morgan clan was involved as more than confusion, albeit they might have learned some things about Jessie from their landlord, who worked for her. They learned the most from Jim Upjohn, who liked to brag about things he knew as well as things he didn't. At first they'd have paid him little mind as they slowly cleaned him out and then got into him for a mess of I.O.U. markers. Boasting he was the son and sole heir of an important cattle baron would have allowed him to run up quite a pile of markers. But of course there came the day when it was time to pay the piper, or in this case a tribe of mighty vicious folk.''

Vail objected, ''Gambling debts are only debts of honor. You can't sue to collect on marker-one in any court I know of.''

Longarm blew smoke out both nostrils like an annoyed bull and Vail shut up as his deputy continued, ''Professional gamblers might have known that, boss. Blacky Morgan had the local rep of dealing with stiffs more serious than suing 'em. I doubt we'll ever know the final fate of the real Jim Upjohn for certain. I know I sure as hell wouldn't tell even the Rangers about any dead bodies they didn't already have on hand for *my* murder trial. The point was that dead or alive the poor loudmouth was in no position to pay off and

293

they wanted the damned money. I told you they'd started out as stage entertainers. So it would have occurred to them before it might the James-Younger gang that the sucker who'd stiffed 'em bore a faint resemblance to one of their own. His real name, as it turns out, is Marcel Morgan. Blacky's first cousin. He's refused to say whether he or Blacky were the real leaders or if he was just picked for his looks. With false buckteeth and his hair changed he could pass at a glance for the real James Upjohn. They'd established poor Jim had no real friends back home.''

Vail protested, ''Aw, come on, impersonating one person sounds wild enough. Are you expecting me to believe they tried to use doubles for both Jessie Starbuck and an old boyfriend?''

Longarm nodded but said, ''Hell, they never got *away* with it, did they? Having one double go home to his dear old dad, murder him, and then fire all the help in his grief was wild enough. The fake made sure few mourners, if any, would show up for the funeral by forgetting to send out invites. Then he quickly courted and wed a local tramp everyone knew a lot better, many a local boy in the biblical sense.''

Vail started to ask a dumb question, nodded, and rumbled, ''I see the twisted sense in that. Anyone mentioning how young Jim had changed so much might be put off by the fact a local gal had married him and had to know her own husband, no matter how odd he acted.''

Longarm nodded and said, ''Meeting neighbors he might not know with a gal on his arm who did know 'em covered for a multitude of slips. When Jessie and me met 'em in Fort Worth she did all the talking while he stayed strong and silent. It even fooled Jessie. She hadn't had a conversation with him in years and thought the change in his manners an improvement.''

Vail nodded but asked, ''In that case why in thunder did they put Jessie through all that misfortune earlier?''

Longarm said, ''They didn't have to. But they thought

they had to, so they did. You see, Jessie hardly knew their ringer and, as I said, folk don't worry about whether a casual acquaintance is the real thing or not unless a slipup inspires 'em to look just a mite closer. With old Hortense doing most of the talking and covering any slips, the fake only had to last long enough to liquidate the estate and light out. But the real Jim Upjohn had told them true and false about Jessie Starbuck. He would have known about that English barmaid who caused so much trouble by posing as Jessie that one short time. That could have been what gave them such a grand notion to begin with. But in his bragging he'd also told 'em he and Jessie had been teenage lovers, and it's one thing to sell a bull to Pirate Peterson and another thing entire to fool an ex-lover within a quarter mile."

Vail brightened and said, "I see. They had to make sure no gal the real Jim Upjohn had ever been that close with showed up at the big state fair! But wasn't trying to use a double for her as well just too risky for a sensible crook to contemplate?"

Longarm shrugged and asked, "Who said they were sensible? Of course it was too risky to get away with. That's why they didn't! Blacky may have felt left out as they made up the double for old Jim. He considered himself an expert impersonator and must have noticed he might be able to pass for her to the casual eye as they spent all that time plotting to take her out of the game any way they could. Had they just waylaid Jessie and fed her to the crabs on the bottom of Galveston Bay, they'd have likely got away with it. They came close enough as it was, and I'm sure glad they attracted my attention to their dirty doings by trying to make sure I chased the poor little gal to Canada."

Vail said, "I imagine Jessie was glad, too. All right, we've got a fake Jim Upjohn selling off the assets of the colonel's estate and a fake Jessie scaring Henry skinnier and trying to lure you up to the Peace River. How come it kept getting even more complicated than that?"

Longarm said, "Simple. Captain Wilson tipped the Galveston vice squad off to the way the gang seemed to be using one of his properties. That saved Jessie, earlier than they wanted her found, dead or alive. They had to stake out the state fair and hope for the best. When Jessie met the fake Jim Upjohn and he saw she'd accepted him as real, he tried to call off their plan to assassinate her before she could give him away. Anyone could see it worked better if everyone in town took him for the real thing long enough for him to just take all the money and run. It ain't half as easy to leave town in the middle of an investigation into the killing of a Texas rancher half as important as Jessie."

Vail nodded and said, "It seems obvious Blacky was unaware of the change in plans when he laid for the poor sweet gal up in her hotel suite."

Longarm nodded and said, "The way that turned out confused all of 'em but old Marcel, hugging himself for being clever enough to pull it off. When he ordered 'em to call it all off and just let Miss Starbuck be, they suspected a double cross. Even an ape can see that once a pal has a carpetbag full of money and a clear escape route, there's just no telling how good a pal he might really be. With Morgan dead the less brighter members of the clan just went for blood revenge. The fake Jim saved Jessie and stood over her blazing back because he saw that he'd never be able to make a quiet bank withdrawal and just vanish into the mists if everyone stayed in town searching high and low for some infernal gang. Changing sides worked out just swell for him. Or it might have, had both me and Jessie been willing to let loose ends dangle. But we weren't. So we caught him. State and county law have already rounded up some of the lesser lights we missed, such as the few hands out to the Upjohn spread they'd replaced the original help with. Hortense says she never liked either Jim all that much, and her testimony ought to help Texas hang the son of a bitch if Texas never finds each and every body."

Vail sighed and said, "Well, the Good Book says the wages of sin are death, even when you sin a heap less sneaky. I ought to make you pay for all the fun you've had neglecting your sworn duty to the department you draw your wages from. But old Alex Starbuck was a pal of mine and I see the day is about shot. So get out of here before I find a floor for you to sweep, and make sure you get to work on time, come morning."

Longarm rose to his considerable height with a nod of thanks, saying, "Well, I reckon I'm about due for a good night's rest after all I've been through for Texas."

He meant it, and he left the Federal Building and headed over to the Parthenon Saloon for some pigs knuckles and a pitcher of suds. But the sun was already low above the Front Range to the west, and he knew he'd feel even more wistful in the soft romantic light of sundown, so he swung the other way to sort of drift up Capitol Hill, wondering what that widow woman on Sherman Avenue might be planning for supper.

Watch for

LONGARM AND THE VIGILANTES

140th novel in the bold LONGARM series

and

**LONE STAR AND
THE DEVIL WORSHIPERS**

96th novel in the exciting LONE STAR series

Coming in August!

LONGARM

Explore the exciting Old West with
one of the men who made it wild!

A special offer for people who enjoy reading the best Westerns published today. If you enjoyed this book, subscribe now and get ...

TWO FREE WESTERNS!
A $5.90 VALUE—NO OBLIGATION

If you enjoyed this book and would like to read more of the very best Westerns being published today, you'll want to subscribe to True Value's Western Home Subscription Service. If you enjoyed the book you just read and want more of the most exciting, adventurous, action packed Westerns, subscribe now.

TWO FREE BOOKS

When you subscribe, we'll send you your first month's shipment of the newest and best 6 Westerns for you to preview. With your first shipment, two of these books will be yours as our introductory gift to you absolutely FREE, regardless of what you decide to do.

Special Subscriber Savings

As a True Value subscriber all regular monthly selections will be billed at the low subscriber price of just $2.45 each. That's at least a savings of $3.00 each month below the publishers price. There is never any shipping, handling or other hidden charges. What's more there is no minimum number of books you must buy, you may return any selection for full credit and you can cancel your subscription at any time. A TRUE VALUE!

Mail the coupon below

To start your subscription and receive 2 FREE WESTERNS, fill out the coupon below and mail it today. We'll send your first shipment which includes 2 FREE BOOKS as soon as we receive it.